Secret

OF THE
HALL

The *Eden* Hall Series

Secret
OF THE
HALL

BOOK 3

VERONICA HELEY

ZONDERVAN™

GRAND RAPIDS, MICHIGAN 49530 USA

ZONDERVAN.COM/
AUTHORTRACKER

ZONDERVAN™

Secret of the Hall
Copyright © 2006 by Veronica Heley

Requests for information should be addressed to:
Zondervan, *Grand Rapids, Michigan 49530*

Library of Congress Cataloging-in-Publication Data

Heley, Veronica.
        Secret of the hall / by Veronica Heley.
            p. cm. — (The Eden Hall series; bk.3)
        ISBN-13: 978-0-310-26561-0 (pbk.)
        ISBN-10: 0-310-26561-4 (pbk.)
            1. Young women—Fiction. 2. Inheritance and succession—Fiction.
        3. Administration of estates—Fiction. 4. Home ownership—Fiction. 5. Villages—
        Fiction. 6. England—Fiction. I. Title.
        PR6070.H6915S43 2005
        823' .92—dc22
                                                                        2005013744

Interior design by Michelle Espinoza

Printed in the United States of America

---

06 07 08 09 10 11 • 17 16 15 14 13 12 11 10 9 8 7 6 5 4 3 2 1

Acknowledgments

Where do ideas come from?

Sometimes a writer gets an idea but has to test it out to make sure it works.

When the idea for *Secret of the Hall* came to me, I told a policeman about it, and he said, "Oh, you were at T——M——when it happened, were you?'

I'd had no idea that the scenes I'd imagined had actually happened at an existing stately home.

My technical advisor for the music world was Paul Balmer. He studied music in Liverpool in the 1960s and went on to be a producer for BBC Radio 1. He is a contributor to *The Penguin Encyclopaedia of Popular Music* and the author of *Stephane Grappelli With and Without Django*, the official biography. He was BAFTA nominated in 2002 and is co-director of *www.musiconearth.co.uk*.

I am very grateful for all the help he has given me.

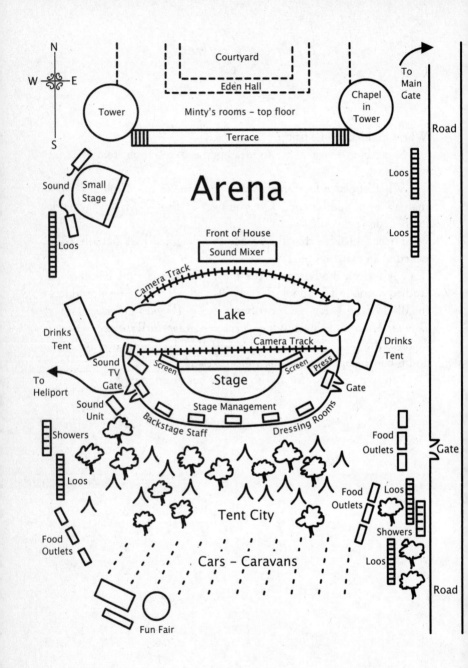

Chapter One

Patrick didn't panic, though Minty could see he wanted to.

He wouldn't have got the call at all if he hadn't left his mobile switched on by mistake. That was strange in itself, because he usually switched it off after work every morning.

The call had come through as they sat in a café in St Mark's Square in Venice. The bronze giants on the Clock Tower had just struck the hour of three and they were discussing, lazily, where they should eat that night.

Minty turned her head away as her husband answered the call. She resented the intrusion on their holiday. The agreement was that Patrick would work for one hour every morning, but from the moment he shut off his phone and closed his laptop, they were to devote themselves to pleasure. Or rather, to getting through the day while avoiding the topic of her miscarriage.

May in Venice. Beautiful. Warm enough to sit outside. Wonderful coffee. Pigeons to feed if you were so inclined. Gondola rides if you wished to be romantic. Art galleries … restaurants … the theatre … so much to distract her.

Patrick being amusing, kind and tender.

Perhaps they'd move on to another city next week. They'd been comparing the merits of Pompeii or Rome, Minty hiding the fact that she didn't care much where they went or what they did. Amid the sumptuousness of Venice, Minty had a sudden flashback to her beloved Eden Hall, the beautiful stately home she'd unexpectedly inherited in England. There it would be much cooler. The trees in the Park would be green and shady.

She knew in her head that coming away with Patrick was the sensible thing to do, given her inability to do anything but sit and stare at the wall after her fall down the stairs.

Had it been a boy or a girl?

Don't think about it.

So now she smiled, dressed herself in pretty clothes and faked enthusiasm for all Patrick's suggestions for passing the time. But that's all they were really doing. Just passing the time.

He wasn't fooled, of course. They'd been childhood sweethearts and knew one another's strengths and weaknesses. He watched her all the time, the outer corners of his eyes wincing when she went through a bad patch.

But she was gradually recovering. Wasn't she?

As her strength returned she'd begun to realise that Patrick was worried about what was happening back in England. His best friend and partner was carrying their busy solicitor's practise by himself, and though Patrick tried to hide it, she gathered that all was not going well.

The upright line between Patrick's brows became more pronounced day by day, while Minty buried the knowledge that he was needed back home, telling herself that she needed more time away, that she wasn't strong enough yet to cope.

Until the phone call came.

He turned slightly away from her as he took the call. His long-fingered hand, playing with his coffee spoon, grew still.

Minty averted her eyes. Whatever the phone call was about, it was nothing to do with her. The agreement was that he should take her away until she was better, and she was only half-way back to normal. She was coping on the surface, yes. But not underneath, where it counted.

The call went on and on. Patrick turned his dark head even farther away from her, concentrating. He didn't speak. Minty's hearing was good. She could tell it wasn't his partner on the phone but a woman, probably his office manager.

The woman was speaking without urgency. Matter of fact. Minty had met her. She was a charming, competent woman. She would deal with — whatever it was.

Patrick took a deep breath. "I'll get the first plane back."

He shut up his phone and turned back to Minty, frowning, knowing he was about to give news she wouldn't want to hear. "Jim's in trouble. You don't need to come back with me. I could fly out again at the weekend."

Jim was his partner. Minty liked him but hardly knew him or his wife, Anthea. They had a frail little daughter who caused them a lot of anxiety. Minty lifted her empty coffee cup to her lips. Her hand was trembling. "Is their baby back in hospital? I thought she was doing quite well at the moment." There; she'd actually said the word "baby" without bursting into tears.

"It's his wife. She had a minor op, nothing much, but she's got a raging infection and they say ... Jim's been called to the hospital. There's a nasty court case brewing at work and a backlog they're not coping with. If you can manage for a few days, I'll go back, see what I can do."

Once she'd have urged him to go, quickly. Once she'd have been really distressed by the news. But now? No, she couldn't yet cope with anyone else's problems. She put her cup down, slowly, very carefully. She wanted to scream and shout that she still wasn't well, that he mustn't leave her, that he'd promised to look after her always.

She clutched at common sense. Patrick would never willingly let her down. If she cried and made a scene, if she asked him to do so, he'd stay ... and let his career and his partner take their chances. But would that be the right thing to do? She'd chosen to follow Christ when she was a small child, and it was not difficult for her to work out what Jesus would do in the circumstances ... which was ... ouch! No, she really did not want to follow Him in this matter.

She prayed, *Lord, help me to be unselfish!* She could feel panic rising in her throat and pushed it down again. Could she manage to stand on her own two feet again? With God's help, perhaps she could. But stay on here without him? No.

"I'll come back with you."

Patrick had light grey eyes which saw farther than most. "Are you sure?"

She shook back her mop of fair hair and forced herself to sound positive. "Yes. It's time I went back, anyway. I haven't a clue what's been going on at the Hall without me. The place might have burned down for all I know."

Patrick summoned the waiter, laying money on the table. His mind was obviously racing ahead, but he knew how to reassure her. "Nothing will have gone wrong with the efficient Annie Phillips in charge. Didn't she run your father's financial empire for years? Running a stately home for a few months will have been a doddle for her. Now if it had been left to your beautiful but daft half-sister ...!"

Minty smiled, as he intended her to do. "Of course Annie will have managed perfectly. Shall I pack while you get the plane tickets organised?"

That was when their luck ran out. The flights to London were all fully booked. Patrick considered hiring a car and driving back up through Europe. He would have done so, if he hadn't known it would be too much for Minty. He enquired about chartering a plane. At times like this it was useful to have money. Then they were told they could take a plane to Amsterdam and change there.

Minty didn't allow herself to think about anything except assembling and packing all the bits and pieces they'd collected during their time away. They'd left in haste with one suitcase each, but now there were six big cases to pack, and even then she had to buy a holdall to cram things in at the last minute. Retail therapy, Patrick had called it, encouraging her to buy a new wardrobe for herself and gifts for everyone back home.

She tried to ring Eden Hall to warn them they were on their way, but the battery on her mobile phone was dead. She hadn't used it since they'd been away.

Patrick tried to make the call for her in the taxi on the way to the airport, but couldn't get through. At the airport they were told they could have seats on an earlier connection to Amsterdam if they hurried, so they bundled themselves on to that.

Amsterdam: cool and impersonal. Busy. Patrick phoned his partner, who wasn't in the office. The news from the hospital was not good, and Jim wasn't expected to come in.

Patrick asked his secretary to let everyone know at Eden Hall that they were on their way back, but might be late that evening ... asking Reggie, the Houseman, to bring the big car to London airport to meet them. They raided the duty-free shop for more gifts to take back home.

Delays. The next flight was overbooked, and they must wait ... should they go to a hotel for the night? Patrick said yes, Minty said they should wait, perhaps seats would become available on another plane.

Patrick tried ringing Eden Hall again but still couldn't get through. He tried to check with his secretary that she'd phoned them, but of course she'd left the office for the night. Minty fell asleep with his arm around her in the airport lounge. And woke in the bleary light of early morning. Patrick half carried her to the plane to Heathrow. He said that if Reggie didn't meet them in London, he'd get a hire car to take them on home to the Cotswolds.

She felt scruffy in her blue linen dress. Linen always creased so badly. Patrick needed a shave; he wasn't a handsome man, but he was tall and bronzed with the Mediterranean sun and had the knack of looking immaculate, no matter what he was wearing ... unlike her.

He couldn't use his mobile on the flight so got out his laptop and started worrying away at it. She tried to sleep again but failed. She was tired, and the nightmare thoughts that she'd been keeping away from her conscious mind came flooding back.

She thought, *Can I bear it?* Going back there ... that plunge down the staircase into the Great Hall?

Don't think about that. Think about how beautiful Eden Hall will be in late May. Will the chestnut trees in the Park still be flowering? Think about the plans you have for opening the Park to visitors. Think about the many good friends you have there. Dear efficient Annie, of course. Nothing could have gone wrong with her in charge. Barr, the Administrator ... fond of a drink but part of the fabric of the Hall, he'd been there so long ... All the people who worked at the Hall or in the village ...

Don't think about the darkness, falling ...

Don't think. You can do it, girl.

Trust in God. Pray a bit more. Trust Patrick, my lovely man, my best friend in all the world. She put her hand in the pocket of his jacket. He smiled and touched her hand without taking his eyes off his laptop.

Heathrow Airport at eight in the morning. Busy. Cold. Their luggage hadn't arrived with them. Perhaps it would be on the next flight?

Patrick was outwardly calm, but a nerve twitched at the corner of his jaw.

He still couldn't raise anyone on the phone either at his partner's home or at the office. Presumably Jim was at the hospital, and it was too early for the office.

No one was answering the phone at Eden Hall, either.

More bad news; there was no car from the Hall waiting for them. Patrick had his laptop; she had a handbag, a sweater and the bag of duty-free presents.

He said, "What shall we do?" He knew what he ought to be doing, which was rushing to Jim's rescue, but he left it to Minty to decide. If she said she couldn't cope, he'd stay with her.

She stood as straight as she could for tiredness. "You go on ahead. I'll wait for the next flight, see if the luggage is on it. Then I'll hire a car and follow."

He checked her over for signs that she could cope, and she forced herself to smile. "I'll be all right. I'll ring you when I get back, and you'll ring me when you've got news of Jim."

He said, "I can buy a razor and a shirt here, but ... I'll be thinking of you." He kissed her quickly and took two strides away. Then rushed back to hold her in his arms for one long, sweet moment, before disengaging himself with an inarticulate murmur and making his way swiftly out of the hall.

Minty heard a woman say to her companion, "Honeymooners!" Minty smiled, because she and Patrick had been married only seven months. It took nine months to produce a baby. Ouch. Turn your thoughts away.

Lord, keep him safe on the journey and be with Jim and Anthea.

The luggage was not on the next flight, but someone said it might be on the plane due in another hour. In the rest-room she tried to pull a comb through her mop of tangled fair hair. Her eyes looked anxious in the mirror. She splashed water on her face to wake herself up. There were blue shadows under her eyes from fatigue, not make-up. She'd never been conventionally beautiful, and the last few months had taken their toll of her. But though she was still too thin, she looked a hundred times better than the dazed scarecrow Patrick had taken away from the Hall.

She couldn't do anything about the creases in her dress, but she had a decent tan and had even begun to put back some of the weight she'd lost after the baby ... stop that thought. She thought she looked a lot better than she felt.

She found a public phone and rang through to the office at Eden Hall, but there was still no one there to answer the phone. She'd have something to say about that when she got back. She bought a paper to catch up on the news. She had some breakfast, though she wasn't hungry. Too tired to be hungry.

At last the luggage arrived. She piled it onto a trolley and rented a car to drive back home.

She longed for her blue and white tiled bathroom with its power shower ... the four-poster bed where she and Patrick slept ... the comfort of their cool green sitting room ... the peace of the family chapel in the tower. The view from their rooms at the top of Eden Hall must be spectacular now, looking down over the great sweep of lawn to the lake fringed with yellow irises ... and the Park beyond, dotted with horse chestnut trees in flower. Surely they'd still be in flower when she got back. She couldn't wait!

And her friends. Serafina, her housekeeper, who'd once looked after Minty's father and who had stayed on after he died. Minty longed for Serafina's cosseting, her tasty cooking. Her earthy common sense.

Then there was capable Annie Phillips, her financier father's right hand for so many years. She was the next best thing to a mother that Minty had, since her own had died so young. Annie could be prickly, but you could rely on her till the end of the world.

Minty had hardly thought of them while she'd been away and was surprised to find how much she was looking forward to seeing them all again.

She slowed down in the winding lanes that ran this way and that across the rolling landscape of the Cotswolds. She had an acute sense of smell, and now she wound down the window to catch passing scents … a newly mown grass verge, wild garlic … the scents of spring.

She passed through a tiny village with golden stone walls and thatched roofs. There were roses tumbling over the doors. Across an ancient stone bridge … into and out of the shadow of an old church set in a graveyard, thick with tilted stones … a smithy, still working to provide hand-crafted weather-vanes and gates.

Sheep on the hills. The oldest parts of Eden Hall had been built on the profits from sheep.

A small town with crazily climbing streets and miscellaneous styles of architecture. This was where Patrick and Jim had their main office, though Patrick also worked half the week in the village at the gates of Eden Hall. She considered dropping into Patrick's town office for news, but decided against it.

She turned off the main road to Eden Hall with a sigh of relief … only to be brought to a halt behind two lorries waiting to go through the gates.

The Hall was open to the public from Wednesday to Sunday, and the gates would then be open all the time. What day was this? She rather thought it might be Tuesday. It was easy to lose track of the days when you were on holiday. They had travelled overnight from Venice, and they'd gone to church yesterday? The day before? She checked with the newspaper she'd bought that morning. Today was Tuesday.

On Tuesdays the Hall was usually shut to visitors. Perhaps there was some charity function being held there tonight?

There was something else new just inside the gates. A solid-looking Portakabin such as those used on building sites, manned by a man in uniform. What were they doing there?

The driver of the first lorry handed down some paperwork. The security guard checked it over and waved him through. The gates opened, and then they closed again. Minty edged her car closer, frowning. Were they hosting royalty, that such precautions were necessary?

The process was repeated with the second lorry. And now a van was pushing its way into the queue, its bumper edging in front of Minty. The driver was aggressive and she didn't want the rented car to be damaged, so she drew her car off to one side, parked and got out.

A large sign nearby advertised that this was Eden Hall, open to the public Wednesdays to Sundays. A hand-painted sign had been tacked over the times of opening, reading—CLOSED TILL FURTHER NOTICE.

Minty rubbed her eyes. Eased her neck and shoulders, stiff from the drive.

Whether it was Monday or Tuesday, that sign should not be there. And neither should that Portakabin.

The van was allowed in, and the gates swung shut once again. The guard locked them shut with a key. Why? They'd never had to lock the gates before. What was going on?

Perhaps ... perhaps it wasn't a bad idea to lock the gates. At night, say. Perhaps the ever-efficient Annie had ordered it done? Yes, that would be it.

But now, at eleven o'clock in the morning, Minty wanted those gates open so that she could get in. She leaned over into the car and sounded her horn.

The security guard looked her up and down. "The Hall's closed."

"Not to me," said Minty, feeling irritable. "I live here. Open up."

He was one of those men who enjoyed power and, she suspected, also enjoyed refusing a woman's request. His head was shaved, and he had a heavy, jowly face. He looked as if he'd played a lot of sport in his youth but was letting himself go in middle age.

He shouted back to someone in the Portakabin. "We've got a right one here, Johnno. Lady Muck. Says it lives here."

Another hulking male came to the door of the Portakabin. Both men had heavily tattooed forearms. Both carried walkie-talkies strapped to their shoulders. The second one inspected Minty's sleeveless dress and tangled blonde hair. And leered.

"Closed, love. Even to you."

Minty clutched at her temper. "I don't know who you are or what you're doing here, but I'm Mrs Sands and I live here. Please, open the gate."

They laughed, loudly and coarsely.

"Who's Mrs Hands when she's at home, then? One of the cleaners? You'll find them in the village, love. Re-lo-ca-ted, as they say."

"For the duration," nodded his companion. "Get lost, right?"

"Look," said Minty, approaching the gates, "my name is Araminta Cardale Sands. Eden Hall is my home. I've been away on holiday. I want ..." Her voice broke. She clenched her hands into fists. She mustn't let them see how near to tears she was. "I've been travelling all night, and ..."

Johnno shook his head. He continued to smile at Minty, not nicely. "Give up, ducky. You're a bit long in the tooth to be hanging round here, anyway. I can tell you for nothing, you've not got what it takes. Right, Len?"

"Right on," said Len, smirking. "Not enough up here or down there, and there's no spark, see what I mean?"

Minty reddened. What did they mean? That she wasn't beautiful enough to be let in? She shook her head to clear it. What on earth were they talking about? "Will you kindly ring the Administrator? He'll vouch for me."

Johnno shrugged. "Humour her."

Len shrugged but spoke into his walkie-talkie, watching Minty the while. "Len here, on the gate. Got a woman, trying to get in. Blonde, late twenties, I should think. Says her name's Mrs Hands, says she lives here ..." Len shook with laughter. Then clicked off his walkie-talkie. "He says he's the Queen of Sheba, too."

Minty blinked. Barr had been at Eden Hall for years and was a part of the landscape. She was very fond of him, and she'd never imagined he'd deny her entry to her own house. "Let me speak to Barr."

"Who's Barr? Hatton's the man. Now if you'll remove yourself? You're blocking the gates and we're expecting another delivery soon."

Len checked that the gate was locked. It was. He and Johnno retired to the Portakabin. Minty shook the gate, but the lock held.

She took a step back, staring around. Was she going mad? Perhaps she was still in the plane, having a nightmare. Security men barring the way in. No Barr? What was going on here?

The sun lay heavily over the land. England in May could be bleak, but this was a fine spring day. The horse chestnut trees which lined the avenue to the house were in full bloom, candles of white with touches of pink. She'd hoped they'd still be in bloom when she returned, and they were. But she'd been shut out of her home.

On the other side of the road lay the river, running swift and strong following the spring rains. She set her back to the gates and looked across the river towards the village. She had friends there. She could knock on the doors of half a dozen houses and they would greet her with pleasure and welcome her indoors.

Or would they? Perhaps they'd stare blankly at her and say, "Never seen you before! Go away!"

She shuddered. Took a deep breath.

This whole situation was crazy, but she was perfectly sane. She would find a phone box and ring Patrick. He would come tearing back and sort it out for her. Her white knight.

No. She wouldn't do that. He had other problems to deal with today, problems that only he could solve.

This was her problem and she would solve it, somehow.

A car thundered along the road with its radio blaring. It had a faulty exhaust. If the police saw that, they'd stop the driver and ... her eye was caught by a billboard along the road towards the village.

EDEN HALL FESTIVAL
INDIE, POP, TRANCE, WORLD & BEYOND
FRIDAY & SATURDAY ... ADMISSION FEES ...
PARKING ... TICKETS FROM ... PHONE NUMBERS ...

What on earth did this mean? She didn't even know what "Indie" meant, for a start. Or "Trance". "World & Beyond" was slightly easier to understand. Presumably these were all different genres of music?

There was a blur of names. Names of different bands, singers, musicians. Some names were written in larger letters than others. She didn't recognise any of the names, but she'd never been particularly interested in popular music.

The dates ... She drew in a long breath. The festival was being held in her home that very week!

Did this explain the presence of the security men? Yes, but where was Barr, and who was this man Hatton they were talking about?

Too many questions. She needed answers. She got back into the car and considered her options. She could go up to the Manor House where her old friends the Woottons lived. They'd cluck over her, smother her. No, she didn't want to be smothered.

Annie. She'd left the Hall in Annie's capable hands. So where was Annie?

Minty hit the dashboard in frustration. If only her mobile had been charged up, she could ring these people and get some answers, but as it was, she was stuck.

What about her personal assistant, Iris? Where was she? Why hadn't Iris answered the phone in the office at Eden Hall? Had she left the Hall for some reason? Iris' father owned a thriving Chinese restaurant in the village; he'd know what had happened ... but did she really want to walk into his place and let everyone know she'd been refused entry to her own home? The humiliation of it!

Who could she turn to?

One after the other, Minty thought of people and discarded them. Too old. Too much of a worrier. But perhaps there was just one person who could tell her what was going on without having hysterics.

Minty started the car and took the road over the ancient bridge to the village. She avoided the High Street, turning up the lane which served the back gardens of the houses and shops.

Patrick spent half his week based in the nearby town and half working from his family's substantial Georgian house in the village.

His extremely efficient secretary was to have continued staffing his office here during his extended holiday with Minty. What was her name? Elizabeth something. Elizabeth had kept in touch with Patrick by phone and e-mail. She'd also been working part-time for Neville Chickward, the local accountant who looked after the books for Eden

Hall. Neville had moved into Patrick's office in his absence. Between them, they should have the answers to Minty's questions.

There was parking for two or, at a pinch, three cars at the bottom of Patrick's garden. One space was occupied by Elizabeth's Mini, but the rest were empty, which meant that Neville wasn't working there today.

Perhaps Elizabeth would also have news of Jim and his wife.

If she was still there.

Minty got out of the car and then held onto it for a moment, feeling giddy. She said aloud, "Pull yourself together, girl. Her car's there, isn't it?"

A Mini is a very reassuring car. Sensible, capable, low cost.

Someone must have been tidying Patrick's garden for him in his absence because it was comparatively weed-free, though a little shaggy around the edges. It was a long narrow courtyard garden, paved with old slabs of stone on which stood an ancient sundial. It was a garden for all seasons—like its master—in that there was something in flower every day of the year.

Patrick had loved this garden.

For the first time Minty wondered why he hadn't asked for space to create a garden of his own at Eden Hall.

She grasped the handle of the door into Patrick's house. Would it open? Would Elizabeth recognise her? She turned the handle and went in.

Chapter Two

The black-and-white tiled floor was just as Minty remembered it and so were the dark panelled walls. The hall ran right through the centre of the house from the garden at the back to the front door on the High Street. Immediately to her left lay the stairs to the living quarters above. Farther along the hall lay the door to Patrick's office. Minty tried the handle. Locked.

The first door on the opposite side of the hallway stood ajar. The room within used to be a library-cum-store-room, but she could see it had been cleared and fitted up as an office. Presumably this was where Neville worked?

From the reception room at the front came the murmur of a woman's voice, saying that she'd pass the message on to Mr Neville tomorrow. So Elizabeth still worked here? Relief!

Minty tapped on the door to reception and it swung open to reveal a well-remembered scene. A bird-like middle-aged woman was seated at a large desk behind a computer, talking into a telephone. She couldn't be more than five feet tall and looked fragile, though Minty knew she was as tough as old boots.

Elizabeth caught sight of Minty and gaped, ignoring the voice on the other end of the phone. A shadow passed across her face. Then she smiled and waved her free hand in a "Hi!" gesture, before bringing the telephone conversation to a close and rising to her feet.

"Mrs Sands! What a surprise! When did you get back? Why didn't you phone? Is Mr Patrick here, too?" Yet in that first moment there'd been uneasiness—possibly even something antagonistic—in Elizabeth's eyes.

Minty shook her head. "He's gone straight to the office in town. I went up to the Hall, but they wouldn't let me in."

"Oh, really? How very odd. Of course, the security people are turning people away all the time, and they wouldn't know who you were. What a welcome home!"

Minty frowned. Elizabeth was making all the right noises, but underneath there was an air of . . . amusement? Satisfaction?

"My goodness," said Elizabeth, "but hasn't there been a lot going on! Oh dear, I'm forgetting my manners. Do take a seat. Would you like a cup of something? You're looking so much better, if I may say so."

Minty relaxed. She was not going mad. There was an explanation for everything, and Elizabeth would give it to her.

Elizabeth busied herself providing coffee and biscuits while she talked. "Of course you've been missed, but Mr Patrick was right to take you away. He said to me, 'Betty'—he's always called me Betty—'I'm worried she'll fade right away if I don't take her off for a bit.' You'd hardly had any honeymoon at all with you both being so busy, and I suppose he was thinking how his mother died so soon after that dreadful scandal, and yet it was all lies . . ."

The phone rang again, and Elizabeth switched it over to an answering machine, still talking. Minty blocked out Elizabeth's voice, remembering only too vividly the lies which had linked her own mother to Patrick's father, and the tragic consequences.

Minty's father—Sir Micah Cardale—had been a worldly wise international financier who'd married the young heiress to Eden Hall in a love match and produced a child, Minty. Unfortunately Sir Micah had a secretary who had aimed to be the next Lady of the Hall. She spread stories that Minty's mother was having an affair with Patrick's father, who was an old family friend, as well as the family's solicitor. Worse was to come. Six months pregnant with her second child, Lady Cardale had discovered her husband in bed with his secretary and had driven wildly away from her birthplace . . . only to crash and be killed in a car accident.

Patrick and his family had been forced out of the village by the ensuing scandal, and the child Minty had been sent to live in the city with relations who cared nothing for her.

Patrick had returned to the village when he grew up and graduated, to re-occupy his family's home and pick up the remains of his father's practice. When Minty herself returned to the Hall, they had fallen in love with one another all over again. In a Cinderella-type ending, Minty had inherited the Hall and married Patrick. They had been fortunate enough to conceive a child straight away . . .

... and lost it.

Elizabeth had her hand on the phone, looking up at the clock. "Now who would it be best to speak to at the Hall? I wonder if I can get hold of Iris. She might be able to get away for lunch and sort it all out for you."

"Tell her to meet me at the gate."

Elizabeth dialled a number taken from a list in a book, but apparently Iris was not available. Elizabeth left a message for her to ring back and turned back to Minty. "I'm sure she won't be long." There was no uneasiness in her face now. Minty wondered if she'd imagined it. She was tired enough.

Elizabeth said, "So, tell me everything. We weren't expecting you back for ages. How is Mr Patrick? He never talks about himself when I speak to him on the phone."

Minty set down her empty cup. "He's fine. We were in Venice yesterday morning when he had a call saying his partner was in trouble. We took what flights we could get, but the luggage went astray. So I stayed behind at the airport to collect it while Patrick went on ahead. He asked them at Jim's office to ring the Hall to tell them we were on our way. I tried to ring, too, but the battery on my mobile is down and when I used a public phone box and tried to ring them, there was no reply."

Elizabeth shook her head. "They've moved offices, got these new numbers."

"What's going on, Elizabeth? When they wouldn't let me into the Hall, I asked for Barr and they said ..."

"Mrs Sands, surely you knew?"

"Call me 'Minty', please. What ought I to have known?"

Elizabeth twiddled with a pencil. "We were told that you were all for it, that you approved." Was there a note of resentment in her voice?

"You mean the festival? I saw the poster for it, but I don't even know what half the words mean. What's 'Indie' and 'Trance', for instance?"

"I had to ask, too. I think 'Indie' is some kind of pop, though don't ask me what. 'Trance' is music to dance to. There's all sorts of acts scheduled—folk, gospel, rock … everything you can think of. I don't suppose you expected it to take off like it has." Elizabeth didn't seem wildly happy about it.

"What's wrong with it?"

Elizabeth shrugged. "I don't even live in the village, thank goodness. You'll have to ask Iris. Or Ms Phillips. She knows all about it."

Minty told herself that was good news. If Annie Phillips was in favour of the festival, then that was all right. Wasn't it?

The phone rang and a familiar voice asked for Elizabeth.

Elizabeth snatched the phone up. "Iris? Yes, I did leave a message for you. Mrs Sands has returned unexpectedly, and they wouldn't let her into the Hall."

Elizabeth listened and put the phone down again. "Iris will be with us in ten minutes. Meanwhile, would you like to visit the cloakroom while I ring the office in town and try to speak to Mr Patrick?"

Elizabeth was avoiding explanations. Minty's perplexity grew. Did Elizabeth mean Minty was supposed to have approved this festival? Well, she supposed she did, in a way. It would bring in a lot of people, which presumably meant entrance fees and catering. There must be a lot of money to be made from it. So why not? Of course it would have been nice to have been consulted about such a big event, but there … hadn't Patrick forbidden her even to think about work while they were away? So how could anyone have asked her about it?

Annie Phillips had power of attorney, and if she had agreed to it, then it must be a good thing.

There'd been a muddle on the gate; the security people had mistaken Barr's name. That was all it was. A simple explanation.

Minty freshened herself up, thinking that she'd been making a mountain out of a molehill. She was feeling quite relaxed until she met Iris in the hallway. Iris hadn't used the front door, as she might have been expected to do, but had come in through the back door from the garden.

Beautiful and remote, Iris was a high flyer with a good degree and business experience who'd worked in London before Minty lured her back to the Hall to be her right hand. Now Iris was sporting a large identity tag and looked worried. But she smiled with what looked like genuine pleasure when she saw Minty.

"Oh, Minty ... thank God!" Iris wasn't a Christian, but like many people she called on God's name automatically when she was distressed.

Minty held out her arms to Iris, and the two women clung to one another. Minty had always felt she could trust Iris as if she were her own sister. Well, actually, Minty didn't trust her half-sister Gemma very far, but she did trust Iris.

Minty had told herself to be calm, but the first thing she said was, "They wouldn't let me into the Hall." Just like a child.

"I heard. I'm so sorry. It's all such a muddle. I don't know where to start, but ... are you all right now, Minty? You're looking so much better, but ... we were told you wouldn't be back, so ..."

Elizabeth appeared, flourishing a key. "Make yourselves comfortable in Mr Patrick's office and I'll get you some lunch. Some sandwiches from the pub?"

"All I want," said Minty, "is to get back home, take a shower, eat some of Serafina's wonderful food and catch up on all the news."

"Serafina. Yes, well," said Iris, losing her smile. "Perhaps we'd better have a snack here first."

Elizabeth led the way into Patrick's office, which was dust free and looked as if he'd just stepped out for the afternoon. Minty hesitated, disliking any delay in returning to the Hall. Iris seated herself in the client's chair in front of Patrick's antique desk, so Minty subsided into his big swivel chair.

"Serafina," said Iris, "is not at the Hall."

Minty stared at Iris. Serafina hardly ever left the Hall. She'd been housekeeper to Minty's father and had seemed happy to stay on to look after Minty. It gave Minty a feeling of insecurity to hear that Serafina was not at the Hall.

"Ms Phillips found a house she liked a couple of miles away and moved in a while back. Serafina joined her."

Minty was silent, readjusting her ideas. She told herself it was selfish of her—and very short-sighted—not to have realised that during the months she'd been away, other people had been getting on with

24

their lives. As they had every right to do. But she would miss Serafina. And Annie, too.

"I wish I'd known," said Minty. "It's only natural that Annie should want to leave her flat at the Hall and buy her own house. She has plenty of money. As for Serafina, she hates to be idle, and I'm sure she'll be happy with Annie. They've worked side by side for so many years. Of course I'll miss them, but I'm pleased for them, too."

"Yes," said Iris, not sounding convinced. "I see the news has come as a surprise to you. I find that strange. We were told that you were being kept informed about, well, everything. That you approved."

"Patrick said I wasn't to be bothered with business until I felt better. I suppose he knew about it but didn't want to worry me." She could understand why Patrick would have kept bad news from her during the first month of their absence, but why hadn't he told her about Serafina on the journey home? Surely it should have been the first thing to spring to his mind?

The door opened and Elizabeth came in with a bag of sandwiches and some soft drinks. "I got them to toast the sandwiches, so eat them while they're hot."

Minty was ravenous. She took a toasted sandwich and bit into it. It was good. Fattening, and probably not good for cholesterol, but who cared under these circumstances? Iris took another sandwich but had hardly finished it by the time Minty had eaten two.

"Start at the beginning, Iris. Assume that I know nothing of what's been happening, because that's the truth."

Iris consulted her almond-shaped fingernails. "The first thing ... are you sure Patrick didn't tell you? Barr fell off the wagon in spectacular fashion, and Annie accepted his resignation."

"Oh ..." Minty let out a long breath. Barr had a tendency to drink too much, but he'd been on the wagon for so long that Minty had thought he'd got his problem under control. "Oh, I am sorry. He was a kind man, and he knew the Hall and all its ways better than anyone."

"We were all sorry when he left. But Annie was right. He couldn't be trusted."

Annie, thought Minty, had never been tempted as Barr had been. Annie was sometimes self-righteous. But probably she'd done the right thing.

Iris continued, "Annie found someone called Clive Hatton to replace Barr as Administrator and to manage the Hall and Estate. He'd been running a place in Scotland for the National Trust. Quite the English gentleman."

Minty narrowed her eyes. Iris' tone had been at odds with her words. Was Iris sneering at Mr Hatton or commending him?

"We soon realised what a difference a professional can make to the running of a stately home. We'd been thinking in terms of hundreds of visitors for events, whereas he thinks of thousands."

Minty guessed, "You don't like him?"

Iris stirred restlessly. "Yes, I do. Of course I do. He's extremely efficient and he gets on well with Neville, who's sorted out the books at the Hall so well. But everyone gets on well with Neville, don't they?"

Was Iris changing the subject? "I like Neville," said Minty, testing the waters.

Iris nodded. She liked Neville, too.

Minty couldn't make out whether Iris liked or loathed Mr Hatton. "So," said Minty, "this festival was Mr Hatton's idea?"

A faint frown appeared on Iris' brow. "The original idea was to have a classical music concert in the open air down by the lake below the house. People would bring picnics and sit on the slope above the lake, and we'd have elegant suppers in a marquee. Annie approved that idea, but somehow … I really don't know how it happened, Gemma …"

"Ah, Gemma," said Minty. She'd wondered where her beautiful but wayward half-sister had come into the picture. "I left her in charge of events but said everything had to get Annie's approval."

"Oh, it did. At first, anyway. Then Annie was offered a place on a government quango — some committee to do with the charity your father founded — and she moved to her new house. So she hasn't been around much lately. Gemma started working more closely with Mr Hatton and …"

"She's sleeping with him?" Minty knew what her half-sister was like. Too many men and too much drink at an early age had left Gemma adrift in life, rushing from one wild experience to another and finding none of them satisfactory.

Iris shrugged, raised her eyebrows. There was no need to reply. Gemma was sleeping with Mr Hatton. "Mr Hatton said we ought to widen the scope of the concert to appeal to a mass audience. The event is to be spread over two days, with people bringing their own tents, sleeping rough, whatever. Toby did the publicity nation-wide. You'd have seen some of it if you'd been in the country, but of course you weren't. Annie was more or less out of the picture by then, but Gemma said you were thrilled with the way things were going."

Minty got up and started pacing the room. "When did she say that?"

Iris had the dates pat.

Minty said, "The last week in March we were hopping on and off boats going round the Greek islands, with just one rucksack between us. No mobile, no laptop. We were out of touch for about a week."

Iris consulted her fingernails again. "There was a lot of pressure on Mr Hatton to go ahead. It is possible, I suppose ..."

"That Gemma did some wishful thinking? That she took my approval for granted?"

Iris met Minty's eyes. "Your approval swung it with the local council, though the village is still worried about so many thousands of people descending upon them."

"Thousands!"

"Tens of thousands, probably. Coming from all over the place. Some flying in from the Continent." Iris' voice went flat. "You didn't know anything about it?"

Minty braced herself. "Well, it isn't so bad. It'll bring a lot of money in, and the disruption to the Hall ... well, there needn't be any, need there? So we're closed to the public till it's over? I'm sure you've organised everything beautifully."

"I like a challenge. Clive's made me responsible for ticket sales, franchising of food outlets, sponsors who want to stage corporate hospitality and invitations to important people. We had to take on extra staff to man the phones day and night. New telephone lines. There wasn't room enough for all of us in the tower office, so we moved out to the north wing, where your father's charity offices used to be."

So that was why Minty hadn't been able to get a reply to her phone calls to the Hall.

"It's bedlam, in a controlled way," said Iris. "Clive has overall responsibility for everything, of course, including security, television coverage and the media. Toby does the publicity—that's driven him ragged. Clive got in touch with a promoter who's responsible for booking the artists, providing the stage management, the stage, installing the power lines for sound and television ... everything."

"Television coverage?" Minty was amazed.

"News coverage for our regional company, definitely. Maybe a snippet or two of national coverage. There'll be DVDs made as well. Everyone who goes in and out of the Hall has to have a security badge. We've had all sorts trying to get in without paying. The security guards have been turning away groupies and sight-seers and autograph hunters already. They thought you were a wannabe singer, I believe."

So that's why they'd been so short with her and said she hadn't got what it took! Yes, but that didn't account for the nasty feeling that was sneaking around the back of her mind. "So what's wrong, Iris?"

"Nothing." Iris smoothed back her hair. "It was difficult to book a first-class lead act at such short notice, but we were fortunate enough to be able to get Maxine. You've never heard of her? No, it's not really your thing, is it. Gemma has known her for ages, met her at a party somewhere, and that swung it for us. Maxine is famous, got quite a following. I can't say that what she does is exactly my scene, but it's all very clever. She's got a voice like ... I don't know how you'd describe it. Seductive, I suppose. She's got charisma. The crowds love her."

"You don't sound as if you approve."

"Oh, I do." But she didn't. Iris tried again. "It's just that sometimes her lyrics are ... oh, I don't know. We've sold an enormous number of tickets just because she's coming. Gemma's besotted. She's got Maxine to promise she can be one of the backing singers ..."

Minty snorted. Gemma was a beautiful girl with a model's figure, but she'd no training as a singer and was definitely not a team player.

"... and in return, Gemma's invited Maxine and her entourage to stay at the Hall for the duration. They're there now, making a video." Iris swallowed. "The thing is, Minty, Maxine was supposed to stay in the guest quarters in the west wing, but Gemma was showing Maxine round the place and she saw your rooms … and demanded to have them."

Minty stared at Iris, who flushed dark red.

Could it be true? Could Minty and Patrick's own suite be taken over by a stranger? The four-poster bed in which she'd been born, and in which she and Patrick slept? The sitting and dining room furnished with the furniture from Patrick's family home?

Minty sat down abruptly.

Iris looked away. "I didn't like it when it happened, either. None of us did. That's why Serafina moved out. But Gemma said you weren't going to be back for ages, and Clive backed her up, of course. You see, if Maxine gets upset and leaves, we'll have no headliner for the festival and might as well cancel. There's too much money been laid out for us to risk that. So … you see?"

"I'm beginning to."

"I realise it's upsetting for you, but Minty—for the sake of the festival and all the money that's involved—do you think you could go back to London for a few days until the festival's over, or stay at a hotel somewhere?"

Minty shook her head.

Iris leaned forward. "I understand how you must feel, but … look, suppose I tell them you're arriving back from holiday tomorrow. I can get Gemma to ease Maxine into the west wing, which is where she should have stayed in the first place. Then you can make your entrance in a couple of days' time and occupy your own rooms without anyone losing face."

Minty took a deep breath. "I need to see Gemma. And meet Mr Hatton."

"Gemma's working with the video unit today. I'll tell Clive." Iris bit her lip. "He's very busy, you know, working a twelve-hour day, sometimes more."

Minty wanted to ask who paid Iris' wages: Mr Hatton or Minty? Come to think of it, she must be paying Mr Hatton's wages, too. Yet Iris was behaving as if Mr Hatton was the boss and not Minty.

Iris looked at her watch. "I must go. I'm really sorry to have had to tell you all this. We all thought you knew, of course. About the festival and Clive, at any rate. I'm glad you're back. I really am."

Minty gave her a searching look. Iris seemed to mean it, but Minty sensed something was being withheld from her.

Minty said, "I take your point about not upsetting Maxine—although really! No, it's done now, and I can see we'll just have to muddle through as best we can. I'll find somewhere else for us to stay tonight. I must speak to Annie, and will you ask Mr Hatton to meet me here at ten tomorrow? You'll keep in touch, won't you? And let me have your new office number."

"Make it eleven tomorrow for Clive. That gives him time to deal with the morning's foul-ups before coming up here."

Iris wrote down her new telephone number and slipped away, leaving by the garden door. Was that so that she wouldn't be seen leaving Patrick's house? Surely Iris knew there were no secrets in a village? Someone would have seen her enter and leave by the back door. So who was she fooling?

It was one too many puzzles for Minty to cope with.

Chapter Three

Elizabeth was busy on the phone again, so Minty climbed the elegant stairs to the reception rooms on the first floor in which Patrick and his family had once lived. Sunlight poured through the tall sash windows, revealing huge, empty, dusty spaces. Most of Patrick's furniture was now up at the Hall, though his kitchen and study were still fully furnished.

Minty followed the stairs to the top floor. Here everything was just as Patrick had left it when he married Minty and moved to the Hall. The main bedroom, the guest room ... his Spartan bachelor bedroom with its single bed ... the bathroom and toilet. Everything was dusty but otherwise in good order.

Minty peered into cupboards on the top landing. There were enough sheets, duvets and towels if she decided to stay the night ... but there were no comfortable chairs to sit in, no table to eat at.

She sat on Patrick's narrow bed and looked at the palm cross he'd tacked on the wall opposite. His Bible was in one of their suitcases in the car below, but he'd left a slender volume of psalms behind in his old room. She picked it up, looking for comfort. The book had been much used and fell open at the twenty-third psalm.

> *The Lord is my shepherd, I shall not be in want.*
> *He makes me lie down in green pastures ... he restores my soul ...*

She repeated aloud, "He restores my soul."

Ever since the miscarriage, she'd battled with lethargy and bouts of despair. Every night, she and Patrick had read their Bible together, he with his arm about her. They'd talked over the notes for that day and prayed. Or rather, Patrick had mused aloud and prayed and she'd listened, unable to feel anything, conscious of the void in her life where the baby should have been.

She hadn't blamed God for the loss of the baby, precisely. Not perhaps in so many words or even thoughts. But she hadn't been able to pray. Instead, Patrick had prayed for healing for her.

Now the words of the psalm caught at her mind and lodged deep. "He restores my soul."

She began to weep, soundlessly at first, and then in noisy gulps. She wept for the child that was to have been, and for her loss of trust in Him. All this time He'd been offering her healing through the Bible, and she'd blocked Him out.

She lay curled up on Patrick's bed and wept, reaching up to God in her mind, offering herself afresh to Him, thanking Him for everything He had done for her. Praising Him.

How she got from sorrow to praise, she didn't know.

At last she lay still and felt a new serenity. She whispered, "He will restore my soul."

She didn't know how long she lay there, but after a while she sat up with renewed strength. She washed, brushed dust off her clothes and went downstairs to see if Elizabeth was free to talk.

"Mrs Sands, would you like some tea now?" Minty noted that Elizabeth had not yet called her anything but the formal "Mrs Sands".

"Oh, and by the way—" Elizabeth went rather pink—"You probably didn't know, but Mr Patrick fixed up a switch on his telephone so that he could speak to me directly from his office if he wished to do so. I didn't realise the switch was on until you and Iris started talking, and I couldn't help hearing what you were saying. Is it true that you didn't know about the festival or the pop group? And that you can't get back into your rooms at the Hall?"

Minty tried to put a good face on it. What was the point of blaming others? Besides, Patrick had probably known all about it and approved. "Just one misunderstanding after another. I don't think anyone's particularly to blame, but I do have some catching up to do. Thank you, Elizabeth; a cuppa would be good. I'm afraid I'm not making much sense at the moment."

"You'll be fine after a good night's sleep. I've been on to the office in town, but I couldn't speak to Mr Patrick because he's in court."

Minty started. Patrick had hardly got back into this country, and he'd had to appear in court already?

"They said it was some very important case, and what with Mr Jim being at the hospital—his wife's still very poorly, I understand—they were at their wits' end, but Mr Patrick can always be relied on to help out."

Very true, thought Minty. He'd gone straight into court? What an effort he must have made to master the details of the case and be ready to feed information to a barrister, while worrying about Jim and Anthea, not to mention their frail little daughter. He must be worrying about Minty, as well.

She decided that she wouldn't scream to him for help. Not this time. This time she must cope by herself. After all, everything at the Hall seemed to be under control, even if some of the detail was not quite what she'd expected.

Tea arrived. Minty asked if Elizabeth could charge up her old mobile and give her an up-to-date list of numbers for the Hall.

Elizabeth said she could. She hovered, moving cups and saucers around on the desk, before bringing herself to say, "I think you should know, Mrs Sands, that just before your spot of trouble, Mr Patrick was asked, formally, if he'd like to go on the Board of the charity which your father had founded. It sounded as if they really wanted him. He was pleased, but of course he had to turn the offer down when you were poorly."

Minty put her cup down with an unsteady hand. Sir Micah Cardale had spent the latter part of his life setting up a charity to further education in deprived areas. The Foundation helped build and resource schools. Minty had automatically been voted onto the Board after her father's death but had felt very much out of place among the financiers and high flyers. She'd always thought Patrick would have been more at home in that world. In fact he'd been asked to serve on the Foundation when they became engaged, but he'd had to turn down the offer when circumstances made it difficult for him to accept. He hadn't told her that they'd made another formal approach to him recently. Elizabeth obviously thought he ought to have accepted, and perhaps she was right.

Was this why Elizabeth had been displaying resentment? Minty felt as if she'd mistaken the last step on the stairs in the dark. Elizabeth disliked her! Minty wasn't used to being disliked. It hurt.

"I'm sorry," she said. "I didn't know."

Elizabeth inclined her head, accepting the apology with reservations.

Minty now had to consider what they should do that night.

Although few people knew it, Patrick was a wealthy man who owned quite a few properties in the area. One was a cottage on the outskirts of the nearby town, which he'd used when working in that direction. Minty and Patrick had used Mill Cottage for their honeymoon because, although it was small, it was quiet and comfortable. Patrick had let it out for the winter months, but perhaps it was now free?

Minty asked Elizabeth if she might use her phone for a moment. And then had to ask her for the number for Mrs Mimms, who lived next door to the cottage and looked after it for Patrick. Luckily Mrs Mimms answered the phone, as chatty as ever.

Yes, the place was empty at the moment, said Mrs Mimms, adding that she'd been popping in to see that all was right and tight because one of the gutters was not quite what it should be, but all was well at the moment and though their tenant had moved on, there was someone else enquiring ...

Minty cut across the flow of words to say that she and Patrick would be using it for a couple of nights, and if Mrs Mimms could possibly get in some milk and bread and perhaps a few eggs, that would be wonderful.

Mrs Mimms said she would, and how lovely it was to hear Mrs Sands' voice again.

So now Minty knew where they could spend the night. She used the office phone to ring Patrick's mobile, but it was switched off as it always was when he was in court. She left a message to say they would be at Mill Cottage that night.

Elizabeth was making herself very busy with her filing, throwing sharp glances at Minty between while. She was—perhaps deliberately?—making Minty feel uncomfortable. "Is there anything else you'd like me to do for you, Mrs Sands?" In other words, please go away and leave me in peace to do my work.

"No, thank you," said Minty. "There's a great many people I ought to phone to say I'm back, but they'll have to wait till I've spoken to Ms Phillips and Mr Hatton."

Elizabeth looked at her with narrowed eyes and spoke more deliberately than usual. "You must have realised what trouble this festival would cause."

Minty was exhausted. She pushed her hair back off her face. "I knew nothing about it till today, but I suppose people will find that hard to believe."

Elizabeth folded her lips. "I'm glad I don't live in the village, that's all. My cousin's husband that's a policeman, he says it's asking for trouble. But there … I suppose Mr Hatton knows what he's doing." She meant the very opposite of what she said; Elizabeth did not think Mr Hatton knew what he was doing.

It was all very confusing. Minty obtained directions to Ms Phillips' house and took the rented car back on the road.

❧

It was springtime. Bluebells spilled in pools of blue under trees which were just putting out new leaves. Starwort spangled the hedgerows with silvery-white flowers. Birds sang their loudest. Somewhere in the distance a cuckoo chimed in.

Minty parked the car in a lay-by. She got out to feel the breeze in her hair and watch the clouds ride smoothly across the sky. Sheep bleated on a far-off hill-top.

A tractor was working somewhere nearby.

A lorry laboured past, trailing blue smoke. All was right with the world, except where man had made a mess of it.

Minty closed her tired eyes, feeling the breeze on her eyelids, listening to the sounds of the countryside, savouring the scent of new mown grass.

> *He has restored my soul. Praise Him, praise Him.*
> *Drop the still dews of quietness upon my soul ...*

The words of the old hymn comforted and strengthened her. She was going to be whole again. The burden of grief and loss that she'd carried for so long was becoming lighter.

"Sufficient to the day is the evil thereof!" That had been her uncle talking down to the child Minty, forbidding her to worry about the morrow. She hadn't believed him then. She wasn't sure she believed him now, but she'd have a try at it.

She got back into the car and drove down into the valley and up the other side to find Annie Phillips' new place. The house had been architect designed, probably in the 1920s when houses were either geometric or curved. This one was geometric, which would suit Annie Phillips' sharp-cornered personality. It was reached by a steep drive off the road. Built on a bluff overlooking the valley below, it would have spectacular views but be buffeted by winds in wintertime.

Minty got out of the car on the hardstanding at the side of the house, and noted freshly sown grass seed laid in swathes around the house. Annie liked everything neat around her. There were no flower beds.

A stone-flagged terrace encircled the house on three sides, with patio furniture laid out on it. Red and white striped awnings helped to shade the ground floor rooms, with mathematically spaced red geraniums in window-boxes echoing their vibrant colour. The front door was a heavyweight, built of light oak. Minty pressed the doorbell.

Annie Phillips herself came to the door. In her fifties, tall and severely dressed in an elegant black suit, Annie looked every inch the successful businesswoman, but on seeing Minty, she took a half step back.

"Araminta! I didn't expect you ... is Patrick with you?" She did seem genuinely pleased to see Minty ... though was that a hint of

VERONICA HELEY

anxiety in her eyes? Minty wondered if she'd imagined it, or if she was growing suspicious of everyone.

"Well, this is a surprise. Are you quite well again now? What a terrible thing that was. I was so sorry. Isn't this place marvellous? Come in, come in. Is Patrick meeting you here?" She led the way, still talking, across a wide hallway into a vast sitting room with views across the valley.

Annie had been spending money. She'd bought angular seating upholstered in a thick white cotton material, and ebonised wooden tables and chairs. The walls were dead white. The only things Minty remembered from Annie's previous quarters were the Chinese silk rugs on the polished floorboards, which gave the room some colour.

"This is beautiful, Annie," said Minty, appreciating the skill and taste which made the room such a picture.

"Your father was always on at me to get a place of my own, but when he was alive I never felt the need. Even after he died. But then you went away and this place came on the market, so ... are you really well now, my dear?"

"I thought so, till I was refused admission to the Hall."

"What?" Annie was shocked. "I don't understand. Oh, but perhaps ... Patrick said you'd be away for another couple of months, and the guards wouldn't know who you were. What a mix-up! I hope you gave them a piece of your mind." Annie gave an artificial little laugh. "I suppose you'll want to pick a bone with me. You left me in charge but ... oh, so many things have happened, and perhaps I haven't been as much on top of things at the Hall as I ought to have been."

Minty was fond of Annie and didn't like to make the older woman feel uncomfortable. "I hear you've been head-hunted for some government post? Congratulations. They couldn't have found anyone better."

Colour tinged Annie's face. "Well, my dear. Thank you. I must admit I was surprised when I was approached, but I couldn't refuse because it's continuing the work your father started, helping to educate those in need, especially in inner cities. It takes up a lot of my time. Not that I grudge that, of course. Your father would have been pleased, wouldn't he? Sometimes when I'm chairing a meeting, I think of him and what he'd have said if he'd been there … and … well, we all have to move forward, don't we?"

"Yes, we do," said Minty, who also missed her father.

Annie said, "I've only just come back from a meeting in Town this morning, haven't even had time to change. What with this and that, I hardly have a moment to myself. And I have to return early next week for another meeting."

"I understand how it is. So, tell me everything. I hear poor Barr overstepped the mark."

"That was a shame. He'd been at the Hall for so long, and I know you were fond of him. But — " a sigh — "he lacked motivation, and without you to chivvy him along, he became cavalier in his attitude to work. He fell behind with his paperwork. Little things. Pointers to his state of mind. Then he was caught drunk driving. Nearly ran over a child in the High Street in the middle of the afternoon! He resigned, of course. Patrick agreed with me that he had to go. Mr Hatton is quite a different kettle of fish, as you'll see. But Patrick will have told you all about that, won't he?"

Patrick should have told her on the plane coming back, but there … he'd been caught up in work so quickly.

No, he should have told her.

Annie looked at an inner door but made no move to call Serafina. In the old days Serafina would appear with trays of strong coffee and plates of delicious cakes as soon as any visitor ventured into her territory. Perhaps she'd gone out for the afternoon?

Minty said, "Tell me about this festival."

Annie frowned. "I don't understand why you thought a pop festival would be such a good idea. I said it would upset the villagers and be a highly risky undertaking, but Gemma said you were all for it. I was made to feel rather foolish, though I suppose my feelings are hardly important in the world view of things. I keep telling myself that your father would have approved such a bold venture, but I must admit I've been rather worried about it."

"I knew nothing about it till I tried to get into the Hall today," said Minty. "I'm not at all sure that Patrick did either."

"Oh." Ms Phillips stared out of the window, evaluating the situation and not liking her conclusions. "You think Gemma indulged in some wishful thinking? But ... how very awkward. I've signed cheques for everything they asked for. Surely Patrick must have approved?"

"Haven't you spoken to him about it?"

"Well, no." Annie didn't fudge the issue. That was not her way. She sat with her knees and ankles together and looked Minty in the eye. "We discussed having a classical concert in the open air and organising a hospitality tent serving food and champagne. That was the week before you went off to the Greek islands, and Patrick said you'd be out of contact for a while. The following week I had to be in London. On my return I went up for a meeting at the Hall. That's when Gemma said the plans had been changed. She said you'd approved." Annie looked into space for a long minute. Then met Minty's eyes. "She's pulled a fast one?"

Minty nodded. "It looks like it."

"What will you do?"

Minty grimaced. "What can I do? Isn't everything too far advanced to cancel? We'll just have to make the best of it. I'm told the village doesn't like it, and I'll have to check on that. I've spoken to Iris, and I've asked Mr Hatton to report to me at Patrick's office tomorrow. Can you join us?"

"Unfortunately I have another appointment. I'll be available, if you wish to phone me, after twelve." She frowned. "Mr Hatton seems very efficient, and Neville Chickward is a steadying influence on the financial side. They tell me these events can make a lot of money ..." Her voice trailed away.

Minty nodded. Despite her brave words, Annie seemed to be as uneasy about it as Minty.

"Iris said that Serafina was living with you?"

Annie sat even more upright than before, if that was possible. "She'll be delighted you're back. She says I don't do justice to her cooking, and to tell the truth, I've grown accustomed to living on my own."

So Serafina had not settled down with Annie? Minty got to her feet, thinking how much she longed for a shower and a good meal. It seemed to have been a long time since she ate a proper meal.

Annie saw her to the front door and waved goodbye. Minty trudged round the corner of the house to her car ... and found Serafina sitting four-square and solid in the passenger seat. There were two extra suitcases on the back seat together with a jumble of boxes and plastic bags.

"Serafina!" Minty felt like bursting into tears. Relief, perhaps? "What are you doing here?"

"Coming with you, of course. You'll turn those nasty people out of the Hall, and then we can be comfortable again."

"I'm going somewhere else tonight, giving them a chance of moving to the west wing without losing face. I've arranged to stay at Mill Cottage and—"

"Suits me. There's two bedrooms, isn't there? I've got my own television and duvet. You show me the kitchen, and I'll get something tasty going for supper for you and Patrick. Don't tell me he won't be hungry after a day in court."

Minty got behind the wheel, still feeling stunned. And relieved. And pleased. And worried. All at once. "How did you know?"

"I've got my methods. When that lot took over, I had a quick word with Chef in the restaurant ..."

"Dear Florence. How is she? How is she managing if the Hall is closed to the public?"

"Mr Hatton asked her to stay on to cook for Maxine and her crowd. There must be twenty of them at least. No, there's more now they've started making the video. Then there's the security guards and the new staff in the office. Oh, there's plenty of mouths to feed. Florence doesn't like what's happening there any more than I do, but we agreed she should stay and do what she could to keep standards up. Her and Reggie, the Houseman—and Hodge, the head gardener. They're still there. We keep in touch by phone every day. So let's get going."

Serafina was dressed in black as usual. She had the build and sallow complexion of her Mediterranean ancestors. She was a formidable woman who'd loved and looked after Sir Micah Cardale and had transferred her loyalty to Minty—and Patrick—after his death. Minty was amazed that Serafina had been routed by the incomers. She wouldn't have thought Serafina would be easy to shift.

"Dear Serafina, I've missed you. But are you sure that you want to come with me now? Mill Cottage is tiny and ..."

Serafina did up her seat-belt. "I left a note for Annie. I've got a nice steak and kidney pie in the cool-box in the back that I'd made for her, but she only wants the lightest of evening meals, which is no compliment to the cook. Best get moving, or it might spoil."

Round the corner came Annie, holding a potted red geranium in one hand and a piece of paper in the other. "She's found my note," said Serafina.

Annie was smiling. What a relief!

Annie handed the geranium to Minty through the car window. "I'm sure you've got plenty of plants of your own at the Hall, but this one seems to be left over."

Minty handed the geranium to Serafina. "Are you sure, Annie?"

"Glad to see the back of her." Smiling. And to Serafina, "You look after Minty, now."

Annie waved them out of the driveway, and Minty turned the car in the direction of Mill Cottage.

Chapter Four

Mill Cottage was ancient, crouching low to the ground. Its heavy oak beams supported a structure which had been old when the foundations of Eden Hall had been laid. Minty and Serafina took the first of the packages out of the car, stepping down from the street into a room which was all unexpected angles within walls almost a yard thick. There was an enormous fireplace, a Welsh dresser with blue and white plates on it, and some comfortable pieces of furniture. When Patrick was around, the table and probably most of the chairs would contain a drift of papers and books, but having been let out over winter, it was unusually tidy.

Serafina took some of her belongings through to the kitchen and the rest upstairs to the back bedroom, while Minty put the geranium on one of the window-sills and fell into a day-dream, listening to the rustling of the stream outside the window. You could always hear water at Mill Cottage. Swollen with rain, the stream nearby rushed and pounded along its course, seeming almost threatening to Minty, overtired as she was.

Minty knew she ought to get moving, sort out the luggage, unpack, have a bath, help Serafina to settle. She was too tired to move. Too tired even to pray, except to say over and over, "Lord, restore my soul ..."

Serafina was strong and could move quietly when she chose, but even she had difficulty getting the big cases out of the car. Minty roused herself to help. Together they got the luggage upstairs, checked that both beds were made up — thank you, Mrs Mimms — and Minty managed to step in and out of the shower without tripping over and injuring herself. She made it to the bed, intending to dress in clean clothes ... and sat down ... then lay back, just for a minute ... and fell asleep.

She woke when Patrick sat on the bed and leaned over to kiss her.

She knuckled her eyelids and returned his kiss, wondering for a moment where she was.

"Clever girl," said Patrick, easing himself out of his jacket. "Coming here is perfect. Peace and quiet. And Serafina! How did you manage to get her here? She says it's steak and kidney pie for supper. Oh, and Jim's been at the hospital all day and intends to sleep there, too. I'm not sure Anthea's going to make it."

"Oh, that's terrible. Poor Anthea. I wish I'd gotten to know her better, but I thought there'd be plenty of time. And poor Jim! How is he coping?"

"So-so." He touched her cheek. "How about you?" He looked worn out. The upright line between his eyebrows had become very marked these last few months, and he'd lost weight.

She knew that she had all sorts of important things to discuss with him, but for the moment she couldn't remember what they were ... and then she did, and frowned.

He yawned, shedding his tie. "Serafina gave me a cup of coffee to keep me awake till supper. Have I got a clean shirt anywhere?"

She eased herself off the bed. "I'll look. Practically everything we've brought back needs washing, but I think ..."

She found a clean shirt in the second suitcase she tried, but when she turned to hand it to him, he'd fallen back onto the pillows and was already asleep, cup of coffee untouched on the bedside table.

"Let him sleep awhile," said Serafina, appearing in the doorway. "You, too. I'll wake you in an hour when supper's ready, but don't expect miracles. This oven lacks fire in its belly, if I'm any judge of the matter."

Minty wriggled into Patrick's arms and felt safe for the first time since she'd been refused admission to her home. From somewhere way back in her childhood she remembered an old lady saying that if you wanted a man to talk sense, you had to feed him first. Smiling, she too fell asleep. Questions could wait. Rest first. Then eat. Then ask questions.

Patrick looked better after two helpings of everything. Serafina fretted that the oven was slow and refused to eat with them, saying that she wanted to watch one of her favourite programmes on the telly. When they'd finished, Patrick pushed his plate away and said, "I only remembered when I got into court. I ought to have told you that Barr had—"

She cut across him. "Where will we stay in London when we go up for meetings at my father's charity?"

He blinked. Felt for the cigarettes which he'd very nearly stopped smoking. Failed to find them. Looked into his empty coffee cup for inspiration. Checked her face, looking doubtful. What he saw there seemed to reassure him. He laughed, eyes gleaming. "Welcome back, Araminta. I've missed you."

She picked up his hand and laid the palm against her cheek. "'He loves not, who alters when he alteration finds.' That's a quote from someone, but ..."

He opened his mouth to tell her, but she forestalled him.

"... I don't care who it was who said it first. What I mean is that I'm not quite there yet, and I didn't really want to come back so soon, but now I am ..." She took a deep breath. "... I'm coping. Not terribly well, but I am coping. I know I've been a heavy burden to carry for the last few months—no, let me finish. I mended slowly ..."

"My darling, you nearly died."

"Did I? I can't remember anything much about it till we got to ... where was it I first ate a square meal? In that restaurant in Normandy? Or was it in Paris? Well, I'm over the worst of it. I know you have other burdens to carry now, and I want you to know that I'm happy about that."

He said, "Praise the Lord." And meant it.

Serafina entered as noiselessly as usual. "I'm clearing the table. He'll want space to work this evening."

Patrick's eyes snapped to his laptop and then back to Minty. "No, Serafina. I'm not working tonight. I won't even ask what we're all doing here at Mill Cottage. Let's all clear the table and wash up and perhaps go for a stroll along the lanes. Take time out. Enjoy being back in this country."

Serafina looked grim. "I don't need help washing up, and I've never believed in pretending black was white. Things are not all right at the Hall, and you ought to know what's been happening."

"Yes, but not this minute. Remember, sometimes things may look black, whereas they're really only grey."

Patrick had his way. He had the knack of putting his life into different compartments and shutting the door on them when he wished. Minty usually found it hard to emulate him, but tonight she found his refusal to talk business refreshing. She found herself unwinding, even though she hadn't realised she'd been tense.

Serafina refused to join them in a stroll around the village, saying she'd rather watch television though the reception was not all it might be.

Patrick made Minty pause at the corner of their lane, watching the house martins wheel and squeal above the roof-tops. House martins usually returned to the same houses every year, but there were no nests under the eaves of Mill Cottage.

In the dusk the white foam of Queen Anne's Lace decorated the verges of the lane. May blossom scented the air with its heavy perfume. A sweet chestnut showered pink petals on them as they passed below it.

They took a roundabout route, with his arm about her waist, matching steps. They paused at the gate of the little church, where someone was practising the organ.

It was a blessed hour, which she knew they would both remember in the troublesome time to come ... for both knew there were troublesome times ahead.

Only when they returned to the cottage and were sitting with their arms around one another on the settee did Patrick turn to her and say, "Shall we talk now? I'm sorry I forgot about Barr going. It must have been a shock. Annie made sure he was all right. He got a lump sum by way of severance pay and he's gone back to the New Forest, where he's got relations."

She nodded, thinking it was probably due to Patrick that Barr had got any severance pay at all.

Patrick said, "The new man, Hatton. Excellent references. I checked and so did Annie. I wish I could have met him first, but ... Annie was desperate. We gave him a six-month contract, renewable. I thought he'd want a long contract, but he said he wanted to meet you before he would commit himself for more than six months. If you get on with him, he stays. If not ... he goes."

Minty screwed up her face. "Iris was ambivalent about him. She says he's efficient, but ... I couldn't make out what she really felt. I'll see him tomorrow, form my own judgement. It appears the village is upset about the festival ..."

"Surely they're not objecting to a classical concert by the lake?"

Minty shook her head. So Patrick hadn't been told about the change of plan. "It appears that Gemma's enthusiasm for a particular pop star has got out of hand. It's now going to be a two-day music festival, nationally advertised."

"Good grief! That'll be an enormous undertaking. Can Hatton bring it off?"

"Iris seems to think so. The only problem is that the star is presently occupying our suite at the Hall."

"What?" He was not amused.

She put her hand on his arm. "It's only for tonight. Gemma thought we'd be away for ages. The pop star will be moved to the west wing tomorrow, and we'll move back in. So now, what about you? Will you accept the offer to join the Board of my father's charity?"

He rubbed his forehead, set his dark head against her fair one. "You know how it is with me and worldly rewards. God never seems interested in furthering my earthly career. I was sounded out for a second time the morning that you had your accident ..."

She stiffened. Then made herself relax.

"... so maybe they'll ask me again, and maybe they won't. Maybe God will open that door for me to go through, and maybe He's got something else in mind."

She mourned for him. "You'd be so good at it, too. Elizabeth's furious with me for getting ill just as the offer came through. I don't think she likes me."

"She has a low view of human nature. Her husband ran off with her best friend, and she lost her little boy in a boating accident."

She guessed he'd referred to the child's death deliberately. For once she'd managed not to react by withdrawing into herself. She supposed she'd always feel a twinge of sorrow when babies were mentioned. Perhaps that was part of growing up, that you could accept that life wasn't always a bed of roses.

She said, "I'm all right. Really. Do you need to spend half an hour on your papers before bed?"

He yawned. "Nasty rape case. Contradictory evidence. Jim's mind doesn't appear to have been as clear as usual when briefing counsel. If you want to go on up to bed, I'll follow in half an hour." Yet his arm didn't slacken around her.

She thought of the careful love-making he'd allowed himself these last few months. She'd tried to disguise the fact that she wasn't interested in it, but of course he'd known. Perhaps she could do something about that now. Why not? She felt a stir of anticipation at the thought of it.

"Patrick, I know you used to daydream about the time when we would be married. Tell me about it."

Patrick looked sheepish. "All men have fantasies. I suppose I might have wondered what it would be like to have you soothe my fevered brow."

"You're feeling feverish at the moment?"

"Incredibly."

She thought this might be interesting. She held out her arms, but as Patrick bent closer, he caught his foot on the coffee table and sent it flying.

Serafina appeared in the doorway. "What happened? Are you hurt?"

Patrick nursed his ankle. "Only in my dignity."

Serafina was not amused. "Minty should be in bed and asleep by now."

"Yes, nanny," said Patrick, but he said it under his breath.

Minty meanwhile was almost crying with frustration. It was true that she was tired, but each time she'd met with a rebuff that day, tension had been piling up inside her. If only Serafina hadn't seen fit to check up on them!

"Come on," said Patrick, helping her to her feet. "Serafina's right, you know. You should have been in bed hours ago."

She wished he was not so careful of her. Patrick had himself well under control, of course. He always did. He would no doubt immerse himself in his work and forget all about her in five minutes, whereas she was going to be put to bed like a naughty small girl, instead of a grown woman with needs.

She scowled at herself in the bathroom mirror and scowled at Patrick when he kissed her good night. She couldn't sleep. She tried his side of the bed, and then hers. She heard Serafina come upstairs and use the bathroom. There was no traffic on the road outside. The stream nearby was running quietly in its banks. She told herself that if she didn't sleep soon she'd be unable to deal with Mr. Hatton in the morning ...

... and woke to find Patrick asleep beside her. A blackbird was heralding the dawn even though it was still dark outside ... well, gun-metal grey, not black night.

Patrick was sleeping "spoons" behind her, his left arm thrown over her protectively. His breathing was even. No dreams or fantasies were disturbing his sleep tonight, but they were still disturbing her. She wriggled around till she was still within his arm, but facing him. He half woke and whispered her name. She laughed, holding him closer till they were once again, joyfully, made one.

Afterwards she lay back, watching the morning light tinge the room with colour. With hope. She smiled and stretched and nestled closer to him. He threw his arm over her, as he had before. They slept.

She woke when he did. Patrick always started the day slowly, stretching, yawning, gradually bringing the morning into focus. But this time he sat upright, eyes wide. "Did I imagine it? I can't believe ... did we?"

She smiled up at him.

"You seduced me!"

"Do you mind?"

"Baggage!" Yes, it seemed he did mind. "You know the doctors said ..."

"To take it easy. But I'm better now."

"You always were the rash one, wanting everything to happen yesterday."

"And you were the one who had to pick up the pieces for me. I know. But I feel marvellous, really I do."

He couldn't so quickly give up the habit of worrying about her. "It's my job to look after you."

"And mine to see that your every need is catered for. Like another go?" She chased him, laughing, into the bathroom.

Chapter Five

Serafina dished up a full English breakfast for Patrick and Minty, although they protested that they weren't used to it after so many months abroad. Patrick ate with one hand while flicking through some papers with the other. Minty ate about half as much as Patrick, pleased to see him demolish everything in sight. Serafina scolded Patrick, saying he was far too thin. Minty agreed and was then scolded for the same reason.

Finally Patrick shoved everything into his briefcase. "I have to go and slay some dragons. How about you?"

"Same here," she said, thinking of what the day might hold for her.

He tapped his briefcase, the line deepening between his eyebrows. "I'm worried about this case. Our client doesn't seem to have much faith in herself. If she goes into the witness box thinking herself even partly to blame, a particularly nasty crime will go unpunished."

Minty said, "You must put on the full armour of God so that you can stand your ground ..."

Patrick joined in, "Wearing the belt of truth and the breastplate of righteousness ..."

"Carrying the shield of faith ..."

"... and praying in the Spirit on all occasions."

Serafina came with Minty to the window to watch Patrick drive off in his much-loved but ancient Rover. Serafina disapproved. "Why doesn't he get a new car?"

Minty shook her head. "He loves it, and he's never seen the point of throwing money around."

Serafina said, "Shall we be here again tonight, or back at the Hall?"

"I don't know." Minty put her arm round the older woman, enjoying her well-remembered lily-of-the-valley scent. "Are you sure you want to throw in your lot with us? Wouldn't life be easier for you back with Annie? My father left you some money. Don't you want to buy a house for yourself and settle down?"

Serafina snorted. "What would I do in a house all by myself? Sit and think of the family I lost and the mistakes I've made in life? No. I like a bit of excitement, and there's always something happening around you and Patrick. Also, you need me, and I like to be needed. I'll nurse your little ones on my knee yet. I'll start supper here and you can ring me when you know where we'll eat it."

Minty had a horrid feeling that getting back into the Hall was going to be difficult. With a sigh she fished out a telephone directory, pulled the phone towards her and started making calls. First she rang her solicitor, but alas, he was away on holiday and wouldn't be back for another week. However, the manager of the bank could see her in half an hour. Patrick always said that the person who held the purse strings was the one who dictated policy, so now she must take the purse strings back in her own hands.

Later that morning she squeezed her rented car into the parking space behind Patrick's house. Two cars were already there. One was Elizabeth's Mini, and the other would belong to Neville, the accountant who dealt with the books for Eden Hall. Minty was fond of roly-poly Neville and looked forward to seeing him again.

She let herself into the hallway and heard Elizabeth talking on the phone in reception. The door to Neville's room was open and he was inside, putting files into a cardboard box.

She tapped on the door and went in, expecting a warm welcome ... but got a frown instead. He'd put on weight since she'd last seen him, but his eyes were as honest and direct as ever.

He said, "Well, this is a surprise. Nice to see you again, Minty. I'm only sorry it's under such tiresome circumstances. I promise I'll be out of here on Friday."

Minty got that creepy feeling again. "You're leaving? Why?"

He turned his shoulder on her. "You got my letter of resignation, didn't you?"

His intercom clicked on and Elizabeth's voice came through. "Coffee, Mr Neville?"

Neville started to say "No," but Minty overrode him. "Good morning, Elizabeth. Yes, please do bring us both some coffee. And perhaps you'll show me how to turn the intercom off."

A pause. The intercom went silent. Minty took the client's chair at Neville's desk. "Now, Neville. What's going on? You haven't really resigned, have you?"

He seemed angry. With her? He continued to take files from a cabinet and stack them in a box. "You know I have."

"I know nothing. Tell me."

He suspended his packing to stare at her. He passed his hand over his forehead, smoothing back fair hair that she noticed with gentle regret was beginning to thin. He seated himself in his big chair behind the desk and pulled on his lower lip, appraising her. Rethinking the situation. Neville was nobody's fool.

He repeated her words. "You know nothing?" His colour was fresh and his face unlined, but if he wasn't careful, he would soon be too plump for good health. "Where do I start?"

"Start with Barr."

"Barr." He laid his hands on his desk, palms down. "Barr was shattered when you lost the baby. He blamed himself for not having gone to look for you earlier. We all felt guilty about that. If the Hall had been open to visitors that day, if Serafina hadn't been tied up with the plumber, if Iris hadn't gone to fetch the new brochures from town ... if any one of us had gone looking for you, as we usually did ten times a day, then you'd have been found earlier. But none of us did. The doctors didn't think you'd pull through at first, and when you did leave hospital, you looked like a ghost."

Minty held back a wince. She knew she'd been found at the bottom of the stairs in the Great Hall, and she thought she remembered falling down them ... but nothing else. The black door opened in front of her. She sent up an arrow prayer.

Lord, be with me! The black door closed again. Relief! She wasn't going down into the pit this time.

Neville continued, "Patrick hardly spoke for days. And you know what the doctors said …"

Actually, she didn't. Couldn't remember that bit at all.

"… so when he said he was going to take you away to recover, we could see it was the right thing to do. But we all felt lost. I'd started an audit because of the mess the accounts had been in when I took over. Barr helped me as best he could, but he was out of his depth. He took it to heart, felt he ought to have served you better.

"I don't know when he started to drink again, but the next thing we knew, he nearly ran over Alice Mount's little girl in the High Street. She'd wriggled out of her pushchair and darted into the road while her mother was opening their front door. Not really anyone's fault, but Barr was breathalysed and … well, that was that. Alice was prepared to forgive and forget. She was angrier with her daughter than with Barr. The police saw it differently.

"So did Barr. He couldn't get over it. I suppose resigning was the right thing to do under the circumstances. I spoke to Ms Phillips and to Patrick, and we agreed to accept Barr's resignation. Patrick arranged for generous severance pay."

Elizabeth brought in some coffee and Minty's re-charged phone. She seemed inclined to linger. Minty thanked her and Elizabeth left, closing the door rather too firmly behind her.

Minty poured coffee for them both. "How often did you contact Patrick?"

"Weekly at first. Come the middle of March, Patrick said you were getting a tan and beginning to relax. Then there was that break when you went off to Greece. After that, things changed. Hatton took charge—as he had every right to do. So if I wanted anything, I bothered him about it, and not Patrick."

She nodded. "Tell me about Mr Hatton."

He ran his hands back over his hair again. "He has all the right qualifications."

A poor answer. "Iris says he gets on well with you."

Neville reddened, said, "Iris …" and looked out of the window.

Minty was intrigued. "You like Iris?"

"The more I see of her, the more I ... but she won't even come out for a meal with me. Tell you the truth, Minty, I thought I had it bad for you at one time, and I'm still very fond of you, don't get me wrong. But Iris does something to me." He tried for a smile. "I'm wasting away for love. Or rather, I'm adding to my waistline, because every time I think of her I get miserable, and then I eat for comfort."

Minty rubbed her forehead. Possibly Iris hadn't told this great baby—for he was a baby in spite of having an acute financial brain—about the time she'd been raped. Perhaps that was still a barrier for her when dealing with men?

Neville was looking at her rather like a puppy hopeful of a treat. "You wouldn't put in a good word for me, would you? I'm honest, well-meaning, comfortably off and anxious to make a life-long commitment, wedding ring and all."

Minty nodded. "I'll sound her out. But I'm meeting Mr Hatton here in half an hour, and I really need to know what you think of him before then."

He threw out one hand in a gesture at once frustrated and despairing. "He looks like a Hooray Henry, more breeding than brains, you know? But he's got brains, all right. He seems to be the genuine article, good family, no hint of anything shady in the background. He's single, runs an expensive car, is always immaculately turned out, has had a number of jobs climbing the career ladder in the heritage business. He has big ideas, but there's nothing wrong with that. The idea of a classical concert in the park had been in place before he came—in fact I think it was my aunt who suggested it first."

Neville's aunt, Mrs Chickward, was a force to be reckoned with in local society. She was always thinking up schemes to benefit charity, and a classical concert would have been exactly her style.

Neville continued, "Then Hatton—or perhaps it was your half-sister Gemma? I don't know; they're very close nowadays—he or they transformed it into a two-day event for popular music. You can put me down as old-fashioned, but I was uneasy about it. Perhaps because I don't like heavy metal music."

"Neville, come off it! Your liking or not liking a particular kind of music wouldn't affect your judgement about it being a good or bad thing for the Hall."

"Why did you let them do it, Minty? How did it get past Patrick? A hundred times I've told myself you've got such a flair for events that it must be all right. The way you've turned the fortunes of Eden Hall around is admirable. The new brochures, new advertising campaign, new chef at the restaurant ... brilliant!

"I can see why you let Gemma continue to run events in your absence. When her head's not turned by this pop star lark, she does the job well enough. Of course the festival could make you a lot of money, but I do think you were ill advised to refuse the police offer to oversee security."

She blinked. "What was that? The police wanted ...?"

"You don't know anything about that, either? You'd better talk to Hatton about it. He's brought in a smallish concern who rent out security guards, and to my mind they lack the experience and the manpower to deal with a big festival.

"That wasn't what drove me to resign, though. Hatton hasn't picked the right policy for Public Indemnity. If there's an accident of any kind — if someone was disabled or killed, for instance — we'd be wiped out for lack of proper insurance.

"I couldn't get Hatton to take me seriously about it. In the end I threatened to go over his head and appeal to Patrick. And I would have done, if Patrick hadn't been so keen to keep his new telephone number and e-mail address to himself. I can understand that he didn't want to be bothered with ..."

"What was that? He hasn't changed them. Why should he?"

"Because he had his mobile and laptop stolen in Greece and Gemma said ..." Neville's voice tailed away. In a flat tone he said, "They weren't stolen?"

Minty shook her head.

Neville assimilated the news, blinking. "What a fool I am! I believed her. So I didn't even try to contact him. I did try to get hold of Ms Phillips. Several times. But she's also been away a lot. When I finally spoke to her, she tore me off a strip. She said she trusted Hatton completely and that I wasn't to bother her unnecessarily. So naturally I resigned."

Minty began to pace the floor. What was wrong with Annie? How could she let things get into this state? Given that Gemma's latest ambition was to be a pop star, it looked as if she'd bent the truth more than a little in order to further her ambition. Gemma could be charming and helpful when it suited her, but she could also be vicious.

She said, "When did you resign?"

"On Monday. I gave the letter to Gemma, who said she was sorry to see me go and asked me to vacate these premises as soon as possible."

Minty glanced at her watch. "Hatton's due any minute now. Look, Neville, I don't know where that resignation letter is, but I'm asking you to forget it. Just to cover ourselves, will you get Elizabeth to rough out another letter confirming your reinstatement? There's a couple of other things. While I was at the bank, I ..."

She outlined what she wanted done, and Neville nodded and said he'd get on to it straight away.

Elizabeth came in to remove the coffee things and announce that Mr Hatton was here with a friend of his, and she didn't understand why they were coming here, rather than meeting up at the Hall. Minty guessed Elizabeth knew exactly what was going on and was enjoying the situation.

"Thanks, Elizabeth. Perhaps you'd show them into Patrick's office and bring us some more coffee?"

Minty pocketed her mobile phone and moved across the hallway to Patrick's office as her visitors appeared.

Clive Hatton was a tall, bony, fawn-coloured man. His smooth, plentiful hair was a light brown, as were his eyes and his skin. He gave the impression of wearing jodhpurs and being about to play polo, but in fact he was clad in expensive if casual clothing. A Hooray Henry with brains, Neville had said. Not to be under-estimated.

Minty disliked him on sight, though she couldn't have said why.

His companion was shortish, darkish and had spent a lot of money on his smile. Who was he and what was he doing here?

"Ah," said Clive Hatton, extending his hand to be shaken with the air of a conquering hero expecting applause. "The Lady of the Hall. At last." He treated her to a practised politician's smile. "We're all delighted to see you back. They tell me the Hall lacks a certain something in your absence. But forgive my manners. May I introduce

Lee Cannon-Jones, an old acquaintance of mine who's kindly agreed to help us out."

Minty held open the door to Patrick's office. "Mr Hatton, I'm delighted to meet you at last. And Mr Cannon-Jones is here as …?" Minty thought she knew, but wanted clarification. If she was right, then Mr Hatton had been more than quick off the mark in replacing Neville. He'd been consulting a crystal ball.

"The Hall's new accountant. You've heard, of course, that Neville has resigned."

"Did he go, or was he pushed?" asked Minty, although she thought she knew the answer to that one. "Never mind. I've asked Neville to stay on, and he's agreed to do so." She took Patrick's big chair behind the desk and waved Mr Hatton to the client's chair.

Mr Hatton's eyes sharpened, and Mr Cannon-Jones looked to his friend for a lead. *Mr Cannon-Jones, I observe you are a yes-man, and I don't want yes-men working for me.*

"Now that's a bit of a facer," said Mr Hatton, taking the chair she'd indicated and crossing long legs one over the other. He wasn't faking his relaxed attitude. He was relaxed, sure that he could get his way. "Why didn't you ask my advice first? You need time to get up to speed again. I understand you were forced to have a complete rest after your breakdown …"

Was it a breakdown? I suppose it was. Is Mr Hatton right? Am I completely off course?

"… and I do understand that Neville's an old friend of yours. But perhaps not quite the man for the job at the Hall nowadays?"

Minty leaned back in her chair as Elizabeth brought in more coffee for them all. "Coffee, Mr Hatton? Mr Cannon-Jones, you must feel you've been brought here under false pretences. I hope we will meet again soon, but for now …?"

Mr Cannon-Jones looked at his friend, who kept his eyes fixed on Minty. The poor man muttered something about a forgotten appointment and faded from the scene. Mr Hatton took his coffee black, with two sugars. Minty left hers to one side.

Let battle commence.

Mr Hatton treated Minty to a white-toothed smile. "May I say how glad I am to see you looking so well? We'd heard you wouldn't be back for some months, and that even then you'd have to be careful not to overdo things."

Minty wondered who'd said that. Gemma, perhaps? Patrick wouldn't have allowed her to go back to work if he'd thought she wasn't up to it.

Mr Hatton allowed his smile to become warmer. "May I also say how much I've admired what you've done at the Hall since you inherited. For an amateur without any background in the business, it was quite remarkable."

Minty leant her elbows on Patrick's desk and rested her chin on her folded hands. So this was the line Mr Hatton was going to take? She had to admit, it was a good one.

"But perhaps," he said, making her a charming little bow, "your illness — though regrettable — has given the Hall a chance to grow. At the present time, with so many old houses failing to pay their way, you need the services of professional men and women. I think I came along at just the right time."

Yes, he had brains. Minty had to admit that. He was making the case that she was not strong enough, or adequately trained to carry the Hall into the future. Perhaps he had a point?

He said, "The festival will create jobs in the neighbourhood. More. It will put the Hall firmly on the tourist map. Promote us into the First Division, as it were." He drank off his coffee and replaced the empty cup on the saucer.

"Of course there will be those frightened by the scale of the event. That's only natural. No one here has any experience of such matters — and of how much revenue they can bring in. Ms Phillips, for instance, was most unsure at first. Naturally. She is of the old school and perhaps not quite ready to move forward into the twenty-first century. She also, I understand, has some health problem?"

Minty felt a chill down her back. Was it possible that the ever reliable Annie was ill? Did that explain why she'd let the reins slip? Annie had been unable to meet her this morning because she had another appointment. Was that an appointment with a doctor? Was it serious? Minty shook the thought away to deal with later.

"Then — " Mr Hatton's tone was indulgent — "Neville couldn't quite get his head around our latest development. Influenced by his aunt, I fear, who'd envisaged a gentle canter through the classics for one of her charitable causes. I respect Neville ..."

You don't sound as if you do.

"... and for a small-town accountant, he's done well. But — forgive me for criticising one of your friends — he's not terribly quick to grasp the larger picture ..."

Still Minty kept silent. She wanted to hear everything. From both sides.

"... which is why I had to find another accountant in a hurry. Mr Cannon-Jones is ..."

Minty shook her head. "I don't like yes-men."

Mr Hatton leaned forward. "Now that's what I like to hear. A great lady who is big enough to admit when she's made a mistake, courageous enough to seize the moment and move into the future with confidence."

Flattery will get you a long way, but not far enough. No, Mr Hatton; I do not like you, though I see that I have to work with you.

Minty leaned back in her chair. "How is Gemma? I expected her to contact me last night, or this morning at the latest."

"Ah, dear Gemma. She sends her apologies. She's working. Filming in the dungeons this morning."

"There are no dungeons at the Hall."

He smiled indulgently. "There are now. In the basement, the old kitchens, you know? Some of the ancient spits do very well as instruments of torture."

Minty blinked. This was something else to look into. "Correct me if I'm wrong. You think this festival will bring long-term good to the Hall? Tell me about the downside."

He was amused. "Of course there are minor inconveniences. If we'd only known you were to return so early — if you'd given us warning — then you'd not have had to find alternative accommodation for the next few days. Undoubtedly some of the village people think themselves hard done by because of the increased traffic, though the shops are making more money than they could have dreamed of, and everyone who has a spare room is letting it out. Then there's the money it'll bring into the Hall. Think what you could do with the profits from this one venture. Your father dabbled in charitable giving, I'm told ..."

Minty blinked again. Was it possible the man didn't know of Sir Micah's nationally respected charity?

"... and I'm told that you personally are always thinking about what you can do for other people." He was very sure of himself. "With your courage and my expertise, we can transform the fortunes of Hall and village."

She stared at him and through him. Yes, she was swayed by the thought of the good she could do with more cash, as he had intended she should be. The village hall needed to be re-built, and the vicarage was in a poor state of repair. She could sponsor holidays for handicapped children, perhaps, and ... lots of things.

But. He was proposing that she be nothing more than a figure-head in future, while he held the real power. Was he right in thinking she was a child playing with grown-up toys and that it was time for her to hand over the responsibility for the Hall to professionals?

"I'll think about what you've said." She stood up. "I've been to the bank this morning. I understand that in my absence you, Ms Phillips and Neville were joint signatories, and that two signatures are needed on all cheques. I've reinstated my signature at the bank. In future two signatures will be needed on all cheques over fifty pounds, and one of those signatures will be mine.

"Two other points. At my request, Neville's looking into the question of Public Indemnity. Whatever happens, we must be properly insured for such a big event. He's also expressed a concern that the security firm you're using lacks enough manpower to control the crowds."

He beamed at her. "Poor Neville. If only he'd asked me I could have put his mind at rest. The security firm is expensive. In events such as these it is usual to ask for volunteers from the rugby clubs in the area, who will provide stewards for a fraction of the cost. Rest assured, that's all in hand."

He stood, smiling, sure of himself. Thinking that with a small concession here or there, he'd won her to his way of thinking. "I'm sure I can count on you being discreet over the next few days? You won't try battering down the gates again?" He was making a joke of it, but she didn't smile.

"I promise not to bring the police in to turn Maxine out, provided that ..."

For the first time he looked alarmed. "Why would you want to do that? We have a contract with these people, giving them free accommodation at the Hall until after their appearance on Sunday night. Legally they've every right to be there."

"I'd like to see a copy of that contract, and I need a word with Gemma. Another thing, would you please make sure that I, my husband and my housekeeper may come and go to the Hall as we please. I'll also need my own car. It may be that I can move into the west wing until such time as ..."

He shrugged. "That's fully occupied by Maxine's people, makeup, hair, wardrobe, personal trainer. Her PA and the dancers are in the flat once occupied by Ms Phillips, while the north wing has been taken over by the backing singers, musicians and technical crew. I was amazed to find how many people we had to accommodate. It's been a headache. Your little Iris has been most helpful, settling them in and dealing with their complaints ..."

Minty set her teeth at the condescending way he spoke of Iris.

"Some of the technical staff are in the holiday cottages, and of course there's people ringing up and wanting accommodation all the time, though most will bring their own tents or caravans. At the moment there isn't a spare bedroom to be had at the Hall." He laughed gently. "I had the odd fancy that the old place likes the buzz of being fully occupied. It brings it to life."

"Most unsatisfactory, Mr Hatton."

"From your point of view. But ..." He spread his hands in despair. "What can we do? We can't turn them out. Perhaps you could go back to London for a while, or to a hotel? Yes, why don't you do that? It would be best if no one in the village learned you were here, even. It might unsettle them."

Minty was grimly amused. "It's clear you've never lived in a village. The moment I returned, everyone knew."

He nodded and made as if to go. Hesitated, turned back to face her, looking serious. "You know, I think I handled this all wrong. I was expecting someone like your sister Gemma ..."

"Half-sister. My father married twice."

"I wish we'd met earlier. You are the kind of woman I've always dreamed of. Is it too late? They say you've thrown yourself away on a small-town solicitor."

Minty's eyes widened with shock. How dare he?

"I only wish ..." He projected a strong physical desire for her, which made her eyes open even wider. "You really have no idea how attractive you are, have you?"

Upon which he left the room, leaving Minty feeling confused, embarrassed, angry and amused in turns.

Chapter Six

The phone rang on Patrick's desk and Minty moved to pick it up, still thinking about Mr Hatton's nerve! Patrick was more inclined nowadays to ask if she was warm enough or fancied something to eat than to pay her a compliment.

Perhaps he ought to do so? He'd other ways of showing his love, even if physical passion wasn't one of them at the moment except—she remembered with a smile—last night. She knew she could rely on him for truthful, if sometimes painfully honest answers.

It was Patrick on the phone. "Are you all right, Minty? The judge has just told the jury to take a rest and has sent us all out. Which probably means he wants to consult the Clerk of the Court on a point of law. So I've got a few minutes."

She twined her fingers round the cable of the telephone. "Mr Hatton was here. He says there's no room for us at the Hall, and I think I believe him. I don't like him, though I can't tell you why."

A thinking pause. "I'd back your instinct, Minty."

She tried to sound amused, though in reality she'd been rather shaken by Mr Hatton. "He made a pass at me."

Would Patrick be angry or jealous? He sounded amused. "So he should. You're a toothsome morsel."

She almost smiled at that and then was indignant. *A toothsome morsel, indeed!* "Patrick, tell me honestly. Am I well enough to cope?"

"A couple of days ago I'd have said you needed more time, but the way you've managed since we've returned—I'd say it's done you good. We're survivors, you and I. Uh oh. The judge wants to resume. Ring you later."

She put the phone down and got out the mirror from her handbag. A toothsome morsel, her? She giggled. She went to the window to see herself better. Yes, there was still a shadow under her eyes, but something—perhaps it was just the stimulation of being back in England?

Perhaps it had been the release the previous night had given them?—had brought a trace of colour in her cheeks. She did indeed look more like her old self.

She was a true blonde, and her eyebrows and eyelashes were too pale for the current fashion, but Patrick said she sometimes "blazed into beauty." That was good enough for her.

She shut the mirror up, staring back down the days to the moment when she herself had realised that she was going to survive. It had been their second day in Greece and Patrick had encouraged her to climb a rocky hill. They'd picnicked under an olive tree so huge and old that she couldn't get her arms round its trunk. A branch had split off from the main trunk, but still attached by a slender link, had continued to bear silvery leaves.

The sky had been clear for once. March in Greece could be treacherous. She'd leaned back against the tree trunk and looked up through the leaves, wondering how old the tree was and what great events had taken place during its lifetime. She'd been clinging to her faith in God by her finger-nails. It was the rock on which she'd built her life and it had not failed her, though she'd been through the dark night of the soul. For the first time since the accident she allowed herself to look forward.

She'd said, "This tree's a survivor. So are you, Patrick. I've just realised that maybe I can survive, too. Do you think we could stay on here a while?"

The original plan had been that they should stay on that island for two or three days and then move on. Patrick had left his mobile phone and laptop in the hotel in Athens.

"Why not?" Patrick had said.

Perhaps that moment on a hill-top in a Greek island had been the point at which everything had gone wrong back here in England. Those few extra days in which they'd been out of contact might have made all the difference to Minty's slow recovery, but it might also have handed the power at Eden Hall to Clive Hatton.

So now it was up to her to minimise the problems which the festival might cause.

She went slowly upstairs to the flat above. Dark marks on the panelled walls showed where furniture had once stood.

There'd been talk of bringing in some second-hand furniture and letting the place to Neville, but he'd moved in with his aunt on the Green instead.

Minty wished there'd still been some furniture there, because then she and Patrick would have had somewhere to stay locally.

The place wasn't really so very dusty. With a good clean ...?

But here came Elizabeth, panting up the stairs after her.

"Mrs Sands, I've Mrs Wootton from the Manor on the phone, and while you were with Mr Hatton some other people rang as well. If you'd only said you wanted to look round here, I'd have told you there's no furniture."

Elizabeth was making it clear that Minty had no right to poke around without her permission.

Minty said, "Thank you, Elizabeth. I'm sorry you had to toil up here. I'll take the call in my husband's study."

Elizabeth didn't like that. Presumably because she couldn't listen in? Minty went into Patrick's study and shut the door after her before picking up the phone to speak to her friend Mrs Wootton.

"Venetia! Lovely to hear from you. Yes, we just got back yesterday, and everything's topsy turvy ..." Venetia and Hugh Wootton were two of her best friends in the village. Venetia was in charge of the stewards who manned the rooms when the Hall was open to the public, and Hugh—lately retired from the army—had gravitated naturally to being on all the local committees. Their son Toby was in charge of publicity for the Hall—and for the festival, too.

Venetia was elegant, intelligent and did most things at the double. "Minty dear, how are you? Someone said they'd seen you in a strange car yesterday, but Toby said you hadn't turned up at the Hall and that even if you had ... well, that's something you'll soon put right, I'm sure. We've all been so worried about you and—no, I mustn't run on like this. Why don't you come straight up to the Manor and have a spot of lunch with us? In an hour, say?"

"I'd love to," said Minty truthfully. Venetia always had her finger on the pulse of village gossip and could be relied on to tell Minty what she needed to know.

"Oh yes, and Hugh says he wants your opinion of something in his garden. As if that was really important at the moment."

Hugh's message was coded. Whereas Venetia tended to flap and fuss, Hugh was a man of few words who made every word count. If he'd issued an invitation to Minty to talk to him in his beloved garden, that meant he had something important to say, preferably without his wife knowing about it.

As Minty put the phone down, Elizabeth charged into the room to hand Minty a number of telephone message notes. "These stairs ...!" Elizabeth retreated before Minty could ask her to do anything more. Her attitude to Minty was hardening. Elizabeth did not approve of Minty moving into her domain.

Who had rung? Gemma, but only to say she was terribly busy filming but hoped to catch up with Minty later. Mrs Chickward, Neville's formidable aunt, who wanted to welcome Minty home but also to discuss what was happening at the Hall.

The Reverend Cecil, from the vicarage: a nice man, possibly a trifle naïve, but a man of God, all the same.

A red-headed whirlwind spun into the room. "Minty, my love!"

Carol was Minty's oldest friend, from way back when they'd been at college together. Her hair was still a flaming aureole of light auburn — never call it ginger! — and her smile as warm as an open fire on a winter's day.

Carol's father was an antiques and jewellery dealer in the City. When Minty inherited the Hall and half the village, he'd opened a second shop there, partly because he thought it would be a good place for trade and partly to have the use of the workshops behind for restoration and repair work. Carol had moved into the flat above the shop and proved herself an excellent businesswoman.

"Why didn't you tell us you were coming back so soon? Are you okay now? Let me look at you!" Carol turned Minty round to face the window. What she saw seemed to worry her.

"I'm much better," said Minty, stifling an urge to throw herself onto Carol's shoulder and weep. "Really."

"Humph! You might be able to pull the wool over some people's eyes, but not mine. What is Patrick doing, letting you come back too soon?"

"He's got problems of his own and really I'm coping very well ..."

"Humph. Well, what can I do to help?"

Minty hesitated. "Do you have the time?"

"My darling, business is booming, but I have an excellent staff. Would you believe ditzy Carol employing staff? I've someone to spell me in the shop when I go out on a buying spree, two fabulous craftsmen in the workshops who are kept busy night and day doing repairs and restoration work, plus a couple of giants with muscles out to here, to heave things around. I'm in clover and totally at your disposal."

Carol seated herself on an upright chair and produced a notepad and pen. "Your orders, madam?"

Minty's mood lifted. "Oh, Carol. I know I should have come to you first off, but I couldn't make out what was happening, and I began to doubt my own sanity. I knew nothing about the festival till I got back and was refused entry to the Hall. Mr Hatton thinks I can help best by keeping out of the way, but ..."

"That creep!"

"Is he a creep?" Minty genuinely wanted to know.

"To be fair, some think he's an archangel sent down from heaven to shower goodies upon them. That's a bit of a mixed metaphor thingy, but you know what I mean."

"You don't agree with them?"

"I'm prejudiced because he tried to slide his hand up my skirt when we first met. But lots of men do that," said Carol, who'd long ago learned how to deal with men's roving hands. "I don't like what he's doing to the village, I suppose. He's giving short-term leases to people selling trashy pop star mementoes and New Age stuff, pendulums and the like. I suppose it's good commercial practice and brings in the money, but I think it devalues the place. He says I don't like it because they're taking trade away from me, but the people who buy that trash would never dream of entering my shop."

Minty digested that in silence. No, she wouldn't have given leases to that sort of trader, if she'd been here.

Carol looked around with an assessing eye. "Lovely rooms. This is Patrick's old study, isn't it? Are you staying here for the time being?"

"I would, if I could find some furniture."

Carol grinned. "I've dropped in at the right moment, haven't I? What period?" She swung through into the big bare living room. "Hm. Well, I've got a late Edwardian bergere three-piece suite in the workshop which needs recovering but is perfectly all right for everyday use. That could go round the fireplace."

She scribbled notes to herself. "There's a gate-leg oak dining table in the store-room. Chairs: I can do a dark oak carver, not bad-looking. Plus three dining chairs which are pretending to be Hepplewhite, but you don't have to believe everything the seller tells you. Rugs? Hmm. A couple of large modern ones in pastel colours, not unpleasing. Pictures? A couple of reasonable quality Dutch flower paintings, oil. A mirror for over the fireplace, a couple of occasional tables, two table lamps and a bookcase. Knowing Patrick, he'll have books everywhere within minutes. I haven't any curtains big enough for these windows, I'm afraid. Anything else?"

"But Carol …! I mean …! I'll pay a hire charge, of course, but … can you really do all that?"

"You ought to have said you'd pay any *reasonable* hire charge, or I might take you to the cleaners. Haven't I taught you anything about business over the years?"

"You taught me everything about friendship."

"That cuts two ways, Minty. Tell Elizabeth to let me in this afternoon, and by tea-time you'll be up and running."

"Carol, you are …" Minty felt for her handkerchief. "Thank you. And I never even asked how you are, yourself."

Carol grinned. "I'm fine. Dad thinks he might take me into formal partnership some day. Mum's had trouble with her knee and the kids are just, well, teenage kids, you know? They all want to come to the festival, needless to say. My flat above the shop is lovely, though a bit small now I've got Iris staying with me …"

Minty stiffened. "Iris has her own cottage at the Hall."

"It wasn't very nice for Iris up at the Hall with all those roadies. One of the dancers is a right pain. Iris actually had to mace one of the cameramen, and dear Reggie — your Houseman — knocked another out because he kept pestering her, and you know what she's like about men getting too close."

"That's awful!"

"You ain't heard nothing yet. When Mr Hatton heard about it, he said Iris must learn to be more of a team player, *and Iris apologised*! Mr Hatton didn't say much to Reggie because he needs Reggie to see to everything practical for him. Mr Hatton's a bully, if you want my humble opinion.

"Anyway, Iris said she'd move back in with her parents at the Chinese restaurant for the time being, but they're up to their eyes in work, open every evening till late, have taken on extra staff to try to cope. I said she could move in with me, and we get on just fine."

Minty tried to sort out her thoughts. "Iris came to see me yesterday. I got the impression she's divided in her loyalties."

"I can't make her out. One moment she says Hatton is the best thing to hit us since sliced bread, and then she reminds me that her parents' lease is due for renewal soon, so she's got to be careful. She says she's thriving on the extra responsibility, works long hours, keeps telling me how much good this festival is going to do to the community. She protests too much, if you ask me. And, if anyone argues, she says it must be all right because you authorised it."

Minty ticked off on her fingers. "I didn't. Patrick didn't. I'm amazed that Annie did. Tell me, is there anything wrong with Annie?"

Carol looked undecided but finally said, "I took your uncle to hospital in town, and we saw her coming out of the oncology department."

Minty blinked. Her Uncle Reuben was here? But ... wait a minute; oncology equalled cancer. "Annie's being treated for cancer?"

"She won't talk about it. But Florence Thornby — Chef — she knows someone who her daughter was at school with, who's a radiotherapist, and it seems that yes, Annie is having radiotherapy."

Minty felt as if she'd been kicked in the stomach. In many ways Annie had taken the place of her long-dead mother. If Annie was to die ... no, it didn't bear thinking about.

Carol read Minty's thoughts. "Cheer up. The word on the street is that it's not particularly serious and she'll probably die of hypothermia before the cancer gets her. They say she keeps the central heating on low to save the pennies, even though she's got pots of money."

Minty nodded. There was a bright side to all this. If Carol had got herself into the village grapevine, it proved she was not only making her business succeed but had been accepted by those who counted hereabouts.

So what about her Uncle Reuben? After her mother's death, Minty had been sent to live with her father's brother, the Reverend Reuben Cardale and his wife. Her uncle's loud voice and Old Testament beliefs had frightened the child almost as much as her aunt's beatings.

Minty had found it hard to forgive their treatment, but after her aunt died she had come to understand that they had just been passing on the way they themselves had been treated as children. She'd also come to realise that her uncle was not a vicious man but had been weak where his wife was concerned. After her death, he'd become curiously shrunken and dependent upon Minty, even going so far as to say she was all he had left in the world.

"What was that about Uncle Reuben? He was going to retire from his parish earlier this year and go into sheltered accommodation."

"He did retire and not before time, if I may say so. Still thinks his dear little wifey will start up from the grave to minister to him. No, forget I said that. She was a beast to you, but he did love her and still misses her. He's become forgetful. He arrived at the Hall one day in March with a vanload of bits and bobs, expecting you to be there to welcome him. If he'd ever been told you were away, it had slipped his memory. Gemma made him welcome, sort of. As much as she is able, I suppose. She is his niece, too, isn't she?

"He was lonely up at the Hall, poor chap, and spent most of his time either in the bookshop or with the Reverend Cecil—who's been really good to him, by the way. I don't quite know how it happened, but your uncle moved into the vicarage with Cecil. We find him in the street sometimes, looking lost. Anyone who knows him shunts him back to the vicarage. He's gone a bit odd, I must admit, but I rather like the old so-and-so."

Minty felt another burden settle on her shoulders. "You took him to hospital?"

Carol pulled a face. "You could smell his feet a mile off. He reminded me of my grandfather, as obstinate as an old mule he was, and his feet stank because he wouldn't let anyone near them. I told your uncle I'd have him put in a home if he didn't let me take him to hospital to have them looked at because he hates the doctor here. Says he's an old fool. It takes one to know one, they say. Of course I wouldn't have tried to have him put away and he knew that, but it made him laugh, and he agreed. So now he's got regular appointments with the chiropodist in town, and I don't mind giving him a lift there and back. I get my hair done while he's at the hospital. It suits us both, so you needn't look so stricken."

There was a disturbance down below. Someone was calling Minty's name, and Elizabeth was trying to hush them. Minty rushed down the stairs with Carol at her heels. Roly-poly Neville shot out of his office with a client at his shoulder, both looking alarmed.

Elizabeth was saying, "Now, Alice, you don't want to make a fuss!"

"Yes, I do!" Alice was holding a hand to her face, which was bleeding. Her T-shirt had been ripped at the neckline and she'd lost a shoe.

Elizabeth was trying to push Alice out of the door. "I repeat, Alice, this is not a hospital and if you want the doctor ..."

"No doctor," said Alice, eyes wild. "Sorry, Minty! I wasn't thinking straight. I thought Patrick might be here and could help. Sorry, Carol. I didn't mean to disturb anyone. If you'll just let me sit here quietly for a moment, I'll think what's best to do."

Alice Mount was a buxom blonde from the council estate with a business degree and a weakness for black men, one of whom had deserted her when she became pregnant. Minty and Alice had become good friends when they'd been cleaning the holiday cottages together. Alice now managed the cottages, living in one with little Marie and her new boy-friend. Dwayne was an electrician whose parents had come over from the Caribbean thirty years ago, but unlike Alice's first love, he was hard-working and planned to marry her in due course.

Neville looked worried. "She's been assaulted. Shall I call the police?"

Minty prised Alice's hand away from her face. Blood was oozing from a cut on her cheek. "Ouch. You're going to have a black eye, Alice. Come into the cloakroom and we'll get you cleaned up. Yes, Neville. Please call them."

"No police," said Alice. Elizabeth folded her arms, indicating she wasn't calling the police either.

Neville's client pulled on his arm, and he looked at his watch and grimaced. "Minty, if you need me?" He retired to his office while Minty and Carol helped Alice into the cloakroom.

Minty said, "Who did this to you, Alice?"

Carol was grim. "I can guess. He thinks any woman under fifty's fair game. It's said he even tried to proposition Mrs Chickward!"

Minty was diverted at the idea of anyone propositioning the stately Mrs Chickward, who must be nearing seventy years of age.

Alice began to weep. "Dwayne mustn't find out. He'll go ballistic! What am I going to do? Oh, that hurts!"

Minty soaked her handkerchief in cold water and applied it to Alice's face again. "I need to know who it was, Alice."

Alice made a visible effort. "It's best you don't. You might think you ought to do something about it and you can't, not really."

"Alice!"

Carol said, "It wasn't a roadie, or she'd have told because they can be brought to heel. It must be Nero." In reply to Minty's questioning look: "The lead dancer in Maxine's group. Six foot two of smooth-muscled black nastiness. Thinks he's God's gift to women, and if a woman doesn't bow down and worship, there's something wrong with her."

Alice's tears welled over. "Iris rang to report a fault on the electrics at Riverside Cottage. There's a sound engineer living there with his partner, quiet enough. Marie's out with a friend today, and I knew the crew were up at the Hall making the video, so I thought it would be all right.

"Nero tried it on with me at the weekend and was furious when I said no. He said he knew I liked black men and was just playing hard to get. He must have been lying in wait somewhere because when I opened the door he barged in behind me. I screamed, but there was no one to hear because Dwayne's working up at the Hall, too.

"Nero said he was going to teach me not to disrespect him. He hit me, knocked me down. I reached out for something, anything ... I got hold of the copper warming pan that hangs on the wall and ... I'm so sorry, Minty, but I think I dented it. It stunned him just enough to make him stagger back and then I ran up here."

"We must ring the police," said Minty.

Carol and Alice gave her identical looks of pity. Alice said, "If he was angry with me before, he'll be livid now. I'll lose my job and so will Dwayne."

"Nonsense," said Minty.

Carol said, "Darling, let me put you in the picture. The man's a menace, but he's flavour of the month up at the Hall. No police, because until the festival's over, no one dares cross Nero for fear of upsetting the famous Maxine. She who must be obeyed. Alice, you'd better rest up, and we'll think where you can go for a bit. Has Dwayne got any relatives in the city that you can stay with until the festival's over?"

Alice shook her head.

Minty laid another cold hankie on Alice's face. "Of course you won't lose your jobs. I'll see to that."

Carol was ever practical. "Alice, I'll lend you another T-shirt and some flip-flops, and we'll wait till Dwayne gets back from work before you go home."

Alice sobbed. "I daren't go back. This house is empty, isn't it? Can't we move in here? He won't look for me here."

Minty was annoyed. "I really don't see why you should be chased out of your own home just because this man thinks he's king of the castle."

Carol patted Alice's hand. "I'll think of something."

Minty straightened up and reached for her mobile phone. "I'll get the number from Elizabeth and have a word with Mr Hatton now."

Elizabeth didn't seem to approve of Minty complaining to Mr Hatton but did provide the relevant phone numbers for his mobile phone and his office. There was no reply to the mobile number, and in the office a woman said Mr Hatton was in conference and could they take a message.

"Mrs Sands here. It's urgent. Tell him to ring me straight away on my mobile."

Alice curled up in a corner of Elizabeth's office. "I'll be all right in a bit. Honest."

Carol said, "I'd better get back to the shop, start getting that furniture over."

With some misgivings, Minty left Alice to make some phone calls in Patrick's office. First she rang the vicarage to ask the Reverend Cecil about her Uncle Reuben. Again, no reply. She left a message on the answerphone that she'd try to get round there later. Then a quick call to Serafina to tell her that Patrick's house would be ready to receive them that evening, and could Serafina organise a minicab to get herself and all their belongings over to the village? Then another call to leave a message on Patrick's mobile to say where they'd be that evening.

There was a host of other things which she felt she ought to be doing but, glancing at the clock, she remembered she was due up at the Manor.

First she must check on Alice. Suppose Alice suddenly took a turn for the worse? Would Elizabeth take responsibility for getting her to the doctor's?

Luckily, even after this short time, Alice was struggling back to normal. Alice was a big strong girl, another survivor. She said, "You've got furniture coming? This place is filthy. You leave it to me. It'll take my mind off things to get the hoover out."

"Promise me that you'll ring the doctor or the hospital if you feel worse?"

"Yes, yes. Don't fuss." Alice hadn't the slightest intention of doing either.

Minty gave up and went out to the car. She couldn't start it. Suddenly, for no particular reason, she fell forward into the black hole.

Depression. That was the name of it.

Deep and dark and cheerless. No hope could survive there. She fought it. She tried to dredge up memories of sun and light dancing on rippling seas. But that was in another world, far away. She would never feel the sun on her skin again. Never feel anything.

Still she fought back. She remembered the olive tree and its silver leaves lifting in the breeze. Patrick spreading his jacket for her to sit on under the tree.

The olive tree was a survivor. Patrick was a survivor.

"I will survive, too."

She remembered that there was a God out there somewhere. *Dear God, let me not be mad.*

As suddenly as it had taken hold of her she came out of the dark place, like a swimmer coming up from deep waters. Her head burst through into light and air and she breathed deeply. There was a bush of honeysuckle just bursting into flower nearby, and she took her fill of its scent.

Light. Sound. She could hear a fledgeling sparrow in the honeysuckle going "Cheek, cheek, cheek."

All glory, praise and honour to You, Hosanna, King.

She turned the key in the ignition, and this time the engine caught. She brushed the hair back from her temples and drove up to the Manor.

Chapter Seven

The Manor was a perfect example of Georgian architecture, situated on the hill above the village. Minty wasn't particularly surprised to see several visitors' cars parked in the drive as she drew up.

Venetia Wootton knew everyone. Not only was she in charge of the team of stewards who worked at the Hall, but she sat on almost as many local committees as her husband.

Dear Hugh—a solid man in every way—met Minty in the hallway, and though not a man normally given to physical demonstration, kissed her on both cheeks and gave her a hug that nearly broke her ribs.

A hubbub of voices was coming from the sitting room.

Venetia erupted into the hall, half pleased to see Minty and half annoyed with her. "So there you are at last! Lovely to see you back. It seems such a long time since ... but come along in. There's a few people dropped in to see you."

Hugh whispered, "Courage, Minty. I'll be in the walled garden when they've finished with you."

Minty watched him depart with a flicker of dismay. Hugh was a good man to have at your back in a fight. And if she wasn't mistaken, a fight there was going to be.

"Come along, come along!" Venetia was a well-preserved and elegant blonde with an impeccable background, but she did tend to chivvy and fuss people. Minty wondered how their son Toby was coping now he'd returned home to live.

A group of formidable women awaited Minty in Venetia's pleasant sitting room.

Mrs Chickward—she must be greeted first—did not rise from her seat to welcome Minty but inclined her head and bestowed a thin smile upon her. Mrs Chickward was Neville's aunt and might well be furious at the treatment he'd been receiving from the Hall lately. Tall, bony and restrained in dress and manner, she represented the best of country traditions, working tirelessly for voluntary organisations.

Opposite Mrs Chickward—they would never be found sitting on the same settee—was her rival in all village affairs. Mrs Collins had the physique and brains of a sergeant major, and though not blessed with a county background, her organising ability made her someone to be reckoned with. She was as garish in dress as Mrs Chickward was sober. Together they represented the Voice of the Village, which was reputed to be against the festival.

"Mrs Collins." Minty found herself tugged down so that the older lady could kiss her cheek. This surprised Minty, till she realised that as usual Mrs Collins was taking the opposite line to Mrs Chickward, whose greeting to Minty had been chilly.

"Lovely to see you, dear. You have lost weight, haven't you? Have one of these delicious sandwiches."

Minty took one and turned to greet the last two members of the group. First was Doris, a sweet but dithery widow whose life was devoted to running the gift shop at the Hall. She'd be against the festival, of course, because the shop must be closed for the duration.

And ... now, this was a surprise! Moira, the landlady of the Pheasant Inn, the biggest and best public house in the village, was seated beside Doris. Big and bulky, peroxided, with eyes as sharp as needles and a generous bosom which hid sound business sense. The pub must be coining money, so she'd presumably be for the festival? How did she come to get included in this meeting?

Moira responded to Minty's greeting with an explanation of sorts. "Mrs Wootton happened to mention she was hoping to see you today when we met in the post office. I'm afraid I invited myself to this meeting."

"Very welcome," murmured Venetia. Insincerely? The landlady hadn't previously been invited to the Manor. So maybe she was against the festival, too?

Minty sat where Venetia indicated.

Mrs Chickward was accustomed to taking the chair at meetings. "Now, my dear. We've all been sent invitations to this pop festival of yours, but ..."

Minty spread her arms wide and said, "Ladies, I didn't know anything at all about it till I got back ... and was refused entrance to my own home!"

"Yes, we heard about that," said Moira thoughtfully, turning the rings over on her fingers. "They thought you were a groupie or some such nonsense."

Five pairs of eyes considered Minty and decided that no sensible person would ever mistake her for a groupie.

Venetia said, "You mean that Patrick didn't tell you?"

"Patrick didn't know, either. I've been trying to find out how we came to be hosting a festival, and all I can say is that there was a failure of communication somewhere along the line. We were out of contact for a week, then Annie seems to be having some health problem ..."

Doris nodded. "Someone said they saw her at the hospital, but when I asked her about it, she bit my head off."

"... Gemma has been seduced by the idea of becoming a pop star, and Mr Hatton has large ideas ..."

Five nods. Mrs Collins threw a glance of triumph in Mrs Chickward's direction. "I never thought you knew the exact details!"

Mrs Chickward waved her hand. "Now, come; I've heard you say that—"

"Ladies," said Minty, round a mouthful of ham sandwich, "if I'd been asked, I don't think I'd have agreed. Somehow or other my consent seems to have been taken for granted."

"You were hijacked by Gemma, you mean," said Venetia. "Tea, coffee? Fruit juice?"

"Fruit juice, thank you," said Minty, taking another sandwich. "I haven't been able to catch up with Gemma yet. Mr Hatton tells me that this festival will put Eden Hall on the map as a tourist attraction and will make a lot of money which can be ploughed back into the community."

"I know the young people are all for it," said Mrs Chickward, looking worried. "Friends and relations I haven't heard from for years have been badgering me to put them up. But there'll be a cost. Mr Hatton's cancelled my May Ball in aid of Oxfam. It'll be the first time in fifteen years that we haven't raised money for them."

"We'll have to think of some way round that," said Minty, knowing how important these charity events were and how long it took to organise them. "Perhaps a Christmas event?"

Venetia placed some fruit juice on a table beside her. "The Hall's closed to visitors so my stewards are out of a job, and I've been informed they're not 'suitable' to help out at the festival. That's understandable since most of them are elderly and retired, but we're all worried about what's going on at the Hall behind our backs. Maxine and her lot don't care anything about antiques or the history of the place."

"To tell the truth," said Minty, "if things hadn't gone so far, I think I'd have tried to get the festival cancelled, but as it is ..."

"It's too late," said Mrs Collins, heavily. "I'm only wondering if the lawns at the Hall will recover in time for our annual garden fête in September."

The landlady was still twisting her rings. "To be fair, it will bring a lot of money into the community. The shops are selling souvenirs and junk food and drinks as if there were no tomorrow. Maxine and her crew have only been here a week, but they're spending freely in the village, and just by being here, they're attracting visitors to the neighbourhood. At the pub we've taken on extra bar staff and increased our takings.

"But there's a downside to this. The litter in the High Street is appalling, and getting everyone out at closing time is a real headache. What's more, our usual customers don't like being pushed into a corner of the snug. Of course the villagers are cashing in wherever they can. There's not a spare room to be let this week anywhere in the neighbourhood, but that's not all roses, either. We don't know where these people come from. I'm advising everyone to put away their ornaments and insure themselves for breakages."

Mrs Chickward was still unhappy. "Neville's worried and been threatening to resign ..."

So she didn't know he'd actually done it? Probably been too frightened of his aunt to tell her.

Minty said, "I spoke to him this morning. There'll be no more talk of resigning, and he'll work with me to minimise the problems." She reached for the last sandwich. "Well, ladies, we have to accept that the festival's going to happen whether we like it or not. I know it's a lot to ask, but will you work with me to limit the damage it can cause the community?"

Mrs Collins tossed her massive head. "What can you do, locked out of the Hall as you are? Which is a disgrace, if I may say so."

A murmur of assent.

"Leave that to me," said Minty, sounding braver than she felt, since she hadn't the faintest idea yet how to get back in. "If we can form a committee to identify problems and suggest how to deal with them. We could meet tomorrow afternoon at, say, five o'clock, at Patrick's office in the village."

"You can count on me, of course," said stately Mrs Chickward. "Especially if we can re-schedule to hold a Christmas ball for Oxfam." She produced an envelope from her handbag. "I'm so glad you and Patrick are back in time to come to my At Home on Saturday. A pity it coincides with the opening of the festival, but of course the date has been in my calendar for months, and the azaleas in my woodland garden will be at their best."

Mrs Chickward opened her house and garden for an early evening party twice a year, to see her azaleas in the spring and her maples in the autumn. Everyone who was anyone would be there.

"You've forgotten my invitation again, dear," said Mrs Collins, who'd only ever been invited once before.

Mrs Chickward smiled with her teeth. "How ever did I forget you, dear? I'll put it in the post tonight."

Doris fluttered, "Of course we're all with you, Minty." Doris would never get an invitation and knew it. Neither would Moira, who gave a grim nod before heaving herself out of her chair and saying she'd best get back.

Venetia said, "Oh, Minty. Don't forget Hugh wants a word before you go."

Minty nodded and hurried after the landlady for a quick word. "You know Alice Mount? She used to work for you in the evenings, didn't she? Well, it seems that ..."

Minty wandered into the walled garden, where Hugh was tying up a clematis which had come adrift from its trellis. "My dear." He dropped his roll of twine into a capacious pocket and drew her close to him. "How are you doing?"

She could always speak the truth to Hugh. "Better, though not quite myself yet. Well enough for Patrick to leave me for short periods of time."

He led the way to a rustic bench. His eyes were a faded grey, direct and honest. "Got something to tell you. Difficult. Don't believe in mumbo jumbo. No imagination, that's me. Probably wouldn't recognise it if it was put under my nose."

Minty was mystified.

Hugh cleared his throat. "Someone in the market heard about it. Told me. Said a man from the Hall was trying to buy a black cockerel. Not any kind of cockerel, mind. Had to be black."

A black cockerel? Mumbo jumbo? Minty tried to put two and two together. "You mean ...?"

"No idea. Could be. Thought you ought to know, put a stop to it, if it is."

Why would anyone want a black cockerel? Except ... a sharp intake of breath. No. Surely not! Not in this day and age. "Do you know who wanted the cockerel?"

Hugh looked unhappy. "I did ask. Chap said it was an off-comer, pale as a slug, expensive car. I don't like the sound of it, Minty. Get young Cecil on to it, if it's true."

Minty nodded. "I don't know anyone like that, but I'll see what I can find out. Now, Hugh, I want to ask you something. What do you think of Mr Hatton?" Did Hugh stiffen? "Come on, Hugh. You had to attend court martial proceedings when you were in the army, and now you're a magistrate. If Mr Hatton came up before you, what crime would he have committed?"

He thought about that, fingering his jaw. Shook his head. "Wrong question, my dear. He wouldn't be in the dock. He'd be on the bench." He tapped her hand. "He does remind me of someone, though. Ambitious. Clever. Got promoted fast. Killed in an accident on the firing range."

"Accident?" repeated Minty. "You mean ... killed by one of his own men? I asked the wrong question. I should have asked why he wasn't popular."

"Efficient soldiers are not always popular." He hesitated. "The man I'm thinking of had no loyalty to anyone except himself."

If there was one thing you could say about Hugh, it was that he was loyal. As was Patrick.

She said, "Right. I've been warned."

He started cutting tulips and late narcissi from the border. "Take these back with you. Might cheer the place up a bit. By the way, they're taking bets in the village on how long it will take you to get back into the Hall."

Minty smiled and said nothing. How on earth was she going to manage it?

As Minty drove back to the village, she tried to put her mind in order.

She couldn't possibly deal with all this by herself. Patrick must find time to help her. He'd know how best to deal with Mr Hatton and the festival and, well, everything. Especially if there was any truth in what Hugh suspected. A black cockerel? Mumbo jumbo? Ouch. Hugh wouldn't have told her about it if he hadn't been pretty sure it meant big trouble.

Then again, Patrick must go with her to see Annie. Was she really ill? Would Serafina have left Annie so quickly if she'd known that Annie was ill? Mm. Possibly. Serafina's loyalty had been first to Sir Micah and then to his daughter, Minty. And there was that word "loyalty" again.

If Mr Hatton was only loyal to himself, then ... what did that mean for the future of Eden Hall?

She parked at the back of Patrick's house, noting that Neville's car had now disappeared. Her mobile rang as she rescued her bouquet of flowers from the car, so she paused to take the call in the garden.

Patrick. "Minty, the judge has let us out to play early, but I've promised to go and sit with Jim in the hospital later on tonight. I'll come back home now so that we can have supper together, perhaps go out somewhere for it? Then I'll get back here afterwards."

He was checking up on her, of course. Making sure she was standing up to the strains of the day.

She said, "Did you get my message? We're in your old house in the village."

"Fine. I've got Mr Lightowler here, from the bookshop. He came over to pick up some stuff from the printers and his car's broken down. He says the five o'clock bus has been taken out of service and the next one isn't due for an hour and a half, so I'll give him a lift. See you soon."

Elizabeth met her in the hallway, looking anxious and flustered. "Mrs Sands, I don't know that Mr Patrick would like what your friend Carol's been doing here, and now Serafina's arrived, making herself quite at home, and I must say that I strongly object to ..."

Carol ran down the stairs, laughing. "Dear Elizabeth, you know you're delighted to have your lord and master back under your thumb."

"Miss Carol!"

Minty thought Carol had a knack of finding out what people were like very quickly. "Elizabeth, you've done wonders caring for this house in my husband's absence. He's looking forward to being back here again this evening. Now, have there been any messages for me? From Mr Hatton? Gemma? No? Then we'd better see what Carol's done, shall we?"

Elizabeth followed Minty and Carol upstairs. Alice was there, polishing an already shining Pembroke table. The place had been transformed.

Minty loved it. "Carol, Alice, you are miracle workers!"

Carol looked pleased. She'd arranged a comfortable-looking if slightly shabby three-piece suite around the fireplace, with two occasional tables between, supporting lamps. Annie's scarlet geranium was in the middle of the dining table, resting in a blue and white pot. A mahogany-framed mirror hung above the fireplace, and a couple of Dutch flower pictures enlivened the walls.

True, the place still looked bare, but that was because Patrick surrounded himself with a litter of books. Even when they'd been in Greece, travelling with one rucksack between them, he'd managed to pack in a new translation of the Bible and some Greek poetry.

Carol took the armful of flowers from Minty. "I know where I can lay my hands on a vase for these."

Serafina appeared from the kitchen, looking at her watch. "He's not going to be late for supper, is he? Lamb chops and new potatoes. I've put your cases upstairs and made my bed up in the spare room, if that's all right."

Elizabeth's mouth was turned down. "He'll hate all this second-hand furniture. He's used to his family antiques."

Carol lifted her eyebrows at Minty and shrugged.

Minty said, "Of course he is, Elizabeth. But what he needs above all at the moment is a quiet, comfortable place in which to relax. When I think there was nothing at all here a couple of hours ago, I'm thrilled with what Carol's done. Thank you, Carol. Now Alice dear, how are you coping?"

"Not bad." Alice had one eye nearly closed but was looking more cheerful in her borrowed cherry-coloured T-shirt and flip-flops. "Dwayne phoned to say this afternoon's filming has been cancelled, but he's still needed to help set up for tomorrow. The filming's probably been cancelled because I laid Nero out. I told Dwayne what happened. He was dead angry, but I made him promise not to try anything with Nero. He agrees we can't risk losing our jobs."

"I'll have a word with Mr Hatton. You're not losing your jobs over this. Now, about tonight ..."

"Now that was a surprise. The landlady of the Pheasant Inn down the road—you remember I used to work there in the evenings? Well, I'm going to help her out for a couple of hours in the kitchen till Dwayne finishes, and he'll join us there. She's had a rowdy couple staying that she's asked to leave, so they've got a spare room which we can use till the festival's over. I'm just hanging around here till my friend brings Marie back from town."

Good, thought Minty. Even Nero wouldn't try anything at the pub.

"The five o'clock bus was cancelled," said Elizabeth, with a trace of satisfaction. "My sister who was coming over for supper's just rung me to say that she's got to get a taxi. So you'll have a long wait."

"I don't think so," said Carol, looking out of the window. They all heard the cough of Patrick's old car. Minty went to the window and couldn't help smiling, despite all the anxieties hovering at the back of her mind.

Patrick's car had all its windows down to allow various packages to be thrust out through them. A child's bike and a pushchair were hanging out of the boot, secured with rope, and what looked like a laundry basket had been lashed to the roof rack.

Arms and heads were protruding from every window, and as Patrick eased himself carefully out of the driving seat—carefully because someone was sitting in the front passenger seat with an enormous parcel on his lap—various children's voices could be heard, demanding to be let out.

"What a scream!" said Carol, amused.

Minty wrestled with the sash window, trying to throw it up and failing. It had got stuck from disuse. "He told me he was giving Mr Lightowler a lift back. He must have seen the others waiting at the bus stop and given them a lift, too."

Alice was waving. "There's my friend with her little boy and Marie. They went into town to look at shoes." She ran down the stairs.

"There's that woman from the post office with her dotty mother."

"And Mr Lightowler from the bookshop. What on earth has he got there?"

With rapid efficiency and good humour, Patrick unlashed pushchair and bike from the boot, helping passengers to alight and brush themselves down. Mr Lightowler was calling out for help, thin legs and arms waving from under the enormous package on his lap.

Elizabeth beamed with pride in her employer, and then scowled. "They take advantage of him. I must get his messages ready." She hurried away as Alice emerged from the house into the garden to scoop up Marie and give her a hug.

Patrick extricated Mr Lightowler with some difficulty and helped him to his feet, while an elderly woman castigated him for not retrieving her basket from the roof rack first. Minty fancied the car groaned with relief when everyone was out. The children were jumping around, excited. Everyone was talking at once. The noise was shattering.

Carol said, "So you're still in love with him?"

Minty didn't reply. She'd always loved Patrick, but she'd never thought of "being in love" with him. For months she'd rested secure in the knowledge that he loved her, while she was unable to do more than exist and hope that one day she'd be able to feel again. To love again. Of course she loved him, but perhaps it needed Carol to point out that she not only loved Patrick, but as of that very moment, she was deeply in love with him as well.

Carol said, "I'll put these flowers in water and get out of your way."

Still standing by his car, Patrick clutched at his pocket. His mobile phone was ringing. He answered it with one hand, while releasing the laundry basket with the other. The children calmed down and left with their mothers. Mr Lightowler departed, as did the woman from the post office and her mother, trundling the basket along between them. Now you could hear the birds cheeping in the garden.

Patrick listened, laughed, spoke into the phone. It looked as if he was making a joke of something that had been said. He delved under his seat to produce briefcase and laptop, switched off his mobile and stowed it away.

Then he sagged against his car, his body expressing a deep weariness. His face settled back into the lines of anxiety he'd been carrying for months. Gone was the decisiveness and humour he'd shown when talking on the phone, and the lightheartedness with which he'd crammed everyone into his car so that they shouldn't have to wait hours for another bus.

He looked so tired it was amazing he was still standing upright. The line between his eyebrows was very marked. He looked a lot older than his years.

Minty thought, *Have I done that to him?*

He looked up and saw her at the window. Instantly he pulled himself upright, managed to smile and wave. Assuming his burdens once more.

She went slowly down the stairs, struggling with herself. What she wanted to do was to run to him, demand that he drop everything to listen to her, to attend to her. She had the right, didn't she? He'd left her alone all day while he went to look after his partner—oh, poor Jim; what was the news there?—and then take over some difficult case or other in court.

She'd coped, though. Hadn't she?

"I've got a surprise for you, Patrick," said Minty. "See what Carol's done for us."

Patrick followed her upstairs. He dropped his jacket in one chair, his laptop and briefcase in another, and looked around in wonder. "Minty, this is amazing! We can move straight back in. If only the garden wasn't looking so ragged, I'd think time had moved backwards." He managed to smile and even to make it look natural.

He said, "Tell me about your day. I was worried about you. I wouldn't have left you but ... this case! I must take a look at the papers tonight. Jim's distraught. They say Anthea could go at any time." He passed his hand across his eyes. "So young! So unexpected. I can hardly believe it. I keep trying to pray for her, but I've been so busy ... which I suppose is no excuse."

Minty touched his arm. "Perhaps we can have a quiet time praying for her after supper—oh, but you have to get back to be with Jim, don't you?"

He nodded. "What time's supper? Is Serafina here?"

"Where else?" said Serafina, leaning on the door to the kitchen. "Half an hour, prompt."

Elizabeth came in, clutching a pile of mail. "Before I go, Mr Patrick, there's one or two things that ..."

"Not tonight, Elizabeth," said Patrick, with a trace of impatience in his voice. "First thing tomorrow, I promise."

Elizabeth was not pleased but put the pile down on the dining table in pointed fashion before leaving.

Now was Minty's opportunity to drag him back to her side. To monopolise him. She could make him sit down beside her and she could tell him everything. Ask him about everything. Trust him to put everything right.

Of course she remembered he'd always needed space and time to himself. That hadn't been difficult to arrange before they married, or even after. Until the accident. Since that day he'd hardly ever been alone, because she'd become distressed if he left her for more than a few minutes at a time.

She marvelled at his patience, at the sacrifice of himself that he'd made for her. She wondered how he'd managed it. He'd had no time to be alone with God. Always having to be aware of Minty's needs. Always ready with a diversion if the black door opened in front of her. Watching her constantly. Putting himself last.

And she'd been just about ready to do it again.

Could she let him go? Stand on her own two feet? Trust in her own strength?

No, she couldn't. The black hole would open up and swallow her.

She had a moment of acute vertigo, and then . . .

. . . and then she remembered that she didn't need to do it in her own strength. If she trusted enough in God's helping hand, if she called on Him, instead of on Patrick, she could do it. For a little while, anyway.

She set her jaw. Sent up an arrow prayer for help. *Help me to say the right thing.*

She said, "My problems can wait. Your garden needs attention. Why don't you go and potter about in it for a while? Unwind. I'll see that you eat and get off again in time to meet up with Jim."

He hadn't expected that. He'd expected to have to support her as usual.

His shoulders relaxed. She hadn't noticed he was so tense, not till he allowed himself to feel free of her burdens for a change.

"Thank you, Minty. That's exactly what I need. If you're sure?"

She wanted to scream that no, she didn't want to set him free even for an instant. But she didn't. She put her hands behind her back and went to see about making up the double bed in the master bedroom.

She wouldn't try to solve all the problems. She'd just let them trickle through her mind, holding them up to God, saying . . . *Look, what am I suppose to do about this? About Mr Hatton and the festival, Venetia and her committee, the strange tale Hugh had told her . . . Alice* and Dwayne ... *her uncle arriving at Eden Hall, forgetting that Minty wasn't there ...*

She tried to make a list of people to see in the right order of importance but kept putting new concerns to the top. *What was wrong with Annie?*

When Minty had finished making up the bed, she let herself sink to her knees and tried to pray. Words, images, fears. All flowed through her brain and some of them caught up in eddies. Knotting themselves up so she couldn't disentangle them.

She spread out her arms on the coverlet and laid her head down. *Father, you know best. Help me to do the right thing. Please be with Patrick. And Jim and Anthea and their little girl ...*

Loyalty.

That word stayed with her.

Chapter Eight

At supper Patrick appeared refreshed by his quiet time in the garden. He admired the way Carol had made the place comfortable for them, said he must pop up to see Hugh's tulips before they were over, and remarked it was good that they'd got back in time for Mrs Chickward's evening At Home because it was an excellent way of meeting up with people one didn't see every day.

He said his day in court had gone better than expected and the judge appeared sympathetic towards his client.

"But Jim ..." He passed his hand over his face. "I think he's drinking, though he swears he isn't. His sister's come over and taken charge of his little daughter, who's pretty bewildered by it all, poor thing. And the paperwork at the office ..." He lifted his shoulders and let them drop.

Minty said, "Didn't you take on another partner this year? Or did I imagine it?"

"That's something else to sort out. We did, but she's been off work with stress for weeks. Jim hadn't told me. I'll try to see her tomorrow. Now tell me about your day. Can you cope?"

Minty forced herself to nod. "Lots of problems, but lots of people to help me. Gemma seems to be involved in making a pop video."

He laughed at that, as she'd intended he should. He shook his head. "Do you see her as a pop star? I'm not sure I do."

"Me, neither." She purposely kept her tone light.

He looked at her hard, trying to assess whether it was safe to leave her for a while. "This festival. It's going to be very big, isn't it? Someone showed me a leaflet about it today. Even I'd heard of some of the acts. Are we expected to be on show, do the host and hostess thing?"

"I'll find out tomorrow. Mr Hatton seems to have everything under control. There's one or two things I'd like to talk through with you, but they can wait and Jim can't."

She waved him off and tried to help Serafina clear the table and wash up.

"I'd rather do this by myself," said Serafina. "You go and sort out that lot up at the Hall."

"All right. First tell me: Is Annie ill?"

Serafina folded her lips. "She says it's not serious and she wants to carry on as usual. She says it's just a little lump that's been removed and she needs some radiotherapy to make sure it doesn't come back. I don't think she's lying. I said you'd want to know, and she said there was no need."

Minty was horrified. "She shouldn't be alone!"

"She likes living alone and she loves her new house. And peace and quiet. She always made a fuss if I turned my television up a speck to hear it better. She's got this new government committee to keep her occupied. She's not like you and me, you know. She doesn't need people. I wouldn't have left her if she'd let me do anything for her, now would I?"

Probably not. Serafina understood loyalty, too.

Minty went into Patrick's study to jot down notes about what had been happening and to make phone calls. A male voice answered the phone at the Hall. Neither Mr Hatton nor Gemma were free to come to the phone at the moment. No, the man couldn't say whether or not her messages had been passed on. Why not try again tomorrow?

Annie wasn't answering her phone, but Minty left a message on the answerphone.

Someone rang the front door bell below. Serafina had retired to the guest room on the top floor, judging by the noise from a television set up there. The volume was turned up high. Was Serafina getting deaf? Something else to check out.

Minty ran down the stairs to find Carol on the doorstep.

"Sorry, love. I ought to have phoned first, but … could you pop over for a bit?"

"If I can find some front door keys." They investigated Elizabeth's desk — wouldn't she be cross when she found out that Minty had been rummaging around in her desk? — and discovered a bunch which turned out to contain keys for the front and garden doors.

"Hold on a mo," said Minty, as they wove their way across a High Street which seemed far busier than usual. She peered into a shop window filled with New Age books and paraphernalia. Crystals, pyramids, junk jewellery, joss sticks. Pop records, videos, posters of dishevelled young men.

Carol shrugged. "Doing quite well. If you like that sort of thing."

"I don't," said Minty, in a flat voice. "What sort of lease have they got?"

"Not long," said Carol, unlocking the door between the antique shop and the Chinese restaurant. She led the way up some steep stairs to a large room overlooking the High Street. The building had appeared Victorian on the outside, but inside its timber framework betrayed an older age.

Iris was sitting on a low window seat, turning a brocaded cushion over and over in her hands—a sign of agitation in one usually calm. She looked up when Minty came in and said, "It's a storm in a teacup, that's all."

A third person was sitting there, hands dangling between his knees, fair hair ruffled. Toby Wootton, Hugh and Venetia's much-loved son, whom Minty had appointed head of publicity for the Hall. A nice-looking man, with a delicately triangular face, a face which was at present very troubled.

"Toby." Minty put a steadying hand on his shoulder, though why he should need steadying, she didn't know. "Tell me."

Iris punched her cushion. "Alice ought to have had more sense. She knows how much depends on our being helpful. She's just not a team player. There are other ways of dealing with Nero."

Carol pushed Minty towards a chintz-covered chair and took another for herself. "Iris, would you call those two silly girls from the council estate team players? They've been hanging around the Hall, pestering the crew for attention. In nine months' time they'll be producing a couple of players of their own, won't they? Without any fathers to support them. What about the schoolboys who've been truanting when they should be taking exams? Are they team players, too?"

"You know very well what I mean," said Iris, turning her head away.

Toby had his eyes on Minty. "Alice and Dwayne are to lose their jobs. Maxine insisted, said Alice had assaulted Nero. He couldn't work this afternoon. They had the whole unit on stand-by, losing money. Everyone was furious. Hatton wanted to prosecute Alice until I pointed out she hasn't any money."

Iris smoothed down her already perfect smooth hairstyle. "I don't know why Carol brought you over, Minty. Alice and Dwayne will be replaced by agency staff. It's a small price to pay."

Carol drawled, "You see the primrose path before you, Minty. Bend a little here, avert your eyes there and ..."

"Nonsense," said Iris, but her pale face flushed.

Minty sat down beside Iris. "Iris, my dear. I've trusted you with my life before now. Tell me the truth."

Iris turned her head away. "What is truth?"

Carol sighed. "Minty, let me explain. Iris thinks that her future—and that of her parents—depends on her ability to 'see the wider picture.' I don't agree."

Iris said, "Compromise is not a bad thing."

Minty grew anxious. "Carol, you've openly criticised what Mr Hatton's doing. Have they been putting pressure on you, too?"

Carol grinned. "My father's no fool. He negotiated a long lease on these premises, and I don't depend on the Hall for my living. It's true Maxine said she wanted to buy some of my most expensive stock, and of course that would help my turnover, but Father trusts my judgement and he won't sack me if she fails to come up with the goods. Toby's another matter. Toby's besotted with Maxine. She's got him crawling round her feet like a puppy."

Toby said in a hoarse voice, "Rubbish!"

Carol flicked her fingers at him. "The poor wee laddie!"

Toby reddened and looked away.

Minty said, "I'll speak to Mr Hatton about Alice. It's Nero who ought to be prosecuted, not her, and neither she nor Dwayne will lose their jobs because of him."

Toby said, "It's easier said than done, getting to speak with him if he doesn't want to speak to you. Look, Minty, I don't like it either, but he's got a point. We can't have someone working for us who assaults our guests. Hatton's contract gives him the right to hire or fire any of us. I pulled it out of the file today to check, and it's there in black and white. While I was about it, I also copied Maxine's contract for you."

He handed it over to Minty, who glanced at the signatures. Maxine's contract was signed by Annie and Hatton.

"Watertight," said Toby.

"Thanks, Toby. I wanted that." She had no pockets in her dress and hadn't thought to bring a handbag. Her keys were hanging on her belt. So she put the contract in her bra. "But I'll still have a word with Mr Hatton, because sacking Alice and Dwayne is wrong."

Carol said, "Yes!" and punched the air.

Iris said, "Minty, you haven't thought this through. The festival starts in three days' time. Clive has all the responsibility of it on his shoulders ... the money that's been invested ... the sponsors, security, everything. He's made it all happen. A hundred times a day there's a crisis for him to solve and we need to support him, not drag him away to deal with trivial problems which have been blown up out of all proportion.

"Alice attacked a guest. Alice must go. I might persuade him to keep Dwayne on, I suppose. He's useful enough. But Alice must find herself another job—and naturally she must move out of her estate cottage."

Minty shook her head. "No way! If Mr Hatton can't spare the time to come down here to speak to me, then I must go up to the Hall and talk to him there. Besides, I want to see for myself just what's going on."

Iris made an involuntary movement but kept her beautiful face blank. Minty looked searchingly at her. Was something going on at the Hall that Iris didn't want her to know about?

Toby looked haggard. "There's nothing for you to see. At least, I suppose the unit's moved things around a bit for the filming, but nothing that can't be put right in a day or so. I can see you wouldn't like the language which the crew uses. They're pretty foul-mouthed, but it's just the way they speak. It doesn't mean anything. Yes, some of them have got up to things you'd probably disapprove of, but we're in a backwater here, aren't we? A bit old-fashioned?"

Carol pointed a finger at him. "What about the man I caught in my doorway, dealing in drugs? He works for Maxine, but he didn't lose his job, did he?"

Toby explained to Minty. "Good lighting cameramen are like gold dust. He'll be more careful in future. Maxine's manager came down in person to apologise to Carol. There's always drugs at these festivals. Nobody thinks anything of it."

Carol put her hands on her hips. "He also remarked that these old buildings are fire hazards, didn't he? And asked if I kept much in the way of varnishes and paints in the workshop. Which of course I do."

Minty was horrified. "He was threatening you!"

Toby looked anguished. "No, of course not. He was interested in what goes on here, that's all."

Carol flicked her fingers at him. "It was a threat, but please note that I was born contrary and don't scare easily. Come on now, Toby. The other day you hinted at something nasty going on at the Hall, though you wouldn't say what it was. You can tell Minty, even if you won't tell me."

Toby shook his head. "You're imagining things."

He was lying. Minty considered her options. "All right, tell me how I get into the Hall."

"You don't," said Iris quickly. Too quickly.

Toby grimaced. "Hatton laid it on the line for us. We haven't got long till we open, and there's a million things to do. Maxine is furious at losing an afternoon's filming because of Alice, and we can't afford to offend our top attraction. So there are to be no visitors to the site. None."

"Money talks," observed Carol, "but lust shrieks aloud."

"It's not ...," said Toby, flushing. "I'm not. Really."

Carol changed the subject abruptly. "Minty, let me show you the rest of the flat. I sleep on the big settee here, but ..." She led the way to a tiny staircase at the back. "This is the way to the attic room, which is now Iris' territory. Here's my kitchen, where I play at being cook now and again, though mostly not. The bathroom next door has a good power shower, and here is my very own bolt-hole, a door through to a tiny patio on the roof of the sticky-out bit of the shop below. This is where I sit and think. Isn't it dinky?"

They stepped out onto a small patio furnished with a comfortable all-weather chair and table under an adjustable parasol. Green tubs had been planted with fragrant lavender bushes, and in the cool dusk it was a charming, secluded spot. A laptop and a mobile phone lay next to a paperback on the table, evidence that Carol did indeed make use of this secluded place.

"Why, this is delightful, Carol." Minty dropped her voice. "Any idea how I can get into the Hall? I need to see for myself what's going on."

Carol also kept her voice low. "I'll look out a couple of things that might help and drop them over to you later this evening; just don't tell the others."

"You fancy Toby, and you want help rescuing him from Maxine?"

"You think I'm in love with that big fool? I should be so stupid."

Minty reserved judgement. If Carol was indeed in love with Toby, she wasn't going to admit it.

Toby was on his feet when they returned to the living room. "I'll be on my way, Carol. Early start tomorrow. I'll see you across the road, Minty."

Minty was amused. "I don't need seeing across the road, Toby. Anyway, I'm going up to the vicarage because I hear my uncle has taken refuge there."

"Then I'll see you to the vicarage."

Toby was right in thinking she could do with a strong shoulder to push her way through the crowd in the street. The Chinese restaurant had a queue of people outside, and even the little coffee shop next door had remained open to serve high teas. The pubs were doing good business, too. Traffic was always slow down this street, but now there seemed more cars than ever trying to park, and groups of people were wandering aimlessly around looking for amusement.

"Toby, why are all these people here days before the festival starts?"

He steered her round a group of boisterous teenage boys. "Apparently it always happens. People with tents and caravans come early to stake their claim to a good pitch before the security people are ready for them. Then there's a band of travellers—watch your purse when you walk around. There's even a small fun fair moved in. We've tried to move them and the travellers on, but they dodge around so much it's hard to keep track of them."

"Amazing!" said Minty.

"Mm. There's designated areas set out in the Park. A huge tent city with caravans behind. Car parking at the back. Blocks of toilets everywhere, of course, though they're not coming till tomorrow. They should have been here yesterday, but there was some kind of hold up."

"What will people have been doing without toilets? Oh. Dig holes?"

Toby nodded. "The smaller stage is up and ready, but they're still working on the big one and the trenches taking the power lines out to it—the trenches have to be at least four inches under the turf, you know. The big marquees go up tomorrow. Some of the smaller tents—for the Press and changing rooms for the artists—haven't even arrived on site yet. A lot of the food stalls are already serving food around tent city. We need to pray for good weather."

A cavalcade of Silverwing motor-bikes roared down the High Street, weaving in and out of traffic.

Minty tried to make sense of what was happening. "Do we get a rake-off from the food outlets?"

"We're supposed to, yes. Hatton's a really sharp businessman, and if you can just hold off for a few days, Minty, it'll all be over and done with. I expect Iris will see that Alice gets another job somewhere else, and as for Carol, well, she's taken a casual remark the wrong way. There's really nothing to worry about, honest."

Minty wondered what Patrick would say if he could hear Toby making excuses for the bullying that Carol and Iris were being subjected to. Toby was a nice man but perhaps a trifle naïve.

As a child he'd helped a bully put Patrick in hospital, then agonised over it for years. Iris had kept quiet after she was raped, for fear that her parents would suffer. Minty wondered if, by giving in once to bullying, Iris and Toby were easier to bully now. They knew from experience that life did exist after you gave in to pressure, even if it wasn't as happy an existence as it might be.

She said, "Toby, you must be going through hell at the moment. Have you told Carol what happened when you and Patrick were children?"

Did he blush? "I told Maxine. She was wonderful about it. She said that some children are just so annoying that ..." He caught himself up. "Well, she doesn't know what Patrick's really like, does she?"

Minty paused beside the shop selling pop memorabilia. "Is that Maxine?" She pointed to a poster of a beautiful girl with a mass of black curls, apparently about to kiss the top of a bottle—or to put it in her mouth. The message the poster was sending was ambiguous.

Toby beamed. "Cool, isn't she? You can't take your eyes off her when she walks into the room. But you have to handle her right. She's cancelled concerts at the last minute before now when something's upset her. I suppose all great artists are like that."

They walked up the High Street, past the ancient church, to the Green where the roads divided. Minty surveyed the chaos of parked and would-be parking cars on the Green, some of which had actually invaded the cricket pitch. A number of caravans were trying to find parking spaces around the Green itself. Mrs Chickward lived in a stately old house fronting the Green. She must be up in arms about this.

She said, "What arrangements have been made for extra policing, and when do they start? How much is that going to add to the costs?"

"There's a very efficient security system in place ..."

"Inside the grounds, yes. I've met them. What about here, in the village?"

"Hatton said ..." Toby looked at the chaos and winced. "You're right. We're going to have to ask for traffic police. You always think so clearly, Minty. It's a shame you've not been involved from the beginning. I'll speak to Hatton about it tomorrow. It will add to the costs, of course."

Minty nodded and ducked into the vicarage doorway. The building looked tired. It needed the services of a builder and decorator, if she was any judge of the matter. Who was responsible for the vicarage? Was it the church authorities, or was it down to her as Lady of the Hall? She must find out.

She'd known the Reverend Cecil for years, because he'd once been a curate of her uncle's in his city parish. Cecil was a modest, not-too-bright bunny of a man, who served God to the best of his ability and sometimes was wiser in his dealings with people than many a scholar. A while back he'd fancied Minty might make him a good little wife and parish helpmeet, and in consequence had been wistful when Minty and Patrick had been married in his church. Nevertheless, he was a man who could be relied upon. Within his limits.

The vicarage bell wasn't working, but application of the heavy doorknocker eventually brought Cecil to the door. Toby waved good-bye and set off up the hill.

"Minty! Mrs Sands, I should say. Someone said you were back, but then someone else said that you weren't staying because you didn't like what was going on, but ... oh, come in, come in. Your uncle's at the church. He spends a lot of time there. 'Wrestling with God', he says. I must admit that I thought he was, well, going over the top, but now ... oh dear, do mind that hole in the carpet. Can I offer you something to eat or drink? I'm afraid there isn't much, because what with this and that, and I've got a meeting in half an hour but ... what can I get you?"

The vicarage had never been well furnished, but surely it had never been as shabby as this. Minty made a mental note to do something about it. "It was very good of you to take my uncle in."

"Carol brought him to me one day. What a treasure she is, to be sure. I wondered whether she would like to come up for a light supper with me one evening, but no, it appears she has already lost her heart to someone, though no one seems to know who. But you came about your uncle. In the old days people used to steer him back to the Hall if they found him wandering in the street, but after the, well, the invasion, he refused to go back there and became quite, well, incoherent is putting it mildly."

"Wasn't Gemma looking after him?"

Cecil became pink about the face and neck. "I'm afraid the young have no patience with the old nowadays. Of course when you get old you do slow down and sometimes can't find the right words, but he always seems comfortable with me. I don't forget how good he was to me years ago when I had doubts about my calling, and he encouraged me to keep on going.

"Carol took him to the doctor here, who gave him some pills, which I'm sorry to say he threw away. I was going to take him to the hospital myself, but then I was tied up with Mrs . . . oh, you probably won't know her, she hardly ever moved out of her council house in all the years I've been here, and then of course she died . . . so as I said, I couldn't take him. So Carol did, and they gave him a check-up and they say there's nothing particularly wrong with him apart from his feet which needed looking at. My own father died when I was in my early teens, you know, and my mother married again, so he's company for me."

Minty gave him an affectionate kiss on his cheek. "Thank you, Cecil. I'll be back in the Hall as soon as the festival's finished, and then I'll be able to look after my uncle myself."

Cecil looked embarrassed. "The thing is, he's happy here. He keeps saying that the Hall is the haunt of the devil and . . . Well, you know, people nowadays don't talk like that, and there's no denying that some people are saying he's lost the plot completely and ought to be put away."

"What do you think, Cecil?"

He ran his tongue over his lips. "I think he's right." He looked at her like a dog that expects to be whipped for wrongdoing, but she nodded encouragement.

He said, "I can't put my finger on it. There's been a spate of petty thefts from the shops, some vandalism, some drunkenness. That man Nero is a menace. It's said the landlady at the pub shut his fingers in her car door. By accident, I'm sure. The traffic's terrible. But none of that's really important, is it? There's a rumour going round that . . . no, it's laughable, really. Some people think all pop stars are in league with the devil, you know."

"I'll judge for myself. Meanwhile, I'm worried that you're support-ing my uncle and yourself on your salary. I'll see you get a cheque to cover his board and lodging for the time he's been living with you, and

I'm going to suggest Alice arranges for someone to come in and cook for you."

"I wasn't asking for money."

"Of course you weren't, but it's only right that my uncle is fed properly and has his home comforts. He has his pension, but I don't suppose it's occurred to him to give you any of it. He probably hasn't even thought to cash it, if I know him."

Cecil shook his head.

"We'll have to sort him out then, won't we? It'll make me feel less guilty about not having him with me for the moment, if you'll accept something from me."

"Thank you, Minty. And God bless you. I hope you can sort everything out—at the Hall, I mean. I've been praying for someone to wake up and do something about—whatever it is—that is, if there is anything. And here you come, the man to the minute . . . at least, the woman to . . . well, you know what I mean."

"Dear Cecil, yes. Now I must go and find my uncle."

Chapter Nine

Minty opened the great door of the church and stepped inside. The walls and roof were of golden stone and there were tall windows of greenish glass all around. Paler stone gravestones had been inserted in the floor of the nave, and there were marble tablets on the walls. There was a tablet to her father on the wall next to that of her mother, and above them more tablets to her mother's family, the Edens.

Someone was moaning. A black-clad figure was rocking to and fro in one of the front pews. The Reverend Reuben Cardale looked unkempt. He'd allowed a beard to grow and hadn't trimmed it. His grey hair fell in elf-locks about his collar. His clothes were rusty black but clean, and he didn't smell of old man.

His eyes were closed. "Oh, Lord. Protect us and save us. Defend us from the evil one ..."

Minty laid a hand on his shoulder. "Dear uncle, it's me. Minty."

"What? Who?" He started and his eyes opened. For one moment Minty thought he didn't recognise her, but then he did.

"What kept you? Don't you realise what's happening here? The whore stalks the streets and turns men's hearts to lust."

There was spittle at the corner of his mouth, and his hands knotted into claws as he raised them to the skies. He was shaking with passion. With rage, or fear?

Minty was alarmed. Cecil had tried to warn her and so had Carol. What she saw now seemed to verge on madness. He grasped her wrist. His eyes were pale and looked at and then through her. "I told them. I warned them. She corrupts everything she touches. Minds and hearts. Sin steals their thoughts and everywhere there is the stench of corruption. For seven days now I have prayed that God would strike her dead, but He has not heard me. I have fasted and prayed, but still she lures them on.

"I've stopped people in the streets and warned them to repent. I've begged them to come in and pray with me, to confess their sins and beg for God's forgiveness. They refuse to listen!"

His voice rose to a shriek. No wonder people shrank from him and thought he might be certifiable. *Yet Cecil thought the old man was right! And Cecil was not mad.*

Minty put her arm about his shoulders. He may have been a harsh guardian in her childhood, yet he was her uncle and she felt responsible for him.

He was quiet now. Even weeping a little. He made no attempt to reach for a handkerchief, and she thought he probably didn't have one. His wife had always attended to every domestic detail for him. Now she was gone, he was adrift in life.

He closed his eyes and folded his hands. He began to move his lips in silent prayer. She joined him in that. *Dear Lord, preserve us from all evil. Strengthen us for the battle that is to come ...*

Minty was surprised at the words that had sprung into her mind. Did evil really threaten the Hall? She'd heard of attempted sexual assault, bullying and drug-dealing. She'd seen traffic chaos and heard of a charity event being cancelled. But all that didn't amount to seeing evil incarnate stalk the streets, did it? Her uncle was well past his sell-by date.

Dear Lord, open our eyes to see clearly. Comfort and strengthen those who feel threatened. Protect the friendless and powerless. Guide Patrick in his new responsibilities. Be with Anthea. Oh, dear, poor Anthea — and Jim. Keep the black door shut. Keep despair at bay. Grant me wisdom to see what is best to be done. Help Carol and ... is she being foolish to defy Hatton? WHAT IS GOING ON AT THE HALL?

Footsteps came down the aisle and there was the Reverend Cecil, full of concern for her uncle.

"There you are, now. You'll have been glad to see Minty again, won't you? Don't you think she's looking much better? We'll all be as right as rain again, now she's back. I've ordered a couple of pizzas for supper. You like the three-cheese one, don't you?"

Reuben Cardale reared up. "Don't treat me like a child. Of course I know my niece. My prayers have been answered, and she has returned to put everything to rights. It's good to see you again, child. You're all I have now. That half-sister of yours, Gemma ..." He shook his head. "Weak as water and heading for destruction. I will continue to pray for her, of course, but I greatly fear it's in vain."

Cecil picked up a walking stick, which Minty hadn't noticed before, and handed it to his one-time mentor. Minty hadn't known her uncle needed a stick nowadays.

Cecil was serious. "Yes, we will all pray. But now, supper awaits, and then I have a meeting."

"Pizza ..." The old man's eyes brightened and he left the church on Cecil's arm, forgetting Minty.

She slipped into the place he'd occupied and let herself be filled with the peace of the church. An oasis of calm and light in the middle of ... what? Were Cecil and her uncle right?

She left the church only to find herself enclosed tightly in a pair of strong arms from behind. To her horror she was lifted right off her feet. What was happening?

Iris had taught her some tricks for dealing with men who tried to take advantage, and she had her bunch of keys already in her hand to let herself into Patrick's house. She told herself to go limp, not to struggle.

"Who's this beauty, walking straight into Nero's arms?"

Her feet were dangling off the pavement. She twisted her head around to see who was holding her. Nero was exactly as Carol had described him: smooth-muscled and very black. And he had a plaster high on his cheek-bone, which looked slightly swollen.

She said, "Put me down, please."

"Nero likes it when little girls beg." Seeing that she made no attempt to struggle, he set her on her feet and turned her to face him. As he did so, she brought her hand up with the keys in it and jabbed at his crotch.

He screamed, a high shriek. He doubled over, covering himself with his hands. Several passers-by stopped to see what was the matter. One of them laughed, though not loudly.

Minty stepped back, out of his reach. "Don't try that again, Mr Nero, or whatever your name is. Otherwise you'll be off filming for more than one afternoon."

He screamed again, but this time there was a bubble of whispered words in the scream. He called her dreadful names, promising vengeance.

She crossed the road, inwardly shaken but outwardly unperturbed, and let herself into Patrick's house. Should she ring the police? Patrick would say that she should, but on the other hand, Nero had definitely come off worst from their encounter. And she felt too shaken to do anything but make herself a cup of tea and sit quietly looking out on the garden for a while.

All was quiet, except for the television turned up high on the top floor. Serafina was making herself comfortable in the spare room. After a while Minty went into Elizabeth's office and switched on her computer to do some research. You could find out almost anything, if you knew where to look. She keyed in the word "Maxine" and waited for the information to unroll in front of her. What she saw gave her a good deal to think about.

She switched off Elizabeth's computer and went upstairs to work in Patrick's study, bringing her notes up to date, and listing a number of points she'd like to discuss with him.

It was getting late. The evenings were still growing lighter, but she was tired and more than ready for bed. The only problem was that Patrick wasn't there yet to share it with her. She turned down the bed in the big front room, had a shower and washed her hair. Serafina's television was turned off and gentle snores could be heard all over the top floor.

She was towelling her hair dry while looking for her favourite nightdress when she heard Patrick's car return. Serafina had unpacked for her—darling Serafina!—but where had she put Minty's nightdress? She heard Patrick talking to someone, taking the stairs one at a time with long rests between.

Had he brought someone home with him? Jim? And if so, what did that mean?

Her hair was in wild tendrils around her head and she still couldn't find her nightdress. She seized the first piece of clothing to hand—one of Patrick's shirts—and shrugged herself into it.

Patrick reached the landing, encouraging his partner up the last few steps. "Just another couple of steps and we're there. Yes, I know you want the toilet. Here we go." He eased Jim into the toilet and closed the door on him. He looked weary to the bone.

Minty said, "Dare I ask ...?"

"She died this evening." He passed his hand over his eyes. "Jim was there till the end. I couldn't leave him there. He's in a bad way. Been drinking, too."

Minty sagged against the wall. "Oh, no. But she was so young! And her little girl! And Jim! How ever is he going to cope? Of course he must stay." She took his hand. "You look worn out yourself. You go and have a shower and I'll make up the bed for him in your old bedroom."

She'd just finished making up the narrow bed when she heard the toilet door open and somebody blunder along the landing. There came a soft but heavy thud ... and then nothing.

She found Patrick just emerging from the bathroom, towelling himself dry. The door to the big front bedroom was open and Jim had fallen diagonally across the double bed. Patrick pulled on Jim's arm and called his name, but it was no good. He'd passed out. Presently his snores began to compete with Serafina's nearby.

Minty put her hands on her hips, threw back her head and laughed. Patrick looked dazed.

She tried to explain. "We're running a hostel for the homeless. First Serafina moves in with us. We nearly had Alice, Dwayne and Marie join us this evening, and I did wonder if we could put my uncle up, too. I feel like the old woman who lived in a shoe, who had so many children she didn't know what to do!"

Patrick gaped. Something happened to his face that she hadn't seen for a long time ... if ever.

"Minty ... you're laughing!"

"Listen to the noise they're making! Patrick? What's the matter?"

"You're laughing!" There were tears in his eyes. "I never thought ..." He blinked hard, tried to pretend he wasn't crying. "Sometimes I've wondered if you'd ever laugh again."

She put her arms about him and held him tight. As tightly as he held her, though he leaned back to make sure that yes, she really was laughing.

She said, "We can't shift Jim so we'd better undress him as best we can and pull the duvet over him. Your old bed will have to bear both of us tonight."

"It's too narrow."

"Don't tell me you didn't have fantasies of my sleeping there with you, all those years when I was growing up in the city and you were living alone here and wondering if we'd ever meet again."

He was still shaken but trying to control himself. "Fantasy number eight for use on high days and holidays. You really are laughing, aren't you?"

"Haven't I laughed at all these last few months?" Looking back, she realised that she hadn't. She'd smiled when she could. But not laughed. She stroked his cheek. "I really am laughing."

Together they made Jim comfortable, and then she led Patrick into his old bedroom.

He said, "I'm too tired to relax. I'll read for a while, then sleep on the settee downstairs."

"Carol could only find us a two-seater settee. We'll manage here."

"Yes, but ..."

She pushed him down onto the bed, where he lay on his side, looking up at her. She slid the shirt off her shoulders, inch by inch. "Do you think you could manage a 'toothsome morsel'?"

"Ah, well. Now you mention it. Perhaps I could." And proved that indeed he could.

When they'd first married, she'd always been first up in the mornings. While he shaved and dressed, she'd read their Bible notes and passage from the Bible aloud. Then they'd sit and pray together, sometimes aloud but more often in silence.

After her miscarriage, he'd taken over reading the daily notes aloud and she'd listened, or tried to listen. And never prayed aloud because she could only think of one prayer then, and that was, *Lord, help me. Let me not be mad.*

Now she sat cross-legged on the bed and read aloud while he got dressed. When she'd finished the Bible reading, they were quiet together. She was thinking of poor Anthea and her little girl, and of Jim. Asking God to hold Jim in His loving arms, to give him hope for the future. And then, amazed with thankfulness, she thought of all God's goodness to herself and Patrick.

He sat on the bed, eyes down, feet in shoes but not yet laced up. Praying. He was a powerful prayer, but it embarrassed him to pray aloud.

She lifted her eyes to the sun, which was beginning to insinuate its rays through the uncurtained window. *Dear Lord, You are so glorious. I can't praise You enough! And thank You! What a wonderful world You have made. More than anything I praise You for giving me so many blessings. Such good friends. Such a beautiful place to live. So much useful work to do.*

Yes, I do thank You for the work you have given me. I ask for wisdom to use Your gifts as You would wish ... and the strength and courage to carry out Your wishes.

Patrick had rested his hand beside her on the bed. She wriggled her fingers into his, and his hand tightened on hers, though he did not speak.

Thank you, Lord, for Patrick. For his integrity and strength of character. For giving himself over to looking after me all this time, neglecting his work, his friends, everything. When I compare what Mr Hatton, Iris, Toby and Carol are saying, with what Patrick would say or do, then I have a yardstick to judge them by, because this man has never bent before injustice.

Patrick's fingers were twined around hers. He lifted his head, taking a deep breath. He said, "I've been thanking God for your laughter. For giving you the strength to deal with everything that's been thrown at you since we came back. I'd been wondering if I was right to let you come back, but ... God is good and—" a gentle sigh—"I've asked Him to look after poor Jim."

He picked up the Bible reading notes. "That bit about not keeping company with evil. It seems as if it was meant for us today."

"No compromise," she said. She shook out the clothes she'd worn the day before and the contract Toby had given her fell out onto the floor. "Ah-ha. Have you time to cast an eye over this?"

Serafina's voice rose from below. "Breakfast's on the table."

He laced up his shoes, frowning. "I'll have a look while I eat."

They knew better than to be late. Minty scrambled into some clothes quickly, decided to put her hair up later, and got down in time to see Patrick reading the last lines of Maxine's contract while finishing off his cereal.

Serafina plumped a full English breakfast in front of both of them and told Minty she was to "eat up, every scrap, put some flesh on those bones."

Patrick began to re-read the contract. Then gave a short laugh and shook his head. "Gemma ought to have had her own solicitor draw this up. What she gets out of it is vaguely worded. 'An opportunity to join the backing group.' Hardly watertight. I wonder what she'll actually end up doing. I'm almost sorry for her."

"What about our rights?"

"Mm? Oh. Paragraph three. 'Suitable accommodation will be provided for Maxine and six members of her household.' Define 'suitable', Minty. How many people has she brought with her? More than six? A second contract should have been drawn up after Maxine saw our quarters and decided to shoot a video at the Hall. But perhaps she thought Gemma was so dazzled with thoughts of stardom that she wouldn't dare object to any alteration of the terms.

"I could drive a coach and horses through this contract. Relocate Maxine where you wish. If you wish. Or leave it till after the festival and shoot her out then."

So it was up to her. She said, "My uncle and Cecil both think there's something nasty going on at the Hall. Hugh thinks so, too. Iris denies it, but Toby isn't sure. Is it my job to interfere?"

"Is 'interfere' the right word?" asked Patrick, reaching for the last piece of toast. "Where do your responsibilities lie?"

Ugh. The Hall and village and everyone who lived in it were her responsibility. Which meant she had to find out exactly what was going on and then decide what to do.

Elizabeth panted up the stairs with a pile of mail for Patrick to answer. He drained the coffee pot while switching into business mode. Minty drank tea and wondered why tea in England tasted so different from that served on the Continent.

Elizabeth opened the post and laid letters in front of him one by one. Patrick scanned them with his usual amazing rapidity. "Tell him no. Say I'll consider this one and write in a few days. Say I'll see these people next week, any day, except— no, I'd better ring you when I get to the other office, see how many days I'll be in court ... is Jim up yet, Serafina?"

Serafina moved noiselessly to replace one pot of coffee with another. "Sleeping like a baby."

"Ah." Patrick's eyes swept up to meet Minty's, and she felt herself go white and shivery. Jim and his wife had a year-old toddler who'd never been in the best of health. How would he cope now?

"My godchild," said Patrick, in the lightest of light tones. "She's been dumped on her aunt, which is a good enough short-term solution."

Babies. The black door opened up. Minty clutched at Patrick's hand, which happened to be thrust towards her just at that very moment. She clung to him. Mastered herself. Let go of him and sat back in her chair. Praise be, she hadn't gone under that time.

He turned back to Elizabeth and his letters. "Yes, I'll do this. This one ... I'll ring from the other office. I'll have to be working from there for a while. I must see our new partner today. Not sure when. Have to try to fit it in somehow. If she could come back to work for even a couple of hours a day, that would help."

He drank another cup of coffee straight off and stood, looking round for his jacket. Elizabeth pushed one more letter at him. "I thought you'd like to see this."

He scanned it. His face went blank. Something important?

He glanced at Minty, then at Elizabeth, and read the letter again. So it was something that would affect both of them.

He opened his mouth, closed it, shook his head at himself. He folded the letter up and put it in his pocket. Elizabeth looked frustrated. "It's important, Mr Patrick."

Patrick sighed. "The timing's all wrong. Again. I don't think Jim will be getting back to work for a while. Will you see to him, Minty?"

He thanked Elizabeth and Serafina, picked up his laptop, mobile and briefcase and went down the stairs, feeling in his pockets for his keys.

Minty collected his jacket — which he'd forgotten, of course — and followed him down to his car.

He threw his things into the passenger seat. "I've just thought of another good prayer. 'Lord, Thou knowest how busy I must be this day. If I forget Thee, do not Thou forget me.'"

"I like that. Where's it from?"

"General Sir Jacob Asterley, on his knees, on the morning of the first battle of the Civil War, 1642."

She liked it, trying it over and over in her head. *If I forget Thee, do not Thou forget me.* Some prayers stuck in the mind more than others. She wondered if Patrick said this prayer every day as he went off to work, and thought he probably did.

His car started up with a slight protesting cough, settled down and idled itself off and away. Minty went back upstairs to find Elizabeth had waited for her.

Elizabeth was not in a good mood. "I see my bunch of spare keys is missing. I assume you took it?" Her tone was not friendly, and Serafina gave her a speculative look.

Minty straightened her back. "That was me. Is there a computer I can use yet?"

Elizabeth bridled. "These things take time, you know."

Minty was careful not to sound as if she was quarrelling with Elizabeth, but needed to make her position clear. "Would you check on it for me, please?"

Elizabeth went off with a heightened colour. Serafina said, "Someone dumped a bag of bits and pieces on the doorstep. I took it in with the milk. Elizabeth will probably complain that I've pinched her milk, but she can always get some more, can't she?"

Minty tried to help Serafina wash up but was shooed out of the kitchen. "And don't come back in. I'm putting the washing machine on this morning. It's not new, but rather like that long man of yours, it's built to last. And," said Serafina, banging plates into the dishwasher, "don't you fret about that god-child of his. God knows you're not ready to take on another woman's baby yet."

Minty nodded, hiding her misery and guilt. *Soon, perhaps. Dear God, make it soon.*

Minty explored the "bag of bits and pieces" and guessed it was from Carol. Among other things there was a brightly coloured skimpy top, a tiny pair of frayed denim shorts, a baseball cap and some huge sun-glasses. Minty had never worn such gear in her life! As a disguise, these things would be perfect. No one would suspect the quiet, modestly dressed Lady of the Hall of appearing in such clothes. The question remained, how to get an identity disc to allow her into the Hall?

There was a thud on the door below and Elizabeth marched up the stairs with a large envelope addressed to Minty. "I suppose you know what was in that letter for Mr Patrick? An invitation to lunch from the District Chairman. You may not have heard of District Chairmen, since you were brought up in the city—" Elizabeth made it sound as if Minty had been brought up in a cesspit—"but that's the top man in local government, over the heads of the mayors and councils of all the parishes and towns hereabouts. Sir Thomas ... well, you won't know the name, will you? But he's retiring and they want Mr Patrick to stand in his place at the next District Council elections. The chairman sounded him out about it after Christmas, and I could see he was interested. But he couldn't accept then because of taking you away, and now I suppose he'll refuse because of Mr Jim."

"Thank you, Elizabeth," said Minty, thinking that Elizabeth was probably right. Patrick had always said that God wasn't interested in his career, except as it might be of use to other people. He was pretty well resigned to it, but this latest twitch on the nerves must be hard on him. First the offer from the Foundation, and now this.

She turned her attention to her own post. The envelope and letter within were of excellent quality, such as Minty had used at the Hall. With a shock, she realised that they had indeed come from her own supply of paper at the Hall. From Maxine, to be precise. Or rather, it had been typed by someone—a secretary?—and signed by Maxine in a spiky hand.

> *Dear Mrs Sands,*
>
> *I must apologise for having turned you out of your charming home. Will you give me a chance to make amends? As you may know, we are busy filming at the moment, but I'm not needed till noon, so would you come and have a cup of coffee with me at eleven? I'll send the car for you so that you have no trouble getting in. I have a proposition to put to you which I trust you will accept.*
>
> *Yours,*
> *Maxine*

The note threw Minty into a state of doubt. She read it over twice. The language was that of a slightly old-fashioned, punctilious hostess. It spoke of practised charm. It wasn't anything like the kind of thing Minty had imagined would come from a pop star. It was disarming. Perhaps the woman would be easier to deal with than everyone had indicated?

Maxine had a proposal for her? Whatever could it be?

She would go. Of course.

Meanwhile she had Jim to check on—still asleep, poor man. And phone calls to make.

She managed to catch Annie Phillips at home. "Dear Annie, may I come up to see you some time today? There's so much to discuss ..."

"I'm quite all right," said Annie in a forbidding tone.

"I'm sure you are," said Minty, trying to soothe.

"I've lived alone and I'll die alone. Not that I'm dying. Not the least of it."

"No, indeed."

"The way gossip takes off! Ridiculous! A tiny lump, a course of radiotherapy. I suppose Serafina told you."

"No. I heard it from two other people."

Silence. Annie said in a softer tone, "I'm sorry, Minty. I get so tired of people asking me how I am. I really am all right. The doctors said there's absolutely nothing to worry about now, provided I have my check-ups on time."

"I'm glad. Life wouldn't be the same without you telling me what to do."

"You don't need telling. Patrick says that you're making a good recovery. How are things up at the Hall?"

"I don't know. They won't let me in to see."

"That's unpardonable. Why ever not? You should sort it out with Mr Hatton. Oh, and by the way, I gather Clive's been having trouble with Neville. Do you know what that's all about?"

"A something and a nothing. Mr Hatton ought to have taken Neville's advice on a financial matter but didn't. I've sorted it. Perhaps I can get hold of Mr Hatton and we could come out to see you this afternoon ..."

"I'm going up to Town for a meeting this afternoon." More silence. "Minty, I think you'd better count me out for the time being. We're preparing a report for the Minister of Education which has to be in next month."

Minty had to accept that Annie was not going to help her. "Ring me when you get back and I'll come out to see you. Look after yourself, won't you?"

Chapter Ten

Minty put the phone down and went up to check on Jim. He was stirring, but only just. She helped him to the bathroom, took his dirty shirt down to Serafina to wash and found him a clean one of Patrick's to wear. He stayed in the bathroom so long that she had time to make another couple of phone calls.

First to Carol. Carol was busy with a customer but was amused to hear Minty's reaction to her proposed disguise. Then to the vicarage. The phone rang and rang and no answerphone clicked in. Minty wrote out a cheque and put it in an envelope, asking Elizabeth to deliver it to Cecil.

She rang the pub and asked if Alice was still there. She was and came to the phone to say that all was well. She'd heard nothing from the Hall. Dwayne had gone up to work there as usual, but the pub was short-handed with all the extra trade that the festival was bringing in, so Alice had been told that they could stay on there as long as they liked. All she had to do was find someone to look after Marie during the day, which she could do now she was earning a proper wage.

So Alice didn't know she was supposed to be getting the sack. Well, that was one thing Minty could put right when she met Maxine.

She sorted out a well-cut linen dress in her favourite blue and was brushing out her hair prior to putting it up when Jim lurched out of the bathroom, holding his head in both hands. She got him into his clothes with some difficulty, treating him as one does a toddler. "No, this arm goes through here … see?" Then she soothed him down the stairs and got some fresh coffee and some aspirin for him. He looked around as if he'd never seen Patrick's rooms before.

He was dry-eyed. Empty-eyed.

Minty sat beside him. "Patrick's gone into the office. He'll ring when he can."

He drank coffee, swallowed aspirins. Didn't speak.

Minty was reminded that Patrick hadn't spoken for days after she'd lost their child. She patted Jim's hand. Sat with him in silence.

There was no clock on the mantelpiece now. A pity. Patrick's clock had gone up to the Hall and was on the mantelpiece in their cool green sitting room there. Minty hoped that dear Reggie had remembered to wind it. Reggie had been her father's driver and was now Houseman in charge of so many practical things around the Hall. Would Maxine be sending Reggie down to collect her? Hm. Probably. He'd be coming for her soon, and she still hadn't put any lipstick on or done her hair.

Which was more important: sitting with Jim, or doing her make-up?

She held back a sigh. She was sure Maxine would be beautifully presented and make Minty feel like a drab little girl.

Jim sat on. Now and then he rubbed the back of his neck and sighed.

Minty looked at her watch. And then beyond her watch to her feet, which were in bedroom slippers. She tried to remember where her good blue sandals might be ... and her matching handbag from Florence.

Jim said, "Got any whisky?"

She shook her head. Patrick liked a bottle of good wine occasionally but rarely drank anything else. Any wine which had once been here was now up at the Hall.

Jim lurched to his feet and steadied himself. His neck muscles thickened and his colour rose. He was working himself up to express his rage and misery. He swept the vase of tulips off the mantelpiece and then went for the geranium in the pot on the dining table, picking it up and throwing it at the wall, where it smashed, scarlet petals floating down and settling on the floorboards. Carol would be cross. Minty made a mental note to see that Carol was properly reimbursed.

"Anthea ... hates ... red ... flowers!" He screamed, fists raised to heaven. "She can't leave me like this!"

"No, I know." Minty tried to put her arms around him, but he fought her off, blundering around the room. The lamp on the coffee table was next to go, swept off, shattering to pieces. Next he picked up a book which Patrick had brought in with him last night and left behind. He tore at it, wrenching at it, fighting it. Finally the binding gave way and he was able to tear leaves out and tear and tear until there was nothing left.

Serafina marched in. "Shall I phone Patrick?"

Minty shook her head. "He'll be in court. We've got to manage ourselves."

Elizabeth arrived, just in time to see Jim attacking the cushions on the settee, throwing them around, trying to tear them apart. He knocked over the coffee table and almost fell. Minty caught him and held him though he tried to make her let go. His first fury was beginning to abate. He began to cry in great jerking breaths ...

"She ... can't ... go ... she can't just ... go like that!"

Minty held him fast, taking one or two nasty punches to her body as she did.

Elizabeth said, "I've never seen such a disgraceful—"

"Hush, Elizabeth," said Minty. "Let him mourn in his own way. Come on now, Jim. Sit down here. Anthea was such a lovely girl, wasn't she ...?" Serafina picked up the ill-treated cushions and replaced them on the settee so that Minty could ease Jim to sit there with her.

"You have no idea how I feel!"

"True. Very true. Tell me about her ..."

Elizabeth said, "There's the car come from the Hall for you, Mrs Sands. They won't like being kept waiting."

Serafina took over from Minty. "There, there. We've got to let Minty go. You stay with Serafina, now ... go on, Minty. I'll stay with him till he's calmer."

"Elizabeth, will you tell them I'll be down in a minute?"

Minty tried to shake the creases out of her linen dress, but it was no good. Linen always did crease badly, even when it was mixed with something else and not supposed to. She ran up the stairs. Wash hands and face. Find another dress. Anything. The moss-green she'd worn the other day. Suitable, but ... where were her sandals? Those old ones would have to do. No time to put tights on, and it was going to be a warm day, anyway, so perhaps that didn't matter. Her hair was a mess. She brushed it out quickly, used a couple of combs to hold it back from her face. Pearl stud earrings.

Handbag. Keys. Lipstick. A quick swipe with the lipstick.

Try to collect her thoughts. What must she remember? Alice and Dwayne. They mustn't suffer. Nero must be curbed somehow.

She sped down the stairs again. Serafina was coping well. Minty blew her a kiss and ran down the next flight. Elizabeth was on the phone, but the front door was open and there was Reggie—dear Reggie—standing by her father's beautiful big car, holding the door open for her.

Reggie was wearing his chauffeur's uniform instead of his usual casual jeans and sweatshirt. He stood, cap in hand, eyes focused somewhere above her, to hand her into the car. Under normal circumstances he'd have shaken her hand warmly, asked how she was feeling. But these circumstances weren't normal, and by his attitude he was telling her that this morning he had to play the part of impersonal servant.

She said, "Nice to see you again, Reggie."

She stepped into the back of the car, noticing that there was someone else already there. Perhaps this other person accounted for the formality in Reggie's manner.

"Axel Schutz. Maxine's manager." He had a slight accent and was perhaps of middle-European descent. He was a pale man with thinning, beige-coloured hair, and he wore a cream linen suit. Also creased, Minty noticed. He looked to be about fifty, and there was a puffy look to his features. Heart condition?

His eyes were the palest blue Minty had ever seen, far paler than hers. His voice was a monotone. He flicked his eyes all over her, head, dress, ankles and feet. His manner made her uneasy. She thought this man probably ate little girls like her for breakfast and wondered for the first time if she'd been foolish to accept Maxine's invitation to the Hall.

"Araminta Cardale Sands. I'm sorry to have kept you waiting."

He touched her hand and dropped it. His hand was moist, clammy. "A beautiful day."

A nasty thought: Was he a knee-groper? She waited till his hand touched her knee—by accident, of course. Then moved her knee away. His knee followed, so she lifted her hand in the air and held it suspended, ready to slap. He got the message and withdrew to the corner of the car.

He put dark glasses on and stared ahead. She kept her eyes ahead, too. Would he speak? Apologise?

No, he wouldn't. Then she got it. Hugh had said a pale slug of a man from the Hall had wanted to buy a black cockerel. Was this the man? Ugh!

She saw that Reggie's back was rigid through the sliding glass partition that she'd never seen pulled across before. Her father and Reggie had been good friends, and she'd always thought Reggie liked her, too. Mr Schutz might be there to make sure that Reggie made no complaints to the Lady of the Hall, but Reggie was telling Minty a great deal through the simplest of body language.

They swept down through the village and through open gates — the security men, one on either side, holding them open till they were inside the Park. They took the route round to the gravel in front of the west wing, where cars were usually banned to preserve the carefully raked gravel. There were no other cars in sight.

Minty looked for signs of disorder, but there were none. The main door into the oak-beamed Great Hall was closed.

As Reggie held the door open for Minty to alight, Mr Schutz climbed nimbly out of the other side. He said, "Maxine wants you to know how much she appreciates the view of the Park from the south side of the house." He led the way at a fast trot round the corner of the great house, walking so fast that Minty had no opportunity to speak to Reggie.

Minty's suite was on the top floor of the south front. Why were they not going through the house to reach it?

On the south side there was a wide, stone-flagged terrace overlooked by the great State Rooms. An elaborate tent, lined with pink silk, had been set up on the terrace. Walking into it from the bright sunlight outside, Minty found it hard at first to see what was inside.

The tent was almost as big as the Chinese Room behind it. A silken carpet had been laid on the flagstones, and the place had been furnished with a daybed from the Red Room, some of Patrick's comfortable Edwardian chairs and two mahogany side tables.

Speakers had been set up on either side of the daybed, and there was a pulse of music in the air, hardly audible yet insidious. As was the curl of incense from a pierced china pot nearby — taken from the Chinese Room and never, to Minty's knowledge, used before. Minty had an unusually keen sense of smell, and the incense clogged her nostrils, threatening to choke her. She could feel it rise to her brain and automatically stepped back towards the light.

A beautiful girl rose from the daybed and came towards her. "You must be the Lady of the Hall. Forgive me, but you are not at all what I expected. I don't think you'd be interested in taking part in one of our videos, would you?"

Minty blinked. The word "odalisque" slid into her mind. Though she was not entirely sure what the word meant, she imagined something exotic and seductive.

For a moment she thought Axel had made a mistake in bringing her to the tent, for this girl was nothing like the poster Minty had seen in the village. Her hair was long and straight, as fine and blonde as Minty's, but probably silkier. It swung far below her waist, unconfined. Then Minty saw that the hair must be a wig, for the girl's other features were the same. She had high Slavic cheekbones and long-tailed, startlingly blue eyes. Her mouth was a luscious shape, very full, revealing perfect teeth. She had no eyebrows at all, unlike the girl in the poster.

Maxine's voice was soft and warm, inviting Minty to laugh with her at their unusual situation. The woman carried the scent of musk with her as she moved. More scent! Also very strong.

Maxine was exquisite: slender and sinuous. She wore a sheer, pale blue robe over … well, nothing at all. Minty's mind told her that of course the woman was wearing a body-stocking. Probably.

Maxine took hold of Minty's hand and drew her close. Minty did not resist.

Maxine pressed Minty's hand in both of hers. "They told me you were beautiful and you are, I suppose … in a restrained way. They told me your eyes were blue, but they aren't sapphire blue, as I'd imagined. I don't think I could copy your colouring."

"I'm not really beautiful. Not like you," said Minty, aware of the haste in which she'd prepared for this meeting. Her lack of grooming contrasted with Maxine's. Maxine was a polished jewel, and Minty a rough-cast semi-precious stone.

Maxine was slightly taller than Minty, who only now realised that she'd put on a pair of flat sandals instead of the heeled ones she'd been looking for. There was something about Maxine which reminded you of sex. Images twined through Minty's mind, of bodies encircling one another on a great bed. The bodies were both white ... and then one of them became black, and Minty wondered if Nero frequented this woman's bed.

Maxine gestured to the Park. "I think you'll agree I've been looking after this well."

Standing this far back, Minty could only see the ornamental stone urns on the balustrade. They'd been filled with flowers, though not ones which Minty would have expected Hodge, her head gardener, to use. Hodge was a geranium-and-lobelia man. Here were great stands of calla lilies and trailing exotica which Minty had seen in catalogues but never in the flesh. There were more urns at the corners of the tent, filled this time with blue agapanthus, which surely must have been forced to be out at this time of the year.

Minty tried to dispel the effect the incense fumes were having on her. She said, quite truthfully, "Superb." A glass was handed to her of something that looked like orange juice but with bubbles in it. She thought the drink might clear her head and gulped down a couple of mouthfuls before she remembered Patrick had always warned her about drinks like that, which might look harmless but were sometimes laced with champagne. She wouldn't drink any more of it.

At the back of the tent a buffet had been laid out, with a miniature refrigerator on top of it. A woman in a black dress was unobtrusively serving the same drink to Maxine. A sort of stile had been built over the window-sill into the Chinese Room behind, so that someone could reach the terrace without going all the way round the house to the front door. An innovation, but a good one.

"You can't see from there," said Maxine, urging Minty to the front of the tent. "I have sensitive skin and have to keep out of the sun, but you go and look."

Minty stepped to the balustrade, shading her eyes. From the terrace the ground swept down in a long grassy slope to the man-made lake, fringed with yellow irises. Beyond the lake rose a huge semi-circular construction sheltering a large stage. Men were swarming all over it. The *tap tap* of hammers echoed up the slope. Huge screens were being set up flanking the main stage. An area between the stage and the lake had been cordoned off and men were at work there, too, though Minty couldn't see exactly what they were doing.

Behind the stage a semi-circle had been fenced off. Men were busy there, setting up a number of tents, some small and some larger. Caravans were being pulled onto the site by jeeps. Machines were excavating trenches ... for power lines?

To the extreme right as she looked down the slope was another stage, not nearly as large as the one by the lake, and with fewer men working on it.

Minty was amazed. "How ever many men does it take to set this up?"

"A small army," said Maxine, amused. "Look, here come the toilets. To be avoided at all costs, I can tell you. We performers have our own in the dressing-rooms, of course." Lorry after lorry, fitted with cranes, were pounding onto the site, lifting out a line of what looked like sentry boxes and setting them down some distance from the stage.

"The beer tents will be set up this afternoon, one on either side of the arena," said Maxine. "I must say Clive has organised everything pretty well."

Minty didn't know how to reply to that. She looked at the drink in her hand and decided she didn't want to risk any more of it, so put it down on a nearby table—taken from the Jacobean State Bedroom.

"You'd prefer coffee? A cold drink?"

Minty shook her head. "No, thank you. I'm glad you invited me here today, because ..."

Maxine placed her hand on Minty's arm. "You must have been upset, returning to find us in your home. I can imagine how you felt."

Minty wondered if she were in Wonderland. This woman was nothing like the terror she'd been made out to be. Only then she remembered Iris' caution, Alice's fear, Carol's bravado. The back of Reggie's neck.

"You're a genuine English lady," murmured Maxine, her hand warm on Minty's arm, her scent filling her nostrils. "Do you think you could teach me how to play the part?"

Minty avoided answering that one. She said, "We have one or two things to discuss. I believe that my half-sister invited you to stay on the understanding that ..."

Maxine put her arm around Minty's shoulders. "A talented girl. I promised her her chance at stardom, and she shall have it. Aren't you proud of her?"

Minty thought of asking Maxine if she really thought Gemma had talent, but decided it was irrelevant. "I'd have been even more proud if she'd asked my permission."

Maxine gave her a friendly hug, which turned Minty's mind to bed once more. How did Maxine do that? Was it some fault in Minty that Maxine made her think of sex?

Maxine said, "Ah, poor little Gemma. She was so distressed, so embarrassed when she heard you were returning early. I told her, your big sister will not refuse you your chance at fame, will she? She will be happy for you." A slight accent? French? No, but something like it.

"That's between her and me. Where's Gemma now?"

"Filming in the courtyard. They'll be needing me soon, but till then let's sit down and get to know one another. I hear you've been very ill and are still not recovered. I can't imagine how it would be to lose your baby and then discover you're barren and can't have another ..."

Minty took half a step back. The tent roof seemed to come down upon her, envelop her in its dusky shadows; the black door opened wide, and she was about to plunge down into it. She fought the darkness back. *Save me, Lord! Out of the depths I cry to Thee!*

The darkness rolled back and she gasped with relief, but the word "barren" continued to thunder through her head. Barren. No more children. No one had told her that. Perhaps they hadn't dared. Was it true? If it was true, Patrick would have protected her from the knowledge, waiting to tell her till she was better ...

Barren! Never to hold a child of her own in her arms?

It was a crushing blow. She put both hands to her head and held on tightly.

Barren. Barren ...

Maxine was guiding her to the daybed, urging her to sit, to drink something. Her scent was overpowering. Maxine's body had become soft, offering the promise of comfort.

Minty preferred Patrick's brand of comfort.

Shakily, she pushed Maxine away. That terrible word continued to echo through her head. She needed time to absorb the pain. To think about what this meant. She needed to be alone, to scream and cry ... as Jim had done and for the same reason. She also was bereaved.

Patrick? How long would he stay with her, knowing she couldn't now bear him a child?

She shuddered. She couldn't think clearly. The musky scent was affecting her brain.

Maxine's arm held her close, comforting her. "You didn't know? Oh, my poor sweet girl. What a shame. I expect you feel like committing suicide at the moment. I wonder why they didn't tell you. I suppose they didn't want to upset you. But you had a right to know. It's going to affect your whole life, isn't it? You can't look at things the same way now, as you might have done if you had children to look forward to ..."

Minty heard her and didn't hear her. It was as if she was hearing two voices at once. Maxine's voice, commiserating with her, and ... another voice. But that second voice was so faint that she couldn't quite make out what it was saying. And then she did hear it. To her surprise, it was her uncle's voice. He must be praying in church, and he was saying something about keeping good company.

No, that was all wrong. That bit about avoiding bad company had been in the Bible reading notes that morning. And she couldn't possibly hear her uncle's voice from where she was now.

"There, now. There, now." Maxine was stroking Minty's arms. "You see, it's not so bad when you've accepted it, is it? I can tell you that a life without children has a great deal to recommend it. You are young and could be pretty if you took a little trouble with yourself. Go round the world. Drown yourself in good works. How does your husband feel about it? He probably feels as I do. Children can tie you down so. He's an attractive man, I hear. I'd like to meet him some time."

Minty pushed herself upright. She'd been wounded almost to death, but she still had her responsibilities. Doggedly she clung to them. Barren or not, she still had a job to do, the Hall and its people to protect. "I'm looking forward to coming back home."

"Ah. That." Maxine lifted her heavy mane of hair from the back of her neck and shook it out in a shining fall. Her action reminded Minty of a shampoo advert. "I've taken a fancy to this place. I can be myself here, without people bothering me. I can film in peace and even hold my own gigs here. Since you won't be having any children to pass it on to, how much do you want for it?"

Another shock. How many more shocks could she take? At least there was an easy answer to this one. Minty stood up, steadying herself. "The Hall is not for sale."

"Oh, come. There's a price for everything. Name yours."

Minty tried to smile and knew she'd only made it as far as a grimace. "I can't sell the Hall. Perhaps you don't know about these things, but there's an entail on it, which means that I only hold it in trust. I can't sell, and if I don't have any children it passes to a relative."

"I was misinformed," said Maxine. The lines of her face sharpened, and she shot a darting glance back at the open window of the room behind them. "Very well, then. I'll rent it from you for, say, ten years."

Minty stiffened her spine. She was so badly wounded in spirit that she thought she'd keel over in a minute, but her only hope of comfort in the future must lie in getting the Hall back.

"I can understand that you think everything in the world is for sale. I understand that you have more money than I have. But you're up against something here which you may not have come across before. I love this place. My family have lived here for centuries. It's my home. So let's talk about when you're going to leave. I have seen a copy of the contract and ..."

"How?" Almost the woman frowned and she shot another dark look behind her. "Well, never mind that now. I've no idea when I shall feel like moving on. We're only half-way through making the video. Then there is the festival at which I am the star attraction. After that I shall be so exhausted that I shall need a good long rest."

"The contract stipulates suitable accommodation for yourself and six members of your household ..."

"I regard my present accommodation as suitable, and naturally we have extra people here if we are to make a video which will include Gemma."

Stalemate. Minty didn't know how to proceed. She couldn't think clearly. That musky scent ...

"I'll tell you what I'll do," said Maxine. "I gather my darling Nero has been injured by one of your girls. Naturally she's been sacked. I was going to sue her for damages. I suggest that you pay me compensation for the money we lost when Nero couldn't work, and we'll drop the charges against her."

Minty couldn't see any point in arguing about details. If she said that Nero had also attacked her, she herself would be in line for damages. She realised she wasn't thinking clearly. She'd been mentally crippled by the news that she was barren. Why hadn't Patrick told her? Out of pity, presumably.

She said, "I'm not playing games with you."

Maxine smiled, her tongue licking her lower lip. "You'd lose if you did. I always win. I want the Hall and I intend to have it."

Minty made it to the front of the tent, out into the sun. She put out her hands to steady herself on the balustrade. The stonework was comforting. She felt the roughness of it under her palm. Reassuring. *Patrick, where are you when I need you?*

She said, "I must go."

"Axel, show Mrs Sands out," said Maxine.

The pale-faced manager appeared from nowhere and gestured for Minty to follow him. She did so. Along the terrace. Glancing up at the tower. At the top of that tower was the family's chapel. Minty longed to be up there now, pouring out her grief to God, asking for strength to deal with this new blow, this almost fatal blow.

Reggie was polishing the car by the front door. He opened the rear door of the car and she got in, closely followed by the manager. They drove off in silence. Minty couldn't think. Couldn't see straight. Her nails dug into her palms. Later, she'd find that she'd drawn blood.

Axel didn't speak during the short journey, but he watched her through his sun-glasses. She looked out of the window, avoiding his gaze. At least he didn't try to put his hand on her knee again.

Reggie drew up outside Patrick's house. He got out and held the door open for her. She got out, too. The manager said to Reggie, "Back to the Hall."

"Your pardon, Mr Schutz," said Reggie, at his most polite. "I've an errand to run for Chef and then it's my lunch hour. If you'd care to wait for about an hour?"

Mr Schutz was not pleased but said, "Drop me at the bottom of the village then, and I'll walk the rest of the way." Reggie got back into the car and drove off, leaving Minty standing on the pavement.

Chapter Eleven

The sun was hot on Minty's head.

The village street straggled down the hill to the bridge over the river, with buildings of all periods and sizes jostling together. Golden Cotswold stone predominated, but there were some late Victorian buildings. By contrast Patrick's beautiful Georgian house was of mellow red brick. Across the road was the cast-iron pillared arcade of shops in which the Chinese restaurant, Carol's antique shop and the new coffee shop were sited. All three looked busy.

The large planters placed at intervals on the wide pavement were full of flowers, trailing geraniums, diascias, osteospermums, lobelias, silver-leafed cinerarias. Pretty. Only someone had pulled out half the plants from the nearest display and dumped them on the pavement, leaving drink cans and plastic food wrappings there instead.

They were not going to make the Prettiest Village final this year.

Minty went into the cool hallway of Patrick's house, because she couldn't think what else to do.

Elizabeth popped out of her office, scolding. "Mr Patrick's been trying to get you on the phone but couldn't get through."

Minty blinked. Her hand went to her handbag. Did she have her newly charged mobile phone with her? No. What had she done with it? Had it fallen out of her pocket when she undressed last night? Had she transferred it to the blue dress she'd worn earlier? And then ... she'd changed again to go up to the Hall. So where was it? She couldn't think. She needed to speak to Patrick urgently. "Can I phone him back?"

"He'll be in court," said Elizabeth, with satisfaction. "But your sister's here to see you, waiting in Mr Patrick's office. And I don't like to complain, but it would be a good thing if you took Mr Jim back to his own home, for I can't be doing with his shouting and disturbing me all the time."

Minty glanced up the stairs, from which she could indeed hear Jim shouting and cursing. Poor man. Could Serafina cope? Minty didn't think she was able to bear anything more at that moment. *I expect you feel like committing suicide.* Now where had that voice come from?

"Welcome back, darling." Minty was enveloped in a musky scent — just like Maxine's? — hugged and dragged into Patrick's office. "Stand back and let me look at you. Oh dear, you do look peaky still. I thought you'd be quite your old self again, after all this time. But isn't it exciting? Aren't you thrilled with what's happening? I am. I never in my wildest dreams thought ..."

Her voice faded out as Minty turned Gemma round to face the window. Gemma tried to laugh. Not very successfully. She'd always had a model's slender proportions, but now she was almost gaunt, and her wonderful red hair had been cropped to a shadow on her skull.

"Don't look at me like that, Minty. It's for the filming, you see. Maxine said we couldn't have two redheads on set so I wear wigs, whatever she thinks best for that day's filming."

Maxine was a redhead? Minty remembered a flowing mane of silky blonde hair and before that, black curls pictured in the poster. Were they both wigs? And what about those startling blue eyes? Had they been contact lenses? If so, why?

Maxine had made some remark about having expected Minty to have eyes of a different blue. Had the woman deliberately made herself up to be a more polished, more beautiful version of Minty? To make her feel inferior? To give herself an edge in their discussions about the Hall?

Minty sat down and passed trembling hands back over her forehead, pushing her hair back from her temples. What was the matter with her? *You must feel like committing suicide ...*

"Can you make me some coffee, Gemma?" Patrick had his own coffee-making machine in his office. He drank a lot of coffee when he was working.

Gemma made a helpless gesture. "Darling, would I know how? Shall I get Elizabeth to make you some? I must say, I don't think it was at all a good idea of yours to come back early. You look as bad as when you came out of hospital."

Thank you, Gemma, for those kind words.

The door opened and Serafina eased herself in with a tray containing one cup of coffee, a mobile phone and some biscuits, which she placed in front of Minty. Serafina ignored Gemma. She'd never had any time for her. Serafina's light lily-of-the-valley perfume couldn't compete with Gemma's heavier scent. The scent of Maxine.

Serafina said, "Jim's not too good. I've called the doctor to see if he could visit, but he can't. He said he'd get back to me, advise me what to do. Patrick rang. He got through to me when he couldn't reach you. Said he was worried about you. He said he'd try to get back this lunchtime if he could. I found your mobile on the floor upstairs."

Minty held onto Serafina's arm, which unaccountably seemed to have got round her. She bowed her head, resting against the older woman for a moment. Then pulled herself upright and tried to smile at Serafina. "Thank you, dear Serafina. I'll be up to see to Jim in a minute."

Serafina nodded, sent Gemma a look of contempt and left as quietly as she'd come.

Minty managed to reach for the coffee a split second before Gemma did. "Did you know that Maxine wants the Hall—for good?" Her hands were shaking, so she used both to hold the cup.

"You should let her have it. Why not?"

Minty drank the coffee and felt marginally better. How was she to deal with Gemma? The girl was so gaunt she'd lost all her beauty. Gemma was paying a high price for her moment of fame. If she was indeed getting any fame out of it, which Minty was beginning to wonder.

"Gemma, you're not looking well …"

"I could say the same about you. Now don't go on at me. I did it all for the best, and you're only cross because you're not going to get the same chance of fame and fortune as me."

Minty closed her eyes for a moment. She'd never wanted fame or fortune. All she'd wanted was the work God had set for her to do at Eden Hall … and Patrick … and a baby. Barren. She was screaming inside. It was tearing her apart. Why hadn't Patrick told her? Something was knocking at the back of her mind about Patrick and a baby, but she couldn't think what it was. She turned back to Gemma, making an effort to seem calm.

"You can't deny you've exceeded your brief—"

"What of it? You're going to come out of it smelling of roses, aren't you? Lots more lolly to throw around. As if our father hadn't left you well off, anyway. I have to look to the future, carve out a career for myself. Maxine has been wonderful to me. So patient. I've learned how to stand in for her while they're setting up, and I'm allowed to appear in all the background shots, and some day when I've had some singing lessons, she'll give me a chance in the backing group."

Minty wanted to yell at the girl. Couldn't she see how Maxine was taking advantage of her? But Minty didn't. She even managed to feel sorry for Gemma. A little.

She said, "For your chance of fame, you've sacrificed something that doesn't belong to you. My home. If Maxine had been confined to the west wing which is set up for visitors, then it wouldn't be so bad ... though I don't think I'd ever have given permission for such a big event as this festival to take place at Eden Hall. We've no experience of such things and ..."

"Clive has." A sullen look.

"Perhaps. But Mr Hatton's only been in the place five minutes, and I'm not at all convinced ..."

"Oh, you're so old-fashioned. Move with the times, girl! Get a life!"

A life. One lost baby. And no more to come. I wish I could think straight. Patrick, I need you!

She tried reason. "Gemma, it's bad business practice to launch into something as big as this without proper provision for all eventualities. Suppose something goes wrong and we make a loss?"

Gemma shrugged. "You can stand it."

Minty was grave. "So you've considered that we could make a loss?"

"Not with Maxine topping the bill. Without her, yes."

"Are you really prepared to sell your soul for a possible ten minutes in the limelight?"

Gemma was defiant. "You can't stop it now."

"I realise that. So. We must have a meeting soon to discuss things like insurance and extra policing..."

"Boring, boring! Count me out."

Minty was getting annoyed. "Do you want to continue being in charge of events at the Hall or don't you?"

Gemma shrugged again. "If Maxine buys or rents the place, there won't be any more events."

"That won't happen," said Minty, feeling more tired than ever.

"Can I go now?" Gemma was fidgeting to be off. "We're filming again this afternoon, and I have to be in make-up in half an hour's time."

She left.

Minty put her head in her hands and sobbed once. Then tried to master herself. It would do no good to give way to grief. She must think about her responsibilities instead. So many people were looking to her for a lead, and she didn't know what to do about any of them.

Here came another of her responsibilities. Alice tapped on the door and came in. Alice needed reassurance that her job was safe, and Minty couldn't give it to her. How had it happened that she had lost control of her employees?

"Alice, I've been up to the Hall to see Maxine, but I've no good news for you yet. Maxine has asked Mr Hatton to sack you both. Naturally I don't agree with that, but—it's difficult. I think the best we can do is to give you and Dwayne a fortnight's holiday."

"Dwayne's needed on the electrics up at the Hall, and I won't be pushed out when I've done nothing wrong."

"I agree. I'm trying to get hold of Mr Hatton, to talk to him about it."

Alice eyed her with compassion. "You look worn out, Minty. You've come back too soon."

"I'll be all right, but I'm worried about you. I had an encounter with Nero myself last night, and I can see what he's like. You're safe at the pub for the time being, aren't you?"

Alice nodded. "I only came up to give you a message from Reggie. He's in the snug at the back of the pub, on his lunch break. Can you pop down to see him?"

"Straight away." Minty was annoyed with herself. Reggie had made it clear to her where he'd be this lunchtime and she'd allowed herself to get so worked up that she'd forgotten. What else had she forgotten? Her mobile. She turned it on and put it in her pocket.

What about Jim? Patrick must be torn into so many pieces at the moment, having to decide whether he ought to be in court, or with Minty, or Jim. Yet he kept his cool and she must keep hers. Why was her mind still so muzzy? She made an effort to push the screaming wound made by the word "barren" into the back of her mind and concentrate on the next thing. Jim. Then Reggie.

"Give me a minute to check on something, Alice, and I'll be right with you."

She ran upstairs to find Serafina standing over Jim, with a glass of water in her hand. Jim had been crying. Serafina was soothing him, patting his shoulder. Jim relaxed, his head lolling back on the settee, closing his eyes.

Serafina drew Minty into the kitchen, closing the door behind them.

"The doctor's receptionist phoned back. The doctor can't get away, but he recommended giving Jim some strong pain-killers. Which I have done. He should be all right for a bit now."

Minty nodded. She ran back down the stairs, checked that her mobile really was switched on and followed Alice through Patrick's pretty garden and down the lane to the garden of the pub. The weather had stayed fine and there were a lot of people in the garden, sitting at tables under umbrellas. The small play area for children was heaving with kids.

Minty remembered that she'd been trying for some time to get a new playground set up for children on the Village Green. This had been opposed by the Cricket Club, who really didn't need the whole Green but were quoting tradition at her. If she did manage to convince them and the festival did make some money, then she could go ahead with that. She thought of the hundreds of men employed on the site in the Park and shuddered. However much was all this costing?

Alice led Minty through the back door of the pub, through the dimness of ancient passages, and then by way of an unobtrusive door into the snug, a small, panelled room with a ceiling dyed khaki from centuries of smoking. It was hot in here, despite the whirr of a modern fan.

Reggie had taken off his cap and unbuttoned his tight chauffeur's uniform. He'd nearly finished the half pint of lager he'd allowed himself and was licking his finger to clean up the crumbs from his sandwich.

Minty realised she was hungry, too. Alice said she'd fetch Minty something tasty and left them. The only other occupants of the room were a couple of domino players in their eighties.

Reggie half rose from his seat on seeing Minty, but she stopped him. Kissed his cheek, accepted a half-embarrassed but hearty hug and sat down beside him.

"It's so good to see you again," she said.

"Me, too," was all the inarticulate Reggie could manage, but the warmth of his grin underlined the message. "You worried me, going up there 'smorning. Axel's a nasty piece of work, but that Maxine is a leech. Sucks the life outa people. You still alive, are you?"

Minty nodded. "Just."

"You should see us! Bobbing and bowing and saying 'Yes, ma'am.' We never bobbed and bowed to your father for all he was a great man, God bless him, and we never bobbed to you, neither."

Minty shook her head. They hadn't. No. But they'd not been afraid of Sir Micah, nor of her. They'd trusted her and they'd been loyal. Were they loyal to Maxine? She thought of Hugh's judgement on a man like Clive Hatton ... shot in the back by his own men. Would they shoot Maxine in the back? Metaphorically speaking, of course.

Reggie said, "You wouldn't believe it if I told you what's going on up at the Hall. You gotta see it yourself. Then you can stop it. Hodge and I and Chef, we've put in a spot of time praying for you to come back. Well, it's maybe not what you'd call praying, 'cos I don't know the proper words and Hodge's language is a bit Anglo-Saxon, if you know what I mean. But his heart's in the right place and he can't abide what she's done to his urns. We don't go to church, mind. But Chef says wishing won't do it. We've got to ask God to do something about it. It's worked, 'cos He's brought you back."

Reggie delved into pockets. "Got it somewhere. Here 'tis." He put an identity badge on a chain on the table and slid it over to her. The photograph on it was of a young woman with fair hair tied up in a ponytail. "Agency girl. Braver than most. Spoke her mind. Got the sack. Took her to the station and put her on a train yesterday. She kept her badge by mistake and gave it to me to give back to Hatton. I told Hatton she'd forgotten to hand it in and must have it with her still. Thought you might find it useful."

Minty took it with a nod. Was her mobile switched on? Yes, it was.

Alice came in with a half pint of shandy and a hot bacon sandwich for Minty. She set to work on it.

Reggie looked at his watch. "Two ways in that I can see. Cadge a lift with supplies. That's Hodge's idea. Problem: it'd have to be with someone as knows you and isn't afraid of losing Maxine's custom. Florist, maybe? Fruit and veg man? Chef's idea was you could go in through tent city if you dress down a bit. Wander around. Mebbe carry a clipboard, say you're checking on the hot dog stands or something. Then come up to the house saying you've got to take the results through to Hatton."

"Why can't *you* tell me what's going on?"

He shuddered. "'Cos I can't believe it. I've gotta go. I'd take you in myself, but they'd spot you straight away."

"What could they do, even if they did spot me?"

"Turf you out. Pretend as they don't know who you are. Like they did the first day, only then I reckon they really didn't know. Then I'd be for the chop, too. And you need me on the inside."

Minty nodded. He buttoned himself up, sighing, for it was a hot day, took his cap and made himself scarce.

Minty checked her phone. Still on. Still no messages. She sat on in the dimness of the snug, trying to come to terms with what Maxine had told her. Praying. Almost falling asleep ... till she was woken by her phone. She started upright, noticing that the tables had all been cleared around her and the other occupants of the snug had vanished.

"Minty?" Patrick, sounding worried.

"Patrick, am I really ...?" She couldn't get the word out.

"Minty? You still there? What's happened? Is Serafina there? Look, I'll get someone to take over here and come and ..."

"No. I'm all right. Just shocked. I've just heard I can't have any more children."

"WHAT? Who ...? What the ...?"

She held her breath.

Patrick brought his voice down from on high. "Now you listen to me, my girl. That's a wicked lie and ... I don't understand ... who said that?"

She began to let her breath out slowly. "Maxine." She discovered she was trembling.

"WHAT!" His voice climbed again. And this was Patrick, who never lost his cool.

She could feel herself begin to uncoil. "It's not true? You see, when she told me that, I ... freaked out, I suppose." She felt tears begin to slide down her cheeks. "I've never been able to remember much of what happened ... after. Not what the doctors said. Nothing."

Patrick bit his words out. "Right. Are you listening now? In words of one syllable. You'd lost a lot of blood. Perhaps banged your head, which accounted for your loss of memory around the time of the accident. They said medication would help with your depression, but it didn't, which was why I took you out of the hospital and bore you away. They said you'd take time to heal. They said it would be better if you didn't get pregnant again for six months. Why do you think I was always so careful when we made love? That is, until ..."

"Of course! I thought something was wrong with what Maxine said, but she confused me so much that I ..."

"Did you eat or drink anything while you were there?"

"She gave me a drink, but I didn't like it and put it down. No, I think it was the incense. It was stifling, and you know how badly I react to strong scents. I couldn't think straight. She lied with such conviction, and I was so befuddled, but I ought to have seen through it. If I'd been thinking clearly, I would have. You've always been so careful right up to ... ah, you're thinking of the other night at the cottage? Whoops!" said Minty, half crying and half hysterical with relief. "You weren't so careful then, were you? That's why you scolded me?"

"I'd do a lot more than scold you if I were with you now. I'd put you over my knee and ... giving me such a fright!" Silence. A calming, peace-bringing silence.

She said, "I'm beginning to recover. She knocked me out, rather. You don't know what she's like. She's charismatic. I didn't expect her to lie. I can see why she said it. She wanted to push me off balance. She wants me to sell her the Hall. Or to rent it to her. She says she always wins."

"Whatever possessed you to go up there by yourself? Why didn't you wait for me? No, what am I saying? You couldn't wait, obviously. How's Jim? I feel so torn ... I can't leave this case, but ... dear Lord above, what am I to do?"

Minty said, "Reggie and Hodge and Chef have all been praying for me to come back and do something. Apparently Hodge's praying is full of Anglo-Saxon words, which shocks the others."

Patrick made a sound which was a cross between a sneeze and a guffaw. "Don't make me laugh. This is serious. I'm due back in court in a minute. It was only a short recess and ... I can't think straight ..."

"I'm all right now. You and I are going to have another child as soon as we possibly can, and I'm going to put on the armour of God and fight a few dragons."

"I've got to go, the judge's coming back. What about Jim?"

"Serafina's looking after him."

"He's in safe hands, then. Good. I'll be back as soon as I can."

※

She pulled and twisted herself into the clothes Carol had sent her. The skimpy top looked ridiculous on her, she thought. The cut-off shorts were incredibly tight and revealed far too much leg. They also revealed the scars of the beatings her aunt had inflicted on her in childhood. She didn't think anyone but Patrick had ever seen her legs so exposed before. Trainers. Clumpy great things, but comfortable. She tied her hair up and back in a ponytail and pulled the baseball cap over her eyes.

The identity tag went round her neck. Thongs went round her wrist. Very yesterday. The outfit was completed by a raffia bag slung across herself, into which she put money, her mobile, a notebook and pen and a tiny camera which Patrick had bought for her on a whim. She wasn't snap happy, but if she needed proof of what was going on at the Hall, then a camera might get it for her.

She looked in the mirror and blushed. "What on earth do I look like?" She tried to cover herself with her hands.

"Stand up straight," said Serafina, materialising in the doorway. "Pretend you're fifteen years old and on the lookout for someone to 'give you a good time'."

"I never wore anything like this when I was fifteen. I can't possibly go outside looking like a ... a groupie."

"Yes, you can. You can do anything you put your mind to. Try wiggling your hips as you walk."

Minty tried and shrieked with laughter. "What would Patrick say if he could see me now?"

"Now there's a man who enjoys surprises. Stand still and let me put some eye liner on you."

Minty let Serafina do her worst, then looked in the mirror. She thought she looked like a panda. "That's too much."

"Nonsense." Serafina darkened and thickened Minty's eyebrows. A bright lipstick went on next, well over the edges of her mouth to reproduce the teenage pout.

"You'd better take this clipboard which I pinched from Elizabeth, and no, she doesn't know I've got it, and I'm not going to tell her and neither are you."

Minty accepted the clipboard, grinning. "Will I do now?"

Serafina was not satisfied. "Have you got a tattoo? One of those transfers would do. And you really ought to have dangly earrings."

Minty giggled. "Want to draw a tattoo on me? Do you think I should chew gum? Will I get through the village without being molested if I go out like this?"

Serafina folded her arms. "I don't approve of your going in there by yourself, but if I'd been your age, I'd have done the same thing."

VERONICA HELEY

"If someone would only tell me what's wrong at the Hall! You could tell me, couldn't you?"

Serafina shook her head. "I might be wrong. I hope I am. What shall I tell Patrick if he rings again?"

"He won't. He's got his own problems." A groan sounded from Jim down below. They listened, but the sound wasn't repeated.

"I'll listen out for him," said Serafina.

Minty sent up a prayer for him. *Dear Lord, remember Jim. And me. Be with me as I go into the lion's den. Or the dragon's. Whichever.*

Chapter Twelve

Minty presented herself at a gate into the Park which was some distance from the house. There was a steady stream of people going in. There were a lot of workmen, in vans and lorries or on foot. There were more cars and caravans, even a coach or two.

The work crew had passes of a different colour from the paying customers. Everyone had to show their tickets or passes at the gate and then had a heat-sealed plastic bracelet clamped around their wrists. That way you could get in and out without argument. Minty was scared they'd spot her because she hadn't got a bracelet on, but it turned out they'd only just arrived that morning, so she just said it was the first time she'd been out to the village and could she have a colour that matched her outfit.

She'd taken the precaution of buying a huge bag of fresh doughnuts to take with her. She told the security man on the gate that they were for the team putting up the big marquees. He took one before letting her in. She remembered to waggle her bottom as she passed through the gate and was rewarded with a sharp slap on her bum. She gritted her teeth and tried to remember to keep waggling as she walked on into the Park.

Tent city was well named. It looked like a refugee camp site. Blocks of chemical toilets had been placed at either end. They looked just like sentry boxes. Farther on there were two shower tents where men were working to connect with water and power supplies. So far, so good, but surely they should have been in place before the first paying customers came on site.

There was a drift of litter around the place already, and because the toilets had arrived late, a lot of private latrine holes had already been dug into the turf. The stench was light but persistent. Presumably it would only get worse. Ugh. And as Mrs Collins had said, would the Park recover in time for the annual garden fête?

An enormous car park stretched beyond tent city. One corner of the car park was occupied by a number of decrepit-looking buses. Travellers? Washing-lines had been put up; dogs sniffed piles of rubbish. Two security men were arguing with some of these caravanners. Were they gypsies or travellers? Getting them to move on would be a headache.

Beyond that again, a small fun fair was under wraps nearby, but beginning—just—to wake up from its afternoon nap. Soon it would be blaring away. Well, it was far enough from the village not to matter.

She looked up at the sky. The fine weather was holding—so far. If it rained, many of these cars and caravans would get bogged down and ... well, that wasn't her problem at the moment.

There were a dozen food stalls already set up and doing good business, and more were coming on site as she watched. The odours from some were not very choice. Three men were having a row about a particularly good site. Who was going to calm them down? The security men? Minty made more notes. How were these food outlets being monitored? She must ask Iris.

A helicopter passed overhead, low enough for her to feel the downdraft. Her father had often arrived at the Hall by helicopter and landed at the helipad which was just beyond the trees, farther into the Park. Presumably most of the artists would arrive and leave that way. Except for Maxine, of course.

And all this two days before the festival was actually due to start. Had extra trains been laid on to bring people here? Buses? Coaches? There was a coach park area set aside. Only three coaches in it so far. It nagged her that there weren't enough security people around, though it made her venture into the Park easier.

She forgot to waggle her bottom every now and then. How did the youngsters keep it up?

Two electric buggies were buzzing back and forth, carting equipment and people around the site. Vans came and left. Scaffolding clanged. Trenches criss-crossed the site. There were workmen everywhere. What a feat of organisation this was! Good for Iris, who presumably had been responsible.

She picked up a leaflet straying in the wind. There was a programme of sorts. On the main stage … blah, blah. And there was an alternative, smaller stage apparently. Was that the one she'd seen close to the house? Alternative comedy? Western-style music? Well, why not?

She wandered down towards the lake and stopped by a fence enclosing a huge semi-circle behind the giant stage. Work was still going on there. Trenches for power lines. Wires snaked all over the place. There was a lot of banging and crashing going on around the stage. Everyone was being stopped at this barrier for an identity check.

The security men on this gate wore a green uniform, different from those on the perimeter.

She pushed one hip out and pretended to be chewing gum while considering whether or not she needed to get into that area. She began to play with her ponytail of hair.

"What's that you got there?" An electrician, wide belt holding an array of tools.

She held out her bag of doughnuts. "Want one? Clive sent me to get them from the village."

He took one. Cast an appreciative eye up and down her. She tried not to blush. "Who or what is Clive?"

She gestured with her chin. "Up at the house. Lord High Everything."

The man shrugged. "This part's stage management. No one gets in here without a proper pass."

"Not even Maxine?"

He grunted. "Nah, we keep everyone out today that's not working on the stage, the cameras or the sound. The Press are almost worse than the performers. That's the Press tent there. Dressing-rooms for the talent further over."

Minty nodded and moved on, nibbling a doughnut, taking in everything she could see. Between the stage and the lake was a sort of trackway. Television and video and sound men had congregated there, arguing about who did what, where and to whom.

On Friday, people would come thronging across the park from tent city until they reached the fence surrounding the stage area. There, they'd divide to left and right, skirt the lake, aiming for the sloping area of grass—the "arena"—below the Hall.

She took the route to the right of the lake and found herself passing within a few feet of a giant tent. She peered inside. It was being fitted out to serve drinks. Generators were being manoeuvred into place to provide power. Casks and crates of beer were being unloaded from lorries. Trestle tables were being set up.

She stood with hands on hips, swivelling round to take in everything that was happening. An identical tent was being set up on the far side of the arena, and that also looked to be sited rather too close to the lake.

"Out of the way!" Another huge lorry was coming through, laden with supplies for the tent. Chairs, tables. Crates of drinks. The lorry stopped just beyond the tent and began to unload.

Minty frowned, measuring distances. It seemed to her that not enough room had been allowed for people to pass between the lake and the drinks tents. Suppose there was a bit of a hold up ... wouldn't there be a stampede as people tried to get away from the arena through that narrow gap? Might not people get crushed?

She stepped inside the tent, trying to locate someone who might be in charge. A student type accosted her. "Not open yet, luv."

She tried to look helpless, holding out the bag of doughnuts. "Clive sent me down to get these."

He nodded, took one and stuffed it in his mouth.

She said, "Aren't you a bit close to the lake? Is there room enough for people to get through?"

"You don't know nothing, do you! The boss doesn't want anyone sneaking past without buying something. He'd have the tent bang across the path if he could. Now, shift yourself. You're in the way."

A security man in blue overalls loomed, and she shifted.

Did that make three different firms covering security? The one on the outside gates, the ones for the stage management part and the one for the drinks tents? She made more notes. That tent was definitely narrowing the path between tent city and the arena. It ought to be moved back at least twenty feet. How many more toilets were there here? Were there enough? How soon would they begin to smell? She supposed it depended on how many people came.

She thought Clive and Iris had done a good job of organisation—with the possible snags of narrow access from the arena, and there not being enough security guards to cover everything.

She looked up at the house. Maxine's tent was still on the terrace, and several people—including a woman in a dark dress—were standing in it, talking. Minty worked her way up the slope, wondering how close to the house she could get before she was discovered.

There were a couple of security men on duty at the foot of the steps leading up to the terrace. Could she bluff her way past them? The group of people who'd been on the terrace went into the house through the open window.

The security men immediately relaxed. The one at this end abandoned his post to stroll across to the other for a chat.

She could sprint up the nearby steps unnoticed. If she was quick.

They'd be sure to see her. Better to be safe than sorry. She could go back to Patrick's house and get out of these horrible clothes. She could tell him what she'd seen and let him deal with—whatever it was that was upsetting people.

No. She'd got this far, and she wasn't going to chicken out now. She wouldn't try to sneak in. She would walk up the steps as if she had every right to be there. If she was stopped, she'd say Clive had told her to report to him. It had worked before. So why not now?

She walked up the steps to the terrace, clipboard to the fore, and peered over the window-sill into the Chinese Room.

There was no one there. The people she'd seen on the terrace had gone through into the house. Again she considered running away, and again she decided not to do so. Yet.

She hopped in over the window-sill and, first listening at the door, passed through the connecting state rooms till she reached the library.

All was still. No one was there, either.

The ropes which normally kept visitors away from the furniture had been removed. Naturally. Maxine had been using these rooms. Furniture had been moved around, ornaments shifted. Nothing seemed to have been broken, but they'd been using candles in the silver sconces on the walls and let them drip down onto the floorboards beneath and, yes, onto the table tops. There were tell-tale wine stains on the priceless furniture, and the rooms had a fusty, dusty air to them, as if they were only occupied at night when the windows were shut fast.

Someone had been playing Scrabble on an occasional table, a human touch which made Minty smile. She got out her camera and snapped the wine rings on the furniture. That would be an insurance job, presumably. She wondered why the housekeeper hadn't made a fuss about the damage and done something to clean it up. But perhaps she was as much in awe of Maxine as everyone else was.

Minty put her ear to the library door and opened it a crack, taking care not to be seen.

The earliest part of the Hall had been built in an L-shape. Later generations had added another two wings, to complete a square surrounding a central courtyard—the Fountain Court. To solve the problem of uniting wings built at different times, there was a tower at each corner containing a staircase.

Minty couldn't see anything but the empty ground floor of the south-east tower. From here she could gain access to the Long Gallery on the east side. Or she could turn left into the arcaded walk or cloisters which surrounded Fountain Court.

There was a lot of noise going on in the courtyard. Presumably they were filming there. Was it the filming which had upset people?

At that time of the afternoon this side of the courtyard, including the cloisters, would be in deep shadow.

Minty hesitated. Would her disguise be good enough to pass if she was seen by someone in the courtyard? Yet she must risk being seen if she was to discover what was going on.

She slipped into the tower—there was still no one about—and through an open door into the cloisters, keeping to the shadows.

A second tent-like structure had been set up around the fountain. Television lights were trained on it, and a camera crew were in action, luckily with their backs to Minty. There were a lot of other people there. Sound technicians? Make-up people? A director?

Frenzied music boomed out. Someone shouted, "Cut!"

The music died. A woman screamed abuse at someone for not coming in on cue. A man's voice argued back. A second man's voice soothed the screamer. Minty couldn't see into the tent from where she stood so she moved around, keeping to the back of the cloisters.

"Let's go again."

"Hold it ... ready ..."

"Turnover ... mark it."

"Shot fifty-seven, take three."

"Go play back!"

Music suddenly boomed out. A woman's seductive voice. "I'm burning ... burning ... burning ..."

And now Minty could see, through a gap in the tent. Maxine was standing in the fountain, tearing at the diaphanous blue gown she'd worn earlier. Her eyes were half closed in languorous fashion, her hips gyrating. She was wearing the black wig Minty had seen in the posters.

The noise was shatteringly loud. There were a lot of people in the courtyard, but they were all concentrating on the filming.

That bold hunter of women, Nero, rose from the depths of the fountain basin. Minty hoped it would stand his weight. It had only been restored that year. Nero slid behind Maxine, running his hands over her body, till they were both writhing to the music. "Burning ... burning ... fill me ... take me ..."

Presumably Maxine was miming words, as she couldn't possibly be singing while being so ... well, athletic. Minty felt her face go red. The loving times she shared with Patrick, usually started with laughter and tenderness, led to passion and ecstasy, and fell away to yet more tenderness accompanied by soft laughter. Laughter had no place here.

What she was watching wasn't love. It seemed nearer hate than love.

Blood-red liquid began to seep over the edge of the bowl of the fountain above.

Minty frowned. What liquid was that? Red wine stained marble. No, surely they wouldn't use wine; it was too expensive. It must be some kind of coloured liquid. She hoped it wouldn't leave any traces.

146

Maxine threw off her gown and turned to the fountain, the liquid dripping down upon her white skin ...

"Cut!" The music died.

Maxine screamed, "I'm not doing it again!"

The director soothed her. "Just one more time?"

Nero got out of the basin and reached for the towel which someone was holding for him.

There was no sign of Gemma. No, wait a minute. Wasn't that her with the clapperboard? What a come down for her! Maxine continued to argue with the director, and Nero to turn his back on her.

Minty slipped back into the tower. The video Maxine was making was nasty. Yes. Very. But was it bad enough to warrant the anxiety which people had been showing? Probably not. So, she must look further.

She dumped the bag containing the few remaining doughnuts and peeped through the door into the Long Gallery. This was a room designed to serve both as an art gallery and to allow gentle exercise on wet days. As a child Minty had played badminton here, but more recently it had seen the ball at which she'd danced with Patrick ... classical music concerts ... and then her joyous wedding reception. They'd planned to hold the christening party here ...

There were two ornate fireplaces in the room, and usually the wide old floorboards glistened with loving care. It was clear to Minty that no cleaning had been done here for quite a while. What was worse, the blinds had all been left up so that sunlight streamed in, which, as Minty had had to learn the hard way, bleached the colour out of furniture and furnishings alike.

The pictures of Minty's ancestors still hung on the walls, but they didn't seem to be enjoying the proximity of the dozens of plastic coffee cups and food packaging which littered the place.

There were some stacks of what looked like props in the middle of the room, and a couple of men were working at some laptop computers set up on trestle tables. Neither looked up as she eased the door open.

She closed the door, careful not to make a noise. Where to next? She'd seen people going into the house from the terrace. They must have gone somewhere. They'd looked like business people, not artists. Had Clive Hatton been among them? Yes, she thought he might have been.

Where would they be? Iris had said the office staff had been moved to the north wing. That's where they'd have gone. Hopefully. Forget the north wing; she wasn't looking for financial irregularities.

On the first floor she paused. Gemma's rooms were on one side, but everyone was used to Gemma's wild ways and wouldn't be getting into a state about them. So no need to look there.

On the other side were the State Bedrooms. Minty walked swiftly through them. The red ropes had been removed; someone was sleeping in the Canopy Bedroom. Everything was rather dusty, there were cups and mugs everywhere and some dirty clothes strewn around. What was the housekeeper thinking of? Minty made a note to track her down.

There was nothing particularly amiss on that floor. Which left her own rooms on the top floor. She took a deep breath. Yes, of course. Whatever it was that had upset people so much must be in the rooms Maxine had taken for her own.

Or, of course, in the family chapel. Minty allowed herself to think about the chapel for the first time and felt the hairs rise on the back of her neck. The chapel was the heart of the house. Had Maxine dared to change anything there?

Minty's feet made no noise in her trainers. She felt like a ghost, drifting up the stairs without a sound. She wondered what would happen if she was caught. There'd be a nasty scene, she supposed. She'd be outnumbered, at their mercy, even though by law she had every right to be there.

Reaching the top floor, she hesitated. She could take the door into her own rooms, or she could open the door to the chapel. She stared at the firmly closed, panelled door of the chapel. Inside that holy place she'd spent many hours praying ... as her mother had done earlier ... and generations of Edens before her.

It was a place set apart, quiet, serene. There were windows on three sides letting in light in the morning, the afternoon and the evening. Everything in the chapel, the altar, the cross, the wall hanging, the table at the side on which stood the ancient family Bible and a perpetually renewed vase of flowers ... all were there to honour God.

Suspicions crashed together in Minty's mind ... the fear so many people had shown ... what was it they didn't want to put into words? What could Maxine have done that would cause distress to so many people?

Answer: she'd attacked the chapel.

Minty opened the door and went in.

No sooner had she closed the door behind her than she fought to get it open again.

She tugged at the handle; it turned but the door refused to open. It did stick sometimes in hot weather. She coughed, retched. Choked. The stench was overpowering.

The chapel was in darkness. Why?

She tried to slow her heartbeat. She couldn't breathe properly. Her brain went into freefall. Was she suffering from the same incense that Maxine had used in the tent?

Presently her eyes became used to the lack of light. There was a faint glimmer coming from the edges of the windows. Enough to let her see where to grope for the light switch. She turned on the light, but something ... some gauzy covering had been swathed around the light bulb and the place was still dim. The stench came at her in waves, mingled with the incense. There were flies everywhere. She brushed them off her bare arms.

The windows had been covered with boards painted black, but someone had done a hasty job and a crack of daylight seeped through here and there.

The altar cloth had been replaced with a piece of black velvet. The wall hanging had vanished. The cross had been hung upside down on the wall. The chairs on which Minty, Patrick and Serafina had sat to worship had been thrown on their backs, piled into a corner. One had a broken leg.

She put her hands round her throat, wheezing.

Swirls of smoke seemed to be rising from the floor around her, clinging to her. She fought them off, though her head told her that they were phantoms, only in her mind. Coils of smoke-laden incense were rising from a bowl on the altar, a bowl which had once been used to hold fresh flowers. The Bible was ...

She couldn't bear to look at it. It had been used for ...

The stench was of sex and rotting flesh and dried blood.

Something lay on the altar, stretched out. Disembowelled. Dead.

She hoped it was only the black cock.

She felt the ceiling was descending upon her.

She was going to faint.

No.

She would not faint. She scrabbled with her back to the door, trying to breathe lightly. The sense of something evil in the room was building up around her.

She cried out, "Christ is risen indeed!"

The evil tide seemed to abate, but now it seemed as if there were whispering voices all around her, ordering her to yield.

"No," she said, speaking more normally but with passion. "I love God the Father, the Son and the Holy Ghost. I worship Him and Him alone. In the name of Jesus, I command you to leave this place and never return."

Something changed in the room. Subtly the mood altered. She felt that she was holding evil at bay, but it was not defeated and it had not departed. If she had not been standing with her back to the door, she might have felt it was behind her.

This was the secret of Eden Hall.

The heart of the Hall had been transformed into a focus for evil, sending out its tendrils to ensnare everyone who ventured into its territory. Corrupting people.

"No," she said aloud. "You shall not win. Jesus triumphed over the worst death that they could devise for Him. And He will triumph here."

Now it was easier to breathe. Her heart rate slowed. She lunged for the nearest window, shriekingly aware that leaving the safety of the door left her open to attack from behind. It was no use telling herself that there was no one else in the room. Every nerve in her body insisted otherwise.

The black boarding at the windows had been crudely cut to size and hammered into place, but there were chinks around it. She tried to pull the boards off with her fingernails, but they resisted her. She used the clipboard—she'd known it would come in useful—as a lever, and eventually, sweating, she managed to pry the first board loose. She hammered the window open and cool sweet air rushed in.

She attacked the boards over the second window and let in more fresh air.

Breathing shallowly, for she could feel that the incense was beginning to affect her, she pulled out her camera and took a dozen frames, praying aloud as she did so.

"Dear Lord, have mercy … help me to be strong … banish the evil … In You I trust and in You alone …"

The sun went behind a cloud and she put the camera away to attack the boards over the third window.

The door swung open behind her.

Chapter Thirteen

Minty spun round. Maxine had changed her costume and was now clad in a purple and black dress, tight to the waist and flaring out below. Her face was dead white with black eyebrows, and she was still wearing her black wig. Her eyes were now black, as were her lipstick and nail varnish.

Her teeth glittered. She was wearing a metal brace on her teeth.

Maxine said, "I didn't recognise you at first. You're brighter than I thought, to get this far. But if you enter the Master's chamber, you have to pay the price."

Minty straightened up, conscious of her unsuitable clothing, but defiant. "This is a holy place, and you have desecrated it. No one can worship the devil and remain their own master. You called this place 'the Master's chamber'. Have you sold your soul to him? Did you realise what you are doing?"

Maxine bared her teeth again. "Do you think you are immune?"

Minty held her head high. "Body and soul, I belong to Christ."

"Yet you can be swayed by concern for others, can't you? I saw that this morning. You were prepared to bargain for little Alice's job. Confess it."

"You told me a lie. It wounded me for a while, but now I'm whole again."

"They tell me you and your husband were childhood sweethearts and that he's devoted to you. Let's make a bargain, you and I. If I can get him to break his marriage vows, you'll let me have the Hall."

Minty laughed. "I refuse to play games with you."

"You're afraid I could take him from you!"

Minty saw the trap. She wouldn't wager Patrick's loyalty. "I don't bet."

"Not even on what you think is a certainty? You don't trust him, then."

Minty looked Maxine in the eye. "My husband and I made our vows before God in church. We prayed together in this room every day. I promise you that soon, very soon, this room will have prayers said in it again, and that you will be gone. I give you notice here and now to quit the Hall and never return."

Maxine jeered. "Will you bring in the police to remove me? I think not. My lawyers would merely have to show them our contract and they would refuse to act."

"You've broken the terms of the contract over and again."

"Axel!"

The pale manager appeared behind her, carrying a cat basket from which came terrified scrabblings.

Minty shivered. "You're going to sacrifice a cat?"

"That was my intention, yes. I've had a better idea. See how you tremble at the thought of a cat being killed! Put the basket down, Axel."

The stench of blood in the room was driving the cat wild. In its terror it screamed and tore at the sides of the basket.

Maxine's voice dropped to a murmur. "What will you give me for the cat's life? What will you do to prevent me from killing it here and now?"

Minty parried the attack. "Nonsense. You'd want to have a full-scale service before you killed a cat. So you won't kill it now, in front of me."

"It's your weak point, my dear. Your concern for others. Naturally I'll use it if I have to. So, what will you give me for the cat's life? Your presence in my backing group at the festival, perhaps?"

Minty shook her head. "Don't be ridiculous!"

"You don't know what I could do to you ... or your husband."

"I will pray for you. But I will not bargain with you."

The woman's face changed to a mask of fury. "Axel. Open the basket and let the cat out. You, woman! This cat is feral. It won't let anyone touch it without tearing them to shreds. If you want the cat, take it ... if you can!"

Axel opened the cat basket with care, standing well back. Rightly so, for a half grown black and white cat shot out, spitting with fear and fury. It streaked for the darkest corner of the room under the chairs and crouched there, ears flattened.

Minty had to acknowledge that Maxine had read her aright. She could not leave the cat there to be killed. But a feral cat would lash out at anyone who approached it. If it was feral. That might be yet another lie of Maxine's. Perhaps it was only a household cat which Axel had found for his mistress.

Normally you'd envelop a trapped and frightened cat in a towel. No towel. Minty glanced down at herself. She couldn't remove any item of her present clothing. What was to be done?

The afternoon breeze was banishing the worst of the stench in the room. Every minute that passed, the air seemed to grow lighter. Minty's eyes went round the room, looking for something which might help.

She saw what she needed and worked out how to use it. The white altar cloth, painstakingly embroidered with drawn-thread work by Minty's grandmother, had been balled up and thrown into a corner. It was stained with something ... Minty did not wish to enquire what.

She retrieved it, shook it out, doubled it over and saw with sorrow that it had been slashed and torn in several places. It could be repaired, perhaps. Perhaps.

She approached the heap of chairs in the corner. The chair on which she used to sit had a broken leg. Don't stop to mourn. Pull it out. Serafina's had a broken back. That left the carved oak chair which Patrick used. It had seen many a year out and had resisted rough usage. Minty's mother had been painted sitting in that chair, and Minty had always intended that one day Patrick would also be painted sitting in it. It was heavy. Almost too heavy for her to lift. The cat was cowering beneath it.

Maxine mocked her. "Say, 'Kitty, kitty; come here, kitty!' Go on, try to calm it in the name of your Beloved Master."

Minty concentrated on the cat, which was growling like a dog, wide-eyed with fear and fury. She knew it would be sensible to walk away, to leave the cat to its fate. But she would not.

She held her left hand out and the cat swiped at it, claws extended, snarling.

With her right hand Minty dropped the altar cloth over it and swooped, picking up the struggling animal. She thrust it, still struggling, into the basket. Then she shut the lid and fastened it with the cat still spitting inside.

"Clever!" Maxine seemed to mean it.

Minty stood up. Unclawed. She wondered if they would try to stop her leaving the room, but they didn't. Perhaps Maxine had a warped sense of fairness. She'd challenged Minty to rescue the cat, and Minty had done so. Therefore, she'd let Minty walk free.

Minty could feel their eyes on her back as she left the chapel and took the stairs downwards. Her mind turned to the quiet peace of her own beautiful rooms on the top floor, but she resisted the temptation to go in and see what Maxine had done there.

She wanted to run but didn't. If she walked around as if she had every right to be there, perhaps no one would question her.

At the bottom of the stairs she turned right and made her way through the Long Gallery. The two men working there looked up, surprised at seeing a stranger. She walked past them, wondering if Maxine would change her mind and send someone after her. She reached the far door unmolested.

God, be with me still. So far they haven't touched me. Praise be.

She refused to let her knees bend. She wasn't clear of the place yet. The cat was restless within the basket. She reached the end of the Long Gallery and took the well-concealed door which led directly into the north wing.

So far, so good. The cat basket was growing heavy. She set it down while she considered what she should do next. The family's kitchen lay nearby but it was closed up and silent. Florence Thornby, Chef, would be working across the courtyard in the restaurant kitchen.

Florence would see her safely away. Or Reggie. Or Hodge.

No, she couldn't involve any of them, because they would be left behind when she escaped. Escaped? From her own home? Well, it did feel like it.

What to do next? She could walk into the Estate Offices which were also in this part of the building and get the Estate Manager or his assistant to help her. Ah, but would they help her, or would they send for Clive Hatton to "deal" with her? Perhaps she was being paranoid, but she was afraid to trust even her own people.

Her car. Her own car was a sturdy estate car, not new but reliable. Reggie had bought it for her because she hadn't been able to picture herself driving around with a chauffeur in her father's limousine. What would Reggie have done with her car after the miscarriage? Garaged it in the inner courtyard beyond the restaurant. Yes. But where would the keys be, and would there be any petrol in its tank?

Well ... Reggie knew she was back and knew she'd been going to attempt an entry, so he might well have left the car ready for her to take away. Perhaps.

She straightened her shoulders and sent up a prayer for help. She walked through the maze of corridors that criss-crossed this, the oldest part of the Hall, into the office that had once been a reception room for her father's visitors. Two girls were working there now and looked up enquiringly when she walked in. She didn't know either of them but favoured them with a smile as if she had every right to be there—which she had, of course. She opened the door to the courtyard and shut it behind her.

The late afternoon sun was sending long shadows across the courtyard. There were people there, some dressed like her, some—presumably men working on the stages—bare-chested in shorts and trainers. The restaurant was busy. The gift shop was closed. There was a faint but distinctive smell of urine coming from the toilets, which obviously hadn't been cleaned properly that day.

What had happened to the housekeeper?

One or two people glanced at her without curiosity as she walked through to the inner courtyard. Was that Chef at the kitchen window? Minty couldn't stop to check. She went straight on as if she owned the place—which of course she did—until she reached the places set aside for family cars. Gemma's car was there, with a dented wing, how unsurprising. There was no sign of Reggie, but ...

Another surprise. Her own car had been taken out of its garage and washed clean. It had been turned round, ready to leave. She tested the back door. It opened. She heaved the cat basket inside. A bunch of keys swung in the ignition, and when she switched on, she could see the tank was full. Everything was as it should be.

Bless you, Reggie.

Now to get out of here. If they stopped her at the gates ... she'd think about that when she got there. The afternoon sunshine was warm on her bare arms. The cat yowled inside its basket.

She met a couple of lorries on the driveway. The security men were checking everyone who arrived ... but they were not being so meticulous about those who were leaving, especially if they had an identity tag and were dressed the way Minty was.

She turned out of the gates into the main road, feeling weak with relief.

She'd done it.

By the time she reached the bridge, she was shaking from relief. Nervous tension had carried her away from the Hall, but now she was falling apart. She clenched her teeth, turning up the back lane, refusing to let herself cry. She was conscious for the first time how tight the skimpy top was around her ribs.

She made it to the parking space at the back of Patrick's house and into the space between Elizabeth's Mini and her rented car. Then she put her arms down on the steering wheel and wept.

It was only when she became conscious of the cat crying in its basket that she lifted her head and sought for a handkerchief—which of course she hadn't got.

"Mrs Sands!" Elizabeth had heard the car arrive and had come out to see why Minty had delayed entering the house. Minty got out of the car on shaky legs, and Elizabeth's tone changed to one of horror. "Mrs Sands! You've never gone out dressed like that!"

Minty knuckled her eyes, sniffed and looked ruefully down at her bare arms and legs. "Betty, I need your help." For the first time, Minty had called the woman by her pet name, and it didn't go down well.

Minty reached back into the car for the cat basket. "I've been up to the Hall and I've got photographs to prove what's going on. It's awful! Betty, this is really important. Can you print out my photographs on your computer straight away? Then I rescued this cat ..."

"I know that cat. It's been living wild on the Green since its owner—an old lady up at the council houses—passed away a few weeks ago. What on earth are you doing with it?"

Minty carried it through into the cool hallway and set it down. "Maxine was going to sacrifice it on the altar up at the Hall."

Elizabeth might never have been touched by any appeal Minty might make to her, but she was a soft touch for an abandoned kitten. She undid the lid and reached inside for the cat before Minty could warn her that the cat might have gone feral.

"There, now!" Elizabeth stroked the kitten, who quivered with fear and made an abortive attempt to free itself from the cloth around it, but didn't rake its rescuer with its claws. "Shall we find you some milk, then? And perhaps ... I think Mr Lightowler at the bookshop next door might have some cat food to spare."

"What a good idea," said Minty. She would quite have liked to adopt the cat herself, but it was clear that Elizabeth was charmed with it. Anything which soothed Elizabeth must be a good thing for Minty.

Serafina appeared, carrying a towelling robe to drape over Minty's shoulders.

"There's messages of all sorts, and you've probably forgotten but Mrs Wootton's coming at five with those two ladies who run everything around here."

Elizabeth put the cat down, and it scooted under her desk. "Oh, and Mr Patrick rang, wanting to know where you were, and I said I was sure I didn't know. And Mr Jim's wanting to see you upstairs ..."

"But *not* dressed like that," said Serafina, smiling grimly. "You've just got time to wash and change ..."

Elizabeth poured some milk into a saucer for the kitten and set it down. "There, there, now, pussy. And before you ask, Mrs Sands, if I've been on to the computer people once, it's been five times and they say it's still not running smoothly ..."

"But you'll download these pictures for me, won't you, dear Betty?"

The kitten warily advanced on the milk, keeping an eye out for catnappers, and shying at shadows ... but still advancing, hunkering down and lapping furiously.

"The poor thing's starved," cried Elizabeth. The phone was ringing but she ignored it. "I'll just pop next door and borrow some cat tins ..."

Minty gave up. She put the camera on Elizabeth's desk and allowed herself to be led upstairs, where a now sober Jim was sitting at the dining room table, talking on his mobile and looking at his watch. He was only a little older than Patrick, but not made of such durable material. Blond, well-built, he normally had a quick sense of humour, but looked now as if he'd never laugh again. He'd been drinking a lot of coffee, to judge by the empty cafetière before him.

Minty excused herself to dash into the cloakroom for a quick wash. The water on her face was soothing. She got rid of all the make-up, pulled the baseball cap off her hair and shook it out. She tried to wriggle out of the top and shorts but they were too tight. Probably the heat had made them stick.

She pulled the towelling robe on and belted it before returning to face Jim.

Serafina had coffee and a hot sandwich waiting for her on the table.

Jim turned off his mobile and tapped the table. "Where have you been?" He sounded angry.

Minty held back a sigh, telling herself it was no wonder if he felt neglected. The bereaved usually have first rights to the time of those around them.

"Something urgent came up. Dear Jim, how are you feeling?"

"Well enough." He barked the words out. "I need to talk to Patrick. I've tried ringing the office, but they said he wasn't there, either. Where is he?"

"In court. I know he's tried ringing you here, but ..."

He looked amazed. "What's he in court for? Oh ... yes. I forgot." He looked haggard. Searched his pockets for something but didn't seem to find it. "What's the date today? I don't seem to ... how long have I been here? I must get back, I suppose ... although I can't think ... has my watch stopped?"

"You've only been here a night and a day. It's Thursday. Patrick took over for you in court."

He thought about that. His eyes—now Minty was close enough to see—were focused on something far away, not on Minty.

He gave a start and said again, "How long have I been here? I must get back, I suppose. There's things to do, people to see. Registering the death ..." He shuddered.

Minty wanted to say that she'd go with him wherever he needed to go. But she couldn't. In half an hour she was expecting the good ladies of the village and she had much to do before then, not least of which was getting out of these tight clothes.

She tried to remember what she knew of Jim. "Don't you have a brother and a sister? Your sister's looking after your little girl, isn't she? You're very welcome to stay on here, of course, but ..."

He made a dismissive gesture. "I've just been on the phone to her. She's all right. Coping. My brother's a busy man. He can't ... well, I shouldn't have asked, I suppose. My mother's been away on holiday but is on her way back. She's going to meet me at the house this evening. My brother-in-law is all right. He'll help me make the arrangements for the ..." He gagged, couldn't say the word "funeral."

"My mother says she'll help me clear out her things, but I'd rather she didn't. She didn't like Anthea much. She says all this is a blessing in disguise ..." His voice broke.

Minty put her hand on his arm.

He shook her off. "I must get going, but I haven't a clue where I left my car."

"I've got a car rental down below. Take that. Turn it in when you can."

He looked at her without seeing her. She wondered if he was fit to drive and decided that he probably wasn't. "Jim, why don't you stay on here for a bit? We've got enough room and ..."

"Got to get back. Got to get things sorted. Arranged. Lots of leave due. Might take it. Why not? Patrick left me in the lurch earlier, so he can take over now."

Minty winced. Patrick had had to take a long leave of absence, yes, in order to look after Minty. But he'd kept in touch all the time, doing at least an hour's work every day by phone and e-mail. Would Jim also work when he was on leave? No.

It was no good playing the Who Owes Who game. It probably would be a good idea for Jim to get away for a while, and Patrick could cope. He'd been planning to see their other partner today, hadn't he? Perhaps that would work out.

"Are you sure you can cope?" asked Minty, handing over the car keys.

"I'm all right. Don't fuss."

Minty nodded. No, fuss didn't help, did it?

She saw Jim off and returned to Patrick's office, furiously making lists of who she must ring. She'd had the first flicker of an idea how to get back into the Hall while she was going round the Park. All those cables ... trenches dug for them ... putting them out of sight. Suppose ...? But she'd need a lot of help. Would everyone agree to try her plan?

⁂

She was clearing up after the meeting with the ladies of the village when Patrick arrived. Chairs were everywhere, lists, photographs.

Patrick kissed her and dumped his laptop and a couple of books he'd acquired from somewhere; he was incapable of passing a second-hand book shop without going in. "Are you all right? I got really worried about you this afternoon, but then the judge got going and I had to concentrate on what he was saying. What's been going on here? I see you've got your own car back and the rental car's gone. Did Jim take it? I've been trying to get him on the phone, but he's switched off."

She held up one finger after the other. "Jim's taken the rental car and will turn it in — *if* he remembers. I'll probably have to remind him. His sister's got the little girl, he's meeting his mother at the house tonight and his brother-in-law has promised to help with the funeral arrangements. Jim's not himself yet and he's planning to take a holiday."

Patrick nodded. He looked at the place where the smashed table lamp had been and at the geranium, which had now been replanted but lacked a couple of the flowers that had been on it that morning. "Jim went berserk?"

"He was angry. Took it out on everything around him."

She'd still been wearing the towelling robe when the members of the committee had begun to arrive and hadn't yet had time to change. "I'm going up for a shower."

Patrick nodded and watched her walk away from him. She knew the robe was a little short. He knew that she never exposed her legs to view if she could help it. She wasn't surprised when he followed her up the stairs and into the bathroom, wearing a crocodile grin.

She felt a blush start in her neck and held the towelling robe closer ... how absurd to feel ashamed of how she'd dressed that day! Gently he lifted the robe off her shoulders and turned her round to survey the glory of the clinging top and tiny shorts.

She hastened to explain. "I had to get into the Hall somehow."

He tried to keep his face straight, but a deep crease always appeared in his cheek when he was trying not to laugh. It did now. "Was this the armour of God?"

She spurted into laughter. "Yes, I suppose it was. Oh, Patrick, you should have seen me walking around with a baseball cap on my head, pretending to chew gum and trying to waggle my hips ... and this stupid top is so tight, I don't think I'll ever get it off!"

Serafina opened the bathroom door and handed in a pair of scissors. "Supper's in half an hour."

Patrick said, "Now this is a fantasy I've never had. You should keep those shorts as a memento."

"It's not funny!" said Minty, torn between tears and laughter. "I think I've been marked for life!"

"The scars of battle," said Patrick. "Keep still, and let's see what I can do to set you free."

Minty made Serafina eat with them as she outlined her plans. The phone kept ringing.

First Reggie rang to say it was okay by him. At that point the Reverend Cecil popped over to see them. He'd left Minty's uncle behind, because he'd fallen asleep after their Chinese takeaway meal. Cecil polished off the remains of Serafina's cooking while Minty brought him up to date.

Hugh rang to say it was all right by him, but he wasn't going to tell Toby. Minty grimaced but thought Hugh was probably wise. Her plan wouldn't work if even a hint of it got out. She had decided not to tell Iris, either. She had an uneasy feeling that Iris might go straight to Hatton.

Chef rang and was her usual forthright, helpful self. She agreed with the plan. She told Minty that the housekeeper had taken herself off for a fortnight to her sister's, as "she couldn't put up with the way that Maxine woman was carrying on." Without the housekeeper, the cleaners had refused to do anything.

Neville came round with the accounts. Patrick and he went over what had been done and what still needed to be seen to. Minty fell asleep in an armchair and only woke when Patrick locked up and turned off the lights.

She stirred then. "Has everyone gone? How many hours till D-Day?"

"Get some sleep while you can. Serafina's in bed already. Neville's just gone back up to his aunt's. She's sent a message saying she's been looking out her father's World War Two revolver. I just hope she hasn't any ammunition for it!"

She twined her arm in his as they went up the stairs together. "We agreed you've got to go into work as usual."

"Missing all the excitement."

She steered him into the big front bedroom. "I thought we'd get a good night's sleep in a big bed for once."

He took off his tie slowly. "I never thought I'd occupy this bed. I remember my father and mother sleeping here. They used to wait till they were in bed before they'd talk about all the bad things that were happening to us."

Minty slapped her forehead. "I'm an idiot. Of course you won't want to sleep here." What anxiety and sorrow this bed must have witnessed!

Sir Micah Cardale's lust for his secretary had done more than drive his wife to her death. The gossip had ruined Patrick's father, who'd fled the village but had never really recovered, while his wife had gently faded away.

Only Patrick had survived to return and fight for his own career—and for Minty.

Minty said, "Your own bed is narrow, but I'm sure we can manage."

Patrick took a deep breath. "I refuse to let the past ruin the present. If you could get back into those shorts, I daresay I could manage to forget everything else."

"Do we really need the shorts?"

"Er ... no, probably not." And they didn't.

Afterwards she lay with her head on his shoulder, thinking about the past ... and what she hoped would happen on the morrow. And how much she owed to her husband. She said, "I promised you so much when we married. I've brought you nothing but trouble."

"I knew what I was doing when I married you."

"I suppose most people thought you gained most by marrying me, but I think you lost a lot. Your independence. A home of your own. A garden."

She felt him hold back a sigh. He didn't deny it. "I'm happy enough wherever I am, so long as I have work — and you."

"It's not right. I promised you a quiet room of your own, but you never got it."

"If it all gets too much for me at the Hall, I can always come back here for an hour or so." His arm tightened around her. "No, I didn't mean that."

"Yes, you did. The thing is that the Hall is not really my home, either. It's somewhere I have to live and look after and pass on in good nick when I die. I know I've tried to make our rooms comfortable, but it's not your home yet, and it ought to be. I wonder ..."

He kissed her forehead. "Now what mischief are you considering?"

"Linenfold panelling. A ceiling not too high and not too low. Polished old oak floorboards. Low bookcases round the walls and a huge desk. Comfortable leather chairs."

She'd aroused his curiosity. "There's nothing like that at the Hall. Except, I suppose, the library. Only, that's not linenfold panelling."

She sat up, excited. "No, but ... you remember that my father closed off the doorway leading into my stepmother's rooms?"

"Because he couldn't bear the sight of her? Well?"

"The door's still there, just plastered over. The rooms on the top floor were only used for guests in her day. The room nearest the tower is one large bedroom at the moment, but you could have it as a library for your very own."

He lay still, but she could feel the excitement rising in him, too. "Linenfold panelling? Is there a proper fireplace as well?"

"There should be. There's chimney stacks going right up that side of the house. You like the idea? Good. Now, about a garden ..."

He laughed and drew her down beside him. "One fantasy at a time, Minty. And remember, you've still got to regain possession."

"Tomorrow," she promised. "Tomorrow."

Chapter Fourteen

They say tomorrow never comes, but this one did.

After the usual Bible reading, Patrick decided to read a certain story from the New Testament. "Jesus at the temple. Then he entered the temple area and began driving out those who were selling. He said, 'My house will be a house of prayer, but you have made it a den of robbers.'"

Minty dressed with care, put her hair up and found some decent high-heeled shoes to wear. Put on her pearl earrings. Wondered where all her good jewellery was. Had Patrick put it in the bank before they went abroad? She must ask him, when this was over.

They ate breakfast in silence. Minty thought Patrick was praying. She was, too. Serafina, who usually had plenty to say, was also quiet.

Minty followed Patrick down to his car and kissed him, holding on to him for longer than usual. He took out his fob watch. "It should have started. Should we hear it from here?"

She shook her head. "The wind's in the wrong direction."

He said, "The judge's summing up should finish this morning. Then he'll send the jury out. If all goes as I think, the jury won't be out long, and I could be back here by mid-afternoon."

She shook her head. "You do the job God has set you and return only when you've finished."

"I'm so torn . . ."

She took his face in her hands. "Now it's you who aren't thinking clearly. God has tested you over the years, offering you advancement in your career with one hand, and the opportunity to help the weak and friendless with the other. You've always chosen to help the weakest people, haven't you? Even this spring when I was ill, you chose to leave your work and turn down the opportunity to work for my father's charity, in order to look after me.

"When Jim needed you, you dropped everything to help him. That was the right thing to do, because I was able by then—with God's help—to stand on my own two feet. Then God gave you another choice; there were three people asking for your help: me, Jim and that poor woman who was going into court so badly prepared. I'm strong enough now. Jim will manage, with his family behind him. You chose to help the one who couldn't help herself, and that was the right choice. I think God is saying now that He wants you to go on helping those who can't help themselves. The charity was set up to further educational projects in deprived areas. They want you to join them, and I think you should. And you should meet the District Chairman and at least discuss what may be involved if you stand for Councillor at the next election."

"You may be right, but I'm still torn."

"Pray for me. And I'll pray for you."

His car started at the second attempt, and she waved him off.

Now to face the music. The powers of evil, regiments of trumpets and kettledrums were going to be brought up against her today. Was she strong enough? She lifted her face to the cloudless blue sky and laughed. If God was with her, who could stand against her?

Elizabeth came in early to feed the kitten, which had refused to leave the shelter of her desk and had spent the night on an old cardigan. Elizabeth had borrowed a litter tray from a neighbour and bought some cat food on her way into the office.

"The poor thing went missing after Mrs Thing's funeral," said Elizabeth. "No one else wants it, so I'll take it home with me when it's learned to trust me."

Minty crouched down beside Elizabeth, who was pushing a bowl of food towards the cat. "It may decide to stay here. What will you call it?"

"Perdita, I think. Lost and found."

The cat's nose twitched at the scent of the food, but it refused to leave the safety of its dark corner.

Minty began to tell Elizabeth what had been planned. Elizabeth said, "You want me to lie to them when they start ringing up?"

Minty hoped she wasn't going to blush. "Yes, please."

"Hm. Well, if it gets you back where you belong …"

The cat decided that it was so hungry it had better take a chance. Keeping an eye on Minty and Elizabeth, it crept far enough out of its corner to eat from the bowl. After it had eaten enough, it retired to its dark corner to wash itself. The two women smiled at one another, united at last by a stray cat.

Neville arrived just as the phone started to ring.

Elizabeth said, "Mr Hatton, is it? Mrs Sands? No, she's not here at the moment. Can I take a message?"

The phone clacked on an urgent, despairing note.

Elizabeth raised her eyebrows. "The burglar alarm's gone off? Really? Well, can't you turn it off? No? How distressing. Well, I suppose you need to find the fuse box and …"

The phone clacked even more furiously.

"Oh, you've done that, have you? Well, I really don't know what else to suggest. Yes, I'll tell Mrs Sands when she returns. Where is she? Somewhere in the village, I suppose. Unless she's gone to court with Mr Sands."

The phone shrieked at her, and Elizabeth said in shocked tones, "Now, don't be like that." And put the receiver down. "Language!"

Minty nodded. "It's started all right. I'll be with Neville in Patrick's office for a while. I just hope they don't think Dwayne had anything to do with it."

Serafina brought in some coffee while Minty and Neville went over the accounts in detail. Minty thought Neville had been a good choice as accountant. He was also a Christian. He'd been as horrified as anyone when Elizabeth had shown everyone the photographs which Elizabeth had printed out for them.

"And the insurances?" said Minty.

"All done. It's costing an arm and a leg, but …"

"Worth it."

Elizabeth came in, looking important. "They've sent Reggie up from the Hall to ask if you know how to turn the burglar alarm off."

Minty laughed. "Send him in. I'll make some more coffee."

Reggie came in, wearing his chauffeur's uniform and grinning. "You should see them all running round like ants! I must say the noise does your head in."

Neville wanted to know, "Where did you break the circuit? And how did you do it without them realising it was you who's sabotaging things?"

"Don't tell him anything, Reggie," said Minty. "It's best that nobody knows except you."

Reggie accepted a mug of coffee and sat down, still grinning. "Mr Sands knows, of course. When Minty asked me if it could be done, it was his making sure that we had a good alarm system that let me see how to do it. That alarm vibrates right through you. After a while it makes you want to run away. You shoulda seen them. Eight o'clock this morning it started, while most of them were still in bed, though Chef was just arriving and Hodge was up and about in the garden.

"I makes myself scarce, like you said. I went up early for petrol in the big car, checking for that unevenness I thought I heard in the engine yesterday. Took the car right up to the garage at the cross-roads. Hadn't got me mobile with me, had I? Stupid of me. I didn't get back till about half nine, say, and they was all over me. Hodge was playing stupid, got big wads of cotton wool stuck in his ears. Chef was about ready to hit Hatton with her rolling pin, saying how could she get breakfast for his lot if she couldn't hear herself think!"

Minty offered chocolate biscuits, and he took several.

"Then Hatton comes down. He was yelling to make himself heard, and I was wondering how he'd stood it that long and I'd only been back five minutes. He wanted to know where had I been, did I know where the main fuses were? Well, a course I knew. I said why hadn't them in the Estate Office told him? But they was out in the Park, that lot, covering their ears. Iris and Toby, they were out there, too. Iris was nearly in tears. Hatton said they'd tried taking out the ordinary fuse for the alarm, but it didn't seem to work.

"No, says I. That's right. It's fitted into the mains, to stop burglars taking out the first lot of fuses. Then, because of all the noise, I couldn't think straight to tell him where the main fuse box was and I asked Hatton didn't he know, and a course he oughta had known, but he didn't. Right waste of space he is. That's when that creepy manager Axel comes down and demands to know when order's to be restored. Order, he says! I'll give him order. And that nasty Nero, him as chases everything that's got boobs.

"Then it comes to me, gradual like, where the main fuse box might be. And I leads them down into the old kitchens. Only I couldn't find the right key for the box. I said to Hatton, he must have it. And Hatton says no. Axel screams at us both to get a move on."

Minty was enjoying this, as was Neville.

"So Hatton has to go back to his flat and search for keys. Sweat was dripping off him by this time. Those bells keep up such a hammering, you can't see straight. Axel said Maxine was lying in bed with ear plugs in . . ."

"Oh." Minty was disappointed.

". . . but she'd said we'd better fix it pronto or they couldn't carry on with the filming. The director of the video crew comes up, and he starts yelling and then he has to run outside to get away from the noise and Hatton screams after him . . ." Reggie was almost crying with laughter by this time.

Neville said, "What happened when they threw the main switch?"

"Nothing." Reggie put his mug down, grinning. "Well, the main power went off, a course, but Mr Sands had said ages ago that we ought to bypass the main switch so that no burglar could throw that and cut the alarm off. I'd got that fixed up months ago, and it works a treat. Throwing the main switch doesn't kill the noise."

Minty said, "I was afraid they'd get some electricians up from the festival site to fix it."

"Hatton went down there on his bended knees and implored them to help, but they said the house was nothing to do with them, and they'd got enough on, and anyway, it doesn't sound so bad from down there."

"Good. What about the police? Have they arrived yet?"

"Police, yes. The security men on the gate wouldn't let them in at first. Hatton had to go down and tell them it was okay to let the police in, which they did. The police said we should get the people who installed the system to come and turn it off. Only, Hatton didn't know who the company was, and by that time the people from the Estate Office and Iris had gone home with a headache."

Minty nodded. It was best that Iris was out of the way.

The previous night Reggie had given Minty the name and telephone number of the people who'd installed the alarm, and she'd rung them straight away to tell their head office that she was going to have a good long test of the installation that morning, so that if they got an emergency call from the Hall, to ignore it.

Minty made some more coffee, and Elizabeth handed it round.

Reggie got to his feet. "Hatton'll find out soon enough who the alarm people are. There are worksheets in the Estate Office, signing out their quarterly checks on the system. So I'd best get back. I'll say I searched the village and you weren't nowhere to be found."

"Bless you, Reggie," said Minty, standing on tiptoe to kiss his cheek. "I'm a little worried that they might turn on Dwayne."

"He's a half-way good electrician, but he don't know the Hall like I do," said Reggie. "Luckily he was in late this morning, long after the noise started, so they know he couldn't have had anything to do with it."

"You weren't there when it started, either, were you?"

Reggie winked. "I know one or two tricks. Your father was always interested in clocks, Minty. He'd have been amused by all these goings-on, wouldn't he? I'll buy some ear plugs for myself and Chef on the way back. When shall I tell Hatton that you'll be back?"

"Half an hour? I've got to get Maxine out of there, and if she's got ear plugs then I'll have to rely on everyone else getting so worked up they'll force her to act. Tell Hatton that I've gone up to the Manor House but should be back in half an hour."

Reggie left.

Minty said, "Now we wait—and pray."

Minty was alone in the office when a commotion at the door heralded Clive Hatton's arrival. Elizabeth ushered him in—but first through the door was Gemma, wringing her hands.

"Oh, Minty! It's so awful! Can you stop it? Clive says you'd know how, but I said you'd never do such a thing, would you?"

Minty remained in her seat, studying a file. "Good morning, Gemma. Good morning, Mr Hatton. Don't tell me there's an emergency that you can't deal with!"

Clive Hatton eased himself into a chair. He'd had a hard morning and it showed, but he was by no means beaten.

Gemma wailed, "Don't you know? There's the most awful ..."

Minty blanked Gemma's voice out and watched Clive Hatton, just as he watched her. As Iris had said, he did have brains.

He said, "You arranged it, didn't you?"

Minty snapped the file shut. "Of course."

Gemma gaped.

Minty said, "Sit down, Gemma, and keep quiet. You're way out of your depth."

Mr Hatton leaned back in his chair. "You also know how to turn it off?"

"Yes. Tea, coffee?"

He ignored her offer of refreshments. "What can you possibly hope to gain? Do you want to stop the festival? No, that would be ridiculous. You'd lose too much money."

"I'm fully insured. Neville saw to that for me."

Gemma looked from one to the other, with her mouth open.

Mr Hatton said, "You went behind my back to insure ...?"

"You ought to have seen to it yourself."

He spread his hands. "There'd be no risk of a loss if you hadn't returned early. I must object in the strongest terms to your interference. It places me in an impossible position."

Minty raised her eyebrows.

He hesitated, reading the danger signals but unable to stop. He knew what fury awaited him back at the Hall if he failed to make Minty back down. "If you have no confidence in me, you only have to say so."

Minty weighed her words. "I can trust you to obey orders. My question is, whose orders are you obeying?"

He reddened. "Do you imply that I am not acting in your best interests? That is unpardonable. I must ask you to retract."

"Otherwise ...?"

"You make my position untenable. I would have no option but to resign ... which would leave you trying to run an event for which you have no experience."

Minty was cautious. "I would accept your resignation like a shot, but I'm thinking of you. Are you really offering to resign within a day of the festival opening? How would that look on your CV? Because people do talk, you know. You couldn't expect a tidbit like that not to be broadcast."

Gemma said, "Oh, Clive ... you don't mean it!"

"Shut up, Gemma." He nibbled his forefinger, watching Minty. "I could equally well blackball you."

Minty opened the file and spread on the desk the photographs of the carnage in the chapel. He gave them a cursory look. Seemed to stop breathing and lose colour. He stood up and stepped over to the desk to examine the photographs more closely. "Who took these? When ...? You were up there yesterday, weren't you? Someone said ... but I didn't believe ...! No, this is a put-up job. You've deliberately faked photographs to blacken Maxine's name."

Minty gathered the photographs together and put them back in the file. "So you didn't know what she was up to? I did wonder, but on the whole I thought you innocent ... of that."

He sat down again, thinking hard.

Gemma whined, "Can I see?" She twitched the file towards herself and opened it. She was shocked, yes. But not horrified, as Clive Hatton had been. If anything, she seemed excited by what she saw.

Clive Hatton decided on a new course of action. "I had nothing to do with what went on in the chapel. I agree, it wouldn't do any good to have those photos linked to my name. So I won't resign."

"Oh, goody!" said Gemma, putting her hand on his arm. He shook it off, concentrating on Minty.

Minty flushed with excitement. Had she won? She mustn't take it for granted. There was a long way to go yet. "Very well. We will agree that you continue in your job for the duration of your contract. So, now that the histrionics are out of the way, what is the purpose of your visit this morning?"

He massaged his jaw, for the first time uncertain of his ground. "To ask you to turn off the alarm, of course. When I finally managed to track down the firm that installed the system, they told me they only took orders from you. They said you'd told them last night you were going to test the alarm this morning and that they needn't concern themselves with a call from me. Who did you use to sabotage the system ... Dwayne?"

"He knew nothing about it, poor lad, and I hope nobody has blamed him for it. I used an old friend, and before you ask how anyone else could have got into the grounds, remember that if I could do it, so could others."

"Do you realise what you've done? Maxine herself is not particularly inconvenienced, but filming has had to stop and everyone has had to vacate the Hall. Heaven only knows what mischief Nero has got up to if he's come up to the village."

"I want to speak to Maxine. I need to ask her to ... ah ... modify her activities." And here Minty placed her hand on the incriminating file.

He was relieved. Got to his feet. "Is that all? Come back to the Hall with me now. I'm sure something can be sorted out."

"This time, she comes here. And it's not quite all, Mr Hatton. There's to be no more videoing at Eden Hall. If there's any argument about that, you may tell the video crew and any hangers-on that I'll speak with them in the restaurant later this afternoon and explain why. I've seen for myself the state that the Hall has fallen into. Also, my housekeeper seems to have taken leave of absence. What do you propose to do about that?"

"I expect she will return when ..."

She cut him short. "I can't wait for her to get back. I'm arranging for a team of professional cleaners to go in to the Hall this afternoon to put the place to rights. You will kindly give the security men orders to let them in. I think there are going to be six — no, make it eight — cars. Here are the licence numbers of the cars concerned. I will be coming in later myself to see that everything has been done to my satisfaction.

Will you please make it clear to the security staff that I, my husband and my housekeeper come and go as we please in future?"

He didn't like it, but he couldn't see any way round it. "Very well. Give me the list."

Minty rose to show him to the door. "Once I'm sure that Maxine can do no more harm, the alarm will be switched off. I must warn you, however, that I know how to switch it on again without leaving this room. You understand?"

He was beaten, and he knew it. He twitched his hand at Gemma, who sulkily left her chair to go to his side. For the first time he looked at Minty with respect. "Mrs Sands ... I ..."

Minty produced a thin smile. "Mr Hatton, perhaps we made a bad start. In time we will get to know one another better."

The front door closed behind them, and Minty allowed herself to relax. The intercom on her desk squawked with glee. Elizabeth had been listening in and recording everything. Also in reception were Neville and Alice Mount.

Minty said, "You heard all that?" A chorus of assent followed.

She said, "We haven't won yet. Keep praying."

She went out into the garden and picked herself a couple of early roses to put in a vase on her desk. Iris appeared from the lane at the back of the houses. She was very pale.

They met by the sundial.

Iris said, "Carol said you'd got photographs showing something nasty's been going on in the chapel, but taking these extreme measures ... are you trying to get Maxine to leave? No, that's ridiculous. You wouldn't risk her walking out and leaving us without a top act—would you?"

Minty just looked at Iris.

Iris reddened. "All right. I know your Puritan conscience won't let you compromise. I'm sure Clive had nothing to do with what went on in the chapel."

"No, I don't think he did."

Iris ran her finger down the gnomon on the sundial. "As soon as the alarm went off, I guessed you'd arranged it, though I can't think how. Through Reggie, I suppose? I didn't know what to do. I told Clive I'd a headache and left. You aren't going to sack him, are you?"

"Why, do you think I should?"

Iris shrugged. "I hope you don't. We need him. Well, give me my orders."

Minty told her what had been planned and what her reason was for thinking that Maxine would not walk out on them. Iris nodded. She'd play along.

Minty wandered upstairs to give a hug to Serafina, who was putting a casserole in the oven to cook. "Iris is on our side, so long as I don't sack Hatton. Where's supper?"

"We can have it here tonight, or up at the Hall. Whichever," said Serafina.

"You'll go in with the team?"

"I wouldn't miss it for anything. Don't forget to give me that little camera of yours before we go."

Minty drifted downstairs again. Waiting was hard on the nerves. Mrs Chickward arrived to swell the number in reception. Venetia Wootton came with Hugh.

"Are we too early, my dear?" Hugh had brought her a huge bunch of white lilac, fragrant and exotic. Minty found a large crystal vase to put them in. Their fragrance stirred the air in the office but was not overpowering.

They waited ... and waited.

How long would Maxine keep her waiting?

Would she, in fact, bother to come?

If she realised the trap that had been set for her, she wouldn't stir one foot outside the Hall.

At twelve Minty sent out for sandwiches for everybody. The landlady of the pub brought them up herself, reporting that there'd been an influx of people fleeing the Hall. Some of them were saying it was young Dwayne who'd sabotaged their work, and wanted to know where he was.

Dwayne turned up on her heels, grinning. "They thought it was me, but I said I wouldna know how! And I wouldn't. What do we do now, then?"

Wait.

Patrick rang. The judge had sent the jury out, and he hoped they wouldn't be too long, though you could never tell with these things.

An hour later Minty's mobile rang. Carol, ringing from Alice and Dwayne's cottage at the bottom of the hill. "Reggie's just driving the big car out of the Hall, turning up the High Street. He'll have a job to park anywhere."

Minty said, "We're off!" All those who were leaving for the Hall went through the hallway and out to their cars. That left Mrs Chickward, Hugh, Elizabeth and Minty alone in the house.

It was very quiet.

Reggie took his time coming up the hill, turning at the top of the street and then coming down so that Maxine could alight from the car straight onto the pavement.

Elizabeth reported his progress from the reception room window. "There's that creepy manager of Maxine's getting out of the car, and he's handing out a woman but ... she's a redhead. What on earth's she wearing?"

Minty sent up an arrow prayer. *Dear Lord, You know how much hangs on this. Help me to say the right words. Strengthen my resolve. Be with me throughout.*

Chapter Fifteen

The door opened, and in came Axel, Maxine's manager, followed by a vision in white and silver. A redhead, as Elizabeth had said. Presumably it was Maxine's own hair this time. Hazel eyes, pale complexion. A long white dress and a surcoat of white and silver.

Minty gasped and felt for the arms of her chair. "My wedding dress!"

"This old rag?" Maxine walked around the office, fingering this and that. She was a little taller than Minty, so the dress came a trifle above her ankles while the surcoat swept the floor behind. It was a beautiful dress and looked good on Maxine.

Minty fought for self-control. She wanted to fall on the woman and tear the dress off her, the dress in which she had walked down the aisle to where Patrick stood tall and straight, waiting for Cecil to say the words which would make them man and wife. She'd known herself to be beautiful that day, wearing that wonderful dress, and seeing the love in his eyes. Afterwards, Patrick had swung her round and round, making the dress swirl out behind her, and they'd laughed and clasped one another ... and Reggie had driven them back to the Hall, where all their friends were waiting to rejoice with them ... and she'd practically danced down the Long Gallery, the train of the sleeveless surcoat swinging out behind her ...

And now ...

How dare Maxine!

Minty realised she was shaking. She unstuck her hands from the arms of her chair and tried to breathe slowly, deeply. Maxine had worn that dress deliberately, to push Minty off balance. These were tactics she'd used before. They'd worked in the past.

But not this time. They fed Minty's anger but also cooled it, because she realised all over again how dangerous this woman was.

Maxine didn't speak but took a chair opposite Minty, leaving Axel to hover in the background. Axel was burdened with a large tote bag with Maxine's initials on it.

Maxine's complexion was flawless, her hair a brilliant aura around her head. No wonder she'd made Gemma shave off her locks, for their hair must be precisely the same shade of auburn. Perhaps Maxine's hair was a trifle on the thin side? Perhaps that was why she chose to wear wigs most of the time?

She looked at Minty from under slumberous eyelids. "I assume you arranged for the alarm to be set off and can stop it again in an instant. I offered you a fair price for the Hall. Why are you making things so difficult for me?"

"The alarm ceased within minutes of your leaving the Hall, but we need to rewrite the terms of the contract."

"You provided suitable accommodation. I'm making a video, and I've given your stupid sister work. What could be fairer than that?"

"There was nothing in the contract about using the Hall to make a video. Or about precisely which rooms you should have. Or about desecrating the chapel."

"Desecrating?" The finely pencilled eyebrows rose. "That's a big word for a little girl. Do you know the meaning of it?"

Minty's chin went up. "You've abused my hospitality. The contract between you and the Hall is terminated."

"Little girl, little girl. You can't afford to upset me. If I go, the festival falls apart."

"I'm fully insured in the event that you don't appear, but I don't think you will refuse to appear, Maxine. I looked up your recent career on the Internet, and it seems to me that you're on the downward slope. You've a reputation for cancelling at the last minute. Fans don't like that, and neither do managers who have to refund tickets. Your bank balance can't be as healthy as you'd like to pretend, either. Your last two albums haven't done well. I think you need to appear at our festival far more than we need to have you."

For the first time, Maxine hesitated. She even glanced towards where Axel stood behind her.

Minty, too, looked at Axel.

He said, "Maxine, it may be that there is some sense in what she says. When you appear, everyone goes mad for you, but it wouldn't do any good for you to cancel again."

Minty let her breath out slowly. It looked as if she had an ally in Axel.

Maxine wasn't admitting anything. "Anyone would think you knew the first thing about my world."

"I'm learning," said Minty.

"If you tear up that contract, I'll sue you."

"I'd prefer to see you go and to collect what I could from the insurance, because what you've done to the Hall sickens me. However, I'll stand by the contract, under certain conditions."

The woman's eyes narrowed. She was, Minty had to admit, amazingly beautiful and also frightening. "You want me to promise not to seduce your husband?"

Minty almost laughed. Did Maxine think to deflect her so easily? "My terms are these. First, there was no provision in your contract for your making videos at the Hall. If you wish to continue making them, you do it elsewhere, and you must include Gemma.

"Secondly, if Nero or any other member of your team breaks the law, either by assaulting someone or by trying to sell them drugs, then the police will be called in."

Maxine lowered her eyelids in disdain and looked away.

"Then," said Minty, "there's the question of 'suitable accommodation' for you. My rooms are not suitable. Our family chapel is not suitable, either." She could feel her breathing quicken at the memory of what this woman had done in the chapel; it would have to be cleansed and re-consecrated before it could be used again. She calmed herself. Shrieking at Maxine wouldn't help.

"You yourself will not set foot in the Hall again. I've arranged for you and one of your entourage—you may choose which one—to be given hospitality with Mrs Chickward, who lives on the Green above the church, until the morning after the festival, when you must leave. As we speak, my team is packing up your belongings and taking them up to her house. The rest of your entourage, including the backing group, may stay on in the west wing at the Hall until the day after the festival—unless, as I said, they abuse my hospitality or break the law, in which case they will leave immediately.

"I'm going back to the Hall shortly to see that the video team and hangers-on leave this evening. Your manager will come with me, to ensure they leave the place as we would wish to find it."

Maxine glanced back at Axel, with the very slightest of frowns marring her forehead. "Your conditions are absurd. You can't expect me to agree with them."

"When my friends went into the Hall they were equipped with cameras and videos to make a record of everything amiss. Please leave a note of your address, so that we can forward you a bill for damages. Is that clear?"

Maxine's face was immobile, but she took hold of the modest neckline of Minty's wedding dress, and tore at it ... and again ... and again ... rending the fabric. With one part of her mind, Minty had to marvel at the strength of the woman. With another part, she wept for the destruction of her lovely gown.

Maxine wasn't wearing anything underneath.

Minty stood, not willing to let Maxine see her distress. "I'll fetch Mrs Chickward for you. She will stay here with you—perhaps you might like some tea or coffee?—while I go up to the Hall. When I've made sure everything of yours has been removed, she'll take you up to her house—which I trust you will treat with more respect than you've treated mine."

Maxine lunged for the vase of white lilac and dashed it to the ground. The vase was made of crystal and didn't break. Minty was reminded of Jim's agony of destruction the day before. Had that been anger, too?

Maxine said, "I'll make you pay for this! I'll take your husband from you, that's what I'll do!"

Minty didn't laugh. The woman meant it and meant to try. *God be with us. God be with Patrick. God protect us all.*

Mrs Chickward and Hugh entered the room. They'd been listening on the intercom, of course. Mrs. Chickward checked when she saw Maxine's bared breast and clucked, "Tsk!" She wore the weary, slightly disgusted expression of a grown-up faced with a toddler's lack of potty-training. Mrs. Chickward was unflappable—as was Hugh, who raised an eyebrow but otherwise appeared unmoved.

Minty said, "Mrs Chickward, this is Maxine. I don't know whether she's Miss, Mrs or Ms. Maxine may not even be her real name, either. Maxine—this is Mrs Chickward, who'll look after you till the festival is over. I'll find some sort of robe for you to wear, as I don't think you need my wedding dress any longer. Mr Schutz, this is Mr Wootton from the Manor. He will accompany us to the Hall now, and when we have finished there, he will take you back to stay with him at the Manor."

"Am I a prisoner, then?" said Maxine, flushing scarlet.

"Certainly not," said Minty. "You're welcome to leave this house whenever you wish. Go wherever you are welcome. Only not to the Hall."

Maxine threw the words at Axel. "Give me my bag." She snatched it from him, then turned her chair round so that she sat with her back to Mrs Chickward. She did not speak or acknowledge her presence in any way.

Mrs Chickward nodded to Minty. "I'll take over now, my dear. Just fetch me something for her to wear, and I'll see to it that your dress is invisibly mended and cleaned. You go and clear up at the Hall."

It occurred to Minty that Mrs Chickward would have made a good prison officer, if she hadn't been born into a county family. Almost, she felt sorry for Maxine. But not quite. She went to fetch something for Maxine to wear that wouldn't be too short for her. A white T-shirt and long blue skirt would be the best bet.

So far, so good. Minty couldn't relax yet. One misstep now and they'd be right back in trouble.

Still no telephone call from Patrick. Was he all right? Had the case gone against his client?

Axel Schutz got into Hugh's car. Minty got into hers. Hugh led the way sedately down the back lane, into the main road—what a lot of traffic! Ah, the festival was due to start tomorrow, wasn't it? Minty tried to remember what time they started tomorrow. Mid-day?

They turned into the Hall through the gates. The security guard checked their car registrations and let them through.

Silence. The alarm was off.

As they went along the driveway, they met two cars and a van coming towards them, taking some of Maxine's people away. Video people? Technicians? Lighting?

Mr Hatton met them in the courtyard. He looked as if he was still in charge—but only just. Iris was at his elbow, unsmiling, uneasy.

Iris said, "Welcome back, Minty. Chef's kept the restaurant open and I think everyone's there now … except for a couple of the video crew who've already gone. I'll be in the Estate Office if you need me."

The man who'd been directing the videos was pacing up and down the courtyard on his mobile. Speaking to Maxine? Hearing the bad news?

The restaurant was stifling with cigarette smoke and the press of too many people in the space. Most looked sullen. Nero wasn't there.

Minty was greeted at the door by Chef—dear Florence—four-square, peroxided and efficient. She indicated that Minty should step up onto a chair and thence to a table so that she could be seen by everybody. Minty made sure that Axel Schutz kept by her side.

"What's going on, then?" was the first question thrown at her. "Where's Maxine?"

Minty raised her hand to quell the murmur that rose from all sides. "I don't suppose you know who I am, but my name is Araminta Cardale Sands, and the Hall is my home. In my absence, some of my rooms were lent to Maxine and her friends. Now that I've returned, I need my home back again."

Silence. A considering silence, but not a hostile one. They were, reluctantly, able to see her point of view.

"Maxine will still be appearing at the festival with her usual backing group, but she has accepted alternative accommodation here in the village. Mr Schutz has also been found a suitable place to stay. Mr Schutz will now explain in detail what this means to each one of you."

She stepped down from the table onto a chair and then to the floor, while Hugh helped Mr Schutz up into her place.

Mr Schutz knew his job, she had to acknowledge that. He accepted what had happened with a good grace and was making the best of it. He singled people out by name, saying who was to stay for the time

SECRET OF THE HALL

being, and who would no longer be needed. He said they should all be grateful to Mrs Sands for giving them accommodation, and he was sure they'd leave their rooms as they would like to find them.

He handed over to the man who'd been directing the videos, who confirmed that there would be no more shooting at the Hall. He said he'd be contacting everyone on his team via their mobiles to let them know where and when the videos were to be finished. He also said he hoped everyone who had to leave that afternoon would see that their quarters were in perfect order ... so that one day they might be invited back.

The crew drifted out. There was some grumbling, of course. Some people didn't know where they'd finish up that evening, but they made arrangements with others to be put up at friends' houses. Some hostile glances were sent Minty's way, but no one challenged her right to reclaim her home.

Minty thanked Mr Schutz and said she'd arrange for someone to come up to his room with him to help him clear his things out. She didn't really think he was the sort to pinch bric a brac and towels, but it was better to be on the safe side. He said he quite understood her position, and he hoped she also understood his. She nodded.

He faded into a doorway and got out his mobile phone. Phoning Maxine? The papers? Minty shrugged. He couldn't do much harm now, could he?

Clive Hatton came forward, smiling relentlessly. Perhaps he wasn't best pleased by the way things were going, but he seemed to have learned on which side his bread was buttered.

"Well done," he said, offering to shake her hand. "What a clever little woman you are, to be sure."

If there was one thing that set her teeth on edge, it was being patronised. "Will you make sure no one leaves with 'souvenirs' of their visit to the Hall?"

"Of course." He wandered off. She wasn't sure she could rely on him, but what choice did she have?

When the restaurant was clear of people, Minty threw her arms round Florence and ordered herself not to weep into her comfortable shoulder. "Dear Florence—no, I must remember to call you 'Chef'. You've been brilliant."

Chef hugged Minty and patted her shoulder. "I did what I had to do, Minty. Thank the good Lord for sending you back when He did, because I don't know what would have happened otherwise. Hodge and Reggie might have blown the place up or something."

"You did right. And you did extra right to keep going. I don't know how I'd have got that woman out of the place if it hadn't been for you lot working for me inside. Now tell me, how soon can we get our housekeeper back?"

One of the restaurant staff began putting chairs on tables preparatory to leaving for the night, so Chef drew Minty to one side. "I've got her mobile number, and we've been keeping in touch. She'll be back as soon as this lot's out of the way."

"Good. Now, how have you been doing? Is your daughter still working for you?"

"Not with Nero around, she isn't. He went for one of my girls the very first day, and I had to threaten him with a frying pan before he let go. She left that afternoon, and I couldn't blame her. My daughter's gone to help one of her sisters in the city, who's having her second baby any minute now. I'll get the girls back when he's out of the way. I got two part-timers in from the village, older women that know how to work, and I might keep them on, we've been that busy."

Chef paused, looking out of the window. "Mr Hatton told me to let Maxine and her crew eat what they liked on the house. I told him no way, because I had my girls' wages to pay and food to buy. The crew were happy enough to pay for their food at reasonable prices, and I've put the money in a separate account, not wanting it to get dribbled away through someone else's fingers, if you take my meaning."

Minty filed that piece of information away. Did Clive Hatton have his fingers in the till? Or was he just lax in controlling expenses?

"Now we'd best get out of their way while they mop the floor," said Chef. Minty obeyed her, returning to the courtyard.

Serafina trundled out of the house, dragging two black sacks after her. Behind her came a fat girl in a tight T-shirt and even tighter leggings, lugging along two enormous suitcases. They dumped the lot by the wall.

Serafina said, "Minty, this is Maxine's make-up artist. She'll fetch Maxine's car, which is round the back, and take herself and Maxine's luggage up to Mrs Chickward's. Just one more bag to come."

Minty dared to ask, "How bad is it up there?"

"The chapel made my flesh creep. I took some more photos, as you said. But the rest of your rooms aren't too bad. Furniture's been shifted, one or two pictures changed around, but the place has been kept clean and tidy. Only, she's been wearing some of your clothes, and I don't think ..."

Minty shuddered. "Burn them."

"Right. Also, you won't want to stay there tonight. The rooms are thick with her scent, and there's joss sticks everywhere. And the bed linen ...!"

Minty felt herself grow pale. "Burn that, too. Do we need a new mattress? We could take the one off the double bed in the spare room." With a pang of regret she remembered how much fun she and Patrick had had in the four-poster bed with its willow-pattern curtains. Could she bear to sleep there again, knowing what Maxine might have got up to?

Then she remembered Patrick saying that he wouldn't let the past ruin his future. She braced herself. "Serafina, that perfume of hers has probably got into the upholstery and the soft furnishings and may be difficult to shift. We could take the rugs out and hang them up somewhere to air, but what about the bed curtains? Could we have them cleaned? We can do without them in this warm weather."

Serafina nodded. "I was going to suggest that."

"Do you think we could move back in tomorrow, if we leave all the windows open overnight?"

Serafina nodded again and returned to the house.

Venetia Wootton hurried up—she always did things at the double. "Oh, Minty dear. I've just come from the chapel and ... ugh! It made my skin creep. Isn't there some kind of law against it? I told Toby he should have a look-see for himself and not be so silly as to trust that woman, but there ... men will always fall for a beautiful face. Now, you asked me to check on the west wing: the people who're staying there haven't made too much mess—all surface litter and dust, if you know what I mean. The gift shop's been locked up all this time, and there doesn't seem to be anything missing. I don't see why we shouldn't open the Hall to visitors again next week."

"Splendid," said Minty, distracted by seeing Mr Schutz still talking on his mobile phone. Who was he talking to? Maxine? Probably. Did it matter?

Venetia also spotted Mr Schutz. "How about you, Mr Schutz? Have you got your things yet? Have you got your own car here? You're staying with us, aren't you? Let me tell you how to get to the Manor."

Mr Schutz finished his phone call and mumbled that he ought to get his things. Venetia said she'd go with him to get them if he liked, and they went off together.

Carol came up, ginger hair aflame in the late afternoon sun, carrying her own camera. "I couldn't believe the chapel was as bad as you said, but it was. I felt sick. Anyway, I got the windows open and that's helped. Now, I've looked through the State Rooms. There are one or two pieces of furniture which are going to need stripping and re-polishing. I've taken preliminary photographs. I could arrange for that to be done in our workshops, if you like. It'll have to be an insurance job, and it'll take ages to get the paperwork through, but they'll be as good as new in the end. I'll come in tomorrow and make a detailed list of the damage."

Mrs Collins came bustling up. "My dear, I've never been so shocked! That darling little chapel! People who do that sort of thing ought to be strung up. Will it have to be de-registered or something? I'll ring the bishop and ask what's to be done. As for the rest, the State Rooms are a disgrace. So neglected! All the pictures in the Long Gallery will have to be taken down and dusted before we hold another function there. The Great Hall's not too bad, though there's some cigarette burns on the padded leather window-seats, can you believe it? Oh, and I've just seen Alice, and she says the public lavatories are a disgrace, though I haven't visited them myself ..."

Alice sped up with Dwayne in tow. "Minty, I've got to pick up Marie, but I'll be back first thing in the morning with one or two people I can trust, and we'll soon get the place looking all right again." She looked sober. "Except for the chapel, and to tell the truth, I just don't know if I could bear to go in there again."

Dwayne ducked his head at her. "Thanks, Mrs Sands. I don't know how you got rid of Nero because I'd have slaughtered him if I'd got the chance, though Alice says he isn't worth going to prison for, so ... thanks."

"Alice, you're a marvel," said Minty. "But remember, you two, that Nero is still around, so you'd better stay at the pub till the festival's over and he's gone." Alice went off with Dwayne's arm around her.

Minty looked around. "Chef, have you seen Nero?"

Chef was putting on her coat and collecting her handbag. "He'll be down the village chasing that silly girl from the council estate. She's only sixteen, but no one's said anything because it keeps him out from under our feet. See you in the morning, Minty. A big day for the Hall. Mr Hatton wants me to cater for his guests as well as keeping the restaurant open for performers and back stage staff."

"What guests?"

Chef shrugged. "Important people he and the sponsors have invited. Ten to one he's underestimated what's needed, but we'll cope somehow, I suppose."

Toby came up, looking like a wet weekend. "You were right, Minty. The chapel! I'd heard a rumour, but didn't believe that Maxine would ... I have to face it. She isn't the woman I thought she was."

Mr Hatton emerged from the house. She smiled at him, thinking this was the time to mend fences. "Mr Hatton, do you have a minute? I need to understand who is responsible for what. Who's in charge of the artists, for instance?"

"The stage management," said Mr Hatton, making it clear that Minty was an ignoramus, "is supplied by the promoter on these occasions. I've asked him to spare a moment to meet you ... and here he is. Billy ... meet the Lady of the Hall. Mrs Sands, this is the man who makes everything happen."

Billy was a small man with a big voice, shrewd as they came, with a trail of youngish men and women behind him, all razor keen and efficient. He shook Minty's hand and said he was delighted to meet her ... provided Maxine turned up to perform.

Minty nodded. "Her manager agrees with you that she should."

"Splendid, splendid!" One of his minions handed him a mobile, and Billy turned away to attend to his phone call.

Minty caught Mr Hatton's arm, since he seemed about to follow Billy. Reaction was catching up with her, but she must make an effort to share her concerns with Mr Hatton. "Please, Mr Hatton. Before you go. Are there really three different sets of security men on the site, and if so, who is in overall charge?"

Clive Hatton patted her arm. "Suppose you let me get on with my job. That's what you pay me for, isn't it?"

She reddened. Was she really being stupid? Possibly. "Yes, but ... I'm worried that the drinks tents are too near the lake."

It was no good. He'd already shaken her off and was concentrating on Billy, who was beckoning to him, nodding and smiling, anxious to get away. Minty found she was actually trembling! But she had to make one more effort.

She called after him. "Mr Hatton! I'll see you at ten tomorrow morning, right?" She wasn't sure he even heard her as he ushered Billy back into the house. Toby, looking anxious, followed them.

Serafina returned with one last plastic bag and a box containing various bits and pieces, just as Maxine's make-up artist carefully drove a white limousine—Maxine's car?—into the courtyard. Hugh helped her load up and manoeuvre the monster out of the courtyard and away, and then followed himself.

Chef locked up and departed in her own, smaller car.

Venetia returned with Mr Schutz. She was carrying his laptop and briefcase, while he dragged a suitcase behind him. They took everything round the corner to load into Mr Schutz's own car, which chugged off, following Venetia in her car out of the Hall grounds. Venetia waved as she left. "I'll be back tomorrow to help clear up."

Two large youngish men loaded equipment into a van with shouts and bangs fit to wake the dead. But there: some men just couldn't work without making a noise.

Minty stood in the courtyard, watching everyone leave. Soon everything would be back to normal. Perhaps. Except that the festival started the following day.

Reggie came up. He'd shed his chauffeur's uniform for his usual casual gear. "Not much damage, considering. Clearing up in the Park's going to be the worst. Some people don't know what a rubbish bin's for."

"Dear Reggie. How ever would I have managed without you?"

He grinned. "Wasn't that a laugh?" He wandered away.

All was quiet. Patrick still hadn't rung. Minty nerved herself to go back into the Hall.

Chapter Sixteen

Until she'd walked through every room, re-visited every corner, she wouldn't feel that the Hall was hers again.

Serafina came with her, through the maze of rooms in the oldest part of the Hall into the deserted Fountain Court, where the flow of red liquid had dried to a trickle. What had they used in the fountain? Not wine, presumably, but some coloured water? Would the fountain need specialist cleaning? She must ask Neville how they were fixed for insurance to cover the damage Maxine and her people had done.

They turned into the Long Gallery, where the portraits seemed to welcome her back again. Dust, more dust. The trestle tables — where had they come from? — a considerable amount of discarded clutter, and junk food packaging. Nothing serious.

The State Rooms . . . now quiet and waiting for . . . voices? For the family to return? Her mother's portrait still hung over the fireplace in the library. Good. The Scrabble board lay unattended. She wondered who'd been playing.

Up the stairs to the top floor, missing out the State Bedrooms. The chapel — she made herself enter and look around. She was not going to be sick. No.

Serafina said, "Do you think Carol's furniture restorers can mend our chairs? I liked that chair. It suited me."

"We'll see about it tomorrow. Serafina, I don't think we can ask anyone else to clear this up. We'll have to do it ourselves."

Serafina nodded. "What makes a woman turn to this?"

"I didn't think people still made pacts with the devil, but perhaps that's what she was doing. Inviting him into her life in exchange for fame and fortune?"

"If the devil lives up to his reputation, she'll get more than she bargained for."

Minty felt the black hole open up before her and swayed on her feet. Alarmed, Serafina grasped her arm and helped her out of the chapel onto the landing.

"What was it? The incense?"

Minty rubbed her forehead, blinking. "I don't know what it is. It comes back and hits me now and then. There, now. I'm all right again. Really. No need to look so anxious. Let's look at the rest of our rooms on this floor."

It wasn't too bad. No. Apart from the incense, she thought she could probably have moved back in that night. The bedroom reeked of Maxine's perfume as well as incense. But the windows were all open, and a light breeze was making headway.

Serafina pulled the bed curtains up and sniffed at them. "A pity we've got to close these windows for the night, but if we don't, and the alarm's switched on again, we'll be in trouble. You're right about the curtains and the rugs. I'll get someone to help me take them down tomorrow."

Some of Minty's clothes were on the floor. She'd taken very little with her when Patrick had whisked her away to the Continent. There lay her favourite cornflower blue skirt, and the silk blouse which she'd worn to Mrs Chickward's last drinks party—which reminded her that an invitation from that good lady was more of an order than a request. What could she wear tomorrow?

Minty didn't even want to touch the clothes which Maxine had worn.

Serafina said, "It was a good thing you didn't let Maxine come back here to pack for herself. Heaven knows what damage she'd have done if she'd realised she was being thrown out."

Minty nodded. The dining room and kitchen were much as they should be. It didn't look as if Maxine had been one for cooking. The spare bedroom had been used—presumably by one of her entourage—but didn't stink of perfume or incense. The furniture had been shifted around in the cool green sitting room, but nothing seemed amiss, except that her father's portrait had been taken off the wall, and some publicity shots of Maxine stuck up there with sticky tape instead.

Minty took them down and replaced her father's portrait. He seemed to approve.

At the end of the suite lay the room she had used as an office. It looked as if Maxine had used it for that purpose, too. The computers were still switched on. Minty checked to see if any viruses had been introduced, but they looked to be working normally.

Serafina tipped up the chair behind the desk and revealed a key which had been hidden beneath the seat. She handed it to Minty. "I locked up your laptop and diary in the bottom drawer of the desk after your accident. I expect you'll need them again now."

Minty nodded and retrieved them. Strange to see them after so long.

She followed Serafina into the tower office, which had once been the headquarters for Toby and Iris. Blank and dusty, none of the computers seem to have been used. Of course, Toby and Iris were working in the offices on the other side of the courtyard nowadays.

Minty wondered if they ought to move back. Would the tower office be a good "den" for Patrick? No. It simply wasn't big enough. He needed space.

She went to the far wall of the tower and ran her hands over where the door into the next wing ought to be. Yes, she could see cracks in the plaster outlining the door. She tapped and thumped. The wall was hollow there. It sounded as if plasterboard had been used to seal the aperture, and that it hadn't been bricked up. Perhaps it wouldn't be a big job to open up that door again.

Her mobile rang. Patrick, at last. He sounded tired but pleased.

"Are you all right, Minty? I've finished here. The jury was out much longer than we thought, but we got the right result. I would have come back straight away, but I thought I'd better check on Jim first."

"I'm fine. Back in the Hall, though our rooms need a thorough clean and airing before we can move back in. We'll have supper back at your place ..."

Serafina gave a little scream. "My casserole! I forgot! Did I turn the oven right down when I left?"

Patrick laughed. "I heard that. Tell Serafina that I'm taking you out to supper and we'll have the casserole tomorrow night if it's still edible. All right? Pick you up in an hour at my old place, right?"

"Right. I'll just finish my rounds and get back in good time."

She dressed with care, wearing one of the outfits they'd bought in Italy, in cream silk with a cocoa-coloured trim. It had a long, swishy skirt, and there was a cream silk jacket to go with it. Patrick's house was filled with a blue haze from the burnt casserole, and Serafina was viciously angry with herself about it. And Elizabeth, it seemed, had noticed something was wrong but hadn't thought it her place to investigate upstairs!

"Never mind, Serafina," said Patrick, dropping laptop, mobile, briefcase and yet another book as he came in. "It proves you're only human, and I've had my doubts about that in the past."

Serafina shrieked at him that he'd better watch it! At which he only laughed. He said, "Everyone makes mistakes, Serafina. Even you. Even me."

"But not me?" asked Minty, entering into the spirit of things.

"Not you, beloved," said Patrick, kissing the tip of her nose, which made her close one eye to see if she needed to put any make-up on it. Serafina told them both to be off before she lost her temper, so they went out, laughing, to the car.

They spoke together. "How was it?"

"How did it go?"

Both laughed. Minty said, "You first. You won the case?"

"The jury found the defendant guilty, which he was. The judge will sentence him next week. Our client is so relieved she's in tears, almost speechless. Went around thanking everyone and shaking their hands, even if they'd had nothing to do with the case. It was a good verdict."

"How about Jim?"

Patrick checked the road before turning off into a narrow lane. "As well as can be expected. His brother-in-law went with him to make the funeral arrangements and register the death. His mother's turned up and told him to pull himself together."

"Oh, dear."

"In a way it's a good thing, because he got so angry with her that it forced him to start making plans to keep out of her way. She proposes moving in with him for a while, when all he wants to do is sit by himself and mope. She won't let him mope. She'll probably drive him back to work, just to get away from her. But first he wants to take some leave."

"Which you've agreed to, of course. What about your new partner? No good?"

"Y—yes. With a bit of encouragement. Jim seems to have been a bit hasty with her, but that's only understandable under the circumstances ... their little girl being so frail and then his wife ..."

Minty waited for the usual black hole to open up in front of her at this mention of the child, but it didn't. *Thank you, Lord.*

She eased the seat-belt over herself. "It's been a long day. I manoeuvred Maxine and her manager out. She says she's going to get back at me. Beware boarders, Mr Sands, for she plans to take you captive."

"I trust you'll rescue me from her clutches, if ever it gets that far."

She smiled. The smile faded.

They'd been going through winding, narrow lanes for a while. When they ate out in the evenings, they often went this way to a remote but popular pub.

She said, trying to keep her voice light, "Are we being followed?"

"Yes. I didn't think you'd noticed."

"You made a diversion." She was uneasy.

A mud-spattered builder's lorry was following them. It was unusual to see a lorry out at this time of the evening, though it did happen occasionally. The lorry's windows were shaded, making it impossible to see who was driving.

She was silent. Patrick concentrated on driving. The Rover was not new, though he looked after it well. He put his foot down and the Rover zoomed down the road, took a right turn with only the slightest of drifts and thundered along the new lane.

The lorry followed, also putting on speed.

He said, keeping his tone light, "They've more power than us. If they get too close, brace yourself."

"What?"

At that moment the lorry put on a spurt of speed and she cried out, bracing herself against the dashboard as the impact came, pushing the Rover along. Patrick fought to keep the car straight. If it was driven into a ditch ...

"Who ...?"

"Hold on!"

Again the crash came. Glass rear lights smashed. The Rover was well built, a strong car and heavy. It held to the road, but how much more of this could it stand?

The lorry tried to come up on their right, trying to nudge them over. Patrick held on to the middle of the road. If they were swept off to the edge, they might well be forced over and ... it didn't bear thinking about. They could be flipped over and ... would the car burst into flames? Why was this happening to them?

Were they being pursued by car thieves? No. Who would want an old Rover, however roadworthy it might be? She didn't understand what was going on. Who would do this to them? Why? It was a nightmare, and she would wake up any minute.

If she'd been driving, she knew they'd have been pushed off the road by now.

Patrick narrowed his eyes, checking the dials on the dashboard for signs of damage. "Hold tight!"

A crossroads was coming up. He indicated to turn right, slowing ... the lorry closed up at speed, its intention clear. It would crash into the back of the Rover as it turned right, sweeping them sideways off the road and leaving them helpless.

She wanted to scream but didn't. Patrick must not be distracted. She must sit still and pray. Pray for all she was worth. Pray that they would live. Pray hard.

She braced herself for what was to come ... and Patrick spun the wheel and took a left turn, leaving only inches to spare as the lorry ploughed straight on.

A scream of brakes.

They were running free. The lorry was slow in turning. It had overshot its mark and was having to back and back, and turn slowly.

Patrick knew the country like the back of his hand. Luckily.

He turned off the lane into another, even narrower road. The countryside hereabouts was a network of tiny lanes, each connecting with one another. Only if you knew the area well would you be able to find your way through.

Minty kept her mouth shut and her chin on her shoulder.

Five minutes later they turned into the pub car park.

Normality. People getting out of their cars, exchanging greetings as parties met up and went into the pub. It was a beautiful evening.

Had it really happened? Had they really been chased through the countryside by a lorry?

Patrick switched off the ignition, his face calm but his eyes seeing more than the old inn with its colourful tubs of flowers. "I left my mobile back at the house."

"I've got mine."

"Good." He got out of the car and inspected the damage. "It's still driveable, but we've no rear lights, which makes us illegal. Let's go in and have a think."

She got out of the car and nearly fell. Too much had been happening that day. She tried to laugh. "I'm not sure I can still walk in a straight line."

Patrick put his hand under her elbow and guided her into the building.

Low beams, huge arrangements of silk flowers, comfortable chairs, pleasantly helpful staff. An aroma of good wines and good food. They used to come here quite often and were acquainted with the manager.

"Good to see you again, Mr Sands … Mrs Sands. Your usual table?" Their usual table overlooked one end of the car park.

They sat, spread their napkins, inspected the giant menus. Minty ordered her hands not to tremble.

Patrick said, "Can you pretend all is well? I think the lorry turned into the car park a moment ago, did a tour to make sure we were here and disappeared again. If I'm right, they're going to wait till we leave and try again."

"How did they know where to come?"

"There's not many places to eat in these parts. An educated guess and some local knowledge?"

She wanted to say she couldn't eat anything, but he was ordering asparagus soup and suggested she have a red onion tart. "I'll have duck's breast afterwards, and what about the sole for you?"

"Lovely," she said, her mouth dry.

Patrick looked up at the waitress. "Now we've had a bit of bad news — family business. We might get a phone call and have to leave in a hurry, so if I give you my card, will you let me pay the bill now? For a sweet and coffee as well. And perhaps half a bottle of the house red for me and some Perrier water for both of us. Add a tip, of course. Can you do that?"

"Of course. What a shame. I'll see to it straight away."

"Thank you."

When the waitress had gone, Patrick said, "Don't look now, but someone's just come in who seems to know you. He's at the bar, drinking, not eating."

She took out her hand mirror and angled it. "Nero." Her hands were still trembling. She forced them to close up the mirror and put it away. "He's the lead dancer in Maxine's group. He likes to jump on women. He jumped on Alice and when she rejected him, he tried to get her sacked, wanted Maxine to sue her. He jumped me and I pushed my keys into his groin." Her teeth were chattering. "I—I expect he's furious because I've stopped their fun and games. I'm sorry."

"Hold hard. Pretend we haven't seen him. Smile if you can. You must be hungry. Have you eaten anything today?"

She tried to smile. Knew she'd not made it. "A sandwich at lunch, I think. It seems a long, long time ago. What do we do about Nero? Call the police? Tell them ..."

"What? We were bumped by a lorry. The number plate was obscured with mud, so we couldn't read it. We couldn't see who was driving, either. We think it might have been a man called Nero who's sitting at the bar here, but we can't prove it. And no, we can't see the lorry now and we don't know where it is. I doubt if the police will come out to rescue us on the grounds that we've been bumped by a lorry. No, we've got here in one piece, and now we've got to think how to get home again — without the Rover."

How could Patrick be so calm?

His soup and her onion tart came. He started on his soup, enjoying it. She picked at the tart, discovered she was hungry. She trusted Patrick to get them out of this mess. He always did get them out of trouble, didn't he? She finished the tart.

"Your mobile," he said. "While we're waiting for the main course, go to the Ladies and see if you can raise Reggie. Tell him what's happened and ask him to bring the big car to the pub. Tell him to wait by the public bar, not the dining room entrance. Understood?"

She nodded. "And then I ring the police?"

"Yes. I don't think they'll come, but at least we'll have registered an 'incident.'"

She picked up her handbag and went out to the Ladies. Reggie answered after a nerve-racking twenty rings. She calmed her breathing to speak coherently, though she felt more like screaming. She repeated the words, "The public bar entrance, not the dining room door."

Reggie was alarmed, but as calm as Patrick. "Give me half an hour. Is that blackguard Nero involved? He come back soon after you left and was raging because you'd stopped the filming and Maxine had promised him his own video. I think he'd been talking to her on the phone. Maybe she's put him up to this."

"But how could he get hold of a lorry? And who's got the local knowledge to help him?"

"His totty in the village, her father's a builder. Is the lorry green, without any name on it?"

Minty leaned heavily against the wall. "Yes. The number plate's got mud all over it, though."

"That's an offence in itself. Half an hour." He rang off.

Minty pushed buttons. "Police, please." And there she struck unlucky, for there'd been a multiple car crash on the main road five miles away and there wasn't anyone to spare to investigate their "incident". Just as Patrick had said.

She went back to the table, trying not to glance towards Nero, who was still sitting at the bar. She even managed to smile and exclaim with delight when their main course came. She reported what she'd learned to Patrick, and he looked up at the clock on the wall to check on the time.

"Eat, drink and be merry," he said, pouring himself a scant half a glass of wine.

"For tonight we die?"

"We might," he admitted. "I'm hoping Nero will think we've put the ramming down to a road rage attack from some person or persons unknown. Since we lost him on the way here and are now behaving normally, he won't suspect we're wise to him or that we're worried about the attack being repeated. He can't know we've connected the dancer Nero with lorries. Let's lull him into a false sense of security, so to speak. Have you any jokes left in your repertoire?"

The sole was delicious, but she couldn't manage the new potatoes that went with it. "No jokes. But how about this? It's a conundrum. Maxine is going to try to get her claws into you. How will she do it? You see, she's staying with Mrs Chickward, and I think she'll try to attend the drinks event tomorrow evening. What will she do to attract you?"

"Turn cartwheels on the lawn? Perform the mamba? Will she come on to me with a long cigarette holder and a husky voice inviting me into the shrubbery?"

How she could laugh under such circumstances, she didn't know.

"We're going to get back all right, Minty. I promise you."

"I'm shaking. Aren't I stupid?"

"No. Very sensible."

"How can you be so calm? You've eaten up every scrap of your food!"

"Practice. Twenty minutes gone. Minty, I think it would be best if you went ahead and got away with Reggie, while I stayed behind to finish my meal. If I sit here stolidly eating my pudding, Nero will think you're coming back and will wait for you to reappear. By the time he discovers his mistake, you'll be back home. He's not interested in me. If I borrow your phone, I could call the garage out to replace the back lights, and drive home safely when he's gone."

"Idiot! I'm not leaving you here. Heaven knows how long it would take the garage to get out here and you'd be stranded, without any transport ..."

"I could call a minicab."

"No. That's final."

"Twenty-five minutes. Very well. I've ordered a crème brûlée each. And coffee. When I say the word, you go out to the Ladies again. Take the door to the left beyond the Ladies, go past the Gents and out into the back of the car park. Walk round the side of the pub till you get to the Public Bar entrance. Wait in the porch there till you see Reggie come. If there's the slightest sign of the lorry ..."

"Or if you see Nero moving?"

"Either. Promise me you'll get into the car with Reggie and high tail it out of here?"

"I'll wait there for you. No argument."

"I shall start on my sweet and keep looking at my watch, giving every sign of annoyance that you've stayed too long in the Ladies. I might even get to eat your sweet, too. Ah, here they come. Delicious. Thank you. And two coffees? Yes.

"Good. Off you go, Minty."

He picked up his spoon. She clutched at her tummy as she got up and grimaced, hoping Nero would think she had a stomach upset. Then almost ran to the Ladies ... out through the door past the Gents ... into the cool air of the evening ... she shivered. She looked around. The car park was well lit. Too well lit for her liking.

There was no sign of the lorry, but father's limousine was nudging its way into the car park and parking — double parking — by the entrance to the Public Bar.

Reggie had made good time.

He opened the door without getting out of the car, and she slid inside.

"Mr Sands?" he said.

"Coming. I'm going to duck down to the floor so no one sees I'm here."

She ducked down. And closed her eyes. And prayed.

Dear Lord above ... dear Lord above ...

As often happened in times of stress, she didn't know what words to use. But words weren't necessary at the moment, were they?

Reggie reversed into a space which seemed too small for that big car. He let the engine idle. You could hardly hear it. He'd opened the partition between the driver and the back of the car. She could hear him shift in his seat. "What happened, Minty?"

She told him. Silence.

"Why didn't Mr Sands call the police?"

"I called them. There's been a pile-up. Also, they'd say it was just road rage that's blown over now the lorry driver's cooled down. Only, I don't believe it."

Reggie was troubled. "Nero knows me and he knows this car."

"Yes, but you're not in chauffeur's uniform now, so he may not recognise you."

Silence.

Patrick opened the car door and got in. "I left Nero still sitting in the bar. Home, Reggie."

They zipped out of the car park and turned right. No lorry followed them.

She began to breathe more easily. Had they imagined they were in danger? The more miles they put between them and the inn, the more she thought they'd misread the situation. Except that Patrick's arm around her was as tight as an iron bar.

"Drop us at my old house, Reggie. And ... thanks."

"I've been thinking," said Reggie. "I'll get Hodge and we'll go back, get someone out to replace the rear lights, and bring the Rover back with us. If they can't replace the lights tonight, we'll get them to tow it to the garage so's it'll be safe."

Patrick thought that over. "There's a risk."

Minty spoke up. "Surely they were after me, not you or Reggie? Whatever you say, I'm going to follow up my complaint tomorrow to the police. You love that car, Patrick. How dare they ram it."

"It won't do it any harm to sit in the car park till tomorrow."

Reggie wasn't so sure. "They might enjoy smashing the windows when they find you've given them the slip."

Patrick's arm jerked about Minty. He really did love his car.

Minty said, "You're right, Reggie. It's just the sort of spiteful thing that Nero would do. Don't go back there, though. There's no need for that. We can ring the garage and get them to tow it away to safety tonight."

Patrick agreed.

Reggie drew up outside Patrick's old house, and they got out. "Thanks, Reggie. See you tomorrow."

Minty stretched. What a day! And what an end to it! Was she wobbly on her feet? Yes, just a little.

Patrick had his key out, letting them into the house. He was anxious to phone the garage straight away. He said he'd pay them double if they got the car out of the car park that night. Minty smiled, tolerant as all good wives are of their husband's love for their cars.

Had Serafina gone to bed? Yes, they could hear her television full on, up in her bedroom. Perhaps she really was getting a bit deaf.

Minty made hot drinks for herself and Patrick. He was clicking the lock of his briefcase on and off. "No, I won't work tonight."

They sat in the light of the one remaining table-lamp, talking of this and that. Deciding they didn't need anything more to eat. Unwinding.

At eleven the phone rang. Patrick answered and went rigid. He listened, answered shortly. Put the phone down. Stared into the distance, tapping the receiver.

He said, "Someone's petrol-bombed my car. The garage dead-heated with the fire brigade. It's burned out. No one saw who did it. The police are on their way."

Chapter Seventeen

Minty couldn't think of any words that would help. He'd bought that car ten years ago, maybe more, when he first went into partnership with Jim. He could have bought new cars for himself, but they hadn't appealed to him.

She remembered him happily unloading his motley crew of passengers the other night. How the car had groaned under the weight but borne it. It had had leather seats and a leather dashboard.

She put her arms about him and held him fast. He was breathing lightly, trying to absorb the hurt.

She wanted to weep but was dry-eyed.

She'd done this to him. She'd been the cause of his losing so much: his home, his child, his garden and now ... his beloved car.

She wondered how he could still bear to look at her.

"It's all right," he said, in tones which informed her that she'd better not argue with him. "It's only a car, when all's said and done. It's not as if either of us was hurt in any way. That's the important thing."

It wasn't, and she knew it.

She said, "Come to bed?" It was the wrong thing to say.

He shook his head. "No, I have to go back there, talk to the police. I'll take your car, if you don't mind."

"I'll come with you."

"No, you won't. You're worn out and anyway, it's not you the police will want to talk to. Go on now."

He pushed her towards the stairs, and she went because she didn't know what else to do. Screaming and crying wouldn't help.

She was so heavily weighted down with sorrow that she could hardly climb the stairs. Serafina's light was out and her television was off. Minty sat on the big bed and wondered if she had the strength to undress. She wanted to pray, but again she couldn't find the words.

Please, Lord. Please.

How terribly stupid she was.

She eased off her shoes, thought hard about pulling down the zip of her dress, washing and getting into bed. If she tried very hard, one step at a time, she might make it. This was the sort of time when the black door opened. But although she half expected it to do so, it didn't. She made herself undress, stumbled to the bathroom, showered thinking it might help. It didn't. Felt her way blindly back to the bed, forgot to turn off the bedside lamp and fell asleep feeling ice cold, rejected.

She woke with a start and felt around for Patrick.

He wasn't there.

The bedside light was still on. She sat upright, remembered what had happened and looked at her watch. It was past one, and he hadn't yet come to bed. Was he still with the police? There was a light on downstairs, so maybe he was back. And maybe not.

She must do something. She didn't know what. Something.

She pulled on the nearest thing to hand — his towelling robe — and went bare-footed down the stairs. His study light was on and he was sitting, fully dressed, at his desk. He'd almost stopped smoking to please her, but now there were three cigarette butts in an ashtray on the desk. She decided she wouldn't chide him for smoking this time. He'd been so good for months ...

He was fast asleep with his head resting on his arm. One hand was outstretched, clutching a piece of paper.

She eased it from his fingers. He stirred but didn't wake.

Then she saw what she was holding. It was the scan which showed their baby in her womb. Alive and kicking.

Across the bottom he'd written "My son."

How many months had he held his own sorrow in check, never once referring to it, but always tender to her grief?

How selfish she'd been, never thinking of his grief for the loss of his child, but only of her own.

She couldn't bear it.

O Lord, help me! How could I have been so unloving towards him? Why didn't I think of his grief at all? Why did I only think of myself?

As if she'd cried out loud, he stirred. Lifted his head, blinked. Sat up and looked around him, remembered what had happened. She saw him take the weight of his sorrow upon himself again.

She needed to grow, to equal his strength. His selflessness.

She held out the scan, showing him that she knew of his grief. He tried to smile, to pretend it didn't mean that much to him. How many times had he hidden his grief from her, pretending that all was well with him?

She said, "Can you forgive me?"

"For what? Is that the time? I came back ... I don't know when. You were asleep and I didn't want to wake you. I sat down for a moment and ... stupid of me."

"Can you forgive me for being such a shallow creature, thinking only of myself?"

He blinked, turned his head away. "Where's my mobile?"

"First the child, and then your car."

He shook his head. "Whither thou goest, I go. What day is it today? Or is it tomorrow?"

He wouldn't accept her plea, perhaps because it might reduce him to tears.

"Let me in, Patrick. Let me share your grief."

"Look at the time. Why didn't you wake me earlier? Shall we go up to bed?"

"Not yet. I've got another conundrum for you. How do you buy a pregnancy testing kit in this village without everyone starting to count on their fingers?"

He brushed that aside. "You want one? Not yet, surely."

"Why not?"

He grinned, not nicely. "The promise of another son, in exchange for an old car? What sort of bargain is that?"

Another son. Oh, this hurt had gone deep. And she'd never even noticed that there was a hurt.

"No bargain. A hope. Something to hang onto. It's all we can do, isn't it? Hope and pray."

He put his hands over his eyes. "Minty, it hurts!"

"Yes, I know." She put her arms around him and this time he accepted them, holding her tightly. Breathing lightly so that the pain wouldn't spread.

She thought he was weeping, though he wouldn't let her see. She turned off his light and together they went up the stairs, supporting one another. He undressed with his back to her. Was he still weeping?

No, perhaps not. He went to wash and came back with a calm face. Such a calm face. Hiding his grief. She turned out the light and held her arms open for him to fall into. And he did.

❧

She woke slowly, wondering why she felt depressed. Not "black hole" depressed. But knowing that when she did wake up properly, she was going to remember something she wouldn't like ... ah. She drew in a breath sharply.

The car. The scan of the baby. Patrick's grief.

"Mm?" He was sitting on the edge of the bed, half-dressed, reading his Bible. Not the Bible reading notes, but his Bible. She sat up and peered over his shoulder. He'd been re-reading the story of David and Bathsheba, who'd broken God's laws and grieved when, as a result, they lost their first child. Was he looking for a parallel?

She said, "But you didn't sin. We neither of us did. At least ... we're not perfect, but surely nothing we did would have made God take our child from us."

"No. We didn't. I was re-reading it because ... oh, I don't know. Looking for easy answers when there aren't any. Perhaps I should have been looking in Job instead. God let him be tested to the limit, but he didn't lose faith. I don't know why God took our son away, but perhaps one day I'll understand."

She said, "I've brought you nothing but trouble. If you'd married some nice, quiet woman who thought the world of you and never stepped out of line ..."

He smiled. "Do you remember when we first met? You were only four, so you probably don't. My mother brought you home with her one day, because your nanny wanted to go shopping by herself. You looked at me as if you could see right through me. You said, 'What are we play-ing?' and put your hand in mine. That was it. I was your slave for life."

"You were probably smiling at me, just as you are now. How could I resist?"

He ran his finger across her lips. "My father warned me about you. He said you'd lead me a merry dance, but that after I'd danced with you I wouldn't want any other partner."

She pressed his hand to her cheek. "I remember you always made time for me, that you taught me to read and write, and the names of flowers and butterflies. We never quarrelled, did we?"

"You've just reminded me how fortunate we've been. I should be praising God for you, rather than railing at Him for the loss of the baby."

"We'll make another, God willing."

"'The Lord gives and the Lord takes away. Praise the Lord.' Well, I can't say it yet."

Nor I, Patrick. Nor I.

Serafina called up the stairs, "Five minutes to breakfast!"

Minty noted with amusement that Patrick eased his thoughts away from home and towards work during breakfast. It usually hap-pened with his second cup of coffee. She thought there was an almost audible switch. One minute he might have been chatting with Minty and Serafina, speed-reading the newspaper, scanning private corre-spondence, and the next he'd be sitting upright, fingering his laptop, wondering aloud where he'd left his mobile phone.

Today the switch happened a little earlier, when he pushed half his sausages and scrambled eggs to one side.

"I have to talk to the police again this morning. They'll want a statement from you, too, Minty. Do you need your car today? Silly question, of course you do."

He was trying to put a good face on his loss.

"Mm, yes. I'll be backwards and forwards all day. Hopefully we can sleep at the Hall tonight. Also I want to get over to see Annie. Sup-pose I ask Reggie to take you in the limo?"

"First day of the festival. Reggie'll be needed. No, I'll get a mini-cab to work. The garage said they'd lend me something to tide me over." He grimaced. "I've just remembered, my heavy walking shoes were in the car, and my waterproof jacket."

Serafina looked at his half-eaten plate. "Eat up. Knowing you, you'll probably forget to eat at lunch-time."

Minty knew it was no use pressing Patrick to eat if he had other things on his mind. "What car will you buy this time? A Porsche?"

"No, no. Nothing flashy. Perhaps a second-hand Volvo that's already been run in. Something comfortable and reliable."

"What about a classic car? A Bentley? A Rolls?"

"What, me in a Rolls?" He laughed, pulled his laptop towards him and then pushed it away. "Minty, I had a police inspector—who's by way of being a friend of mine—on my back yesterday, worried about the low level of security at the festival. He's tried to tell Hatton there's no way he can control large crowds with his present force, but Hatton's not listening. The inspector's seen what can happen when something goes wrong and there's a big surge of people."

"I agree. I'm seeing Hatton this morning, and I'll try to talk some sense into him."

As soon as the minicab had taken Patrick off to town, Minty realised she and Patrick had forgotten their Bible reading notes that morning. Would God please look after them—and everyone else today? Please?

Minty worked with Serafina to clear breakfast and pack their things once again. Carol joined them, red hair aflame with excitement, saying she'd help ferry stuff up to the Hall and get them settled in.

The phone kept ringing. Neville wanted to know how he could help. Venetia Wootton said she'd be bringing some of her stewards in to see what needed doing in the State Rooms. Mrs Chickward reported that Maxine had been driven off in her car by her make-up artist, and her hostess didn't have a clue where they'd gone and couldn't do anything about it, because of the party that evening.

Ouch, thought Minty. *I'd forgotten her party. Black mark, Minty!*

Minty tried to raise Mr Hatton on his mobile to confirm their appointment and failed. It was switched off. Toby and Iris were up at the Hall early, but she couldn't get either of them on the phone, either.

She reminded herself that this was the first day of the festival. Mr Hatton and his team had been planning this for months, and probably the best thing she could do was keep out of the way.

Minty and Serafina packed up her car, and with Carol following in hers, they drove along to the Hall. The sky was grey. Perhaps it would rain. Oh dear.

The roads were already jamming up with festival goers. Everyone was in holiday humour. There was a hum in the air. Faces were tight with anticipation. The festival goers turned left at the main road and went along the outside of the Park to the gates Minty had used two days before.

The security guards let Minty and Carol through the main gates, now placarded with notices that this entrance was only for official guests with the correct badges, and for "Artists." The stars would arrive by helicopter to avoid traffic jams, so these artists would be the backing singers, musicians and their like. The two security guards Minty had encountered before had now swollen to four. Would that be enough?

As Minty drove along the Avenue to the Hall, she caught glimpses through the trees of the crowds beginning to throng in the Park. However many people were there going to be?

The courtyard was being kept clear of cars by Reggie, who was being firm but courteous with everyone, sending all the artists round to the visitors' car park, but letting Minty and Carol through into the far courtyard where the family cars were kept.

The kitchens were busier than ever. Chef waved to Minty as she arrived and yelled that she had four extra helpers but could do with a hand if anyone had one to spare. Doris had opened up the gift shop. Minty wondered if that was a good idea. Surely the only people allowed in this part of the Hall today would be backstage staff and performers, and would they really want to go into the gift shop?

Alice was there already, supervising a couple of women from the village as they cleaned toilets and distributed black plastic bags for rubbish. Good for Alice.

Venetia Wootton arrived immediately after Minty, her Steward badge very prominent on her grey two piece, directing members of her team into the house and firmly closing the door on a wild-haired couple who demanded to know where the dressing-rooms might be. It was Minty who directed them to the stage management area, reflecting that if she had no precise function that day, she might well volunteer to act as sign-post for the lost and strayed.

Hugh Wootton strolled up, pulling on a bright yellow tabard which said "Steward" in much larger letters than those on Venetia's badge. He saluted Minty. "Reporting for duty, ma'am. Going to sort out the car park."

Iris whisked across the courtyard, clipboard in hand, wearing a badge which gave her a long title. "Minty, I need to talk to you about meeting and greeting the VIPs and the sponsors later on, but I can't stop now. I'll catch up with you, right? The phones never stop, and the girls in the office are running on caffeine drips!"

An electric buggy festooned with placards rolled into view, collected a man with a toolbox and rolled away again.

Mr Hatton was nowhere to be seen. Men and women were rushing here and there, cables snaked, large men with walkie-talkies stalked, mobiles trilled.

"Wow!" said Carol, humping suitcases. "If it's chaos this side of the house, what's it like in the arena?"

"Do you want to go and see?" asked Minty, catching the excitement herself.

"No," said Carol. "Well, not yet, anyway."

A man walked past them, talking on his mobile. "If he's had a hissy fit …"

Serafina said, "Let's get out of this madhouse."

❧

From Minty's rooms high on the south front, they could see and hear everything. The clouds were clearing from the sky, but it was on the cool side. That, thought Minty, was a good thing, because the slope below was exposed to the sun. People would bake if it was hot and would have no cover if it rained.

The huge semi-circle of a stage dominated the far side of the lake, with two enormous screens on either side of it … on which to project magnified images of the stars? There were gantries on either side of the main stage, and another on the terrace immediately below the house. Engineers swarmed. A semi-circular path had been taped off on this side of the lake, protected by a couple of burly stewards. A television camera on a wheeled platform was being run along the taped-off path … there and back again. A similar track was being tested out just below the stage itself.

Minty reflected that Billy certainly knew his job. The areas under his control appeared to be efficiently run. Could she say the same about Hatton and his arrangements?

Carol gasped. "Minty, however many people are you expecting?"

The slope below them was already crowded with people, some sitting but most standing.

"Too many," muttered Minty, anxiously trying to count how many stewards and security people were marshalling the enormous crowd. She got out her mobile and tried Mr Hatton again. Nothing. She debated whether to go in search of him or not, but just then saw the electric buggy nosing its way through the crowd below … carrying Mr Hatton and … Toby?

Serafina said, "Come on. Let's get the bedroom stripped. We can go sight-seeing afterwards."

"You can see everything from here," said Carol, obediently unhooking curtains but keeping an eye on what was happening outside.

A sudden *boo-oom*! Someone was testing equipment.

Amplified voices.

More people surging onto the slope. Minty tried to make out if the lake had been properly cordoned off. Suppose some youngsters took it into their silly heads to go skinny-dipping? Or paddling? And got into trouble?

She tried to get Iris, but her phone was only taking messages. Minty left a message but wondered, not for the first time, whom Iris owed allegiance to nowadays. Eventually she got through to Venetia, who was in the library.

"All's well, Minty," said Venetia. "Alice has managed to find some of the original band of cleaners—what a treasure that girl is, to be sure—and we're all working together to put the rooms to rights. I'm making a list of damages, mostly cigarette burns and wine stains. Not too bad."

"Venetia, listen. I'm worried about the safety of the house. There's such a large crowd out there, and if anything was to go wrong ..."

Venetia was cheerful about it. "They're enjoying themselves, and why not?"

"If there's a downpour of rain, what will they do? They'll try to take shelter in the house. I know the steps up to the terrace have been roped off and there's a couple of stewards on duty there. That would deter the usual picnickers, but not the thousands we've got on the slope below. If they rushed the steps, they'd be able to reach the house in no time at all."

"Ouch," said Venetia, seeing the point straight away.

"Suppose you ask the stewards to check that all windows are securely locked, and where we've got shutters, to close them. They could also lower the blinds inside. Maxine had some kind of stile made to get over the window-sill into the house from the terrace. That ought to be removed, too. Then there's some good furniture in Maxine's tent outside ..."

"I'll see to it straight away."

Minty, Carol and Serafina bagged up bed-linen, pillows, duvet, rugs, bed and window curtains, all of which stank of incense. Minty hung her head out of the window for a couple of minutes now and then to recover. Serafina got her a camomile tea. They humped the stained mattress and all the bags along to the tower office, which gave access to the lift. They could dispose of them later.

The bedroom smelt fresher when they'd done that.

The mattress, pillows and duvet from the spare bedroom went onto the four-poster, dressed with a clean set of linen. Luckily they could leave the windows open all day.

Then they tackled Serafina's bedroom, which overlooked the Fountain Courtyard. Maxine's make-up artist had slept there but not made much mess. A haze of scent hung in the air, but it wasn't as bad as the main bedroom.

At intervals Minty tried to raise Mr Hatton. And failed. She suspected he was keeping his mobile off to avoid having to talk to her. Maybe he was right. Maybe he knew what he was doing, and she'd only be complicating matters—matters about which she knew nothing—if she insisted on talking to him.

"Oh, look!" shrieked Carol, who kept being drawn to the windows to see what was happening. There were cheers from down below as kaleidoscopically changing lights were thrown onto the two big screens on either side of the stage.

Minty and Carol moved into the kitchen, but Serafina soon packed them out again, saying that she knew better than anyone what went in there. The sitting room wasn't too bad, though a couple of cushions had to be thrown out, as they stank of incense. The dining room was clean enough and there was less smell of incense there.

The chapel. Minty wondered if she could bear to go in there again. If she couldn't face it, then she had no right to ask anyone else to do so. Even with the windows open, the place stank, and not just of incense. She said, "Carol, you don't need to come in with me, but I've got to see what needs to be done."

Carol followed her in and gulped. "Do I look as pale as I feel?"

Minty handed her some rubber gloves. "Whoever faints first is a wimp."

Minty began to pray aloud. "Dear Lord, help! Your Son drove the thieves out of the temple! Give us the strength to drive the evil out of . . . oh!" She broke off with a sob as she came to the altar, where flies had settled on the sacrifice.

Carol cleared her throat. "You can do it! I can't, but you can!"

Minty closed her eyes and prayed. *Dear Lord, give me courage!* She held her breath, unfocused her eyes and swept the lot, black velvet cloth, sacrifice and all, off the altar and into a black plastic bag. The air seemed lighter for its disappearance.

"Attagirl!" said Carol, shakily. "If I were a drinking man, I'd ask if you had any brandy in the house, but as it is—have a peppermint?

Oh!" She'd come across sheets of paper torn from the old Bible. Her voice wobbled. "Could we save the pages? Perhaps a specialist ...?" She answered her own question. "No. Do we chuck the whole book? It's only New Testament pages that have gone." She began to get angry. "How could they! Don't they realise what they're doing? An early Bible like this costs thousands of pounds. It's criminal damage, never mind sacrilege!"

Minty brushed the back of her hand across her eyes. Generations of Edens right down to herself and Patrick had gone to that book for the Word of God. "Don't think about it. Pack the torn leaves into a separate bag and we'll deal with them later."

"Okay." Carol's voice sounded strange, forced. "I suggest that we wash down all the woodwork, panelling and all, with a mixture of vinegar and water. It's better than anything else for old wood."

Minty nodded. She was beginning to feel oppressed by the chapel, too. She unhooked the cross which had been upside down over the altar. It felt gritty under her fingers. Her great-grandfather had brought it back from Italy in the early years of the last century.

Carol said, "Minty ... I can't ... Minty!"

Carol was pressed up against the window, frightened eyes wide.

"Minty, if I move ... it's going to get me ...!"

Minty remembered how she'd felt when she first entered the chapel, as if something was behind her, and if she moved away from the wall, it would surely "get" her. Tears were running down Carol's cheeks. The air between them in the room seemed to swirl. Minty held the cross up before her and dived across the room to put an arm around Carol's shoulders.

She shouted, "In the name of Jesus!" The air seemed to clear a little. Minty dragged Carol to the door ... which had stuck again. She wrestled it open and got them out into the clean air of the tower.

Carol leaned against the door, her face glistening white. Minty hugged her, trying to shake off the evil which still clung to the chapel.

Serafina appeared. "It's best you two keep out of the chapel till the church has dealt with it."

Minty could smell Serafina's lily-of-the-valley scent. It helped to wipe out the memory of what had happened. *Lord, we are broken in spirit by what we've seen and suffered. Heal us to carry out the tasks You set for us to do.*

Carol looked down at her hands, which still held the mutilated leaves from the Bible.

Serafina drew in her breath. "It was from that book that I first learned that God loves me." She raised both fists and closed her eyes. "Let God hear me! By the strength and might of the one true God, I curse the woman who has done—"

Minty stopped her. "Don't. God will punish her as He thinks fit."

Serafina was on fire with righteous indignation. "She deserves …!"

Minty shook her head. "God knows what's been happening, and He will decide what is to be done. So don't curse her."

Serafina departed, muttering under her breath.

Carol said, in a tiny voice, "I didn't know I could be so frightened."

"Nor I," said Minty. "Let's go and sit down for a while. I'll ring Cecil at the vicarage, see if he's found out what needs to be done in the chapel. Serafina's right. It's not our job to tackle it."

Carol's colour came back slowly. Serafina served them coffee in the cool green sitting room, and even consented to sit down with them for a while. Minty rang Cecil and reported what had happened. He said he was on to it, and to leave it to him.

Venetia rang up to say her stewards had been right through the rooms open to the public, and they had all been secured against boarders. She was leaving now but would see Minty again that evening at Mrs Chickward's.

Carol and Minty were resting peacefully when suddenly …

… sound boomed out from below. A voice squawked something. There were cheers from below. An engineer turned up the sound, and both girls jumped as a man began to make announcements. More cheers. Finally a group started to play on the big stage.

Carol winced. She raised her voice to a shout. "Is it going to be as loud as that all the time?" She dragged herself to the window to look out.

Minty yelled back, "Do you think we'll get any sleep tonight? What time does it stop?"

They both started to laugh, rather shakily. Time to move on to the next job.

Chapter Eighteen

By half past twelve they'd got all the rooms on that floor — except the chapel — in good order once again, so Carol fetched sandwiches from the restaurant below.

"Chef's working like a robot, with her helpers running themselves ragged around her. The restaurant has a queue out of the door, and did I get some black looks when I went straight to the kitchen door to get served! Doris has locked up the gift shop and gone to help clear tables in the restaurant."

"Good for her!" said Minty, from around a sandwich.

"That nice girl Alice seems to be everywhere, directing operations. She's put a cleaner on the toilets full time, as one kept backing up. Reggie's driving an electric buggy, ferrying staff to and from the stage management area."

"Mr Hatton? Iris?"

"Doris says they're out and about, rushing around like scalded cats. Iris is looking after the Press with Toby. I only saw him for a second; he'd come back to sort out some trouble at the gate. Someone had forgotten their pass."

"It happens," said Minty, knowing human nature.

Carol had recovered enough to be sharp about what she'd seen. "Toby's complaining that he ought to be dealing with the Press, not Iris. But I think Hatton's right; Toby knows how to get press releases out, but Iris is better up front."

Carol thought clearly, even where Toby was concerned.

Boom, boom, boom. Drum beats, electric guitars, wired-up keyboards ... pretty women dancing up and down ... an even prettier man in slashed jeans, singing in a light-weight, amplified voice.

Minty went to the window and counted stewards' tabards. Again. They were all yellow and easy to spot. Big, burly men. Good.

Serafina—forbidding the girls to help her—went into the chapel to bring out the broken chair and added it to the pile at the top of the tower. Minty accused herself of cowardice but was glad she hadn't had to do that.

"Now," said Serafina, looking around the sitting room, frowning. "All we need is some flowers. Where's that lilac Mr Wootton brought, and did we bring up that pot of geraniums that Annie gave you?"

"I think I left them in the dining room," said Carol. Her mobile trilled, and she answered it. "Minty, do you need me this afternoon? My father's arrived at the shop and wants to look over the stock with me. I could come back later, if you like."

Minty shook her head. "I can cope now. I'm going to be out and about this afternoon, anyway. Give your father my love. And Carol ... thank you, for everything."

"Even for passing out on you?" Carol was almost back to her usual self as she blew Serafina a kiss and made her way out.

Serafina said, "I'm taking a rest, and then I'll see about supper."

Minty stood at the window, looking down on the crowds below. Her uncle had been vocal about the evil at the Hall before anyone else had dared to talk openly about it. She wondered if the efficient Mrs Collins had managed to contact the bishop about cleansing the chapel. And what would that flamboyant lady be wearing to Mrs Chickward's that evening? And what was Minty herself going to wear?

The music stopped banging out from the main stage. Relief! More announcements. More cheers. The crowd below shifted its focus.

Another type of music started up, much closer to the house. A small group of large black men were now performing on the small stage to the right of the arena. Their music was more relaxed, softer, less raucous. There even seemed to be some laughter. The crowd loved it.

Minty worked it out that using the small stage allowed time for a changeover on the main stage across the lake.

Minty was in two minds. Did she shut the windows to keep the music from hurting her ears, or keep the windows open to help disperse the incense? She elected to leave the windows open. And tried to raise Mr Hatton again. Nothing. Iris, nothing. She wondered if they'd had the guile to get hold of a second mobile phone so that they could keep in touch with others, but not with her.

Minty couldn't remember having seen Gemma around that day. Perhaps this would be a good moment to find out what was happening to her. Minty took the stairs down to the first floor and tapped on the door of Gemma's rooms.

Gemma opened the door slowly, concealing herself behind it. "Oh, it's you!"

She left the door open and retreated into her sitting room.

Minty gasped. What on earth was Gemma wearing?

"Like it?" Gemma did a twirl. She was wearing a purple sequinned corset, fish-net tights and a towering headdress of ostrich feather plumes in pink.

Gemma posed, turning herself this way and that before a full-length mirror. "I need to carry a whip with this outfit, don't I?"

Over a nearby chair was draped the purple and black dress Maxine had worn when she confronted Minty in the chapel, and her diaphanous blue gown—complete with body stocking—hung on a costume rail nearby, together with four or five other costumes, scarlet, bright green, orange. A number of jeans, some slashed, some sequinned, also hung from the rail, with a variety of eye-catching tops. There were wigs everywhere: blonde curly wigs, a long black one, braided ones ... masks, shoes, leggings ...

Minty blinked. "These are Maxine's. What are they doing here?"

"When I heard you were throwing her out, I skidded up to your rooms and grabbed her stage costumes. Most of them, anyway. I told her dresser that she couldn't possibly take them all up to Mrs Chickward's and that they'd be safe with me. We're exactly the same size now I've lost some weight, except for our feet." Gemma tore off the headdress. "The one I really like is the purple and black Gothic dress, but her mouth's a different shape and I can't wear the braces on my teeth."

Minty shuddered. "I don't know how you could bear to touch it. She wore that when she did terrible things in the chapel."

"I'm not superstitious. Help me out of this."

Minty had noticed before that Gemma had no imagination. She started to help Gemma out of the corset. "Do I detect a hint of black-mail? You've got her costumes, so she's got to let you appear on stage with her tomorrow?"

Gemma picked up a long, jagged skirt. "She's said I can dance with Nero at the back of the stage during her last number. I wanted to sing in the backing group, but they've all been together for ages, so they won't let me. You thought I couldn't see that Maxine was trying to freeze me out, but I could. I just couldn't work out what to do about it—till you gave me the opportunity to get hold of these clothes."

Gemma pulled on the skirt and picked up a long black wig, which she fitted on her own sleek head. "I'd better warn you that Maxine is going to wear her curly blonde wig tonight with a white blouse and jeans, to see how many people she can fool into thinking she's you at the party. So you'd better watch out for her."

Minty blinked. Whatever would Maxine try next? "What costume will she wear on stage?"

Gemma held up well-cut denims and a low-cut top with flame-coloured streamers floating from the long sleeves. "She'll wear this outfit for starters, with the curly black wig, dark lipstick and black nail polish, because that's the way she looks in all her recent publicity stills. That's when she sings, 'I'm on fire.' She rips that off in the wings while Nero does his belly-dancing. Then she wears that sequinned dress over there, which zips up the back. Easy to get on and off. After that number her dresser has two minutes twenty seconds to transform her into a Goth, and she can do it, believe me.

"When Maxine comes on in the Goth costume she'll bring the house down. That's when she sings 'Reality'. I'll be wearing another black and purple dress, not as well-made as hers, of course. I'll be made up like her, and dance behind her with Nero. He pretends to kill me in the dance. Then she whips out a gun and shoots him.

"Don't look so horrified. It's not a real gun, though she has got one of those, of course, that she got last time she was in the States. It's perfectly all right to shoot a real gun on private property. In any case, what she'll be using on stage is a starter pistol which is loud enough to make everyone jump ... and then she straddles Nero as he's pretending to die. The message is that women have to face reality and take control to survive."

Minty blinked. "By killing your partner? That's an extreme take on reality. Have you had enough time to practise with Nero?"

"I've watched the other women take turns doing it with him. I've had the songs dinned into me morning, noon and night for days. I can dance well enough. I can even sing well enough, if they'd only give me a chance. Maybe I'll get to do it on the video tomorrow."

"What video? I said no more videoing at the Hall."

Gemma shrugged, angling to see her backside in the mirror. "You've banned them from the Hall, but not from the neighbourhood. Axel is finding us somewhere else to finish off." She strutted around, hands on hips.

Minty was fascinated. Gemma was such a curious mixture of weakness and aggression that you could never tell what she might choose to do next.

Minty set out to check on the house. The State Bedrooms first. Everything looked in order except that the canopy bed was still unmade. Axel had been sleeping there, hadn't he? She stripped the bed and pulled the coverings back over it, dumping the used linen by the lift in the tower.

Every now and then she drifted to the window to see what was happening outside. The act on the smaller stage finished. A girl with long blonde hair and the tightest jeans Minty had ever seen was now on the big stage, backed up by a troupe of prancing young men who may or may not have been playing the instruments they were holding. Minty wondered if she was being picky. Surely they wouldn't mime to their own records on such an occasion, would they?

The television crews were moving their equipment around in smooth arcs, recording everything. Who had authorised television? Were they going to be on national or local news bulletins? Or was it a private company making a video for sale? And who would get the money from that? So many unanswered questions.

Minty took the stairs down to the State Rooms on the ground floor to check that the stewards had left the shutters closed and the blinds down. Which they had. The furniture which had been in the tent was now inside, but looking rather the worse for wear. Drink and food stained. Yuk. More work for Carol.

Mrs Collins rang through to give her apologies, but she couldn't make it to the Hall to help today; her dressmaker had failed to finish her new outfit for Mrs Chickward's party as promised, and Mrs Collins would have to go all the way to town to collect it, would you believe? Minty was soothing.

The crowd was good-natured. There was a sudden shower of light rain, but it didn't seem to deter them at all. They waved their arms in the air and screamed along with the act. The girl singer was cheered.

Minty smelt cigarettes in the library. Who had dared to smoke in there? This old house would go up like tinder if anyone dropped a live cigarette butt. She opened the shutters and let the blinds up to investigate. She found a couple of cigarette butts in a glass bowl someone had used for an ashtray. Hatton? Axel? Billy? She removed the evidence. The stewards ought to have spotted that, but if the shutters had been closed and they hadn't got a good sense of smell, they might easily have missed it.

She went to the window to close the shutters again and noticed that the small stage was now occupied by an older man, sitting down, playing a guitar — and how he could play! The crowd was entranced.

Her mobile rang. Patrick. "Where are you, Minty? There's been the devil to pay here. They brought Nero and his girl-friend in for questioning this morning. He insists that he didn't fire my car, although he admits he rammed it. He couldn't get out of that, because the police checked the lorry he'd borrowed for the evening and found evidence that he did. He said he only rammed my car to give you a fright, because you'd tried to knife him . . ."

"What!"

"They couldn't get hold of you — where have you been? They tried the Hall, but no one would admit to having seen you. So with no back-up statement from you, Maxine got him out on bail."

Minty bit her lip. This was not good news. "I've been here all day. It's true that I jabbed him with my keys when he grabbed me. I know I ought to have reported it then, but . . . one doesn't."

"Don't I know it! Women rarely do report assaults."

He didn't say that she ought to have known better. She knew it. "What happens now?"

"Apparently we can't prove he torched my car because no one saw him do it. Nero's talking of suing the police for wrongful arrest. Any sign of him?"

"No. The festival's started. It's cheerful but noisy. I'm worried about crowd control. There's a lot of large young men out there, but ..."

"They usually call on the local rugby clubs to provide stewards. What happened when you spoke to Hatton?"

"He's not answering his phone, and I don't know where he is or what he's up to. I ought to have made a bigger effort. I'll go down now and try to find him."

Patrick was anxious. "I expect Hatton's bringing in more stewards as time goes on. Shall I try him?"

Minty hated to involve Patrick. It was her job to look after the Hall. "No, I'll do it. It's a good thing we're out this evening, because the noise is terrifying!"

"Ah. I'd forgotten Mrs Chickward's party. I'll go back to my place first, see if I can find a clean shirt. Or can you bring one up for me? Seven o'clock?"

Minty switched from one worry to another. "Do you think Maxine will be at the party, since she's 'lodging' with Mrs Chickward?"

"You think she's going to make me a proposition I can't refuse? I'm flattered, I suppose. I must practise my leer."

"You don't know what she's like. She terrifies me."

"You're not easy to frighten. I'll watch out for her, I promise."

He was making light of the matter, but Minty wasn't so easily calmed. Too much had happened that day ... and the day before ... and the day before that.

She said, "I'll find Hatton," and rang off.

A small, youngish girl had come onto the big stage with a group of dancers who were better trained and rehearsed than the others. What a show they put on ... it was magnificent.

Minty wondered if she'd been wrong to think the festival a bad idea. Then she did her head count of stewards again and wondered what sort of shifts they were working. Suppose they were on duty for eight hours—and that was a long shift—then what happened when they went off duty? And where were they being fed? Along with the backstage staff in the restaurant?

The crowd was swelling all the time. Minty had thought the slope well-populated before, but it was getting more and more crowded. Surely they wouldn't keep on admitting people to this limited space?

Every now and then there was a bunching-up of people trying to get past the drinks tents into the arena. And still more people entered the site.

Minty closed the shutters and pulled down the blind. She tried to ring Mr Hatton again. Still nothing. At the library door she paused, thinking hard. There was no connecting corridor on this side of the house, the State Rooms being arranged like a railway carriage, one leading out of the other. So if you locked the library door and the door of the Chinese Room at the far end, no one could get in. They were usually kept locked on the days the public were denied entry.

Who had keys to all the rooms? Well, she did, normally. What would have happened to her big bunch of keys? Answer: Serafina would have them. She went upstairs again. Serafina's bedroom door was shut, but Minty could hear that her television was on. Minty tapped on the door and waited. Serafina might or might not be asleep. It was wrong to disturb her. She would go away, leave Serafina in peace.

The door opened and Serafina stood there, wearing a violently coloured kimono instead of her usual black.

Minty gaped. "Sorry to disturb you. I wonder, do you have my keys?"

Serafina produced them. "Your man said not to give them to you until you asked for them." She closed the door again.

Returning to the ground floor, Minty locked all the doors between the State Rooms and was just leaving the tower for the Fountain Court when she came face to face with Iris. Iris was trundling a drinks trolley along the cloisters, followed by a hefty young man carrying a crate of soft drinks.

"It's nice to catch up with you at last, Iris. Is your mobile out of order?"

Iris started. "Oh. I must have switched it off by accident. So much to do today. I did tell you we were hosting a reception — drinks and nibbles for the sponsors and other VIPs, didn't I? They were supposed to have a tent down below, but it's been commandeered for a dressing-room for the performers. So we'll use the library."

"I don't think that's a good idea for security reasons," said Minty. "The crowd outside is too close for comfort. Which is why I've just locked it up."

Iris frowned. "The stewards did say something about not using these rooms, but I thought ..." Her face cleared. "Well, you won't object if we use your rooms at the top instead, will you? There's a much better view, and that'll impress our guests no end. Chef will grumble at having to send the food up there, but I'll tell her you authorised it. You're out this evening, so it won't inconvenience you at all, and I don't suppose you'll want to move back till the festival's over."

Iris preceded the burly man into the lift.

Minty didn't want to make a scene, so she followed. "I'd better warn Serafina. And yes, we are planning to sleep here tonight."

Iris said nothing to that but exclaimed in horror when she saw the pile of rubbish bags and broken chairs at the top of the tower. "We'll have to get that rubbish moved before anyone comes."

"That 'rubbish' is things of mine that Maxine has contaminated, and it's going for cleaning or repair. Put a screen round it if you want it hidden."

Iris looked at the burly man, who nodded, dropped his load in the sitting room and vanished. Iris sited her trolley at the far end of the room with care. "You must admit the festival's an enormous success. Look how many people have come! Billy wants to come back again next year. Isn't that marvellous? Or — " with a change of tactic — "are you cross because you hadn't thought of it?"

Minty dealt with that one straight away. "It did cross my mind, yes. But no, I can say in all honesty that that's not what's worrying me."

"Then why the long face?" Iris was being impertinent. Iris was uneasy and trying to hide it.

Minty joined her at the window. "I can't believe the Health and Safety people approved that layout."

Iris frowned. "We showed them the plans right from the beginning. We had to, to get approval for the festival. Of course, as time went on, some small alterations were necessary."

Minty gave Iris a hard look. "Those tents on either side of the lake restrict access to the main arena. There's only a narrow corridor for all those people to funnel through. It would only take one person to trip and fall to cause a crush in which people could be killed! No wonder the police are worried."

Iris was pale, but then, Iris was usually pale. "The police? Oh, we don't need them. Did you know they tried to get in to see you today? Something about taking a statement from you about Nero. Been up to his usual tricks, has he? I'd have thought you'd have known how to deal with him without bringing in the police. We need him. Maxine needs him. She said she'd refuse to perform if he wasn't released, so naturally we did what we could to smooth things over. I was sure you'd agree with us, when you'd calmed down. So we told them you weren't here."

"You did *what*?"

Iris almost wriggled. "Depend upon it, Nero will soon be in pursuit of someone else and will forget all about suing you."

"Suing me? Nero torched Patrick's car!"

Iris hadn't known that. She bit her lip, looked away. "Oh, that's ... not good. But presumably Patrick's covered by insurance."

"Iris, you *know* how Patrick feels about his car. He's devastated. And if Nero could do that and get away with it, what will he try next?"

Iris didn't want to think about that. "Well, to get back to what you said earlier, it would cost far too much to involve the police."

"More than the Hall is worth? Suppose there's a hold-up somewhere down there and people charge up the slope to get into the Hall?"

"Now you're being melodramatic. Nothing like that's going to happen. The stewards—"

"Have been on duty since early morning. There aren't enough of them even when they're all there, and when they take a comfort or food break, there are even less. I know. I've been watching and trying to contact Mr Hatton all day. And you."

Iris was sullen. "Clive knows what he's doing."

"By his own admission this is the biggest event he's handled so far."

Iris bit her lip. "I'm sure you're worrying unnecessarily." She glanced at her watch. "Our guests will be arriving soon." She pulled out a mobile phone. "I'd better alert Chef to the change of plan. I'll see what she says about serving the food from the dining room. I can't think why you didn't wait to move in till everything was over."

Minty realised, with regret, that Iris was no longer her loving friend and tactful employee. Would it do any good to sack her, here and now? No, probably not. But things could never be the same between them.

Iris seemed to feel this, too. "You see, Minty, things have changed. They were bound to, after your accident. New men, new thinking. We have to move forward, think of the future. I can see it's hard for you, but then, you've still got to take it easy, haven't you?"

"Is that what Clive told you? Wishful thinking, Iris. I'm fine. I'll warn Serafina and get changed, ready to receive the guests when they arrive."

Iris opened her mouth and closed it again, busying herself with arranging bottles and cans on the trolley. Minty wondered if Iris had thought to act as hostess. Perhaps she had. *Too bad, Iris. Mummy's back, and Mummy's not playing games.*

Minty glanced out of the window. There were too many precious lives at stake down there to play games.

❦

The reception for the guests went well enough. Minty dressed in a low-cut gauzy blue dress over a matching blue slip. Patrick had given her a cashmere pashmina to wear with it, and after a little search she found some high-heeled sandals to match. She put her hair up and wore her pearl earrings, reminding herself to ask Patrick what he'd done with her engagement ring and the opals her father had given her.

Serafina threw a sulk at having "her" rooms invaded and retired to her room with the television turned up high. Chef sent up relays of girls to serve appetising food, while Iris and her burly helper dispensed drinks.

If Clive Hatton had been hoping for Minty's absence, he hid it well. As people arrived, he brought them over to introduce them to her. Many of them she'd met before at local functions, but a few hadn't a clue who she was, and to them she had to explain over and over again that she was Araminta Cardale Sands, owner of the Hall, and that she'd just returned from holiday.

It annoyed her that everyone assumed she'd returned especially for the festival, and that quite a few of them had the nerve to ask for Maxine. Maxine was the star attraction. They were all looking forward to Maxine's performing the following night. The sub-text was, Why wasn't the star of the show there to welcome them?

Minty ducked all questions about Maxine. She smiled and enquired after their health if she had met them before, and asked their names and what they did, if she hadn't. She acted hostess as graciously as she could. There was nothing else to be done but wait her chance to speak to Clive Hatton, which she did manage eventually, wriggle though he might to avoid her.

"Those tents," she said, leading him over to the window. "If we don't get them moved back, say, twenty or thirty feet, tonight, I'm afraid there'll be trouble. Too many people will try to get through too small a gap. Will you arrange it, please?"

He smiled and patted her arm. "Those tents are put there for a reason, my dear. Our sponsors insisted everyone has access to them, coming and going. Food and drink, that's where the money lies. You can't be expected to know these things, can you? You keep right on doing what you do best, which is being a charming hostess, and leave all the detail to me."

"It's not a detail," she said, keeping calm. "It's a disaster waiting to happen. Please see they're moved back overnight."

He looked over her head. "I don't think our sponsors would agree to that, and in any case, they've been put up by a firm who won't be back on site till they come in to remove the tents after the festival's over. May I ask if there's any chance of your relenting and allowing

Maxine to join us? So many of our guests were looking forward to meeting her tonight."

"Maxine is not allowed back into the Hall under any circumstances, so I'm afraid they're going to be disappointed. Mr Hatton, I am serious about those tents. Get onto the firm that put them up, and offer overtime to get them back."

"My dear, you really must leave these matters to me." He patted her arm again and drew yet another well-fed man forward to be introduced to her. Minty seethed internally, but outwardly she smiled and was polite. She looked at her watch and decided she might as well go for all the good she was doing there. Iris watched as she left. Iris could now take over as hostess. Bully for Iris.

Minty felt helpless. As she left the Hall, the noise from the festival followed her. It was muffled by the building, but it was still there.

Chapter Nineteen

Minty left the Hall on foot, carrying a clean shirt for Patrick in a paper bag. The music followed her as she turned up the hill into the village. The roads were solid with stationary cars and trucks, the pavements thronged with people on foot.

She wondered how the Press and the invited guests hoped to leave the Hall after the reception. People of all ages were still trying to get into the festival. Toddlers were carried on shoulders, aging hippies shuffled along, teenagers sang in noisy groups, middle-aged people recalled their younger lives.

She couldn't think what to do about the festival, or Clive Hatton, or Iris. Or Gemma. She couldn't help laughing, thinking how Gemma had neatly pinched all those costumes. Perhaps her little sister wasn't so helpless after all.

Passing Carol's antiques shop, she paused to watch a couple of men fitting a grille over the windows. Carol was taking precautions. Very wise, but it did sink the heart rather to think that it was necessary in this once quiet village.

Carol was standing in the window, hands on hips, red hair aflame, making sure the men did a good job. When she saw Minty, she waved and blew her a kiss. Carol was doing all right.

Her mobile rang. Patrick. "Minty, I'm going to be a few minutes late. The roads are gridlocked. I'll lock the car up and walk down. Right?"

She felt the need to pray, so she slipped into the ancient church at the top of the High Street and knelt in a pew at the back.

Someone had already done the flowers for the weekend services. Great spikes of white stocks and lilies scented the air, but the scent was not strong enough to worry her. As sometimes happened, she couldn't think of the right words to use.

Dear Lord, have mercy. Lord, have mercy. Mercy, Lord.

The quiet of the church calmed her. She could hear distant noises of traffic and people shouting, but in here there was nothing but the occasional "tick" as the wood of ancient timbers shifted. Sunlight patched the floors, slanting through the old windows with their tint of green.

Dear Lord ... all those people! I feel they're at risk. I don't know what to do! Help me. Have mercy on me, on them.

Above her head to the right was the stone tablet in memory of her mother, driven to her death by her husband's adultery. Next to it and matching it was her father's memorial. He'd suffered for his sins, he'd repented and was at rest.

It was Maxine who'd brought evil to the Hall, wasn't it? Or had the evil begun before Maxine arrived? Had it started with Clive Hatton's ambition? And Gemma's?

What did Hatton or Gemma care about the safety of all those people they'd drawn to the site? They were not acting responsibly.

The buck stops here.

Ouch. Did that mean that Minty was really responsible? Probably.

That was tough. Because if Minty was in charge, then she was responsible for the safety of everyone at the festival. What was she going to do about that?

She couldn't do anything more than she had, could she? She'd asked for the two tents to be taken down, and her request—she knew—was going to be ignored.

She could bring in the police over everyone's heads. Yes. But if Hatton didn't accept her authority, he might well refuse to act with the police, and then ...

Visions of the present stewards fighting with the police ... innocent people screaming, getting hurt. Children being trampled underfoot.

She groaned and covered her eyes. It didn't bear thinking about.

She *must* think about it. If she was responsible, then she had to bring in the police and somehow force Hatton to agree to work with them. Pay for them.

And get those tents down.

Perhaps Patrick would have an idea how to cope? No, it wasn't fair to involve him. He had his own problems to cope with: a neglected practise, one partner sunk in grief and another ineffective. His car. Oh, how could she have forgotten his car?

And the loss of their child.

For the first time she dared to look along the wall beyond her mother's tablet. She'd never asked what had happened to the body of her child, but she'd assumed that Patrick would do the right thing, and he had.

"Infant son of Patrick and Araminta Cardale Sands. Safe in God's hands."

She wept.

She left the church to find the High Street gridlocked. Mrs Chickward wouldn't be pleased if half her guests were unable to reach her house.

Betty was packing up to go home when Minty turned her key in the lock. "Oh, Mrs Sands, will you look at Purdy? That's what I call the little cat. She came right out from under the desk just now to use her litter tray, and she's eaten almost all the food I've put down for her." Betty didn't usually work on a Saturday, and Minty suspected she'd done so today in order to keep the kitten company.

The two women crouched down to peer at Purdy, who certainly looked less bedraggled than she had been. "She's stopped shivering," said Betty. "No one else wants her so she'll be company for me. I'll have to take her to the vet's on Monday to get her checked over, but she's going to make it, isn't she?"

Minty smiled and nodded. She didn't really mind that the kitten was not going to be hers. Not really.

Patrick arrived on foot, only five minutes late. "I left the car at the railway station and walked down. It's a rented car, but you'll be pleased to hear that I'm negotiating for an almost-new Volvo estate." He threw her a soft chamois leather bag. "Here's some of your baubles. I got them out of the bank today—was half afraid I'd be mugged for them on the way home. I think the opals might go better with that outfit than the pearls."

She opened the bag with a cry of pleasure, for there were her stunningly beautiful diamond engagement ring, and the set of opals which had once been her mother's and which her father had given her.

Patrick's voice changed. "You've been crying." He always noticed.

She tried to smile. "I was in the church and saw the tablet on the wall. I've never been able to ask before, but were you able to hold our baby?"

Every muscle in his face tightened. "For a few minutes, yes. I baptised him myself. I don't know whether that was the right thing to do, but it seemed so at the time. Then the doctors said you were slipping away, so I gave him to Cecil ... yes, Cecil arrived just then."

"I nearly died, didn't I? But you wouldn't let go." She clung to him. "And our baby? Where ...?"

"In the churchyard up on the hill. Cecil took the service. It was supposed to be private, but your uncle came and Hugh Wootton. Also Mrs Chickward. That was a surprise. I thought at first she'd come because it was the correct thing to do, and she always does the correct thing. But no: she cried and tried to hide her tears. She's really fond of you, Minty. Who else came? Florence, your Chef. Alice Mount. Carol would have come but I asked her to take my place at your side that morning. You were still in intensive care, you see. Reggie drove me there and back, saying I wasn't fit to drive myself, which I wasn't. I'm not sure he was, either, come to think of it. He nearly ran over someone on the return journey. I'll take you up there some day soon."

"Thank you. I'm almost well now, aren't I?"

"Well enough to face the Deputy Chief Constable? I don't know if you remember, but you met him at a charity evening a while back. He'll be at Mrs Chickward's tonight and wants a word with you. Oh, and you'll be amused to hear that Nero has formally withdrawn his complaint against you."

"Big of him. Are the police going to prosecute him?"

"They will if we can make out a good enough case against him, but at the moment they've no proof it was him. I'm trying to be positive. I was insured. I could do with a new car. But it makes me very angry to think he can do such a thing and get away with it."

She held him at arm's length. "Me, too. Now, Patrick, I know the Hall is my business, but I'm not so stupid that I won't scream for help when I need it. About the festival. Things have got way out of hand. Too many people, too few security guards, exits too few and too narrow. I'm scared what will happen if I bring the police in to take charge, and I'm scared what will happen if I don't. Oh yes, and I'm scared what Maxine will try to do to you tonight."

"I've been practising my leer." He pulled a hideous face. "Is that the sort of reaction she usually gets?"

Minty hiccuped, covered her eyes with both hands, wiped tears away and allowed herself to smile. "Er—no. Not quite. Promise you'll scream for help if you need it?"

"Mm. Clean shirt?"

While Patrick was changing, she rang Cecil and asked him if he'd come up with a plan for cleansing the chapel.

He was hesitant. "Minty, I've no experience of such matters. I'll have to ask the bishop. I think I'd better come up to the Hall early tomorrow and see for myself what's going on."

Mrs Chickward's garden was immense, stretching far behind the house and ending eventually in a small wood, which was, of course, private. In the autumn she gave a party to show off her maples, but in the late spring it was her azaleas and rhododendrons which were on show. Most women—however fashionably dressed—knew better than to wear stiletto heels to Mrs Chickward's parties, but Mrs Collins was not one of their number. She met Minty and Patrick as they turned into the gate.

"My dears!" she cried, diamonds winking in the early evening sunlight. "Isn't this all too heavenly?"

Minty blinked and pinched Patrick's arm, since he seemed uncharacteristically to be lost for words. Mrs Collins was always flamboyant but today had surpassed herself. The trip to the dressmaker's had been worth it if her intention was to out-glitter everyone in sight. Purple and green shot silk, lace and sequins were the order of the day, with a skirt that dipped into points here and there around her chubby ankles. To crown it all, Mrs Collins was wearing a feather-trimmed purple hat! No one wore hats to Mrs Chickward's parties. It was a hat which wouldn't be out of place in the Royal Enclosure at Ascot, and anywhere else would be considered a disaster.

"Mrs Collins," said Minty in a voice which trembled, "only you could carry off such an ensemble."

Mrs Collins accepted this as a compliment, which indeed it was. "Oh, and before I forget. About that little problem you have in the chapel, the bishop says that Cecil must speak to him personally, and then he'll send a specialist to deal with it."

On that note, she sailed ahead of them into Mrs Chickward's residence.

"Stately as a galleon," sang Patrick, almost but not quite under his breath.

Minty dug her elbow into his ribs and told him to behave himself.

So it was that they were both smiling as they were greeted by Mrs Chickward, accepted a couple of fruit juices … and came face to face with Maxine.

It was Minty's turn to lose her tongue. Shock, mostly. And outrage. Gemma had warned her, but Minty hadn't realised exactly how closely Maxine could imitate — and surpass — her in looks.

Maxine was at her most dazzling. She was wearing a blonde wig, with the hair piled high on her head. Her make-up was light, her contact lenses were blue, her white shirt was modest but expensive and her jeans clung just as jeans should. She was the very picture of modesty — and beauty. Her figure was superb. Her voice low and caressing. "So this is the man I've been hearing so much about." She took Patrick's arm and drew him through the French windows into the garden. She'd been waiting for him, of course.

She looked up at Patrick as if he were the only man in the world. "They tell me you have ambitions to become a judge. Come and tell me all about it. I know so many people that I'm sure I can help you."

Minty gaped. How simple Maxine made it look! You studied your victim's wife and presented yourself like her, you found out what the victim wanted most in life, and you offered both as a package. What was more, Maxine outshone Minty in every way. Maxine's beauty was ethereal, whereas Minty suspected that she herself had lost most of what good looks she'd ever had. Maxine's figure was perfect. Her perfume clouded the air.

Minty wanted to choke, to scream, to attack Maxine with raking fingernails.

Maxine knew that, of course. The glance she sent Minty was one of triumph.

Someone swept Minty round in a bear-hug, and she found herself face to face with Mr Lightowler from the bookshop, enthusiastic as ever about his latest project, which he must tell Minty about immediately! What did she think of a children's readathon for charity, to be held in the summer holidays?

She looked around and Maxine had disappeared. So had Patrick.

Almost, Minty panicked. She couldn't see either of them anywhere. But here came Hugh Wootton, complaining that he'd stood in the car park at the Hall for hours directing traffic and there hadn't seemed to be anyone to take over from him, so he'd just reported back to the Information desk that he was going off duty and gone. "Enough's enough, my dear," he said.

"I agree," said Minty, who'd spotted Maxine on the far side of the lawn, chatting to some people whose name she ought to know but couldn't for the life of her remember. Patrick was not with her. Or was he?

The gardens were thronged with people, though Mrs Chickward was lamenting loudly that there were not as many as usual. "The traffic! This festival! People have had to leave their cars miles away ..."

Minty spotted a man she knew slightly, one of Patrick's friends. "Lovely to see you again. Aren't the gardens superb? Have you seen Patrick anywhere? I seem to have lost him."

"Wasn't he with that stunning blonde a moment ago?"

"Excuse me." A tall, lean, middle-aged man whom she half recognised interposed himself between them. "Deputy Chief Constable," he said, taking her arm. "Shall we take a turn in the shrubbery?"

What could she say but "I'd be delighted," and look over her shoulder to see if she could spot Patrick as she was led into the depths of the wood. The azaleas were indeed stunning, but she couldn't concentrate on anything, for worrying about Patrick.

The Deputy Chief Constable was talking. "... for your own good, my dear, as I can see you're not up to scratch in these matters. Ah. A seat in time, as they say."

"I'd be grateful for any advice you can give me," said Minty, accepting a seat on an old wooden bench. He proceeded to lecture her as if he was addressing a Neighbourhood Watch group of concerned householders. "Operational Support," he said. "That's what we offered right from the beginning, when we first heard about it." His opinion of Mr Hatton was even lower than Minty's. The Deputy Chief Constable was of the steam-roller variety of speakers. His voice didn't boom. It drilled. Did she know how much the tickets for these events could sell at? A hundred pounds each. Sometimes more. Did she know that the plastic loos which had been hired for the site could be set on fire quite easily? Could she imagine what sort of injuries could be caused by arson in the loos?

Then, "Your security team isn't taking glass bottles off people as they let them in. Disastrous! Every glass bottle is a potential weapon. Have you thought of the injuries that can be caused by the broken neck of a bottle? Of course you haven't. The beer tents should be providing individual plastic cups, but are they? No, they are not. First rule of safety. No glass."

Minty said, "You have some plain clothes people on site?"

"Under-cover police. Of course. We moved in with the first campers. Drugs, you know. Theft. Always happens. My men are equipped with mobile phones, the lot. Keeping an eye on a couple of fellas on the Most Wanted list. Upwards of twenty thousand there this afternoon, I hear. Bound to be double that tomorrow."

"I returned from holiday to find everything arranged. I've no experience of such ..."

"Understood. But no excuses. You'll be held responsible if there's a riot."

She grimaced. "I understand that."

"Too many people. Too small a site. Not enough exits. Or loos. Mark my words, they're digging their own latrines as we speak. Going to cut up the Park. Advice? Give us a free hand to take over. Say the word, and I cancel all leave. We double up your security with our men and then withdraw your men. I've already given the word for us to take over traffic control, even though we've not been officially notified about the event. Roads are all snarled up already, aren't they? Devil of a job to get through this evening. Can't have that. Got to keep the traffic moving."

"Thank you. I appreciate that."

"Next thing, block off all the access roads. Bring in the helicopter. Mounted police, sweep through the Park. Dogs, of course. That should do it."

"Mounted police? Dogs? Helicopters? But ... there are so many families in there with children of all ages. They'd panic! The presence of police in riot gear would surely bring about exactly the conditions we want to avoid."

He patted her hand. "Bound to be casualties in a war, my dear. Think of the Hall, eh? Can't have anything happen to that, can we?"

Minty wondered if he was right. Surely her priority must be to save the Hall? Then she thought of small children running and screaming, with dogs at their heels. Surely the police wouldn't be so ham-fisted! Dogs, mounted horses, helicopter; these were tools that one could use in controlled fashion. To keep control of a situation which might never develop into chaos.

She wavered. Which was more important: the Hall or the people in the Park?

"Just say the word, my dear, and we'll take over."

She wasn't sure she wanted him to take over. Granted, the present security system was far from perfect, but ...

"Only one problem," he said. "My men say you've allowed tents to be put up in the Park. We don't like tents. We can't use mounted police when there's tents all over the place. Get the horses' legs tangled up in the guy ropes. But we can use mounted police in the main arena, sweep everyone down the slope clear of the house."

She thought of the two sponsorship tents which narrowed the exits from the arena, and in her mind's eye she could see the stampedes for safety, children being dragged along, falling, being crushed underfoot ...

No. She couldn't have that. *Pray, Minty. Pray. There must be another way.*

She stood up. "I understand what you've said, and I appreciate your taking the trouble to warn me. Let me have a number where I can contact you. I must speak to Mr Hatton tonight, and then I'll ring you, if I may."

"Day or night, my dear." He bowed over her hand and disappeared. Where was Patrick?

At her elbow. And looking quite normal, not flustered or red in the face as he might well have been if he'd been tangling with Maxine. "Had enough of being lectured? Come out into the sunlight. It's chilly under the trees, and you're shivering."

"Where have you been? I was so worried about you."

"Out and about. Not with Maxine, if that's what you mean. Were you given the lecture on Operational Support?"

"He's right, of course, but I can't see myself authorising mounted police to drive people from the arena. People would get hurt." She shook his arm. "What about Maxine? I heard her offer to make you a judge, if you would only 'service' her. What did you say to her?"

"Mm? Oh, something about her being a good imitation, but I preferred the original."

Minty gaped. "But she's beautiful!"

Patrick smiled down at her. "Beautiful, maybe. Terrifyingly efficient. But not lovely. Not half as lovely inside and out as you, my sweet heart." As usual, he made two words out of the endearment: sweet heart.

Patrick would never be thought a handsome man, though he'd be considered distinguished in old age. But his grey eyes — which could look hard at times — told her that he was constant in love. She thought, *I'll remember this moment: Patrick standing tall and dark against the blue of the sky and the splendour of the azaleas. I'll remember it for ever.*

She intended to say, "I love you." But what came out was, "You're a good man, Patrick Sands."

He was embarrassed. He laughed, ducked his head. Blushed. "At this moment, I'm a very hungry man. Did you say Serafina has some food for us this evening?"

"Refreshments in the dining room," said Mrs Chickward, clapping her hands to get everyone's attention. "A little bit of this and that to stay the appetite. Come along, everyone. Fall to."

Patrick and Minty obeyed and found themselves seats in a corner, where roly-poly Neville joined them.

Neville's usually placid countenance was lined with a frown. "Minty, Patrick. Glad to see you. Everyone's talking about Maxine. She's being coy, saying she hasn't made up her mind whether or not to appear tomorrow. She's a stunning little piece, isn't she? Hard to handle though, I imagine."

Minty carefully didn't look at Patrick. "There are problems, Neville, but as far as I know, Maxine has every intention of appearing tomorrow."

She felt she was being watched and looked up to see Maxine staring at her from across the room. Minty threw back her head and gave Maxine look for look. Then turned back to Patrick. "Any ideas how to get the two sponsors' tents moved before there's a stampede and people get hurt?"

"I haven't been back to the Hall yet, remember. I can't visualise the layout. Can you draw me a plan?"

Mrs Chickward's paper napkins were, of course, of the finest quality. Minty spread one out and sketched the layout from tent city, up through the Park to the stage management area, past the lake with the two drinks tents one on either side ... to the sloping arena below the house.

Patrick whistled. "I see what you mean. Have these tents got a boarded-over floor? No? Power lines? No? Generators? Right. Give me a minute. Let me think something through." He went off into a brown study.

Neville was watching the door.

"Dear Neville, Iris isn't coming," said Minty, understanding his hopes and fears. "I'm not at all sure she's been invited, either. She's acting hostess for the Press and VIPs up at the Hall ... which is where I ought to be right at this minute. Why don't you come back with us now?"

"Right, woman! Do you want those tents moved, or don't you?" said Patrick, coming back to life. They thanked Mrs Chickward for the evening and with Neville in tow, took the back lane down to the main road, to avoid the throng in the High Street.

Chapter Twenty

VIPs were directed to the main entrance to the Hall, where a queue had formed to have their invitations scrutinised before being allowed in. As they waited to be allowed in, Patrick was singled out by a very thin man, who seemed to know him well. Patrick introduced him to Minty, who only caught the words, "...stringer for the dailies." Press? Yes. He had a large Press badge dangling from his lapel.

"What's all this about the chapel? And where's the star of the show?" said the newcomer.

"Maxine is eyeing up the talent at a private party," said Patrick.

"I wanted a picture of her without her stage make-up," said the journalist. "Lovely place you have here, Mrs Sands. I understand you've only just returned from a lengthy holiday and this is your first venture into the festival field. What do you think of it?"

Minty chose her words with care. "I've never seen so many people enjoying themselves. It's fantastic."

"I'll quote you on that. Now, if we can have a picture or two of you, showing you as the Lady of the Hall ... then we can put one of the luscious Maxine next to it ...?"

"Showing Ancient and Modern, you mean?" said Minty, smiling.

"Not at all," said the journalist, and the look he gave her was not only thoughtful but also appreciative. "Perhaps another caption might be 'The Lady and the ...'?"

"Tramp?" Patrick was mildly amused. "You'd never get away with it, Tom. But of course Minty will pose for you."

"Inside the Great Hall?" asked Tom. "That would be best."

The security man on the door gave them one look and said, "No invites, no entry. And the Press tent is beyond the lake."

"I'm getting bored with this," said Minty. "Check with Iris or Clive Hatton or Toby Wootton. Mr and Mrs Cardale Sands. We're hosts here, not guests, and this gentleman comes in with us."

This security guard possessed a few more brain cells than the ones who'd refused Minty entry before; or perhaps she'd gained in confidence since then. He said, "Yes, I've heard about you." And let them through into the Hall.

The Great Hall was always dark. Minty's eyes went to the foot of the carved wooden staircase. That was where she'd been found after her fall. For a moment she suffered another attack of vertigo, imagining herself falling . . . falling . . .

Then she caught herself up, realised Patrick's hand was under her arm and turned to Tom with a brilliant smile. "Where would you like me to pose?"

A middling-sized man had sneaked in after Tom, holding a camera. Tom posed her in one of the window-embrasures, and his cameraman took a couple of shots.

"So what's all this about Maxine, then?" Tom was nothing if not persistent. Minty expected Patrick to send him away, but instead he invited Tom up to their rooms for a drink. Presumably Patrick had some plan in mind. Even in the Great Hall, the noise from the festival could be heard, and as they took the lift to their rooms, Minty had the feeling that the Hall was enduring rather than enjoying the performance. But maybe that was a reflection of what she herself felt.

As they left the lift, Minty noticed that all the spoilt things they'd removed after Maxine's occupation had been neatly screened off. Good.

Once inside their rooms Patrick went to the window to check on the situation below. Minty pointed out the location of the two tents, and he nodded. "Tom, let me get you a drink?"

Their beautiful green sitting room was more crowded than ever before. Some early arrivals had now left, but their place had been taken by others—including some who had also been at Mrs Chickward's party. The noise level almost defeated the sound rising from the stage below. Surely people would start going home soon.

Tom stuck close to Minty's elbow. "All right, so Maxine isn't on show tonight. Understood. But there's all sorts of stories going around about her. One is that she's walking out of the festival tomorrow.

Something to do with the chapel? You wouldn't like to fill me in on that, would you?"

Minty suppressed a shudder. She did not think it would be a good idea to have the desecration of the chapel spread over the tabloid press.

Patrick said, "Our private chapel?" He put the right amount of bewilderment in his voice. "I hadn't heard that one. Hang about for half an hour and I might be able to dig up a proper story for you, Tom."

Tom said, "Like that, is it? Make it worth my time, then."

Patrick disappeared into the throng, and Minty introduced Tom to Iris, who was still acting hostess. Neville tagged miserably along, wanting to get Iris into a corner by himself, but never succeeding.

Serafina had been unable to resist appearing at the reception and was now supervising a table of hot snacks. How on earth had Chef had the time to create these, on top of everything else she was doing? Two young waitresses were deftly removing empties and offering trays of drinks. Paid for by the Hall? Or by the sponsors?

Serafina signalled to Minty and said there was a casserole in the oven for her and Patrick when everyone had gone.

Down in the arena people were dancing and shouting and waving their arms about to the music of a group on the stage. The sound seemed to get louder as the evening wore on. Was that possible, or just a sign that she was getting tired?

Minty caught glimpses of Patrick working the room, stopping to talk to a man here and a woman there. She also saw Mr Hatton talking to a prosperous looking man in a corner. And she saw Hatton's eyes following Patrick around. So Hatton knew who Patrick was. Good. Another crate of drinks appeared from the direction of the lift, and Minty remembered the warning about allowing glass onto the site.

"Splendid," said Patrick, materialising beside her side and beckoning Tom over. "Not much of a story for you I'm afraid, Tom, though you might get a paragraph out of it. As you know, we've two big sponsors for food and drink tents at the festival. Their tents were placed at what was thought to be an adequate distance from the main stage, but the festival has been so successful, they're getting worried about access.

"Knowing that even more people are expected tomorrow, they've decided that, to avoid an incident, they must move their tents back a good way. As soon as they stop serving tonight—in about half an hour—the tents are to be struck and relocated. It will mean their working through the night, but they'll share the cost of that with the Hall. You might want to point out how public-spirited this is of them."

Tom drifted over to the nearest window and looked out. He sighed, shook his head. Nodded. Looked cynical. "Patrick, you know very well that's not the sort of story I was looking for. Our readers want some scandal about Maxine. Or the chapel. I smell a cover up. Are you sure Maxine is going to appear tomorrow?"

"Definitely."

"What was all that about the chapel?"

Patrick said, "You want to take a photo of the chapel? Of course you may if you wish, but I don't think there's anything there to interest your readers."

"Ah," said Tom, draining his glass. "I take it that there *was* something amiss, but you've seen to it. All right, I'll play ball, if I can have an exclusive interview with Maxine tomorrow."

"I can't promise," said Patrick. "But I can't see her refusing, can you?"

Minty said, "She's supposed to be finishing off a video somewhere local tomorrow. Perhaps you can catch her on location."

"Catch who on location?" said Gemma, appearing at their side. She was wearing the long dark wig, the skimpiest of tops, the tightest of jeans and a lot of make-up. Tom did a double-take. "You're not ...?"

Gemma laughed, showing perfect teeth. "No, I'm not Maxine. I'm Gemma Cardale, Minty's sister, and I'm going to be singing in Maxine's backing group tomorrow."

"Now there's a story I can use," said Tom. "Let's have a couple of shots of you and Mrs Sands together ... and perhaps a word or two about how you came to be in the business?" He disappeared into the throng with Gemma, in search of his camera-man.

Minty let out a long breath. "Gemma doesn't miss a trick, does she? Well, good for her. After the way she's been treated, she deserves a break."

Neville came up, looking anxious. "Minty, you're right about those marquees. As soon as this set finishes on stage, there's going to be an almighty queue of people drifting back to their tents and caravans, and they'll all have to feed through those two gaps. People will end up being pushed into the lake, or try to get behind the marquees and get blocked by the loos."

"It's all right," said Patrick. "Or at least, it will be, with a bit of luck. I've got the sponsors to agree we move the tents overnight."

Minty was filled with admiration. "Patrick, however did you manage it?"

"Blackmail, of course. The sponsors like a festival because it's good publicity for them, not to mention good sales. The slightest hint of adverse publicity and they take fright. I told them Tom was here following up a tip that there was going to be a bad accident because of their tents, and they were horrified. They didn't mind risking people's lives for the sake of profit, but the thought that the Press might get hold of the story . . ." He rolled his eyes. "It's all a question of how you present the facts to the jury, my lord."

"Suppose Tom does find someone who knows what Maxine did to the chapel?"

"I rather hope he doesn't, because it would make the Hall notorious, instead of famous. An air of mystery is fine; the sordid truth would have made our sponsors pull out straight away." He grinned. "And now, my love, you'd better break the news to Mr Hatton that he's not going to get much sleep tonight."

Minty beckoned Clive Hatton over. "A word with you in my office, please?"

He followed her, looking anxious. As did Patrick, Neville and Iris.

Minty closed the door on the hubbub next door. "Mr Hatton, the sponsors have been persuaded to have their tents re-sited in the interests of public safety."

Mr Hatton snapped back, "Impossible! And quite unnecessary. Besides, I've already told you that the firm who put up the tents can't return tonight."

She picked up the phone and held it out to him. "I'm sure you have an emergency number for them. Will you ring them now, please, and explain the situation? Use this phone so that we can all hear what's being said."

For a moment she thought he'd refuse, but eventually he took the phone, consulted a list of numbers in his mobile and dialled. Perhaps he hoped the firm would refuse to help, and that would get Minty off his back. Minty pressed a switch to allow everyone in the room to hear the conversation.

"Mr Turnbull ... sorry to drag you away from the television, but there's been a bit of a problem here. Someone's complained that the sponsors' tents are too close to ..."

"Thought so!" A man's deep voice, rough ... from smoking? "Just woken up to the fact that they're risking accidents and law suits all round, are they? Har har."

Mr Hatton ground his teeth. "We've been asked to take them down tonight, move them back maybe fifty feet. I've told them it's just not possible ..."

"We-e-ll ... I wouldn't go as far as to say impossible. I might be able to get hold of my foreman and a couple of the men and get them to you in a couple of hours ... but it means overtime. And we'd need more men to help, men who'd be prepared to do what they're told."

Minty said, "Ask him how many more men he wants."

Mr Turnbull heard her. "Is that the Lady of the Hall? I hear she's a cracker! If she can rustle up maybe four more men, and they're prepared to follow orders ... no, tell you what, I'll come myself. But we'll need feeding and watering, right? Give me a couple of hours to get organised. If you can get the tents cleared, we could start at—what's the time now?—tell the security guards on the gate that we'll be there at one. And get some lights fixed up so we can work all night. Right?"

Minty called out, "Double overtime! And bacon sandwiches, right?"

"I heard that," said Mr Turnbull, laughing. "Now, we've got another problem. We've got another job on tomorrow, and my foreman and most of the men will be needed on that. If I spare one of my men to stay behind to direct operations, can you get your team to put the tents back up?"

"Hope so," said Minty.

Mr Turnbull said, "And hot tea. Three sugars for me. Right?" and rang off.

Hatton put the phone down, looking sour.

Minty said, "Thank you, Mr Hatton. Now, we can't force anyone to work overnight, but if you'd get your stewards together and offer them overtime if they'll agree to help out …? Neville, can we afford it?"

Neville consulted the computer in his head and nodded. "Worth it, Minty. Now, I'm not much good at the physical stuff, but I'm game for a few hours on the food and drink side, preparing tea and coffee, maybe some packet soup, if you've got such a thing."

"I'll muck in wherever needed," said Patrick, "though I've just remembered — to my extreme annoyance — that all my tools were in the boot of my car."

Serafina had joined them, unheard. "Minty, have you the keys to the restaurant? You have? Good. I had a nap earlier, so I could open up the restaurant with Neville to serve hot drinks and sandwiches. We'll have to feed the security men and people humping stuff to and from the tents as well."

"I need a nap myself first," said Minty, feeling dragged down. "But I'll take over for a couple of hours at, say, four o'clock. I'll see the loos are all right, as well."

"Oh, hang about," said Neville. "Can't we get someone else to do the loos?"

He looked at Iris, who looked away.

Minty mourned the lost days of her close friendship with Iris. In the old days Iris would have offered to help, but not now.

"One more thing," said Patrick, looking out of the window. "I think the band's about to produce their last encore. Hatton, can you get someone to make an announcement from the stage about leaving the arena slowly? Perhaps send extra stewards down there to see no one gets pushed into the lake?"

Mr Hatton said stiffly, "The stock from the tents had better go into the gift shop …"

"Not big enough," said Minty. "Put it into the Great Hall where we can keep an eye on it."

"Lights!" Mr Hatton made for the lift. "Iris, are you coming? Find Reggie for me, will you? And then ..."

Mr Hatton and Iris got into the lift and disappeared.

Patrick put his arm round Minty. "Well done. Don't think I hadn't noticed you flagging, because I have. Go and charm the sponsors for a few more minutes, have something to eat and get off to bed. I'll come up later."

Minty thought, *Thank the Lord for answering my prayer.*

Minty fell asleep as soon as she lifted her feet up onto the bed. The alarm woke her at four. Patrick hadn't come to bed by that time, and in fact he never made it.

Minty pulled on a sweater, jeans and trainers and worked in the kitchens till six, when young Toby Wootton came stumbling in to take over from her. Instead of going back to bed, she made the rounds of the Hall and gardens as she always used to do early in the morning.

At seven Minty phoned Chef to tell her what had been happening overnight, apologise for the state of her kitchen and deliver the bad news that they'd run out of milk. Chef, predictably, tore Minty off a strip for not calling her in earlier. Chef had her own anxieties. Mr Hatton had apparently miscalculated the number of guests and stewards who'd needed to be fed the previous day, and she'd run dangerously low on staples such as coffee, fresh fruit and vegetables.

Chef had been up at four that morning, baking, and she'd bring all she'd prepared in with her but couldn't spare the time to go shopping herself, so could Minty find someone to do so for her? Minty agreed, wondering who to send.

At eight, Minty showered and found clean jeans and a good white T-shirt to wear. Patrick appeared, saying he was prepared to work on, if he could only have a shave and something to eat.

"Best eat while you can," said Serafina, dishing up a large breakfast.

"Praise be, no one got hurt in the retreat from the arena last night," said Patrick, rubbing the back of his neck to ease tension. "If I never see another tent pole in my life, that'll be soon enough."

The sun shone and it hadn't rained in the night. Reggie, Patrick, three of the stewards and the security men had worked under supervision through the night to hump the stock over to the Great Hall, take down the marquees, remove them to a safe distance and start to reassemble them. Four more stewards had volunteered to come in and help at seven thirty, and three had actually turned up. Patrick was now allocated to other duties, but it looked as if the tents would be up, re-stocked and ready to serve drinks by noon.

Minty sat on the window-ledge, toast in one hand and tea in the other. With one part of her mind she was admiring the view while mentally reviewing a list of jobs still to be done. Patrick sat at the table, grumbling mildly about the lack of a newspaper and finishing off the sausages and bacon which Minty hadn't felt like eating.

People wandered around the site, chatting, playing with the children, eating whatever they'd brought with them or been able to buy at the various food stalls.

Neville had gone home to his aunt's at three that morning but promised to be back at half past eight to keep an eye on the booking office and supervise the transfer of the cash takings to the night safe of the bank. Neville was not pleased that Mr Hatton had been keeping the takings in the ancient safe in his quarters.

Litter blew about the site, but the sky was serene.

Minty switched to prayer. *Dear Lord, whatever the day brings, help us to follow the right path. Be with us always.*

Patrick said, "Has anyone seen my mobile?"

Mr Hatton crashed in on this peaceful scene. He bore the look of a man who'd laboured long and mightily for hours. Even his normally smooth hair was dishevelled.

He spoke through his teeth. "I don't think you realise quite what you've done. We won't get those tents re-stocked before noon, so we've lost the good will of our sponsors. They'll never sign up with us again. As for our work force …!"

"Good morning, Mr Hatton," said Minty. "Tea or coffee?"

Patrick pushed back his chair. "Well, you won't need me."

"We were doing perfectly all right until you interfered!" Mr Hatton aimed his words at Patrick rather than Minty.

Minty shook her head at him. "Mr Hatton, the buck stops with me, not my husband. You were saying you thought the sponsors were unhappy with the new arrangements? Far from it, I assure you. I talked to them both last night. They quite understood why the tents had to be moved back and said they'd be delighted to be associated with some of our larger charity events in future.

"Apparently we were supposed to provide them with a hospitality tent down in the grounds, but it never materialized, so they are very happy to be allowed up here instead. And they sent compliments to the Chef on the food."

"I told her we didn't need anything exotic ..."

"Good food makes satisfied customers. The only problem was that you told Chef to cater for forty guests and eighty came. I imagine there'll be about the same number today? Now about the stewards who worked through the night. Why didn't you tell them I was offering overtime? They were on the point of downing tools and going home when Patrick turned up and told them what had been arranged. He looked for you but couldn't find you anywhere. Yet another failure of communication?"

"I was out and about."

"I've arranged for the men who volunteered for extra duties to be given a free lunch in the restaurant and then go off duty. I left yet another message on your phone about that. You really must check your batteries."

He screeched, "We're not made of money!"

"We're making enough to pay them and avoid accidents. It was greed that put the tents too close in the first place. The sponsors didn't want to miss a single person passing through to the arena. Yes, it's cost us something to resolve the problem, but better that than dozens of law suits for injuries."

"What are we to do for stewards this morning? We've none left to man the car park or protect the camera team!"

"You're exaggerating, of course. I can see several. I know the security guards are still on duty at the gates because I've checked. As to the rest, the first of the police will be reporting for duty in half an hour."

"The police! We don't need ..."

"I'll come down with you for the briefing in the courtyard. The police will all be in place long before the festival programme starts again at twelve. Which leaves your stewards free for lighter duties today—which they richly deserve."

Patrick looked amused. "I have my orders, too, Mr Hatton. I have to rescue my car and raid the supermarket in town for supplies for Chef."

Mr Hatton yelled, "I resign!" Seating himself in the nearest chair, he crossed his arms and leaned back with a defiant gesture.

Patrick shrugged, kissed Minty, said, "Don't overdo it," and departed.

Minty abandoned her window-seat to help Serafina clear the table.

Mr Hatton spoke through his teeth. "Didn't you hear me? I'm walk-ing off the job this minute, and nothing you can say will stop me!"

Minty said, "Poor Mr Hatton. You look as tired as I feel. Coffee or tea?"

He thumped the table, which caused Serafina to give him a black look.

"Coffee, I think," said Minty to Serafina. She seated herself oppo-site Mr Hatton.

Should she let him go, or try to keep him? She didn't like him much, and she wasn't sure his morals were whiter than white, but could she manage without him? Was he counting on the fact that she couldn't?

He said, "You went behind my back! You undermined my position."

Minty sighed. "Mr Hatton, it won't help to throw accusations around. I could retort that *you* went behind *my* back, and that *you* undermined *my* position. I could also say that from the moment I returned, you've brushed my concerns aside as if they were of no impor-tance. I could say all that. Instead, I'm offering you some coffee and a quiet moment to review the situation."

He remained defiant. "I am not in the habit of taking orders from people who don't know what they're talking about."

"I always take advice before acting, Mr Hatton, and I trust that you will, too. Now, would you like milk and sugar with your coffee, or will you take it black?"

Serafina served coffee, rolled her eyes at Minty, and departed.

Mr Hatton glared at the coffee as if trying to mesmerise it. Minty pushed the milk and sugar towards him and removed her gaze to the window. The sun was shining, the tents had been removed to a safe distance ... and Maxine was somewhere out there, filming.

Minty had managed a quick word with Hodge, the head gardener, that morning. Hodge said he thought "something's going on" in the disused barn at the far side of the walled garden. Hodge didn't like Maxine, because she didn't share his love of geraniums and had ordered exotic plantings instead. Hodge was a wily old bird. He'd promised to find out where Maxine was and let Minty know.

Minty had forbidden Maxine the Hall, but Maxine could say that the outbuildings had not been included in the ban. Ought Minty to do something about that? Ought she to tell Maxine that the Press wanted an interview with her? Or—a nice thought—would Gemma put Maxine in the picture?

Mr Hatton drank his coffee black. He smoothed back his hair, dusted some dirt from his sleeve. Took a few mental paces back towards regaining his normal, civilised demeanour.

"I'm still resigning," he said. "Unless ..."

Minty waited. She thought Mr Hatton still hadn't realised that the Lady of the Hall was back in charge.

He said, "I've had an attractive offer from a much larger stately home. A ten-year contract, for a start. A flat and a car, of course. But they want me to start immediately. I told them that I still had some months to go on my contract here, but in view of our differences, I'm thinking of forfeiting those few months of salary and taking up their offer."

She said, "Congratulations," while thinking hard. Did he really have such an offer on the table? Was he just trying it on?

He glared at her. "I don't want to leave you in the lurch with the festival still running, but you've forced my hand. I ask myself, how would you manage if I walked out on you now?"

Minty said, "With difficulty. I suppose I could upgrade Iris' post to ..."

"That girl! What experience does she have of such events?"

Minty forebore to add that from what she'd heard, he hadn't any experience of running such large events, either.

"Unless ...?"

He inched his chair forward. "A ten-year contract. A better flat, of course. The one Ms Annie had would do me fine. And a car. Expenses. Health insurance. A free hand to arrange what events I think would be best for the Hall. And no interference from you."

"Mr Hatton, the door's behind you."

He blinked. He hadn't expected her to turn him down so promptly, if at all.

"I don't understand. It's a very reasonable package and entirely to your benefit."

"I can't agree to your having a free hand with events. Granted, I may make mistakes, but I'm prepared to learn from them. Let me make myself clear. I own the Hall—or rather, I have been entrusted with the Hall. It's my life's work to look after it and to hand it on to my successor in as good a state as I can. You look on it as a money-spinner. Given your position here, that is not an unreasonable point of view, but from time to time it may conflict with mine. Now, do you wish to continue working for me or not?"

"It would be absurd to disregard this other offer."

"If it exists." Ah, it had been a mistake to say that.

His mouth tightened. "Are you calling me a liar?"

She must back down or she'd lose him. "No. If you feel you must take up this other offer, then of course you must do so. I would quite understand. If you wish to stay, then we renegotiate your contract."

He leaned forward, thinking he'd won. "You agree then to ..."

"Another six months in which we'll have to see how we go. You stay in your present quarters. You may have the use of an estate car if you wish, but it will remain the property of the Hall. The usual expenses, holidays, pension allowance, etcetera. All events originate with me and are discussed at weekly meetings with the senior members of the estate. Lastly, you take your orders from me, and if I find you've been creaming off money in any direction, I call the police in. Understood?"

He reddened. "You cannot seriously think ..."

"Yes. I do." She caught back her temper, which was threatening to leap out of control. "Mr Hatton, would I be right in thinking you've never worked for a woman before, and that it makes you uneasy?"

He blinked rapidly. "Women are generally not capable of business."

She could see him decide to turn on the charm. Perhaps it usually worked for him. He smiled at her, warmly. Insincerely. "But you, of course, are something else. I've never come across someone like you before. So ..."

"Let's get to the point. I haven't worked with anyone like you before, either. Shall we make it a new experience for both of us?"

His smile vanished. She heard voices. She looked at her watch and stood up. "Mr Hatton, we can discuss this again when the festival is over. I left word at the gate that I was expecting the Reverend Cecil for an important meeting, and I think he's just arrived."

Chapter Twenty-One

Not one, but three people had arrived. Minty was alarmed. "Why, Uncle Reuben, whatever are you doing here? You don't look at all well." She steered him to a chair.

Minty's uncle was trembling, leaning on his stick. He looked as if he'd been up all night. His hair was unbrushed, and he hadn't shaved.

Cecil followed, looking anxious.

Behind them came red-headed Carol. "Oh, Minty, I'm sorry but I couldn't stop him. He insists on seeing the chapel for himself."

Cecil murmured to Minty, "I told him what you'd found, thinking he could advise me what to say to the bishop, and I thought he'd have a stroke. I rang Carol and asked her to help me with him, but he won't listen to her, either."

Minty's uncle pounded on the floor with his stick. "There is nothing in heaven or earth can separate me from the love of God!" His eyes looked through them, searching the room for … what? At the second try he seemed able to focus on Minty and held out his hand to her.

"God spoke to me in the night. I fasted and prayed. He said that He still had work for me to do here. Sometimes … of late … I've wondered how soon He'd let me join your aunt. But His timing is not ours."

Cecil murmured, "I told him everything had to go through the bishop, but he said that was a waste of time, as he was here and intends to conduct an exorcism himself!"

"Surely, there's only a few people licensed for that," said Minty, also in an undertone. "Besides, I understand these things can be dangerous, and he doesn't look at all well."

Cecil gave her a look which meant, *You're telling me!*

Serafina materialised, holding a glass of water, which she put in the old man's hand and raised to his lips. "There, now. A glass of water won't break your fast, and when you've done what needs to be done, you'll be able to rest."

They'd forgotten Mr Hatton, who was edging his way to the door, smiling uneasily. "Well, I'll be off then ... lots to do ... people to see ... police to brief ... busy, busy."

"Mr Hatton! Wait for me." Minty made as if to follow him and then hesitated, looking back at the others. "I ought to go with Mr Hatton. But I ought to show you the chapel, too."

"You must learn to delegate, my dear," said Carol, deciding the matter for her. "I'll go with Cecil and your uncle to the chapel so that they can work out what needs to be done—never fear, I'm not stepping inside that hell-hole again—and you go charm the hired help. Before you ask: yes, someone is looking after the shop. My father's got the whole family down for the day. He'll stay in the shop while the rest of them go to the festival. My younger brother can't talk about anything but Maxine, Maxine, Maxine. He's even got a poster of her up in his bedroom. I've tried telling him what she's really like, but he doesn't believe me."

"You leave it to us, Minty," said Serafina. "If I remember rightly, we need holy water and salt. We'll see the place put to rights, and I'll look after your uncle for you. He can take a nap when he's done."

Minty's uncle wavered to his feet, pointing himself in the direction of the far door and the chapel. "In the name of Jesus Christ, Saviour and Redeemer ... my strength shall be as the strength of ten ..."

"He's rambling," said Cecil, distressed.

"He's a man of God. As you are, Cecil," said Minty. "Go with God, both of you, and do whatever is needed to be done."

Cecil nodded and composed himself. Minty knew that many people thought him a light-weight pastor of souls, but she knew that he was also a man of God. Now as she watched, she saw him gather strength from his faith.

"I wonder if he's remembered to bring the salt?" said Serafina. She collected a jug of water and the salt-cellar and followed them.

Carol remarked, more to herself than to Minty, "I do get myself into the strangest situations, don't I?"

Minty nodded. They both did.

Minty wrenched her mind away from what might be happening in the chapel where evil still lurked, switched her mind back to Mr Hatton and followed him down in the lift.

Had she been wise to ask him to stay on for a while? Would she ever be able to trust him fully, or even come to like him? He probably felt the same way about her. If he was wise, he'd take a short contract and look around for something better suited to his talents, such as they were. Of course that meant she could look around for someone else, too.

Well, to business ... she would introduce herself to the assembled policemen and then ... and then ... what next?

What next was that Hodge sidled up to her. She'd just left the kitchens, where she'd asked Chef to provide a free lunch for the police as well as those who'd worked overnight, and assured her that Patrick had gone for fresh supplies.

Hodge was wearing stout leather gloves, which was unusual since his skin was as tough as the leather itself. "Minty, they're in the barn at the back, like I said. Her wanted a bed of hay to lie on. Got her some straw. Then her wanted me to pick her some of them big leaves that grows down by the river. So I did."

He went off, laughing so hard he had to wipe his eyes.

What was so funny about that? Minty knew her Hodge. Hodge didn't like Maxine. Had Hodge played some kind of trick on Maxine? What "leaves" exactly had he got for her? Down by the river ... what grew down there? Ah, the gunneras, which looked rather like enormous rhubarb plants. Yes, Minty could well imagine Maxine having one held above her head as she lay on the straw.

Perhaps she was pretending to be Titania, queen of the fairies? Minty suppressed a giggle. Hmph. Some fairy.

But Hodge's laughter had made her uneasy. Minty made her way round the back of the walled garden to some disused outbuildings. One day she planned to turn them into extra tourist facilities, but for the moment they were empty, dry, deserted.

The huge doors to the barn were closed, but a smaller door had been cut into one side, and Minty went through that to cries of "Quiet!" and "Cut!" And "Take five."

A man was pleading, "Maxine, please use the hand away from the camera when you stroke him, right?"

Minty closed the door behind her, trying not to make a noise. This end of the barn was dim. A number of people stood around, but she could barely make out who they were.

The far end of the barn, however, was aglow with television lights. They lit up a pretty little scene, a rural idyll. A number of bales of straw had been built up to form a throne on which Maxine sat, with Nero's head in her lap. Maxine was wearing her black curly wig and a scarlet, very low-cut top over a denim skirt slit to the thigh.

In one corner a machine was playing one of Maxine's songs. Something about "Take what you want." The technician cut the sound and pressed buttons to reset the machine.

Nobody took any notice of Minty standing at the back.

She drew in her breath. Either to add colour to the scene or give the impression that she was sitting on a throne, large green leaves had been placed on the straw bales at Maxine's back. Minty had to admit that they created a charming picture frame for her but ... *the frame was poisoned!* Minty understood now why Hodge had been wearing gloves.

"Hi," murmured someone close by. Gemma, wearing a red top and denim skirt similar to Maxine's. Presumably Gemma'd been standing in for Maxine again. "Come to turn us out? You didn't forbid us to use the barn."

"You broke the spirit of our agreement, but no, that's not what's bothering me. Don't you see what plant she's got there?"

Gemma shrugged. "Never paid any attention to stuff like that."

"Giant Hogweed. It spreads along river banks. The leaves are highly toxic and can give people a nasty rash."

Gemma looked at Maxine, surrounded by the leaves, and laughed. "Well, serve her right."

"Won't you warn her?"

"You warn her, if you're so worried about her health."

A man turned his head and shouted at them to be quiet or get out.

Minty bit her lip, struggling with herself. She felt nothing but loathing for Maxine, who had brought evil to the Hall. She'd spread her poison everywhere, like the sticky trail of a snail. Minty remembered what Maxine had done in the chapel: the horror on the altar, the reversed cross, the broken chair and the torn Bible. Minty had told Serafina that God would punish Maxine.

Punished she would be, if she let the leaves touch her bare skin. At the moment she was fairly well protected by her outfit.

There was absolutely no reason for Minty to worry about Maxine. Let her take her chances.

The director gave the signal, the technician started the playback and Maxine's voice filled the barn, honey-sweet with a message dripping acid. "Take what you want, but don't forget to pay me ..."

Nero writhed, looking up Maxine as she mimed to the song. She raised her left hand to force his head away from her and the director shouted, "Cut! Not that hand, Maxine! I told you before! The hand away from the camera!"

Maxine thrust Nero away from her and stood. "What can you expect, it's so hot in here!" Minty filtered out the expletives Maxine used between every other word. It was a shock to hear her swear like that because she'd not done it in front of Minty before.

"I need a drink." Someone offered Maxine a cup from a flask of coffee.

Maxine knocked it aside "Not that sort of drink, stupid. Can't we get some air into this place? It's stifling."

Before Minty could stop her, Maxine picked up one of the giant leaves and began to fan herself with it.

Minty pushed forward, crying, "Stop! Don't touch it!"

"What?" Maxine turned on her, recognised her. "Who's this? The Lady of the Hall come to spy on me? Go back to bed, sweetie. You look as if you need it. Hasn't anyone ever told you that bags under the eyes are most unattractive?"

Minty felt her temper climb but clutched it down again. "Those leaves are poisonous. They can give you a bad rash, especially in sunlight or strong light."

Maxine laughed. "Do you really think to frighten me into stopping the filming? Jealous of me, are you? Remind me to send you a copy of the video when it comes out. Come on, everyone. Back to work."

Maxine threw herself back into place, stroking her face with the leaf while watching Minty the while. "See. It doesn't dare to harm me!"

Minty turned and walked out, wondering if Gemma would follow her. No Gemma.

Hodge was standing outside, beside a wheelbarrow full of geraniums. Of course. Presumably he was on his way to tear out Maxine's exotic flowers and replace them with his favourites. Minty decided she wasn't going to interfere; she liked geraniums herself.

He said, "How's she coping?"

"She wouldn't listen when I warned her. Hodge, you ought not to have done that."

Hodge trundled his wheelbarrow away, laughing.

Minty leaned against the barn door, torn between satisfaction and a feeling that she ought to have done more to stop Maxine being hurt. Then Minty thought that Maxine was so poisonous herself that she probably wouldn't be affected. Nor Nero, either.

She took a couple of steps away from the barn, and only then did it strike her that if Maxine did have a bad reaction to the Hogweed, she might not be able to appear that evening! Oh. She hesitated. Ought she to go back, to reinforce her warning?

She shook her head. No. It was too late. Maxine either was or was not going to be affected. It was too late to do anything but pray for everyone involved. It didn't bear thinking what might happen in that crowd on the slopes if they heard that Maxine wasn't going to appear.

God willing, everything would be all right.

She pulled out her list of Things to Do and went to see about replenishing the soft drinks they'd need for the sponsors and their guests. Would Patrick be able to bring back enough food and drink in time?

By this time tomorrow, it would all be safely over. Wouldn't it?

Leaving the barn, she skirted the walled garden until she came to the terrace of cottages which had once formed part of the stable block. These were now occupied by staff. Reggie had one cottage, Hodge another ... and the third had been occupied by Iris until she'd taken herself off to Carol's.

As Minty turned the corner, she saw Iris dart out of her cottage and, with her back to Minty, look towards the courtyard where the family's cars were kept. There was something in Iris' attitude which stopped Minty from calling out to her. For one thing, Iris wasn't wearing any shoes.

Two seconds later, Iris ushered Clive Hatton out of her cottage. Clive thrust his shirt back inside his trousers and hurried off to the main courtyard.

Iris watched him go, arms tight around her body.

Minty felt extremely tired. She'd been up half the night. There were so many burdens on her shoulders ... and now?

She must have made a sound, for Iris turned her head and saw her. Iris was crying.

Minty felt like slapping Iris, and then she felt sorry for her. Minty put her arm about her old friend and guided her back into the cottage. There were used wine glasses and the remains of sandwiches on the table. Iris' shoes were under the chair nearby. No wonder Clive Hatton had been elusive lately. And last night? Had he been with Iris last night, instead of helping to move the tents? Did a liaison between them explain why Iris had always taken his side?

All this time Minty had thought Clive was sleeping with Gemma. Possibly he'd been sleeping with both of them?

But for Iris to fall for such an obvious charmer! With her history of rape and distrust of men! It was a discovery full of sorrow.

Iris said, "You don't need to tell me how stupid I am. I know he isn't worth it. The moment you came back and asked me about him, I knew."

"Why did you sleep with him, if you knew what he was like?"

"Because he said he loved me. Because I've always dreamed of marrying well. Because I was lonely. I know those are poor excuses. I love him and I despise him, and I don't know which is worse."

"Why were you crying?"

"He just told me he's leaving as soon as he can find another post. He says he can't work for you, and I suppose I understand that. I hoped he'd take me with him, but of course he won't. I'd be an embarrassment to him. He's made that quite clear."

Minty rocked Iris in her arms, thinking how surprising people were. Here was Iris, who had always seemed so icily in control of herself, allowing herself to fall for a con artist. Just like any other poor bemused woman. And completely missing the fact that Neville Chickward was besotted with her. Would it be a good idea to mention Neville's name now?

"Iris, you know that Neville ..."

Iris made a dismissive gesture. She was not interested in Neville. She disentangled herself to find a box of tissues. Blew her nose. Ran her fingers through her hair. Looked around her. Drew her dignity around her again.

Iris said, "You'll want me to go as well, won't you?"

"No. You've always played a huge part of my plans for the Hall. Of course I don't want you to go." She remembered how unhelpful Iris had been lately and added, "Unless you're looking for a more high powered job?"

Iris shook her head. "I've learned my lesson. Clive was talking pie in the sky about staging enormous festivals, getting internationally known. It won't happen here, and I'm not sure it ever will happen for him. He's fine on paperwork and ordering people about, but he's none too keen on getting his hands dirty. I saw that last night. Patrick was heaving on ropes with Reggie and everyone else, while Clive was whispering to me to come back here with him. I knew I ought to be helping you, but instead I agreed to do what Clive wanted. And despised myself for it."

"You've been using this cottage all along?"

"No, only the last couple of days, after you threw the technicians out. We used to meet in his rooms at first, but then a couple of rowdy cameramen moved into the housekeeper's flat next door, and Clive wanted us to be discreet. He said it was for my sake, but I think it really was for his. I suspect he has other women to keep happy." She was bitter. Iris saw only too clearly what a fool she'd been.

"Gemma?"

Iris nodded. "Maxine, too, I think. Though I can't be sure. I used to think Maxine slept with Nero, but now I think she just likes to give the impression that she does." She checked her appearance in a mirror, found her shoes and put them on. "What happens now?"

"We go back on duty. You organise everything for the reception, just as you did last night. Patrick's gone for fresh supplies, but until he gets back, we'll be short of everything. I'll join you upstairs as soon as I've checked with Cecil and my uncle."

No point in alarming Iris by saying that Maxine might be in no position to make the evening's performance. Minty looked at her watch. The police should all be in position by now, and with a bit of luck the food and drink tents would be up and serving in their new positions. She'd swing by them on her way upstairs, make sure there were no other problems to solve.

Iris echoed her thoughts. "I haven't been pulling my weight. So many things can go wrong on an operation like this, and I've let Toby and Reggie deal with a lot of them." She looked straight at Minty. "I must be straight with you. If he asks me to go with him tomorrow, I will. You can't trust me any more."

"Oh, Iris. No good can come of it, but ... no, I won't lecture. I will pray for you."

"You Christians think that's the answer to everything in life. Well, it isn't."

"It is for us," said Minty, quietly. "You're still hurting. Give yourself time."

"And death to all faithless men?" Iris tried to smile.

"Right," said Minty. "You check the drinks situation, I'll check the manpower, and we'll meet upstairs as soon as possible."

Litter was a problem in the Park. Everywhere. There weren't enough bins, and some people didn't seem to know what a litter bin was for, anyway. Drinks cans were everywhere. Minty remembered that hint about removing glass bottles from those who came in, and checked that the men on the gate would do that. Of course, it didn't solve the problem of the bottles that had already been allowed in.

She checked that the food and drinks outlets were serving in plastic cups and found that they were. Good. The sponsors' tents were up and re-stocking. They promised to be serving again within the hour.

She checked the restaurant, serving the first sitting of free dinners ... lovely food, cheerful helpers. Venetia Wootton had dragooned some of her house stewards into helping out. Chef was smilingly in charge but anxious to receive the supplies Patrick had gone for. She'd scrounged milk from all over the place, but there was still not enough to go round.

Minty checked the loos, all sparkling clean and sweet-smelling with a bunch of real flowers in each. She was amused to see that Alice Mount had found a dragon of a woman to look after the loos, charging twenty pence a time. Which said dragon would undoubtedly keep for herself. Worth it.

She checked with the police inspector; there'd been a minor scuffle between two teenage boys over an underage girl, a couple of drugs offences, a theft, two children who'd strayed and been restored to their parents. She was horrified to discover that no one had thought to provide the St John's Ambulance people with tea or coffee, but had to ask them to fetch it themselves from the restaurant because she hadn't anyone to spare to take drinks around.

The sound engineers were checking all their equipment. The first of the day's performers were being ushered to the electric cart, which was not being driven by Reggie, but by a slightly jaded Hugh Wootton. Hugh insisted he was fine but agreed he was looking forward to the end of the day. Minty promised to find Reggie to take over from him, but then discovered that stalwart was deep in worried conversation with some electricians and couldn't leave.

Would Hodge drive the buggy? If he was cleaned up, he might. She sped back to the gardens, found him in the greenhouses and bargained with him—she wouldn't tell Maxine that Hodge had knowingly given her toxic leaves, if he got himself cleaned up and did it. He was afraid of Maxine, as he might well be, considering what he'd just done. So he promised he'd do it. She'd known he would, but wondered ruefully whether blackmail was ever justified. *Please, God, You do understand, don't you?*

She spotted Neville in the Information office; busy, concentrating. But not distressed. Good.

She took the lift to the top floor.

She looked down at herself. Jeans and T-shirt. Cleanish, but not particularly appropriate for the Lady of the Hall. She really needed to change into something more formal before plunging into the crowd in the sitting room, but hadn't the time.

Toby Wootton raised a hand in greeting as she passed through the outer office. He had happily abandoned his post in the kitchens and was dealing with some knotty point on his old computer. It was interesting to see how quickly he'd abandoned his new office downstairs and returned to the tower office as soon as Minty was back.

Iris, self-contained and chilly in her black and white office garb, was restocking her trolley in the sitting room with soft drinks.

Clive Hatton wasn't there. Where was he? In bed with someone? No, surely not now. Everything in her rooms was as it should be. No cries of alarm from Maxine.

Minty slid past Iris into the dining room, where the old table was bare, awaiting the next batch of food being sent up from the kitchens below.

Serafina was sitting at the big table in the kitchen beyond. Serafina never sat down during the day; it had been one of the things Minty had tried in vain to change. Today was an exception. She was no longer young and had not only sat down but had fallen asleep.

A commotion at the door. The sponsors had turned up early; Minty thought they were probably anxious to get first pick of the food, but Patrick hadn't arrived back yet, and the dining table was still empty. Iris couldn't even serve teas and coffees until more milk arrived.

Visitors began to arrive, some invited by the sponsors and some by Mr Hatton. One and all they exclaimed at the beauty of the Hall and oh, my dear, wasn't this the most marvellous sight, they could see everything from up here! But the traffic . . . ! Where did you leave your car, my dear?

Minty circulated, smiling, listening, accepting compliments.

Containers of milk appeared; tea and coffee were served.

Patrick arrived, relaxed, smiling. Mission accomplished.

Chef sent up two waitresses with the first lot of food. Delicious smells wafted through the sitting room, and the guests' eyes brightened.

Minty went to check on Serafina, who jerked awake. "How long have I been asleep? Don't you need a nap, too? Oh, I forgot. Your uncle's fast asleep in your bed. Cecil's gone. And Carol. A tiring business, but we managed it between us. I suppose the bishop will need to re-consecrate the chapel some time, but we can use it again now."

"Oh, but ... they shouldn't ..."

"Your uncle was set upon doing it and it wasn't right to stop him. It took it out of him, of course, and that's why he's sleeping. Done him the power of good, I wouldn't wonder. Made him feel he still had a part to play in life."

Minty went quietly through to her bedroom, where her uncle slept on the four-poster bed. He lay so still, with his hands clasped on his chest, that she feared everything had been too much for him, and he'd thankfully gone beyond this life into the next.

Chapter Twenty-Two

Minty stood there, looking down on her uncle. She was too tired to think straight. She hoped he hadn't died. They had unfinished business between them still ... though death did often take people who still had something to say to one another. He'd not been a kind guardian when she'd been taken to live with him as a child. He'd allowed her aunt to take a leather belt to her, to brow-beat her ... almost to kill her spirit. He hadn't seen anything wrong in it.

He'd changed since his wife died. Had begun to lean on Minty, to need her. No, she really didn't want him to die yet.

Besides — and here hysteria began to point out the funny side of the situation — where would she and Patrick sleep tonight if her uncle continued to occupy the best bed? They'd slept in so many places recently, she'd gone to such great lengths to regain the use of their bedroom, that she couldn't bear the thought of having to find somewhere else to sleep.

All was well. He was still breathing. He stirred and opened his eyes, looking around him with a puzzled air.

"Is this where my brother — your father — died?"

She collected herself. "No, he had an invalid bed in what is now my office. But at one time, yes, he used to sleep in this bed with my mother." *And with his mistress. Oh dear, I didn't want to think about that.*

Reuben Cardale was fully dressed under the coverlet, except for his shoes. He struggled to sit upright, and Minty helped him. He seemed calm and rational again, thank goodness.

"Has Cecil gone home? Poor lad. He hardly expected to be assisting at an exorcism today." He gave a hoarse laugh. Minty hadn't known he could laugh. "That Serafina of yours. Splendid woman. The right sort to have at your back in a fight with the enemy."

"You shouldn't have ..."

"Nonsense. That's what I came here for, to help you. Poor little Gemma, too, I suppose ... though she's a lost child, if ever I saw one. I did wonder if God would allow me to go home after we'd cleared the chapel, but it appears I'm still here."

"I was worried about you."

"I'd rather wear out than rust out. Well, well. Help me get off this bed. I must be off to the vicarage. Cecil will be looking out for me."

"Let me show you to the bathroom first. You need to have a wash and brush up, then something to eat. After that we'll talk."

She found him clean towels, checked for a razor and soap. "I thought you'd stay here now that I'm back and able to look after you. You could have Annie's old suite of rooms over the restaurant."

He began to take off his coat but got stuck. Minty helped him. "No, no. I like it up at the vicarage. I like pottering about the village, into the church and out again. Dropping into the café for lunch or a coffee when I want it. Having a chat with Mr Lightowler at the bookshop, assisting Cecil at the services. It's all pretty much on the level, you see. Cecil's given up his dining room for me to have a bedroom downstairs, and there's a toilet on the ground floor. Perfect for an old man."

"But ..."

He patted her hand. "You can leave me to have a shave now. I appreciate your kindness, and there's no denying I did once think I could make my home here at the Hall. But it's a long way up the hill to the church when your legs don't work too well."

As Minty closed the door behind him, she thought that everyone in the village would think she'd turned the old man out, and would judge her accordingly. She supposed that didn't matter. What he said made sense. She must check that Cecil didn't mind, and see they had someone from the village to look after them ... and arrange for his pension ...

She stripped off her own clothes, dived into Serafina's bathroom for a quick shower, and donned a white broidery anglaise dress over a dark blue slip. It looked fresh and was becoming. She reflected that Maxine would probably call the dress "dowdy." Well, so be it.

If only Maxine hadn't been affected by the Hogweed. What were they going to do if she had been?

Minty's uncle emerged from the bathroom while Minty was brushing out her hair and putting it up. He looked better than he had, but still ravaged by time and experience.

"Hand me my stick, there's a good girl, and I'll be on my way. I want to be out of earshot when that caterwauling starts up again outside."

She kissed his cheek and handed him his stick. "Come next door and have a bite to eat while I organise you some transport." Problem: the roads were gridlocked.

She had an idea which made her laugh. "Do you fancy being driven up the hill in an electric buggy? We've got one downstairs that we might be able to spare for half an hour, and I think it could go on the pavements if the roads are all blocked."

He liked the idea. He flourished his stick. "Why not? I fancy the idea of driving up and down the street in one of them."

Did he mean now, or for good? She didn't care. Then, even as she took his arm, the black door opened up in front of her and she had to clutch at him to prevent herself from falling. It only lasted a couple of seconds before she was back to normal, though breathing hard.

"What was that?" He'd been leaning on his stick and luckily hadn't fallen.

"I've been having—visual disturbances, I think you'd call them. Ever since the baby ..." Her mouth went dry. "Pray for me, Uncle?"

"I do, my dear. I do." He looked anxious.

She did her best to smile at him. "I'm all right now, really."

She opened the door to the dining room to find it full of people, all laughing and chatting. And what was this? Enormous chicken and mushroom pies, mounds of risotto and great platters of cold meats had been set on the table, with bowls of salads and heaps of garlic bread, all being served to the throng by Alice Mount—who sent Minty a wink when she saw her. And here came Serafina, carrying in great bowls of fresh fruit salad and cream.

"Dear Alice," said Minty, giving her a hug. "You seem able to turn your hand to anything!"

Alice handed Minty a plate full of food. "Patrick told me to make sure you ate something, and to see that Serafina gets a nap this afternoon. He's gone down to help Neville with the money. Oh, and Dwayne says there's some kind of problem with the wiring, but Reggie thinks he can sort it out for this afternoon, though they might be a few minutes late starting."

The Reverend Cardale surveyed the room with distaste and said in a loud voice, "Sodom and Gomorrah!"

"Well, not precisely," said Minty, trying not to giggle but wishing that Patrick could have been there to share the joke. She must remember to tell him later. She handed her uncle the plate of food Alice had given her and steered him to a seat nearby. A kindly woman, whom Minty had often seen helping out at church, handed him a knife and fork and told him to "Eat up, there's a dear!"

Minty was amused. She could see that her uncle was about to become a Village Institution, his eccentricities tolerated and his courage admired. He'd be a source of pride in the neighbourhood. They'd tell one another, "We've got a right old one here, we have!"

Minty took another plate of food and started to work the room. There were many people there she'd met in the course of the charity events she'd run at the Hall, and some whom she knew through Patrick. She heard the scratchy, carping voice of the Deputy Chief Constable before she saw him. He was pleased with her, said he liked a "gal" who knew when to take good advice, but did she realise that the portable toilets had been sited in the wrong place . . . ?

It was too late to do anything about that now. What was done, was done.

If Reggie could fix the electrics . . . if Maxine was not affected by the Hogweed . . . if it didn't rain . . .

Talking, listening, smiling, eating a mouthful now and then, she worked the room till she came to her office, through which people were still arriving to join the throng.

Tom, the reporter, caught her arm. How had he managed to get in again? And did it matter? "Did you get to see Maxine? What about my interview with her?"

"She was filming in the barn on the other side of the walled garden this morning. She may still be there."

He nodded. Disappeared. Toby was there, chatting away to some people he knew. Of course, the Woottons of the Manor knew everyone.

Minty switched on the computer on her desk—hoping it hadn't gone into a sulk at being left unused for so long—and got onto the Internet to research Giant Hogweed. Maybe it didn't affect everyone. She knew Hodge regarded it as a pest and dug out the plants if they appeared anywhere in the garden.

The seeds are carried by rivers and streams, and the plants can grow to an enormous height, dwarfing men. Its leaves look like cow parsley but are much larger. The sap contains a substance which makes the skin react to ultra-violet light.

Such as the sun. Such as the lights they'd been using for filming? *Severe burns can be caused … swelling … blistering … appearing between fifteen and twenty hours after contact … long-lasting effects may develop,* etcetera.

Minty tried to work out when … if … Maxine was going to be affected. Minty had gone to the barn about ten that morning. Ten plus fifteen equalled one o'clock tomorrow morning, which meant that Maxine would make the performance that evening.

Of course, if Maxine's skin was extra sensitive she might react earlier. But no, she'd been wearing heavy make-up, hadn't she? It was going to be all right. Probably.

The only thing was: at what time that morning had Hodge supplied the leaves and Maxine handled them?

It must be all right. A quick glance out of the window showed Minty that if she'd thought the arena full before, she hadn't seen anything yet. There was a noise like a bull elephant on the rampage, and sound—she wouldn't call it music, precisely—burst out over the landscape. The day's proceedings were under way with a boy band doing their utmost to damage the ear drums of everyone within a mile.

Back in the sitting room, Minty's uncle was looking peaky. White-faced. Minty beckoned to Toby and asked if he'd take her uncle downstairs, find Hodge, commandeer an electric buggy and get her uncle returned to the vicarage.

"Poor old soul, yes, of course," said Toby, who was a good man at heart, even if he did admire Maxine over much.

Clive Hatton appeared, laughing, at ease, taking the credit for everything. Iris re-appeared—best not ask where she'd been—and took over the job of hostess as Minty made her way back down through the suite till she could finally close the door in her own bedroom.

Alone at last! She smiled, wondering how many of her ancestors had crept away from their guests to find sanctuary in their bedroom and say, "Alone at last!"

She stumbled to the bed, stretched out, curled up into a fetal position, wondered where Patrick was and fell asleep. She dreamed of guns and a honey-sweet voice singing of death and destruction ... and leaves which stung like nettles ...

Patrick kissed her awake. "My little cracker!"

She sat upright with a jerk. "Did Gemma say 'That gun' or 'The gun'?"

"Dreaming?"

She shook her head to clear it. "Nightmare. We should be all right, I think, but a spot of prayer wouldn't come amiss. Are you really here, or am I still asleep?"

"Possibly." He kissed her again. "Roll over. My turn for a nap. Guess who's turned up? My partner, Jim. And his mother. She's a right tartar, and I don't blame him for not wanting to spend much time with her. They're in the sitting room, glaring at one another. Your turn to play peacemaker. Wake me when you need me."

As he got onto the bed, she got off it. He'd taken off his jacket and shoes. It was too hot to pull the coverlet over him, so she smoothed the hair back from his forehead instead, thinking how much these last few months had taken out of him. Other people might think him unchanged, but she sorrowed for the slight hollows in his cheeks and the frown line between his eyes.

God grant you a peaceful sleep. God reward you for all the good things you do. God be with you ... and with me ... and also with Maxine.

She tidied her hair, put on a little lipstick—she was looking pale—and went back to the party.

The boy band had disappeared from the main stage, and a gospel choir were just finishing up on the second stage near the house. Everything seemed to be proceeding to plan.

Tea time. Alice was dispensing tea and cakes, tiny scones, bite-sized tartlets, chunks of fragrant fruit cake. Chef deserved a bonus, if anyone did.

There'd been a slight shower of rain, but the sun was shining again. Everyone was in a good humour. Perhaps they'd make it through to the end of the day without trouble. Perhaps all the precautions she'd taken had been unnecessary. That's what Clive Hatton was saying, anyway.

Minty was in that state of exhaustion which meant she felt neither pleasure nor pain. She was a robot, responding in the correct way to whatever was required of her.

Supper time. Chef sent up tasty canapés, and Iris was dispensing wine and soft drinks. Alice cut up quiches, served wedges of game pie. Serafina added some pizzas of her own making. Coffee appeared.

On the main stage an older woman with a thickening waist but bags of charisma sang a capella, backed up by close harmony from a well-rehearsed team of men and women. The crowd was enraptured, swaying in time to the music.

Patrick joined the party, having slept longer than he intended. Like her, he worked the crowd, laughing, joking, eating little but with eyes everywhere.

Minty saw Clive Hatton chatting up a wealthy divorcée. Iris was trying not to show that it mattered to her what Clive did.

As soon as Axel, Maxine's manager, appeared in the doorway, Minty knew why he'd come. She moved towards him as he peered around, looking for her. "She's asking for you."

Minty nodded. She looked out of the window. Nine o'clock and it was still light. Maxine had reacted earlier than expected.

Patrick arrived at her elbow. Minty said, "Maxine's asking for me."

Patrick's eyes narrowed; he put his coffee cup down and said, "I'll come, too. My friend Tom's been bugging me for an interview with her, but so far she's refused to see him."

As they entered the lift, Minty said, "There may be a very good reason for that. Isn't that so, Axel?"

He nodded, wiped his neck with his hand. "Do you think there'll be a thunderstorm? She's in the flat above the restaurant."

Down in the courtyard they could see that the restaurant was still full of people. How on earth did Chef keep going? How ever many covers had she provided this last week? So many free meals for the stewards and the police. If they came out of this breaking even, they'd do well.

They climbed the narrow stairs to the flat which had once been Annie's. Minty reflected that perhaps her uncle had been right to refuse these quarters. Those stairs would be a killer to a man whose legs were not altogether under control.

Maxine was supposed to be the final act that night, the climax of the festival, the much-anticipated star. Several of Maxine's entourage had been sleeping in Annie's flat, and it was natural enough that she'd found her way there. Someone had fixed up a sound link so that they could hear what was happening on the stage, which was of course out of sight and sound, on the other side of the Hall.

Annie's long living room was filled with tense, angry people. The air echoed with the sound of arguments, stilled as Minty came into sight. Gemma was by the window, looking out, smoking a cigarette. She was wearing the long black and purple dress in which she was supposed to dance with Nero that night.

Nero came out of the bedroom as they arrived. When he saw who'd arrived, he almost went back inside, but instead ran the back of his hand across his mouth, straightened his shoulders and came towards them. He didn't seem to have been affected by the Hogweed, for his skin was clear.

He said, "Okay, so I did torch your car, but I didn't mean it. At least, I did mean to scorch the door, because Maxine had wound me up to get my own back on you. But I didn't intend to go so far. The bottle slid out of my hand under the car and exploded. You have to believe me. It was a joke, sort of, and I swear what's happened to her now is nothing to do with me."

Patrick's eyebrows peaked and his hand tightened round Minty's arm, but he didn't speak.

Minty said, "Why would she blame you?"

He was eager to exculpate himself. "She said I ought to have known. But I didn't, honest."

274

"From the beginning," said Patrick.

Nero rubbed the back of his hand across his mouth again. "I was sleeping over in the village. She rang me early this morning, said she was bored. She wanted to get back at you for turning her out. My friend's father is a builder and decorator. Maxine said to get hold of some black paint from him and meet her at the bridge at the bottom of the village. There's a sort of temple affair in the grounds of the Hall here, all white. Maxine planned to paint her name all over it."

Minty shuddered. That temple was very dear to her and to Patrick.

"We got into the Park all right. The security guards know I'm in and out with different girls. To get to the temple without being seen we followed the river in a big loop way beyond the Hall. That's when she spotted these leaves. Big, they were. She wanted one to do a fan dance with, there and then. You don't argue with Maxine when she wants something. But I couldn't break a leaf off. She tried, too. She mashed the stem up but couldn't snap it off. I hadn't a knife on me, so she sent me to get one.

"I reminded her about the temple, but she threw the paint into the river and said this was more important. So I went and found the gardener and told him what she wanted."

"Hodge? An oldish man?"

"Old. He told her not to touch the leaves. Said they were Giant something. Bad news, anyway."

"Giant Hogweed," said Minty, relieved that Hodge had warned Maxine after all. "Go on."

"Maxine thought the gardener was getting at her because she'd told him what to do with his geraniums. So she sent him back for a basket and stood over him while he cut a whole stack of leaves for her. I noticed he wore gloves when he cut them, but I knew better than to say anything to her. She played around with them all morning. Well, you saw."

Minty said, "Was the sun shining when she picked them up?"

He looked puzzled. "Sure."

"You handled them as well, did you? What were you wearing?"

He shrugged. "A long-sleeved sweater, jogging pants. No, I didn't handle them much, no. They were hers, you see. She had all sorts of plans for them. She wanted to make a bed of leaves to lie on and ..."

"What was she wearing?"

"A sleeveless vest, shorts, trainers. Why?"

"If the sap touches your skin when you're in the sun, you burn. It takes between fifteen and twenty hours to take effect. You don't seem to have been affected yet, but I suggest you take off all your clothes and go and stand in the shower for a while. Wash the clothes you wore this morning, before you wear them again."

He made for the bathroom, looking scared.

Axel groaned. "It's worse than I thought." He held the bedroom door open for Minty and Patrick to go through.

Maxine was sitting in front of the mirror, with her dresser hovering over her. Maxine had been dressing for the performance. She had the flame-ribboned top on over tight jeans. But no wig. Her close-cropped head looked naked.

She turned slowly round as they came in.

Her face was swelling, the skin blistering. Her eyes had almost disappeared. Her neck and bosom were also affected, as were what could be seen of her arms.

"You did this to me!"

Minty shook her head. "You did it to yourself. Hodge warned you. So did I."

Patrick said, "She needs a doctor." He got out his mobile.

"She won't hear of it," said Axel.

Maxine screamed, bringing her fists down on the dressing-table. "I'm going on stage, I tell you!" And then, pitifully, "Get these clothes off me!"

Minty would have started forward to help, but Patrick stopped her. "Don't touch her."

Maxine was tearing at the clothes, dragging her fingernails across her skin in an effort to get the top off ... and then the jeans. She stood there, panting, wearing nothing but a slip of a bra and a thong. The skin on her legs was also blistering.

Gemma came in without knocking. She looked delighted with the way things were going.

The middle-aged dresser found a long, dark dressing-gown and wrapped Maxine in it. "There, there. Let me put some cream on ..."

"She should go to hospital," said Patrick. "Perhaps a burns unit can do something to help her."

"No-o-o!" Maxine screamed. "Give me an injection, anything! I've got to go on! Help me! I can't see properly!"

Indeed, her eyelids were still swelling.

Minty drew in her breath. "Maxine, you must go to hospital."

"You're wrong! I will go on! I will!" She swept everything off the dressing-table and began to swear.

Minty glanced out of the window. It was still light, but dusk was beginning to close in on them. "Axel, where's Billy? He's got to be told that Maxine can't go on."

Maxine screamed like a trapped animal.

Patrick said, "I'm ringing for an ambulance, no matter what. But it's going to take time for it to get here from town, because the roads are all blocked. Perhaps we could get a helicopter to take her off? Meanwhile I'll send someone to ask the St John Ambulance people for help."

Axel gave a stiff nod. Patrick left, pulling out his mobile phone.

Maxine threw off her robe and stood in front of the full-length mirror. Four-letter words shot out of her mouth like bullets. She back-handed the mirror, which fell and shattered. She laughed wildly.

Then she did something which would bring shudders to Minty for days to come. Maxine sprang at Minty and held her close, kissing her full on the lips. Minty recoiled, fighting to free herself. Axel shouted and the dresser screamed, but it was Gemma who, after a moment of horror, picked up Maxine's robe and threw it over her head, blinding her completely.

Maxine let go of Minty to struggle free of the robe. Minty stepped back, still feeling the impact of Maxine's body against her, Maxine's mouth against hers ...

"Get in the shower, Minty," said Gemma. "Move!"

Minty moved. She stumbled out of the room and into the en suite bathroom. Nero had gone but his clothes were still on the floor. Minty stepped into the shower fully dressed and let it run and run and ...

... and prayed.

She felt slimed with evil.

She towelled herself dry, dress and all. Her shoes and her dress were ruined. Well, tough. Her hair had come down. She combed it back and let it lie loose to dry in the air.

Dear Lord, help me. Help her. In spite of everything, look after her. I can't imagine a worse fate than what awaits her …

Minty returned to the sitting room and not to the bedroom.

Patrick returned, took one look at Minty, and said, "What's the matter?"

"Maxine kissed me. It's all right, really." She struggled not to cry. "I've been in the shower, that's why I'm so wet." Patrick put his arms around her and held her tight. She let herself tremble. He held her even more closely.

The backing group, the dancers, the musicians were all huddled together.

Billy panted up the stairs, accompanied as usual by a pair of aides. "Trouble with Maxine? Can't you deal with it? What's she up to now?"

Axel and Gemma came out of the bedroom, his arm about her. So. A new alliance.

Axel explained, "Billy, it's the hand of God, honest! She's not playing up. She's covered with sores. An allergy. She can't possibly go on!"

Minty was still shivering. She looked out of the window at the sky, which was beginning to grow dull as evening approached.

Patrick said, "An ambulance is on its way, but it may take some time to get here because the roads are gridlocked. I warned them not to use their siren within the Park and to come straight here to the courtyard. The helicopter would be the quickest way of getting her to hospital, but it's ferrying a group of artists away at the moment. We can get her into it when it returns, but that won't be for a while."

Nero despaired. "We're finished."

"The show must go on," said Axel, sweating even though the evening was cool. "We can't disappoint our fans."

Billy looked stricken. "I can't go out there and tell them she's ill! I'd be lynched. You've got some police on duty, but if there's a big surge of people, all angry … why, anything could happen. You can't reason with them. They'll destroy anybody and anything that moves

... storm the stage, set fire to it ... wreck all the cars in the car park. They love fire. It just takes one maniac to hold up a blazing T-shirt on a stick, and they'll all be at it. Children get hurt, people scream, but that only seems to make them worse. You need riot police if that happens, and the damage ... it can run into millions! They could fire the Hall, anything!"

He was putting Minty's worst fears into words.

"It won't happen if I take her place," said Gemma, with a creamy smile.

Chapter Twenty-Three

Now how did I know she'd say that? Minty leaned back against Patrick's shoulder.

"She couldn't possibly take Maxine's place!" Nero laughed, short and sharp. "Granted, she could wear her clothes and wigs, but ..." His voice trailed away.

"Haven't I stood in for her many times?" said Gemma. "I'll mime to her tapes, as she does when she's filming. Of course I can pass myself off as her. I know the way she moves, and I can fool anyone at a distance. Give me half an hour to practise with Nero, and I'll save the day for you."

The festival director looked dubious. "They'd spot you a mile off."

"No, they won't," said Gemma. "Not wearing her wig and made up like her. We're the same height and I've been standing in for her for ever. If you like, I could wear a mask. There are plenty of masks among her things."

A St John Ambulance man came panting up the stairs and was directed into the bedroom.

Axel mopped his forehead. "I suppose it might work, if ... we could wait till it gets a bit darker. Give us an hour to practise. Billy, can you get the act before her to play an extra set?"

Minty said, "We mustn't cheat people. They came to see Maxine, and we must tell them what's happened."

Billy exchanged looks with Axel. Gemma continued to smile.

"Very well," said Axel, yielding—perhaps too quickly? "We'll make some sort of announcement, tell them it's Maxine's little sister or something."

Billy switched his eyes to Nero. "What do you think?"

Nero was naked except for a pair of briefs. He was, Minty had to admit, a fantastically structured figure of manhood. She'd thought before that he hadn't much of a brain, but it appeared he had enough to sum up the situation and sway the rest of the group.

He looked around at everyone. "Let's see if Gemma can do it, before we sneak out the back door and go home without any money. Let's do the one set with her, here and now with the backing group. If she can carry it off, we go for it. If she's too amateur, then we leave before the crowd gets to us. Right?"

"It's different in front of a big audience," objected Billy, scraping his chin, which could do with a shave. "Suppose she gets stage fright!"

"I won't," said Gemma. Such was her superb self-confidence that even though they all knew stage fright could attack anyone at any time, they went along with it.

Maxine's dresser shot out of the bedroom, weeping, closely followed by the St John Ambulance man, who was shaking his head. "She's in a bad way. If you soak some cloths in water and put them on the burns to keep them cool and wet, it might help, but she won't let me touch her, so ... Someone ought to stay with her, try to keep her calm till the ambulance gets here, but I've got to get back, right? We're busy enough as it is."

Everyone looked at the dresser, who shook her head violently. "I can't! Don't ask me! It's horrible!"

Axel put an arm out to detain the ambulance man. "You won't speak of this to anyone, understood?"

"There's a reporter hanging around outside. Asked me who I was being called to when I came up here. You'd better tell him to button his lip, too." He clattered off down the stairs.

Patrick looked thoughtful. "That'll be Tom, I expect. If Gemma makes a breakthrough tonight, it would be a big story for him."

"Keep him under wraps till we finish," said Billy. He switched his eyes to one of his aides. "Get the boys who are now on stage to play an extra set. They'll love that." He switched his eyes to the other aide. "When they come off, tell the electricians to blow a fuse somewhere. Buy us some time. Right?" The aides fled.

Axel was organising the backing group. "We'll run through the first number, sound and all, and see if she can do it. Gemma, you mime along, right?"

Minty said, "What about Maxine's costumes? Are they still in the bedroom?"

The dresser shook her head. "I won't go back in there ..."

"You will if I come with you," said Minty, steeling herself. She held out her hand to the dresser, who hesitated but took it, following Minty through the door.

Maxine was crouched on the floor in a foetal position, moaning. Whining like a dog. Alone with her pain.

Minty picked up the flame-ribboned top and whispered to the dresser that it would need washing before Gemma wore it. The woman was trembling but managed to snatch up some of Maxine's costumes and the dark wig, before fleeing with them back into the other room.

Maxine's recorded voice filtered through the door to them, honey-sweet and dangerous.

Minty heard Nero shout, "No, no! Not like that, Gemma. I thought you said you could do it!"

Maxine growled like a dog worrying a bone.

Minty wanted to get out of there, but fast. She could still feel the imprint of Maxine's lips on hers. Ugh!

Yesterday Maxine had been at the top of her profession. Today she grovelled on the floor. Abandoned by everyone. Her manager—who would obviously soon be Gemma's manager—had discarded her. So had her entourage.

Maxine's body, where the sap had not touched her, was smooth, but where it had, great weals and blisters disfigured her.

Minty shivered.

What did you do for burns? The St John's man had said you put wet cloths on them. Minty couldn't bear to touch Maxine. "Let me help you. If you get into the shower ..."

Maxine didn't move. She squealed. Like a pig.

Minty backed to the door and stood there, with her hands flat against it. She closed her eyes and tried to pray. *Dear Lord above, help me. Help her ...*

"Do you dare pray for me?" Maxine's voice was no longer honey-sweet, but deep. A bass voice, coming from a frail woman's body. It didn't sound like Maxine's voice. It sounded like ...

Minty heard herself whimper. Then remembered her uncle declaiming that he had the power of ten men when he called on God for help.

"Yes," she said, in as firm a voice as she could manage. "I pray for all creatures great and small, for everyone that is sick. For all those who have turned away from God and ..."

Maxine shrieked and covered her ears.

"For all those who have turned away from God," Minty repeated. "I pray for those who wished ill on others, and those who tried to destroy everything that was good around them. I will pray for you even if you curse me for it!"

A stream of obscenities ripped from Maxine's mouth, but she did not stir from her crouching position.

Minty bowed her head in prayer. "Dear God above, who loves every single person on this earth, who loves us more than we can ever understand ... if it is not too late to save this poor creature Maxine ..."

"It is! It is too late!" screamed Maxine. "I promised. I swore. I am beyond you. I laugh at you ..." She brayed like a hyena.

Minty covered her ears and went on praying. "I know that it is never too late. All you have to do is cry upon the name of Jesus!"

"I spit on the name of Jesus!" screamed the voice, and then a weak child's voice said, "Help me!"

Minty raised her head in hope but did not move from the door. "If you truly wish for help, it will be given to you."

The figure convulsed with painful laughter.

"Please," said Minty. "Get into the shower. It will help ..."

Maxine screamed at Minty, "Get out!"

Minty opened the door and fled, to be caught up in Patrick's arms. Music crashed around her. Maxine's voice rose and fell. Minty dug her fingers into Patrick's body and hid her eyes against his shoulder.

"Hush," he said. He carried her through into the kitchen, sitting her down on a tall stool.

Minty took a couple of deep breaths and pushed the sound of Maxine's laughter way back into her head, asking God to heal her. Wondering if she'd been a fool to pray for that poor lost creature.

Patrick ran the cold tap to get her a drink of water. Good man, Patrick. He always knew what she needed. She gulped the water. Felt marginally better.

The kitchen had always been immaculate in Annie's day. After days under siege by the performers, it resembled a litter bin. Annie would have been horrified.

Minty said, "I told her it would help if she got into the shower, but she wouldn't listen. I tried to pray for her. I thought there was perhaps some spark of good still within her. Maybe there is. Or maybe she's just fooling me. I don't suppose it did any good."

"We can't know that." He put his arm around her shoulders. "Gemma's not doing too badly. She wouldn't fool a pea-brain at the moment, but she likes an audience, and maybe she'll blossom once she gets on stage."

"I suppose I ought to pray for her, too, even though I'm uneasy about her taking Maxine's place."

"They're talking about introducing her as Maxine's sister. That might work. Look, I've got to find Tom and get him to hold off till after the concert." He inspected her from top to toe. "I think we'd better go back to the reception. We can't do any good here, and we ought to be meeting and greeting people up there instead. We could get in across the court, take the stairs and reach our bedroom that way. Clean clothes, wash and brush up, and we'll be ready to join in the oohs and aahs when the lights go out."

"I don't want to leave Maxine. Or at least, I do, but ..."

Axel appeared in the doorway. "The ambulance has just arrived. They'd been called to deal with an incident in the village—bumped cars, nothing serious—so they were almost on the spot. The police have been alerted to get them away quickly. Just as well, because the helicopter's not even on its way back yet."

Patrick said, "Let her go, Minty. If there's a spark of human goodness left in her, then God will find it out."

The paramedics were calm and efficient, but they had to tranquillise Maxine before they could get her onto a stretcher. Minty averted her eyes as Maxine was borne through the living room and away from her past life.

Throughout Maxine's removal, Gemma continued to practise. And practise. None of her entourage volunteered to accompany Maxine to hospital.

As Minty and Patrick left the flat, she remembered Hugh's story about the soldier who'd been shot by his own men . . .

Patrick went straight back to the reception, but Minty needed to change. Patrick had said she should go up-market, rather than dress down, so she put on an ivory lace dress that she'd bought in Italy. Although her hands trembled, she managed to put her hair up again and don her pearl earrings. She thought she looked a lot better than she felt.

The moment she stopped concentrating on what she was doing, her mind leaped back to the moment when Maxine had pressed her lips to her . . . and she shuddered. Would she ever be able to forget it? She felt . . . tarnished.

She knew she ought to go straight back to the guests but decided to steal a few minutes first in the chapel. Would it be clean again? Did Maxine's influence still linger there?

It was fine. Stripped to its bare bones, it carried no trace of past horrors. It was not just a room now, but a room filled with peaceful joy, the joy of Christ. The cross was back in its proper place, and Patrick's carved oak chair was waiting for her.

She held up her arms to the cross and closed her eyes, offering up everything that had happened to Him, praising Him, thanking Him for delivering them all from evil. Asking for a blessing.

She was only in the chapel for a few minutes, but she came out feeling serene.

Now she could act the part of the hostess with the mostest.

Her rooms were more crowded than ever as everyone anticipated the climax of the festival. Questions were asked about where Minty had been. Visiting Maxine, they assumed? What a coup to have managed to get Maxine for the festival, and weren't they all fortunate to be there to see her perform.

All the windows in the suite had been thrown open. The night air cooled those within, but outside in the arena people were pulling on jackets and winding the children into outer clothing.

So many innocent lives. Lord, protect us. Protect them. Look after Maxine.

At long last, and considerably later than advertised, the boys on stage wound down their act and took their bows.

Whistles, clapping, cheering.

The singers left the stage for their dressing-room tent. Minty saw the electric buggy winding its way from the Hall to the stage area, with several people on board. Maxine's dresser with all her gear? Her musicians? It wasn't Hodge driving now, was it? Was Hugh back in the car? Minty crossed her fingers, told herself not to be superstitious. She really didn't want dear Hugh to be in the thick of a mob of angry people if anything went wrong. She smiled at the District Councillor, who had graciously honoured the Hall with her presence, and answered yet another question about her travels round the Mediterranean.

The buggy reached the stage area, decanted its passengers, and started on its return journey. It was getting dark now, but perhaps not quite dark enough. The people below began a cheerful chant, "We want Maxine. We want Maxine. We want Maxine."

With the suddenness of a clap of thunder, all the lights on stage went out.

Silence spread through the crowd. Some uneasy laughter.

The Hall lights were still on.

Up on the top floor, people turned to one another, amazed and intrigued. What could have gone wrong?

Patrick was helping Iris pour drinks. "I suppose some sound engineer has pushed the volume up too high and blown a fuse!"

Some laughter. Some annoyance. Everyone was being good-natured about it.

Down below, something magical happened. Thousands upon thousands of cigarette lighters flickered on. The whole slope was dotted with lights.

On the top floor, everyone crowded to the windows to see.

"What a sight!" breathed a ditzy blonde who was older than she tried to make out.

The Deputy Chief Constable—didn't he have a home to go to?—produced a nasal version of a laugh. "Pretty, what?"

"Very pretty," said Minty, assuming this was Billy's work. She excused herself for a moment, dashed into her bedroom and phoned through to Annie's flat. "Pick up, someone. Pick up!"

A woman picked up the phone. One of the backing group. Minty asked, "How long are you going to be?"

The sound became muffled as the woman covered the phone over with her hand, but still Minty could hear her relaying the question to Nero. And him answering, "As long as it takes!"

Minty told herself to count to ten, slowly. Breathe in. Breathe out. She returned to her guests and there, lo and behold, was Mrs Chickward, magisterially making her way around the room.

"Araminta, my dear, you look lovely, though perhaps a little tired. And where is my tiresome guest, Maxine? She's last on the bill, I gather, and I thought I'd like to see what she was like in action."

"Mrs Chickward." Minty kissed the older lady affectionately. "You were most kind to put her up. I don't know who else I could have asked. Have you had a drink yet? You know the Deputy Chief Constable, of course?"

Patrick turned up at her elbow. "Keep smiling, Minty. That's it. Nothing to worry about. I wish we had a store of candles we could pass out to the crowd. If we ever do this again ... oh, there you are, Jim. What have you done with your mother?"

"Dumped her in the lake," said Jim, who seemed to have been drinking rather more than was good for him. "I wish. Stupid woman. Keeps telling me I'm going to be all right. She was like this when my father died, too. No tears, no regrets. Stiff upper lip, she calls it."

"Dear Jim," said Minty. "Come and sit down in this quiet corner and tell me all about it. I can't imagine how awful it must be for you."

Jim began to pull faces. Was he trying not to cry? Minty steered him to a corner seat and offered him some food, which he refused. There was more food coming in all the time. However had Chef managed it? Minty glimpsed two of Chef's usual waitresses, and was that Chef's daughter, back from the city?

Clive Hatton appeared at her elbow. Drunk, to judge by his glassy-eyed stare. "Bitten off more than you can chew? I always said a woman can't run an event like this. By the way, I've a week's holiday due, and I'm taking off in the morning. And before you ask, I've no idea when I'll be back, if ever."

"Fine, so long as you leave Iris behind."

"Iris?" He barked out a laugh. It was clear he had no intention of taking Iris with him.

Iris had overheard and looked stricken, all over again. Minty would have gone to Iris' side, but Iris wasn't allowing anyone to see her misery and had turned away.

Here came Carol, with her antiques dealer father, laughing at some joke or other. He shook Minty's hand, kissed her on both cheeks and said how much his family had been enjoying the festival so far. His young son was ecstatic, had wriggled his way right to the front by the stage, and goodness only knows when they'd be able to retrieve him.

Another hostage to fortune.

The crowd outside settled down to wait, murmuring, not unhappy. Because the stage lights were out, you could now see stars in the sky ... and tentatively through some light cloud ... came the moon.

Minty did some more praying as she worked round the room ... only to come face to face with Ms Annie Phillips herself! Sitting on a settee, looking as composed as ever.

"Annie, my dearest! I didn't expect you." Minty managed to insert herself on the settee beside Annie. "This isn't your kind of thing at all, is it?"

"Certainly not." Annie was as usual sitting ramrod straight with her knees and ankles together. "But I wanted to know what kind of a pig's ear you were making of it. So far, so good. But in my opinion, you've let far too many people into the grounds ..."

"I agree," said Minty. "I don't like it, and I shan't have a quiet moment till they've all been got off the site without incident. But what about you? Are you all right? I've been hearing ..."

"Tittle tattle. Of course I'm all right. You must come up to see me next week, and we must discuss how much time you propose to give to your father's charity in future ..."

Venetia Wootton, as soignée as ever, complaining merrily that she hadn't seen either Toby or her husband for hours ...

It only remained for Mrs Collins to arrive ... and here she was, larger than life, as usual, in black and scarlet! *Black and scarlet?* Where did she get her clothes? And how had all these people got in? Had they been invited? Another point to raise at the debriefing.

"Aaah!" The sound rose as a giant sigh from the arena as the lights went on again. There was some laughter, rippling across the face of the crowd. They were still very good-natured.

But there was no sign of Gemma.

Minty looked out for Patrick. Where was he? Masterminding events? Or overwhelmed by them?

Smile, Minty, smile.

"We want Maxine. We want Maxine. We want Maxine."

Yes, the crowd was still good-natured, but becoming a little impatient. They were cheerfully calling Maxine's name now. Soon they'd be yelling, and stamping and ...

Ah, the buggy was moving at last. Who was driving? *Oh, no! Not Patrick! No, please, God. Let it not be Patrick.*

Yet who else would be brave enough to take Gemma on such a dangerous mission? *Dear Lord, keep him safe.*

A figure in scarlet and red, her costume streaming with red and orange ribbons, was standing up at the back of the buggy, waving to the crowd. Gemma. She was wearing the curly black wig and a sparkling mask over her eyes. She was laughing.

Reckless Gemma, riding to the rescue.

Around the buggy, surrounding her on every side, came the dancers and the backing group.

The crowd began to roar her name. "Maxine. Maxine. MAXINE! MAXINE!"

Gemma waved both arms, laughing.

From where she stood high above, Minty could see that Gemma was enjoying herself. Perhaps ... perhaps it was going to work?

Helped by the stewards, the crowd parted to let the party through, and closed in behind it again.

"Maxine! We want Maxine!"

Thud, thud of feet.

"MAXINE! We want MAXINE!"

Thud, thud.

Behind and around Minty everyone crowded to the windows.

The crowd began to roar. **"MAXINE, MAXINE, MAXINE!"**
Thud, thud, thud.

Some youngsters began to scream. "MAXINE! Look this way! MAXINE! M, A, X, I, N, E!"

The buggy reached the stage. Minty willed Patrick to return, to leave Gemma there to face the fans.

But of course he did nothing of the kind. He sat there, arms crossed, relaxed. Waiting for whatever would happen.

Minty's fingernails dug into her palms. *Dear Lord, keep him safe!*

Gemma sprang up onto the stage without needing a helping hand, while the others went round to the side, to reach backstage by the normal route. Leaving Patrick alone in the buggy.

Gemma took the front of the stage, bowing low. Acknowledging their greetings. Laughing. Holding out her arms to her fans.

Except, of course, that they were not her fans.

Minty waited for the announcement, keyed up to expect the worst. Would the crowd turn on Gemma and tear her to pieces? And Patrick? *Please, dear Lord ...*

The musicians had by now taken up their places. The backing group fingered their mikes.

Nero led Gemma to centre stage. Some of the stars had been wearing headsets, which meant they could move around freely and still be heard. Gemma was, too. It looked professional, but presumably it was there only for effect.

The crowd applauded. They quieted down, holding their breath, waiting for their idol to strut her stuff.

Who was going to make the announcement?

Axel insinuated himself beside Minty, mopping at his brow. "She's enjoying it too much. Maxine despises her audience."

Minty said, "The crowd loves it." *Oughtn't Axel to be down there with Gemma, looking after her? Or did he think it would be safer up here ... in case something went wrong?*

Nero was taking control. He seemed to be enjoying himself, too. He signalled to the drummer ... and the pounding notes of the first set rang out. Gemma opened her mouth a fraction too soon ... and then the honey-sweet tones of Maxine swelled out over the crowd. "I'm burning ..."

There'd been no announcement! Was that intentional?

Minty clutched Axel's arm. "Why wasn't there an announcement?" But she knew why, of course. He was hoping there'd be no need, that the crowd would accept Gemma as Maxine. But could Gemma really fool them?

The crowd stilled; one or two screams went unheeded. Gemma stood very still, miming to Maxine's voice, letting the first eight bars speak for themselves. Then she threw up her head and opened her arms wide to the crowd as the guitarist took over the tune.

The crowd went mad. They loved it. They loved her.

At least, they thought they did.

The guests crowded to the windows, peering over one another's shoulders, smiling, nodding to one another.

Gemma was encouraged by their applause. She reached out to the crowd, playing them for all she was worth. Minty could have sworn that she was also crooning the words. "Burning ... for you ... burning with desire ... set me on fire ..."

Minty thought, *No one's going to tell them that this isn't Maxine herself, but a substitute. We've cheated them!*

Chapter Twenty-Four

Gemma began to work the stage, now turning her back on Nero, now pretending to sing to him direct. Nero, to do him justice, played up to her. The backing group was brilliant, shivering deliciously in their tight black dresses, their voices blending like melting toffee. The dancers were everywhere, well-rehearsed, agile.

Axel murmured, "Gemma's twisting it. The crowd expect bittersweet. Will they go for sugar instead?"

Apparently they did.

The end of the first set ... the musicians worked themselves into a frenzy as Gemma slipped off the stage for her first change of costume ... Nero pranced and shook himself about, doing what Gemma had called his "belly-dance."

The crowd loved it, but they screamed and roared their approval when Gemma came back in a tight-fitting sequined dress, way above the knees. Still the black wig. The lights went down, and she sang softly, standing very still. "I'm always alone." The dancers stood still. The backing group provided a hum of harmony. Nero vanished.

Axel said, in a hushed voice, "Can she really hold them?"

"She likes taking risks," said Minty, feeling breathless.

The crowd liked it well enough. They swayed and swung their arms. But there was a subtle sense of dissatisfaction rippling through their applause when the song came to an end. Gemma was doing her best, but she lacked Maxine's charisma.

Gemma knew it. She disappeared after a cursory bow, and Nero brought in the musicians with a crash, pretending to conduct them. He was hamming it up. The crowd loved it. They began to clap along to the beat ... were the musicians really playing live, or were they miming? It was hard to tell.

Gemma returned wearing the purple and black dress, with the black wig over a whitened face. No mask. Gemma liked taking risks, didn't she! The crowd fell silent, believing this was the Maxine they knew.

The song started slowly. Gemma made few gestures, but let her clown's face express grief. Behind her Nero started to dance with one of the dancers, who'd slipped into the second purple and black dress ... the dress that Gemma had been intending to wear.

"... pay for what you take ..."

The crowd began to stamp and wave as the tempo increased, and then increased again. The noise must be deafening down there in the arena. Suddenly Gemma turned her back on the crowd, holding up the fake gun ... a roll of drums and a crash of cymbals ... and she fired directly at Nero!

The musicians stopped, mid-gesture.

Gemma held the pose. Smoke drifted from the mouth of the gun.

Nero slipped down, blood oozing through the hand he held to his shoulder.

A gasp ran through the crowd, and there was a wavering movement, a ripple passing across the slope.

Minty took a sharp breath in and held it. It couldn't have been a real gun, could it?

A hoarse voice said, "He deserved it. He slept with everyone!"

Was that Maxine's voice? Was it Gemma's? Was Gemma exacting revenge for his two-timing her? Was her headset live?

The crowd was uncertain. Gemma lifted both her arms into the air and threw back her head as the music crashed in again.

Minty knew that at this point Gemma was supposed to writhe over Nero's body, but Gemma was taking her time over it. She paced slowly round the stage till she came to where Nero lay in his dancing partner's arms.

Gemma stood over Nero and shouted, "Die!"

She held the gun pointed at his breast till the song finished.

Minty was uneasy. Axel was having trouble with his breathing. Was he asthmatic? Nero should now get up, take a bow and walk off stage. But ... had Maxine—Gemma—been given the wrong gun? It was supposed to be a starter pistol, but hadn't Gemma said something about Maxine bringing back a real gun from the States? Had that bullet been for real?

Gemma returned to the footlights and took a bow. Behind her Nero got to his feet and bowed, too. Minty noticed that he was supported by the dancer. But perhaps other people wouldn't notice it.

The crowd decided they'd seen a brilliant act. They screamed and shouted and stamped. "More, more!"

Had Gemma practised anything else?

Nero disappeared off stage, leaning on the dancer.

Could Gemma produce another song? Did she know any more?

Gemma raised her hands for quiet. Amazingly, the noise of the crowd lessened.

Gemma took a chance. She spoke in her own voice, which was deeper than that of Maxine. Yes, her headset was alive.

"Sing along with me ... 'We'll meet again, don't know where, don't know when ...'"

Her own voice was rich and warm and spot on key. Minty felt tears creep into her eyes, for that lost child Gemma *could* sing after a fashion. Standing there in that dramatic dress and make-up, she was able to hold the crowd and get them to sing along with her—for a while.

The musicians began to pick up the tune and follow her. It was an old song, full of sentiment, taking many of them back to the Second World War years, when it was the signature tune for all those parted by the need to fight. A promise of happier days to come when they would all meet again.

It was very far from what Maxine would have sung, but it worked. The crowd was bemused, but more and more began to sing along with Gemma. Here and there they began to sway in time to the music, with its promise that they would all meet again, that there would be better times in store ...

Gemma let the song drift away into the darkness.

There was an almost full moon.

"The show's over for tonight, folks. Take care as you go," said Gemma to the huge crowd. "Drive safely. We'll see you all again soon."

Now what did she mean by that? Tomorrow's newspapers would be full of the deception. Minty could imagine the headlines, "Maxine in crisis care!" Or would they think that Gemma was really Maxine? Or what?

It was working. Some people were slowly beginning to peel away from the edges of the crowd to trickle back out of the arena, yawning, smiling, quarrelling, tiredly making their way back to their tents and caravans and cars.

The lights went off on the stage, but more and more people were crowding forward, calling for Maxine, wanting her autograph, a piece of her dress, to touch her. How was Gemma to get away?

The buggy began its slow journey back to the house, surrounded by stewards, with Patrick driving. Patrick wouldn't have left Gemma behind, but Minty couldn't see any Maxine-like figure on board. Nero was sitting on the buggy with one of the dancers. Minty, watching from above, saw a black-clad figure with close-cut auburn hair walking behind the buggy with one or two of the backing group. Gemma?

Had that gunshot been for real? Was that why Nero was riding on the buggy?

Minty looked for the St John Ambulance post and saw two men making their way as fast as they could towards the house. Had Patrick managed to alert them, using his mobile? Had Gemma known that gun was for real? Or had the dresser in her haste simply picked up the wrong gun by mistake?

Axel said, "We seem to have got away with it. Your sister's not a bad little actress, Mrs Sands. I'd better go and arrange for some press interviews ... I told that reporter he could have an exclusive with Maxine after the show ... he'll get more than he bargained for ... we should make the national press with this ..."

He disappeared. Minty watched the painfully slow progress of the buggy up the slope. No one had yet realised that "Maxine" had slipped through the crowd. Would they make it? Yes ... they were at the head of the slope. Patrick was continuing round the house, would end up in the courtyard.

Minty wanted to rush downstairs and beat him up, scold him for putting himself into danger like that. How could he give her such a fright!

She began to work the room, saying, "Yes, wasn't that wonderful" and "See you again soon" to everyone there.

The Deputy Chief Constable barked, "Was that gun for real?" He answered his own question. "Well, on private property ... let's assume it wasn't." Everyone else assumed it was just a trick. Minty just smiled and tried not to look out of the window too often. Everyone was talking about Maxine and her "new direction." Some of them liked it, some didn't.

Down by the stage there was a knot of youngish men who'd had too much to drink. They got onto the stage and began tearing the place apart. A contingent of police appeared, with dogs! Oh, no!

But it was all right.

The Deputy Chief Constable was chuckling away at Minty's shoulder as she stood at the window. "My men know their business. A good thing you brought us in."

"Yes, indeed," said Minty, wondering how soon the fans would realise they'd been cheated.

A group of young men had congregated near one of the drinks tents. Suddenly there was a flare of light. One young man was hurling a blazing T-shirt into the tent. The security guard grappled with him, but his companions fled, screaming with laughter, up the slope.

Minty froze. Were her worst fears about to be realised? The leading youth was stopped by a policeman, but his fellows got through, climbing the steps to the terrace with ... cans of beer in their hands?

Smash! A heavy can of beer smashed into the old glass of the library window ... followed by cheers and a stampede of police ... tussling with the yobs ... another smash! A second window.

Thank the Lord that she'd taken the precautions of having the shutters closed inside the ground-floor rooms!

The police had the youths under control, hauling two of them off, screaming abuse, while the others fled, laughing. The rest of the retreating crowd had their chins on their shoulders, hastening children along, trying to get away ... would there be room enough for them all to pass between the tents and the lake?

Yes, just about.

Mrs Chickward observed that in her experience children always suffered from too much excitement. "There'll be tears before nightfall, as my old nanny used to say." Minty's rooms began to empty.

Down in the arena, there were isolated spots of resistance as the police began to move down from the house to clear the site. Litter blew in the breeze. A few drops of rain fell, persuading all but the most hardy that they should seek shelter.

"A splendid evening, dear," said the District Councillor. "Aren't our police wonderful?"

"We must do this again sometime," said one of the sponsors.

Where was Patrick?

Jim was asleep in one corner, his mother grimly sitting beside him. Minty supposed they could sleep at Patrick's old house if they couldn't get back to town that night.

Iris looked worn out but kept going.

The clearing up was going to be a mammoth task.

Down below there was a scuffle and some shouting. A woman screamed. "Naughty, naughty boys," trilled Mrs Collins, preparing to depart. "They'll spend the night in the cells, no doubt."

Patrick appeared, calm, smiling. He kissed Minty's cheek and said, "Yes, I know I oughtn't to have done it. But I didn't want poor Hugh to be pulled apart by the fans if anything went wrong."

Gemma arrived some time later, having given Tom got his exclusive and arranged for a press conference on the morrow. Dressed all in black and without wig or dramatic make-up, she was still riding high on excitement. "Are you going to thank me for saving the day, sister mine?"

"Yes," said Minty. "I am. And I hope you get a good contract out of it."

"You couldn't have done it!"

"No, indeed." Minty decided this was not the moment to say that she didn't approve of the way the crowd had been fooled.

Gemma was still as tightly wound up as a spring. "I don't understand about that gun, though. It was supposed to be a starting pistol. Luckily I'm a rotten shot. Poor Nero's got a nasty flesh wound, but he says he'll forgive me if I give him a contract to accompany me on my next gig."

So Gemma was well launched on a new career? Bully for her.

The whole thing had left a nasty taste in Minty's mouth, and as she made it clear at the debriefing, "Never again!"

The final twist to the story occurred at the end of March the following year.

It had been a hard winter though there hadn't been much snow. Aconites and drifts of snowdrops clustered under the trees in the avenue, where the horse chestnut leaves were beginning to unfurl.

Frost had crystallised the grass in the Park and caused the tyres of the guests to crunch as they drove down the avenue and parked as near to the Hall as they could. Some favoured ones even parked on the gravel outside the Great Hall itself.

The first function of the season—a twenty-first birthday party —was in full swing in the Great Hall. The Great Hall was a much sought after venue for private parties nowadays, and the great thing was, as Minty said, that neither she nor Patrick needed to be in attendance. Pots of hyacinths scented the air and mingled with the tempting aroma of the buffet which Chef had prepared.

One uninvited guest was not in evening dress but black leather. Her red hair blazed, though not as brightly as her temper when she failed to get into her suite. She took the lift to the top floor. Neither Patrick nor Minty were in their usual rooms, but she found Serafina dozing in front of her television.

"Where's my sister?"

Serafina struggled awake. "Gemma? We weren't expecting you. They're having a quiet evening to themselves, in Patrick's study on the other side of the tower but ... you can't go in there ...!"

Gemma didn't hear the warning. She retraced her steps to the tower and went through the reinstated door without knocking.

The room was larger than usual for a bedroom in a Jacobean house, with linenfold panelling and a ceiling painted in red and green diamond shapes between the heavy beams that upheld the roof. The broad oak floorboards glimmered in the firelight.

The furniture was from all periods, roomy and comfortable, with a number of bookcases lining the walls, and more books in a pile on Patrick's desk. Heavy curtains shut out the bitter cold of the night.

The room was lit by softly shaded table lamps. One cast light upon Minty, dressed in her favourite cornflower blue, as she nursed a dark-haired baby at her breast. She glowed with happiness, her hair loose about her shoulders.

Patrick was studying some papers at a large antique desk nearby. Minty mourned that his new responsibilities took up so much of his time, but he looked as if he was thriving on it.

At the sound of the door closing, they both looked around.

"Gemma?" Minty stood, lifting the baby to her shoulder. "I thought you were settled in London and working abroad. We did send your things on to the right address, didn't we? You should have let us know you were coming."

"The Australian tour was cancelled at the last minute. The christening's tomorrow, isn't it? How could I miss being godmother?"

Minty exchanged a glance with Patrick. "Well ..."

Gemma poked the baby with a scarlet-painted fingernail. "Looks like Patrick, poor thing. Is it a boy?"

"A girl," said Minty.

The baby opened enormous dark grey eyes, inspected Gemma, decided she didn't like what she saw and closed her eyes again.

"Oh," said Gemma. "My mistake. She'll go far with those eyes."

"We managed one of each," said Patrick, trying to hide his pride. "That's Miss Cardale Sands, and this—" he indicated a fair-haired baby asleep in the crook of his arm—"is our son."

"Good grief!" Gemma bent over the fair-haired boy. "This one looks just like the Edens in the portrait gallery. Two for the price of one, eh? Well, no harm done, then."

Minty looked puzzled. Patrick pushed his papers aside. "What do you mean, Gemma? 'No harm done'?"

Serafina came in with a buxom young woman. "Time for the twins to be in their beds." Minty and Patrick reluctantly handed the babies over. The twins protested but were soon soothed. Serafina asked, "Will Gemma be staying the night?"

Gemma seated herself on the arm of the settee and swung a leather-clad leg. "Acting nanny now, Serafina? And you—what's your name? Chef's daughter, aren't you? Used to serve in the restaurant till big bad Nero scared you away. Do you like being a nanny?"

"Love it," was the response. Gemma was no favourite with the staff. The two women retreated with the babies.

"Minty wanted to look after the twins herself," explained Patrick, "but Serafina wouldn't hear of it, said she couldn't have Minty being worn out by them. So now we share them."

Gemma was bored with the subject. "Any brandy? It's cold out. Oh, and there's something wrong with my key. I couldn't get into my suite just now."

Minty went to stand by the fireplace. "What did you mean, 'No harm done'?"

Gemma looked uneasy. "I thought you knew. It was just a bit of a lark, that's all. I was dead sorry afterwards. But now you've got a couple of replacements ... well ..." She shrugged.

Minty seemed to stop breathing. Her face drained of colour.

Patrick pushed back his chair but kept his enquiry casual. "What did you do, Gemma?"

Gemma shrugged. "Minty was being so stupid about everything. So elder sister. I'd been sniffing a spot of something. Well, so what? She'd never tried it. Didn't know what it was like. So I thought, why not give her a thrill? I had a couple of tabs which someone had given me at a party, so I popped one in her coffee. Woowee! What a laugh!"

Minty put out a hand to the mantelpiece. Patrick seemed frozen in his chair.

Minty whispered, "You put something in my coffee ... for a laugh?"

Gemma swung her foot again. "You should have seen yourself. 'I can fly!' you said. I laughed so much I got the hiccups. How was I to know that you'd try flying down the stairs?"

Minty gulped air, her face ashen.

Silence.

Patrick had also gone pale, but he managed to control his voice. "You saw that Minty had been affected by the drug—what was it? LSD? And you left her alone, without waiting to see if she was all right?"

"Well, I got the hiccups, didn't I? And then I got a phone call and ... don't look at me like that. I didn't mean any harm. So where's my brandy?"

Minty groped for the arm of the settee. Patrick sprang to her side, helping her to sit down.

Patrick ignored Gemma to stroke Minty's hands. "Think of the babies. Don't let her upset you."

Gemma was investigating a jug on a side-table. "Ugh. Water."

Minty held onto Patrick's hand, her mind rushing back to her fall down the stairs, so often and so hideously giving her flashbacks, which had only gradually faded. No wonder the drugs the doctors had given her had failed to work! She must still have been suffering from whatever it was that Gemma had given her. The months abroad ... the damage to her nervous system slowly healing, but her absence causing chaos at the Hall ... dear Barr getting drunk and resigning ... Serafina moving out to live with Annie and both of them hating it ... their housekeeper walking out ... the unfair burden thrown on Patrick's partner ... Clive Hatton moving in with his half-baked ideas ... unsettling Iris ...

And then the festival. Thousands of people put at risk because the arena wasn't big enough to hold them in safety. It was only by God's grace that people weren't killed. And Maxine. The desecration of the chapel. Maxine's hospitalisation and the end of her career. The doctors said her skin was always going to be sensitive to sunlight, and she'd probably never get back on stage. Clive Hatton was still with them but looking for another job.

Minty found she'd been gripping Patrick's hand so hard that her fingers were bloodless. "Gemma, don't you have any idea of how much damage you caused? Patrick and I went down into hell, and it's only through the grace of God that we came out of it. And so many other people's lives were affected by what you did."

Gemma shrugged. "Oh, don't give me that. It wasn't my fault. You could have fallen down those stairs at any time. I suppose I could have gone back to see if you were all right, but I was distracted. Serafina should have looked after you better. I've suffered, too, remember. I thought I could make it into the big time in show business, but nothing's worked out. If I only had money, I could have funded the Australian tour. But there, I don't suppose it's any good looking to you for a handout. Is it?"

Patrick turned away to look down into the fire, resting his head on his arm against the chimney-breast.

Minty said, "You killed our child!"

"No, not killed. You had a miscarriage. Everyone knows that's nothing much, nowadays. I suffered, too," said Gemma, stung into defending herself. "I was really quite upset when you lost the baby."

Minty lifted her hands and let them drop. She turned her eyes away from Gemma and gazed into the fire, saying to Patrick, "Get her out of here."

Patrick said, "Gemma, you caused the death of our child and nearly killed Minty. You've shown no remorse or even understanding of what you've done. You could go to prison for a long time, but we don't wish you any harm. We won't go to the police with what we know. But please understand that you are no longer welcome at the Hall, either to visit or to stay."

Gemma's cheeks burned red.

Patrick looked at the clock on the mantelpiece. "It's getting late. Let me show you to our guest room. Your old suite is being redecorated for renting out to summer visitors. You will not, naturally, be invited to join us for the christening, and we would be grateful if you would leave the Hall before we return from church tomorrow."

Gemma had one last throw to make. "You call yourself Christians? You have to forgive me!"

Patrick held the door open for Gemma, who made as if to appeal to Minty. Minty turned her head away. Gemma gave up and followed Patrick out of the door.

When Patrick returned, he found Minty sitting in the same place, looking into the fire. He sat beside her and took her hand. She tried to smile at him.

He said, "Was I too hard on her?"

She shook her head. "There's something in the Bible about fools doing more harm than evil men. That's Gemma. She never takes responsibility for her actions. Will she ever change, do you think?"

"It'll be hard to pray for her, though I suppose we have to try."

"I was thinking about Job. He suffered but never lost his faith in God. When his sufferings ceased, God gave him more children and riches, more than he'd had before. We didn't lose our faith . . ."

Patrick admitted, "I came pretty close to it once or twice."

"But you didn't. The Hall was not damaged, except superficially. No one was seriously hurt during the festival—except Maxine. We had a bad time, but we've survived, and now we've been blessed with two healthy children. Not one, but two. God is good."

Patrick reminded her, "The Lord gives and the Lord takes away. Blessed be the Lord?"

She touched his cheek. "No, I can't say that yet. But perhaps one day I will."

THE Eden HALL SERIES
Master
OF THE
HALL
ZONDERVAN
VERONICA HELEY

Enjoy an Excerpt from *Master of the Hall*,
the Next Book in the Eden Hall Series.

Chapter 1

It was a bad decision. Minty knew it straight away. And what would it lead to? A victory for God, or ... a descent into hell.

Something flickered at the back of the other woman's eyes. Was it triumph?

✤

These two women had a history. A couple of years ago Minty —heartsick after a miscarriage—had returned home to find a music festival being staged there. The notorious star Maxine had not only taken over Eden Hall itself, but had corrupted the hearts and minds of everyone around her. She'd even dared to desecrate the family chapel.

Now she was back, and asking for a job!

Minty walked over to the library window, giving her time to think. She was worn out. How many times had the twins got her up last night? And how was she to deal with Patrick's desire for more children? She really couldn't face being pregnant again, but she dreaded telling him that. She loved him so much; he was everything she'd ever wanted in a man. She realised that her present behaviour must be frustrating for him, but she didn't know how to explain ...

She shut off that line of thought. It was no use going round and round in circles. There was work to be done.

She pushed back the heavy velvet curtains on either side of the tall windows, to let as much light as possible into the library. A stand of heavy-headed chrysanthemums had been arranged behind one of the leather settees, scenting the air. Something about the flowers stirred a query at the back of her mind. She must investigate, later.

The late afternoon sun warmed the magnificent sweep of lawn below the great house. Down, down to the lake, and beyond. There had been a storm a couple of nights ago which had stripped the last leaves from the trees in the Park, and brought down a great oak on the other side of the house. Patrick was in mourning for the oak, because he often took an early morning walk in that direction. She hadn't yet had time to visit the site.

The splendour of the library lay in shadow behind her, with only a few gleams of gold lightening the darkness of the ranks of leather-bound books. Above the marble fireplace was the portrait of Minty's mother, that pale flower who had died young. Minty's likeness to her mother was very marked, in that both were fair-haired with piercing blue eyes, but Minty's chin announced a stronger, more resilient character and the cross she wore on a chain round her neck was no mere ornament.

By contrast, Maxine was a creature of the shadows, with a capacity for evil. She was an adept at playing games. Despite the damage to her face, she was still a beautiful woman. She'd once boasted she could take Minty's husband away from her. So what was she really after now?

❧

Minty—Mrs Araminta Cardale Sands—had inherited the beautiful but run-down Eden Hall some years ago, and after a struggle had begun to make the stately home pay its way. She'd married her childhood sweetheart in the teeth of opposition from her family who had thought she could do better than a country solicitor, and it had proved to be the best thing she ever did. After a traumatic miscarriage, they'd produced twins who were now two hurtling bundles of energy and a proper handful.

Looking after the twins took up all her time. If she'd had no other responsibilities this might have been all right, but lately Patrick had begun to hint that she was neglecting the Hall and, perhaps, him as well.

She'd given him short shrift. "I'm short of sleep, that's all. I don't understand why you keep on about it. Haven't you always said that running the Hall is my concern, not yours?"

Patrick was not only a solicitor with a thriving practice in a nearby town, but also a businessman with many outside interests, and it was unusual for him to interfere. Yet he had persisted, the upright line between his eyes deepening. "I can't watch you running yourself into the ground and not say anything."

She'd ended that discussion by walking away, muttering that it was ridiculous to say that she was spoiling the twins. If she hadn't been so tired, she'd have lost her temper with him. She'd been to all the boring weekly business meetings at the Hall. Well, perhaps not the last two, because one of the twins hadn't been well and the other had been playing up. But apart from that . . .

Oh, and they'd had a stomach upset after she'd taken them to the toddlers group in the village. And perhaps . . .

She grimaced. Perhaps she hadn't been for quite a while. But Patrick should mind his own business.

When Chef's daughter had offered to take the twins out into the Park for an hour, it had been on the tip of Minty's tongue to refuse, because she'd been looking forward to doing that herself. Then she thought what a pleasure it would be to have an hour to herself to snatch some sleep, and agreed to let them go.

But Patrick's nagging—yes, he had been nagging!—made her drag herself along to the tower office, instead of diving under the duvet.

She wasn't going to the office to check up on things. No, of course not. Just to pass the time of day with Iris, her wonderful PA. Only, Iris hadn't been there, and Toby Wootton, he of the triangular face and misleading appearance of fragility, had paperwork spread over every surface including the floor. Toby was in charge of the publicity and promotional material for the Hall, and very good at his job he was, too.

"Hello, stranger," he said, which made her wince. "No twins today?"

"They're out in the park with Gloria—Chef's daughter—you know? It gives me an hour's peace and quiet."

She drifted to the window which gave onto the Park. A flight of ducks took off from the lake. Was that a tiny scarlet-clad figure running round the far verge, followed by one in blue? Being chased by a laughing Gloria? Minty wished she were down there with them.

Toby was amused. "Those two have enough energy to run a nuclear power station. Did you realise they've learned to operate the lift? You remember you asked if they could sit quietly in here with me and do some drawing while you helped Serafina with the housework? I didn't realise they were plotting something until I heard the lift doors opening and saw them disappear inside."

This was frightening news. If they could operate the lift, the twins could roam wherever they wanted through the great house and even ... horrors! ... stray onto the driveway in front of passing traffic!

The four wings of the centuries old Hall had been built in a square round the Fountain Court. To solve the problem of access at different levels, there was a staircase in the tower at each of the four corners. Minty and Patrick occupied the top floor overlooking the lake, but were gradually spreading into rooms on either side. As soon as the twins became mobile, Patrick had the staircases partitioned off, with handles on each door at adult shoulder height. The tower which housed the office on its top floor also contained a lift, but everyone had thought the operating panel too high for the twins to reach.

Minty checked the height of the buttons on the lift.

"They dragged that chair across and stood on it." Toby was amused. Toby wasn't married and didn't have to worry about what children could get up to.

Minty looked across to the door leading to Patrick's sanctum in the adjacent wing, which he allowed nobody else but Minty to enter. A month ago Patrick had had a combination lock put high up on that door.

Minty couldn't think straight. "We can't move the buttons on the lift. What can we do to stop them getting out?"

Toby humoured her. "There's a lock on the door into your rooms, isn't there? Any idea where the keys are?"

"Of course. I'll see if I can find them. Sorry. Short of sleep."

There was a slightly uncomfortable silence, then Toby—who'd stopped work on his papers—said, "If you're looking for Iris, she's gone off somewhere with Clive. I'm a bit bothered, actually, because there's a couple of women coming for interviews this afternoon. Also, Chef's been phoning through, wanting to talk to her. Iris didn't say where she'd be, did she?"

Minty shook her head. This was something else to worry about. Clive Hatton, their Administrator, had made it clear he'd no intention of marrying Iris. Unfortunately, that otherwise sensible woman believed one day he'd change his mind. She'd had other men interested in her—in particular their delightful if rotund accountant—but she'd never wavered in her devotion to Clive. Maybe they'd gone off somewhere to . . .

Minty stopped that thought. Once before Iris had put Clive before her loyalty to Minty and the Hall. Surely, she wouldn't do that again?

"What's that about Chef?" Chef—Florence Thornby—had been one of the mainstays of the Hall for ages. Minty rather thought Patrick had said something about Chef recently, but she hadn't taken any notice because it was no business of his what Chef did.

Toby shrugged. "I don't suppose it's anything. I'm a bit bothered about these two women, though."

"What jobs have they come for?" Minty realised she ought to have known, but she didn't mind showing her ignorance to Toby, who was an old friend. Well, not so old, really. He'd been at school with Patrick. He was also looking at her in a slightly hang-dog way, almost furtive. Was he, too, up to something?

When she didn't feel so tired, she must find out what was worrying him.

He scrabbled to find some papers on Iris's desk. "One of them wants a job in the gift shop. School leaver. Doris in the gift shop says she knows the girl and thinks she'd be all right. Actually, Doris is pretty desperate for help in the run-up to Christmas, so if the girl's not got two heads, we should take her." He showed Minty an application form filled out in a round hand.

"The other wants . . ." He frowned, checking through the application form. "I'm not sure. Office skills? Computer literate. I don't think we've got any vacancies in the estate office at the moment, have we? Iris hasn't said anything about their needing help. She must have forgotten they were coming."

Minty smoothed back her unruly fair hair, and looked down at her white shirt and blue jeans. She wasn't exactly dressed to interview people, but did that matter? "I was supposed to be having a rest, but I suppose I could see them."

The phone rang on Iris' desk, and Minty picked it up. Someone from the estate office reported that two people had arrived to see Iris. The voice thought that Iris had gone off in her car with Clive and hadn't come back yet. What were they to do?

Minty made a decision. "I'll see them up here."

Toby raised his hands in horror. "Can't you take them somewhere else? It's taken me all afternoon to get this lot sorted."

Minty regarded the sea of papers with bemusement. "What is it, anyway?"

"New brochure. You know."

She didn't know, but hadn't time to investigate. She turned back to the phone. "The house isn't open to visitors today, is it? Take them along to the library. I'll be there in five minutes."

She scooped up the two application forms and picked her way through the papers to the lift, leaving Toby to his sorting.

Reaching the courtyard down below, she wondered whether she ought to have gone and changed her clothes, brushed her hair, and put on some make-up. She didn't exactly look the part of Lady of the Hall at the moment, did she? Patrick had complained recently that she ought to spend more time on herself, but really she was too exhausted to care.

One of the girls from the estate office was hovering in the doorway of the library, anxious to get back to her work. Or to leave early, perhaps? Minty thanked her, and said she'd show the applicants out herself. A movement on the opposite side of the courtyard caught her eye. Who was there? The house was closed to visitors today, so . . . but the movement was not repeated and she dismissed it from her mind.

The library was dim, with the shutters only half open. Minty put the paperwork down on the vast desk in the centre of the room, and went to pull the shutters open and let up the blinds. The sun was bright outside, but inside the room shadows masked the glory of the stuccoed ceiling and the gilt tooling on the leather-bound books.

A dark-haired teenager was standing nervously by the desk, while the other woman had faded into the background. The younger applicant was eighteen and trying to look older, wearing a black trouser suit which had probably been bought for the interview. Her hair was brushed and her nails well shaped and not bitten. Minty got her to sit down and went through her application. The girl was nervous. She'd left school in the summer. She'd thought of going to college but couldn't bear the thought of more lessons and anyway she'd got a boyfriend who was working in one of the pubs in the village, so she didn't want to go far from home. She'd helped Doris out in the shop a couple of times on Saturdays, and she'd really liked it, with all the pretty things they had to sell. And yes, she'd been taught how to manage the till and she could start straight away.

Minty thought the girl might stick with the job for a year, with luck. But, as Doris was desperate for help, Minty said she'd get a contract sorted out ready for the girl to start immediately. The girl was pleased, red-cheeked, smiling. She bounced out of the room, saying she knew her way out.

Minty waited for the other woman to approach the desk.

And drew in a long breath.

"I know you."

The ex-pop star Maxine cast down her eyes. "No one else did."

Maxine's own hair had been a light auburn in colour, cut short because it was a trifle on the thin side. Most of the time she'd worn wigs. Her clothing had been flamboyant. She'd been a sex symbol who despised and dominated her back-up group and dancers. For her most famous act she'd dressed like a Goth in black and purple, with a metal brace on her teeth.

Minty glanced down at the application form, and read off the name. "Judith Kent."

"My real name."

Judith Kent was dressed in a plain grey sweater over a calf-length brown skirt. She wore sensible shoes and carried a dull brown handbag, rather the worse for wear. She wore glasses which were no fashion statement, and her hair—or it might be a wig?—was mouse-colour, not particularly thick and cut to frame her face without being in any way come-hitherish.

On her very last day at the Hall, and entirely through her own wilfulness, her face and arms had been extensively burned by contact with a toxic plant. Now her skin looked smooth, but maybe that was the result of skilfully applied makeup. There had been some damage. Missing eyebrows had been flicked on with a skilful hand. The eyelashes were sparse. In the past she had worn a musky scent, but now she didn't seem to be wearing any at all.

The low, seductive voice was the same, as was the slender figure and classically perfect profile. She had camouflaged herself, but she was still a beautiful woman.

She sat opposite Minty, completely at ease.

Minty fidgeted. It might seem to an onlooker that it was she who was interviewing Minty, not the other way round.

Minty suppressed a shiver. The woman could do her no more harm, could she? Granted, Maxine had nearly destroyed everything that was good in the Hall. She'd even threatened Minty's marriage at one point.

Minty looked down at her hands. She'd crumpled the application form between her fingers. She put the form down on the desk, and straightened it out.

"Why...?" She tried again. "Why are you here?"

"Where else would I go? It's taken a series of skin grafts to look even as good as this. My voice isn't what it was and I don't have the stamina for the club circuit. My agent, the accountants, the recording companies ... they don't want to know me any more." She shrugged. "I had everything once, didn't I? Now all I've got is a second-hand caravan and a couple of hundred pounds. The caravan's in your car park, by the way."

Minty wanted to say that the wages of sin were death, but couldn't bring herself to crow over someone who'd lost so much. Pity fought with outrage. She bit back some hasty words and shook her head. "How could you think I'd help you, after what you tried to do here?"

"I didn't succeed, though, did I? You stopped me, and yes, I'm glad that you did. In my old life, I could have had anything I wanted, and none of it satisfied. I tried drink, drugs, sex, chasing new sensations ..." She shrugged.

Minty couldn't restrain herself. "You performed a Black Mass here in our chapel. Don't deny it!"

"All that's behind me."

Minty stood to end the interview. "I don't believe you."

Judith flicked a slender gold chain out from the neck of her sweater. On it hung a tiny gold cross. "You wear a cross. So do I."

Slowly, Minty sat down again. Was it just another ornament?

Judith nodded. "I saw the light, as they say."

Was she sending herself up, or did she mean it? Minty said, "You can't expect me to believe that."

"It's true." She looked away. "It's not easy to talk about it, even now."

Minty was silent, waiting.

Judith's tone became mock-serious. "Well, there I was in hospital, being persecuted by this woman in the next bed. She'd been blinded in an accident, but she wasn't going quietly. She demanded that the chaplain visit her every day. She was a right pest, you know? As if I wasn't in enough trouble, she wanted me to read to her from her Bible. The nurses were always too busy, but I wasn't, was I?"

Judith's tone slid out of self-mockery into sincerity. "You can imagine how I felt after the things I'd done ... the thing I'd become. I treated her to a right mouthful, but she went on and on at me and one of the nurses told me she was dying, so in the end, I read her a bit. Just to keep her quiet, you know?"

Her voice became reflective. "She wanted me to read to her about a man being forgiven, even though he'd committed terrible crimes. I read on and on, and when she fell asleep, I took her Bible back to my own bed with me and I read some more. That night she died and I still had her Bible."

Judith seemed to be telling the truth, but she wouldn't meet Minty's eyes. "When the chaplain came, I tried to give it to him, said I'd no right to it. He said she'd no family, that I should keep it. I don't know how, but he got me to talk, to confess. Gradually, the load was taken from me and I began to live again. He baptised me in the chapel at the hospital. Then it was time for me to move on. Only I didn't know where.

"He said that being sorry for my sins wasn't enough. That I should try to make up for the evil I'd done. I kept thinking of this place. I told him about it, about you and what I'd tried to do here. He said I should pray about it, that maybe God wanted me to face up to my sins by returning here and offering to work for you.

"So I drove here by easy stages. I arrived in the village a week ago, and then lost my nerve, couldn't get any further. I parked the caravan down by the river and mooched around, asking for a job. Any job. I'm not up to heavy work, as you can probably see, and there wasn't anything else. But there were all sorts of rumours flying around about the Hall . . ."

"What rumours?" Judith was adding to Minty's unease.

Judith waved her hand. "That the Hall was heading for disaster. Then someone in the village said you were short-handed up at the Hall, and it seemed an opening was being made for me. If you turn me away, I don't know where I'll go, or what I'll do."

Again came that flicker at the back of her eyes. Or maybe it was just the flash of her spectacles? As the sun faded from the sky, the room had become darker. Minty leaned forward to switch on a table lamp.

Judith flinched as the light struck her face. Then she made herself turn towards Minty, exposing her face to the light. Now Minty could see that her skin was far from flawless. She was filled with pity for the girl.

"My new face. Do you like it?" Judith's tone was hard.

"But Maxine—Judith—we have no need of a singer here."

"Those days are gone. I'm computer literate, took all sorts of courses between hospital visits, till the money ran out. I could help to look after your children."

Minty recoiled. "I'm not letting you near my children."

Tears came into Judith's eyes. Minty remembered that Maxine had been an accomplished actress. Perhaps she could cry at will?

"You don't trust me." Judith got to her feet. "I suppose I can hardly blame you, though I thought, if you really were a Christian, that you'd give me a chance to show that I've changed." Her voice broke.

No, Minty didn't trust her. And yet—it would be against her better judgement—wouldn't it be right to offer a helping hand? What would Jesus have done? Forgiven her? He'd forgiven those who'd truly repented, but there was a big question mark in Minty's mind. She'd experienced Maxine hell-bent on destruction. Several times she'd been almost seduced by Maxine's softly spoken words.

Also, Minty wasn't Jesus, and she had to think of the broader picture.

Suppose she found Judith a place under someone who could be trusted to look after her? Florence, their chef, was a strong woman and a practising Christian. She was always in need of help; but Judith had said she wasn't up to a physically demanding job, and she certainly didn't look it. What was it that Chef wanted to talk to Iris about? Something Patrick had tried to tell her ... no, it eluded her.

Minty turned over the application form, while Judith stood on the far side of the desk. "Office work?" said Minty. "References?"

Judith smiled derisively. "I completed the courses but I've had no work experience. I got hold of a copy of your brochure on the Hall. Suppose I learn it by heart and take parties round?"

She had a point. They had volunteer stewards in every room, but no one to take parties around. It would undoubtedly be an asset to the Hall if they did. But Toby's mother, Venetia Wootton, was in charge of the stewards at the Hall and had observed the desecration Maxine had wrought in the chapel. Venetia would never agree to employing Judith. Venetia was a Christian and committed churchgoer, true. But she was not that flexible. Also, her only son Toby had once been smitten by Maxine, and even though he'd recoiled from her when he'd seen the signs of satanic practices in the chapel, Venetia wouldn't want him coming into contact with the girl again. And neither would Minty's old friend Carol, who'd had her eye on Toby for a long time.

Minty pushed the application to one side. "I think I'd better ask my husband about this. See if he can suggest something."

Judith looked down. "I thought your husband was a country solicitor who never interfered with the running the Hall."

"That's true, but . . ."

"You have everything, and I have nothing. You have this beautiful house and adoring servants. You have a faithful husband and twins; an heir and a spare, as they say. I could make a start here, in the library. There's dust on all the bookshelves and the books aren't in any sort of order. I could do something about that for you."

Minty looked around her. What Judith said was true. "We can't start spring cleaning the house until after Christmas when we close to visitors for three months. Every few years we have a specialist come in, take down the books and examine them page by page for damage. It's true you could do that, but not till you've been trained."

"I could catalogue them. I could find out how on the internet. I have a lap-top. If you'd trust me, I could even make a preliminary assessment if there's any damage that needs looking at."

Minty bit her lip. The books did need cataloguing. Patrick was the only person who ever took a book out from the library, and goodness knows what was lurking in bottom drawers and at the back of the shelves.

"Just give me a small wage to start with. Enough to buy food. Let me keep the caravan in the car park. That's all I ask. For His sake, if not for mine."

Minty covered her eyes, putting her elbows on the desk. When in doubt, pray. It was difficult, but not impossible, but she had to try. *Please, Lord. Tell me what to do. I can't judge . . . I'm bewildered . . . I'm so tired, I can't think straight. Would you forgive her?"*

She took her hands away from her face. "Would you be prepared to come up to the chapel with me now? To swear on the Bible that you mean to follow Christ in future?"

A faint smile. "Of course. I thought you'd want something like that."

"You say you've been here a week. Did you go to church last Sunday?"

A slight hesitation. "Yes, but only when no one else was there. I was afraid someone might recognise me, and ask me to explain myself. I wasn't sure I could."

"You'd find the vicar sympathetic. He's old for his years and he's seen all sorts. Besides, there's my uncle ... he's retired now, but he still helps with the services ... you might find he's got more time to help you."

Judith inclined her head.

Minty glanced over the application form. "Give me the name and address of the college where you learned IT skills, and of the consultant and the chaplain at the hospital."

Judith filled in the details. Minty still wasn't sure that she was doing the right thing but she said, "Subject to my taking up your references, I'll put you on probation for a week. Minimum wage. You can keep your caravan in the car park. But you leave if there's the slightest hint of trouble. Right?"

"One more thing," said Judith. "You won't tell anyone who I am, will you? I need a clean break with the past."

"I can't promise. One or two people may have to know."

"I'm relying on you."

Minty felt wretched. She was almost sure she'd made a mistake, and what Patrick would say, she didn't like to think. Something flickered at the back of Judith's eyes. Triumph? And then it was gone.

We want to hear from you. Please send your comments about this book to us in care of zreview@zondervan.com. Thank you.

GRAND RAPIDS, MICHIGAN 49530 USA

WWW.ZONDERVAN.COM